Path of Gold

A.J. Mackenzie is the pseudonym of Marilyn Livingstone and Morgen Witzel, a husband-and-wife team of writers and historians. Morgen has an MA in renaissance diplomacy, and Marilyn has a PhD in medieval economic history. They have written two books of medieval history and several novels, including the Simon Merrivale Mysteries, set in medieval Europe. Marilyn Livingstone was diagnosed with cancer in 2022 and passed away in September 2023.

Also by A.J. MacKenzie

The War of 1812 Epics

The Ballad of John MacLea
The Hunt for the North Star
Invasion

The Hundred Years' War

A Flight of Arrows
A Clash of Lions
The Fallen Sword

The Simon Merrivale Mysteries

By Treason We Perish
City of Woe
Path of Gold

Path of Gold

A.J. MACKENZIE

CANELO

First published in the United Kingdom in 2025 by

Canelo, an imprint of
Canelo Digital Publishing Limited,
20 Vauxhall Bridge Road,
London SW1V 2SA
United Kingdom

A Penguin Random House Company
The authorised representative in the EEA is Dorling Kindersley Verlag GmbH. Arnulfstr. 124, 80636 Munich, Germany

Copyright © A.J. MacKenzie 2025

The moral right of A.J. MacKenzie to be identified as the creator of this work has been asserted in accordance with the Copyright, Designs and Patents Act, 1988.
All rights reserved. No part of this publication may be reproduced or transmitted in any form or by any means, electronic or mechanical, including photocopy, recording, or any information storage and retrieval system, without permission in writing from the publisher.
No part of this book may be used or reproduced in any manner for the purpose of training artificial intelligence technologies or systems. In accordance with Article 4(3) of the DSM Directive 2019/790, Canelo expressly reserves this work from the text and data mining exception.

A CIP catalogue record for this book is available from the British Library.

Print ISBN 978 1 80436 690 5
Ebook ISBN 978 1 80436 697 4

This book is a work of fiction. Names, characters, businesses, organizations, places and events are either the product of the author's imagination or are used fictitiously. Any resemblance to actual persons, living or dead, events or locales is entirely coincidental.

Cover design by Blacksheep Design

Cover images © Alamy, Depositphotos

Printed and bound in Great Britain by Clays Ltd, Elcograf S.p.A.

Look for more great books at
www.canelo.co | www.dk.com

To Jane and Ian, good friends and travelling companions.

And as always, for Marilyn.

Now in the east, the shining light behold!
The sun has oped a lustrous path of gold.

– Moshe ibn Ezra (born in Garnāta *c.*1055), *Nachum: Spring Songs*

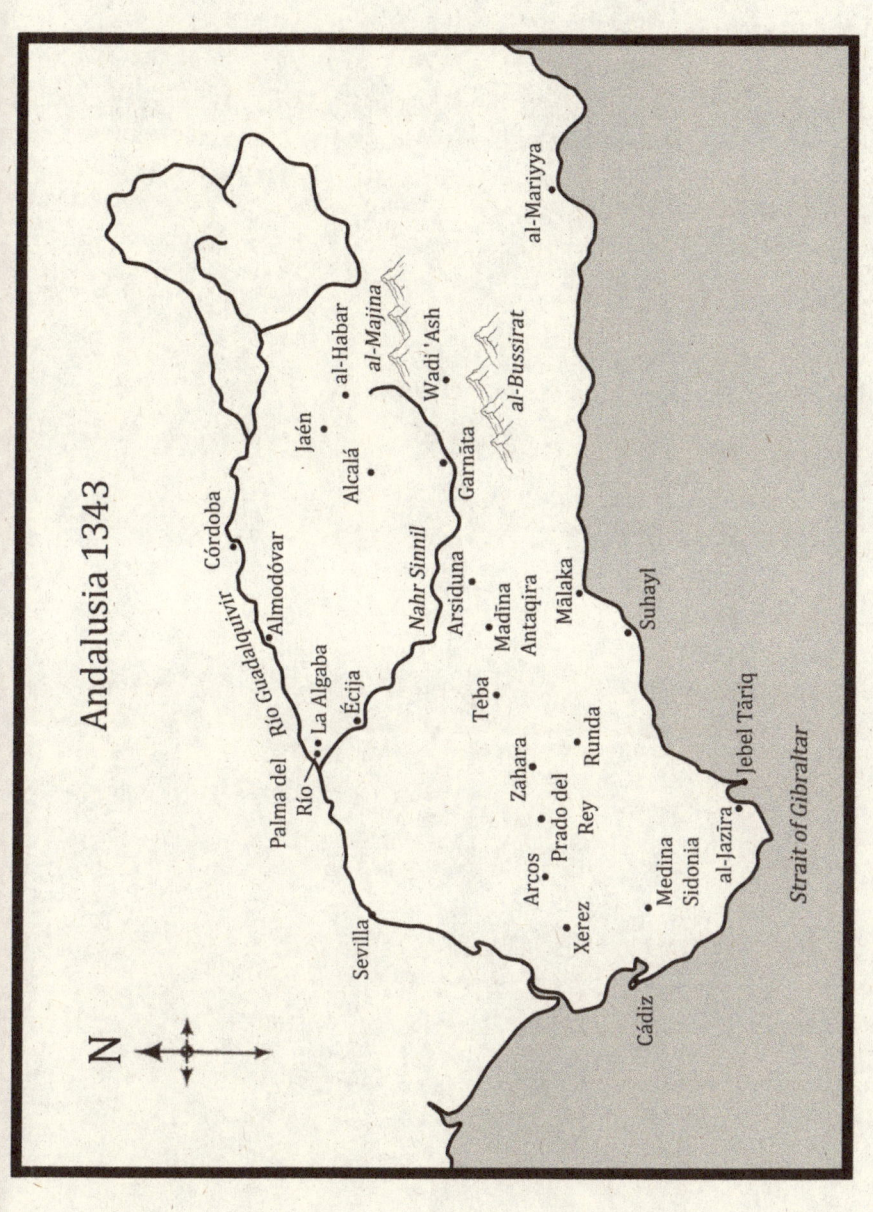

Dramatis Personae

English embassy

Henry of Grosmont, Earl of Derby
Eleanor of Lancaster, his sister, mistress of the Earl of Arundel
Richard Fitzalan, Earl of Arundel
Sir John Sully of Iddesleigh
Simon Merrivale, King's Messenger and later herald to the Earl of Derby
Jacme (Jac) de Ficaris, his secretary
Warin of Hexworthy, his groom

Court of Castile

Alfonso XI, king of Castile
María of Portugal, his wife (currently residing in Córdoba)
Leonor de Guzmán, King Alfonso's mistress
Donato di Pacino de' Peruzzi, the king's banker
Don Juan Manuel, philosopher and military commander
Juan Núñez de Prado, Grand Master of the Order of Calatrava
Fra Pero de Garcíez, Knight of the Order of Calatrava

Others

Fra Moriale (Jean de Montréal), Knight of Saint John and mercenary captain
Juan Moreno, former saffron grower
Philippe of Évreux, king of Navarre

Guilhem-Arnaut de Irunberri, commander of King Philippe's escort
Diago, slave in the water mine at Runda
Euric, leader of the troglodyte people of Wadi 'Ash

Court of Garnāta

Sultan Yūsuf ibn Ismail, sultan of Garnāta
Sultana Fātima bint Muhammad bint al-Ahmar, the sultan's grandmother
Faraj ibn Muhammad, commander of Sultana Fātima's bodyguard
Rīm, Sultan Yūsuf's concubine
Buthayna, Sultan Yūsuf's concubine
Abū Nu'aym Ridwan, *hajib* (chancellor) of Garnāta
Abū al-Hasan ibn al-Jayyāb, vizier of Garnāta
Lisān ad-Dīn ibn al-Khatīb, his secretary
Auria, slave in the *harīm*

Soldiers

Ghilas, a captured Amazigh warrior
Peiro d'Iguna, Navarrese man-at-arms
Sifredo de Berriz, Navarrese man-at-arms
Hamou Ou Akka ibn Zayani, commander of the Warriors of the Faithful
Aksal ben Mellal, one of the Warriors of the Faithful
Mouha ben Tirga, one of the Warriors of the Faithful
Damya bint Hamou Tin Mal (Kahina), commander of the Imazighen at the Hisn al-Nājmi
Jidji, one of her warriors
Yufayyur, one of her warriors

Involved in the salt trade

Abdallah al-Mu'min al-Rumani, *musharaf* (superintendent) of the salt works in Garnāta

Kāsim al-'Aswad, merchant and caravan master from Murrākush
Mauro (Enrique Cavador), slave and salt miner

Scholars, priests, writers and physicians

Dámaso Reyes, physician to Queen María
Lorenço de Alameda, physician to King Philippe of Navarre
Asach de Sharīsh, scholar in Xerez de la Frontera
Brother Sebastián, Trinitarian friar
Rabbi Levi ben Gershon, philosopher, mathematician and astronomer
Duran ben Shlomo Catalan, scholar, translator and wrestler
'Ali ibn al-Rāzī, physician in Garnāta

A note on languages and names

The usual polyglot mix of languages appears in this book, including Latin, Castilian Spanish, Ligurian Euskara (Basque), Arabic and Tamazight (Berber). We have rendered most of these in modern form, not wishing to get involved in intricacies such as the differences between Maghrebi Arabic and Andalusi Arabic, though we have allowed a few historic forms: for example, *fidalgo*, the medieval equivalent of *hidalgo* (nobleman) and *mio çid* and *mi çaida* which are historic forms of 'my lord' and 'my lady,' themselves loanwords from Arabic where the equivalents are *saīdi* and *saīda*. Translating and transliterating Arabic is not always easy, and we used several dictionaries and software programmes to arrive at solutions that we thought would be both accurate and easy to follow. Any errors in translation of any language are of course our responsibility.

The macrons above vowels in Arabic indicate a broad vowel, hence Rīm is pronounced Reem, and so on. The accents above vowels in Spanish indicate a stressed syllable, so CORdoba, AlCAZar, and so on.

Names of countries and places were a bit of a minefield. For the Spanish kingdoms we opted for their familiar modern forms, Castile instead of Castilla, Navarre instead of Navarra or Nafarroa, Portugal instead of Portugale, and so on. Towns and cities in Spain, on the other hand, have usually been given their modern Spanish form, including Sevilla instead of Seville; exceptionally, Jerez de la Frontera is referred to as Xerez, which was the common name until the late nineteenth century (and is still the name of the city's football club). *Spaine*, derived from the Latin Hispania, was reportedly in use in English as early as 1200, but Hispania or Ispania would have been more common at the time; we have opted for the simpler 'Spain'.

Spanish characters refer to Granada, but most of the rest of the people in the book refer to it by its Arabic name, Garnāta (there are other versions of the name). Morocco is very much a modern Western coinage; until very recently the country was referred to by the name of its former capital, Marrakesh, and we have opted for this or the Arabic version, Murrākush, for the country as well as the city. The people known usually as Berbers have been given their proper name, Imazighen (*sing.* Amazigh), and their language is Tamazight.

The term 'Moor' can be controversial, but it was widely used at the time to denote Arab or Imazighen inhabitants of Andalusia and North Africa, rather as 'Saracen' was used in the Middle East. We have put the term into the mouths of some of our characters where appropriate, but have not used it in the narrative.

Towns and cities still subject to the sultan of Garnāta are referred to by their Arabic names unless (usually) the speaker is Spanish; thus a Castilian will refer to Algeciras but everyone else talks about al-Jazīra. The table below gives a correlation of Arabic to modern Spanish names.

Places in the Emirate of Granada

Arsiduna: Archidona
Bayana: Baena
al-Bayyāzīn: Albaicín
Garnāta: Granada
al-Habar: Cambil★
al-Hajar: Láchar
Istigga: Écija
Jannat al-Arīf: Generalife (palace)
al-Jazīra al-Khadrā: Algeciras

Jebel Tāriq: Gibraltar
Madīna Antaqira: Antequera
al-Mallāha: La Malahá
Mālaka: Málaga
al-Mariyya: Almería
Mutrayil: Motril
Al-Qal'a al-Hamrā: Alhambra, the Red Fortress (palace)
Runda: Ronda
Suhayl: Fuengirola
Teba/Hisn al-Nājmi: Teba/Castillo de las Estrellas (Castle of the Stars)
Wadi 'Ash: Guadix
Zahara: Zahara de la Sierra

Places now in Castilian hands

al-Ghaba: La Algaba
Hims al-Andalus: Sevilla (Seville)
Istigga: Écija
Jayyān: Jaén
al-Mudāwar: Almodóvar
Qādis: Cádiz
al-Qal'at: Alcalá la Real
Qurtuba: Córdoba
Sharīsh: Xerez de la Frontera (modern Jerez)

Geographical features

al-Balata: Pico Veleta (mountain)
al-Bussarat: Sierra Nevada (mountain range)
al-Mājīna: Sierra Mágina (mountain range)
al-Qasabah: Alcazaba (mountain)
al-Tell★★: Mulhacén (mountain)
Nahr al-Kebir: Río Guadalquivir (river)
Nahr Malih: Río Salado (river)
Nahr Sinnil: Río Genil (river)

Rawīka al-Ushāaqa: Peña de los Enamorados (mountain)

Places in North Africa

Sabta: Ceuta
Murrākush: Marrakesh

Basque place names and Spanish equivalents

Iruña: Pamplona
Irunberri: Lumbier

* Although in some accounts Cambil and al-Habar are two separate castles, built on opposite sides of the river.

** This is speculative. The later Arabic name of the mountain is Jebel Mawla al-Hassan, but this name refers to an emir of Granada who reigned more than a century later. The Hill is a local nickname for Mulhacén, which we think – with very little evidence – may have been closer to the original name. We have translated this as al-Tell.

The Green Island

1

7th of September, 1343

'The Pillars of Hercules,' said Fra Moriale. 'In ancient times, some people thought that the world ended here.'

Standing on the afterdeck of the galley *Santa Creu*, Simon Merrivale shaded his eyes against the morning sun and gazed out over the sea. A mile away to the right, a mountain rose sharply from the water, a steep limestone cliff crowned with stone towers and walls. Red banners glimmered from the ramparts, tiny specks like jewels against the deep blue of the sky. Another mountain lay dead ahead, rearing up out of the blanket of haze and sea spray that blurred the horizon. Between the two mountains was a narrow strait, with the promise of the open Atlantic on its far side.

'Perhaps it does,' Merrivale said. 'Perhaps this is the end of one world, and the beginning of another.'

Jacme de Ficaris, the third man on the afterdeck, smiled a little. 'You may be more right than you know. These two mountains are the Jebel Tāriq, or Gibraltar as the Castilians call it, and the Jebel Musa. Two realms collide here, Castile of the Christians and the Muslim kingdoms of Garnāta and Murrākush. When we arrive at al-Jazīra, you will find yourself in a place unlike anywhere you have seen before.'

Fra Moriale made an impatient gesture.

A restless pragmatist, he had little time for flights of fancy. 'As Ecclesiastes tells us, there is no new thing under the sun,' he said. 'Al-Jazīra is just another city under siege. We've all seen them, a dozen times or more. Keep your eyes on the prize, and don't let yourselves be distracted by novelties.'

Fra Moriale paused for a moment, watching the white cliffs of the Jebel Tāriq slide by. He called out to the shipmaster, his deep voice booming along the gangway above the long ranks of rowing benches. 'You'll need to increase your stroke rate, *padrun*. As soon as we round the point, we'll hit a very fast current coming in from the west. We need to drive through that, and quickly.'

'*Aè, signur. Capo! Colp rapido!*' A drum began to beat. Down on the rowing benches the oarsmen, muscular brown men from Liguria and Sardinia, moved in mechanical unison, pulling the long gleaming oars through the water, lifting them in clouds of spray and settling into the next stroke. *Santa Creu*'s wooden hull creaked a little as she picked up speed. Fra Moriale turned back to Merrivale.

'What will you do when we reach al-Jazīra?' he asked.

Merrivale paused. 'It depends on what we find at al-Jazīra,' he said finally. 'I know only that the man I am searching for, Donato de' Peruzzi, has gone to Spain. My assumption is that he would go to the court of King Alfonso of Castile, who is laying siege to al-Jazīra, because Peruzzi likes to be close to the centre of power. But I could be wrong.'

Fra Moriale scratched his ear. 'Why do you want to find Peruzzi?' he asked.

'Because he is a threat to my country and my king.' Merrivale paused again. 'And, there is a personal matter.'

'Ah,' said Moriale. 'This is about Savoy. Are you still pining for the fair Yolande?'

Merrivale's hands clenched for a moment. 'Mind your own business.'

'That is exactly what I am doing. Why do you think I agreed to give you passage to al-Jazīra, Simó? Out of the goodness of my heart?'

'You don't have one.'

Fra Moriale chuckled. 'You know exactly why. I am searching for Peruzzi too, but my reasons are entirely dispassionate. I have heard a rumour that Peruzzi has a supply of gold coming out of Africa into Spain. I want to get my hands on it.'

Merrivale said nothing. 'Peruzzi betrayed you,' Fra Moriale continued. 'I know, I was there, in the service of the lord of Monaco. I watched it all happen. You aimed too high, my friend. You tried to turn Savoy into a kingdom, with John of Bohemia at its head, and you wanted the king's daughter for yourself. Peruzzi saw your weakness, and sold you out to your enemies.'

'I know,' Merrivale mimicked. 'I was there. I watched it all happen.'

Fra Moriale gazed up at the castle on the crest of the Jebel Tāriq, tapping his fingers on the hilt of his sword. 'Let us make a bargain,' he said finally. 'We work together to find Peruzzi and the gold. When we do, we split the gold between us. You take half and give it to your king, and I will take the rest and use it to raise my army and found my kingdom. And you can take whatever revenge on Peruzzi that you like.'

'You are assuming there is a great deal of gold,' said Ficaris.

'Of course there is a great deal of gold,' Fra Moriale said, a little impatiently. 'Otherwise, Peruzzi would not be bothering. He is a banker who deals in millions, not petty coinage.'

'What are you not telling me?' Merrivale demanded.

Fra Moriale turned to face Merrivale. 'You are correct in your thinking. Donato de' Peruzzi is at the court of Castile. Not only that, but King Alfonso has appointed him as his personal banker, charged with raising money to pay for the king's war against the Moors.'

Merrivale's fists clenched again. 'How do you know this?' he asked.

'I had a chance encounter with an old friend in Genoa, a Knight of Saint John who joined the Order at the same time as myself. His father was an archbishop, and he himself is now prior of the Order in Portugal with thirty-two acknowledged children. A very generous man, you might say.'

Knights of Saint John took vows of celibacy. So, for that matter, did archbishops. 'How many children do you have?' Merrivale asked.

'A few, here and there. Nothing to boast about. But we are digressing. My friend the prior corresponds with the Order of Saint John's headquarters on the island of Rhodes, which is how he heard the news. Peruzzi used to be the Order's banker, and he still has connections on Rhodes. After you drove him out of Florence, he returned to Rhodes where he spent some time closeted with the Order's treasurer, setting up new banking arrangements. He then departed for Castile. Well, Simó? What about my offer?'

There was a long silence, broken by the creak of the oars and water rushing past the hull of the *Santa Creu*. The southern point of the Jebel Tāriq was coming closer, and already they could feel the power of the current rushing in from the Atlantic. Merrivale turned to Ficaris. 'Would you accept if you were me?' he asked.

'You know perfectly well what will happen,' Ficaris said calmly. 'Once you find the gold, he will elbow you aside and take it all for himself.'

Fra Moriale spread his hands. 'What can I say? God made me as I am. On the other hand, Jac, Master Merrivale is a very clever man. I am sure he will find some way to thwart me. So, what do you say, Simó? Do we have a bargain?'

Merrivale looked up at the sky for a moment. 'We do,' he said. 'And may God help us both.'

The southern point of Jebel Tāriq slid past and away astern. *Santa Creu* shuddered in the current rushing in from the open sea, and for a moment she yawed, the oarsmen struggling to set their oars. The shipmaster snapped at the helmsmen, who dragged hard on the tiller and brought the big galley back on course. Beyond the rock lay a deep bay backed with rugged blue hills. On its far side, the white walls and towers of a city shimmered in the strong light.

Warin of Hexworthy, Merrivale's groom and servant, came up onto the afterdeck, looking at the city. 'Is that al-Jazīra, sir?'

'It is,' said Ficaris. 'Al-Jazīra al-Khudra, the Green Island. It was a fine city, once, but King Alfonso has been laying siege to it for more than a year. Hard to say how much of the finery is left.'

The camp of the besieging army surrounded the city, spreading up the nearby hillsides. The camp itself was in turn surrounded by a wooden palisade. A row of galleys lay drawn up on the beach. Nearer at hand, on *Santa Creu*'s starboard side, another fortified camp lay at the foot of the rock of Jebel Tāriq, facing the city across the bay. Scarlet and gold banners flew from its ramparts.

'That is the Moorish army from Garnāta,' Ficaris said. 'Or Granada, as the Castilians say. Never underestimate them. They may be infidels but they are hard fighters. One company in particular, called the Warriors of the Faithful, are famed for their ruthlessness.' He paused for a moment. 'As I said, it's another world.'

Santa Creu was moving deeper into the bay now, the current slackening a little. Merrivale looked back out into the strait and saw another vessel, smaller than *Santa Creu*, with a turquoise-painted hull and a single lateen sail, just entering the bay.

'That is a Moorish ship,' Ficaris said suddenly.

Fra Moriale's eyes narrowed. 'I know that ship,' he said. 'She's from Sebta, on the far side of the strait.'

'Running supplies into al-Jazīra?' Ficaris asked.

'Possibly. Let's find out.' Moriale called to the shipmaster. '*Padrun! Gira! Colp deguerra! Batè a quart!*'

The drum thudded urgently. Men ran along the gangway, some clustering around the stone-thrower on its turntable just in front of the mast, others pulling the cover off the Greek fire siphon on the forecastle. The brass tube of the siphon shone brilliantly in the sun. Crossbowmen took up positions on the afterdeck and along the gangway between the rowing benches, crouching and winding their bows. The oarsmen increased their stroke to battle speed, driving *Santa Creu* around and back towards the other ship, her bow slicing through the waves.

The other ship was turning too, trying to run further inshore, but as she drew closer to the rock of the Jebel Tāriq the wind began to drop. Her sail flapped and she lost way, rolling in the swells. Her crew hauled frantically on the halyards, trying to fill the sail again as the *Santa Creu* bore down on them. Fra Moriale signalled to the shipmaster and the big galley slowed. The crew of the Greek fire siphon swivelled the weapon hopefully, waiting for the order that would send tongues of oily flame arching through the air and turn the little ship into an inferno.

A man in long brown robes and dark blue headscarf stood up on the afterdeck of the other ship and shouted in Castilian Spanish. 'I come in peace! I seek passage to the Christian camp at Algeciras!'

Merrivale raised his eyebrows. 'Algeciras?'

'Al-Jazīra,' said Ficaris. 'The Spaniards always mangle Moorish names. I suspect they do it on purpose.'

'I come in peace!' the man in the boat repeated. 'For the love of God, let me pass!'

Santa Creu was quite close now, enough to see the other man clearly. Merrivale studied him for a moment. Brown-skinned, black-haired with a closely trimmed beard; well, that described quite a few men around the Middle Sea, but something about this man prodded his memory. Cupping his hands around his mouth, Merrivale shouted back. 'Who are you, stranger? What is your business here?'

'My name is Juan Moreno,' came the answer. 'I am a Castilian. Please allow me to pass to Algeciras!'

Merrivale turned to Fra Moriale. 'I know this man.'

'Let's have a word with him, then.' Fra Moriale raised his own voice. 'Bring your vessel alongside, Señor Moreno, and come aboard. Leave your weapons behind.'

'What happens to my crew?'

'If you come in peace, they will suffer no harm. *Padrun!* Tell the oarsmen to rest oars.'

Still struggling with the light wind, the smaller ship came alongside the galley's stern and Moreno climbed up to the afterdeck. He looked older than Merrivale remembered; his face was weary and there were wrinkles around his eyes, and two streaks of silver on the front of his beard. His brown robe was patched and faded, and looked as if it had seen hard travel. A worn leather satchel was slung over one shoulder.

'Good morning, Señor Moreno,' Merrivale said quietly. 'It has been a long time.'

Moreno stared blankly, his mouth open. Several moments passed before recognition dawned. 'Señor Merrivale,' he said. 'Yes, a long time indeed.'

'Four years since we met in London,' Merrivale said. 'May I ask what brings you here, *señor*?'

'I am searching for someone who is lost,' he said. 'My sister's son.'

'Just a moment,' Fra Moriale interrupted. 'How do you know Señor Merrivale?'

'We were both in the service of Queen Isabella, the queen mother in England,' Moreno said. 'I am an *azafráno*, a grower of saffron. Her Grace had invested in the saffron trade, and I was one of her advisors. I took the post to raise money so I could find my sister and her son, and set them free.'

Water slapped against the hulls of both ships. The crews waited in silence. 'What happened to your sister?' asked Fra Moriale.

'She married a man named Cavador, who worked in a *salina*, a salt mine near the village of Prado del Rey. Some years ago, raiders from Granada destroyed the village. My sister's husband was killed, and she and her son were taken away and sold as slaves. I was a poor labourer at the time, unable to help them, but I vowed that when I had enough money I would find them.'

Ficaris stirred a little.

'Did you succeed?' asked Fra Moriale.

Moreno sighed a little, and Merrivale saw the pain in his eyes. 'It took me a long time to find their trail,' he said. 'They had been sold on several times, first in Granada and then to a slave dealer across the water in Marrakesh. I followed them there.'

'That must have been dangerous,' said Merrivale.

'Not so much as you might think. Some of my ancestors were Moors, and I can easily pass for one. I speak both Arabic and Tamazight. And also, these are my family, Señor Merrivale. If I could save them, I was willing to run any risk.' He paused. 'After many months of searching, I finally traced them to the city of Marrakesh. There I learned that my sister had died a year earlier.'

'Sweet Jesus,' Ficaris said softly.

'How did you know it was her?' Merrivale asked gently.

Moreno opened his satchel and pulled out an object which he handed to Merrivale. It was a crucifix, made of hard translucent stone. Light shone through the stone, flashing in little rainbows. Time had worn and smoothed the image, and the details of the body of the crucified Christ were blurred, although the face remained sharp.

'What is it made of?' Merrivale asked. 'Crystal?'

Moreno shook his head. 'Rock salt. The workers in the *salinas* carve them as acts of devotion. This was an heirloom in the family of my sister's husband, and he gave it to her when they were married.' He sighed. 'In Marrakesh, my sister was sold as a domestic servant, to a family who were fond of her and respected her faith. When she died, they kept the crucifix in hopes that one day it could be returned to her own people.'

'And your nephew?'

'By this point he had grown to be a young man. He was sold separately from his mother, to a merchant and caravan master named Kāsim al-'Aswad. Kāsim owned many of the caravans that ran from Marrakesh over the mountains to Sijilmasa, and from there, south across the great desert to the cities on the far side. My nephew served in those caravans for four years.'

'In which case he may well be dead,' Ficaris said. His voice was sombre. 'Those caravans are brutal and hard. Many of the slaves who cross the desert never return.'

'My nephew survived,' Moreno said. 'I found people who had seen him alive. I tried to find Kāsim in order to pay my nephew's ransom, but I was too late. Earlier this year, Kāsim supported a failed uprising against the sultan of Marrakesh. He was outlawed and fled the country with his household, hoping to take refuge in Granada. I traced them as far as Sebta on the northern coast of Marrakesh, where I learned they had taken passage on a ship bound for Granada. But they never reached their destination.'

'What happened?' asked Merrivale.

'Their ship was captured by a Castilian galley. Kāsim was killed, and the rest of his household were sold as slaves in Castile. And so, I am still trying to trace my nephew. I will not rest, *señores*, not until I have found him.'

You are like a bloodhound, a woman had once said to Merrivale. *Once you have the scent, you will never give up the chase.* He looked at Moreno, seeing the grief and sorrow and grim determination in his eyes, and knew that he was looking at another like himself.

The woman, whose name was Yolande of Bohemia, had predicted correctly that this trait would get Merrivale into trouble. He hoped that this was not true of Moreno.

Fra Moriale shrugged. 'It should be easy enough to find him, Señor Moreno. Your nephew will have told his captors that he is a Christian, and they will have set him free.'

'Not necessarily,' Ficaris said quietly. 'Slaves are valuable. Owners do not always want to give them up.'

'Whatever has happened, I must know the truth,' Moreno said. 'Please allow me to pass to Algeciras, *señores*. I have spent four years on this quest, and I must see it to the end.'

An impulse from nowhere came into Merrivale's mind. 'I will help you,' he said.

Fra Moriale frowned. 'Señor Moreno, I would like a word in private with Señor Merrivale. Will you oblige us?'

Moreno nodded. 'A moment,' Merrivale said. 'Your nephew, *señor*. What is his name?'

'He was christened Enrique,' Moreno said. 'Enrique Cavador. But as a child, he was always called Mauro.'

Moreno turned and walked forward towards the catapult turntable. 'What is it?' Merrivale asked.

'Listening to Señor Moreno talk about the caravans has given me an idea. We know Peruzzi is bringing in gold from Africa. But people do not just give gold away, Simó. Peruzzi is offering something in exchange. Have you considered what that might be?'

He had a point, Merrivale thought. 'What do the caravans carry on their journey south?'

'Many things, but the main commodity is salt. The caravans run from Murrākush over the mountains to Sijilmasa, and from there across the desert to Timbuktu in the empire of Mali. Gold is plentiful in Timbuktu, because the mine owners pay tribute to the emperor. Salt, on the other hand, is scarce and much valued. People say that in Timbuktu, salt is worth its weight in gold.'

Merrivale considered this. He had never heard of Sijilmasa, or Mali, and knew nothing of Timbuktu beyond the name, but it sounded plausible. Salt had many uses apart from food: curing meat and fish, making cheese and butter, salting hides before tanning, medicines. Back in England, dealers in salt were often wealthy men. 'Peruzzi is shipping salt to Timbuktu, whose rulers pay for it in gold,' he said. 'But where would Peruzzi find the salt?'

'Perhaps here,' said Ficaris, pointing at the mountains around the bay. 'There are many *salinas* in Castile, and they produce the finest salt in the world. But the production and sale of salt is a royal monopoly.'

'Kings farm monopolies, especially when their treasuries are empty,' Merrivale said, still thinking. 'They hand over control of the trade, and its future revenues, in exchange for ready money. That would explain why Peruzzi came to Castile... Here is a hypothesis: King Alfonso has handed over control of the salt trade to Peruzzi in exchange for gold to fight the Moors. Peruzzi sells the salt in Africa and receives payment in gold.'

Fra Moriale nodded. 'Señor Moreno's nephew served in the caravans. He must know what routes they travelled, what cargoes they carried and for whom. He might be useful to us, Simó. Help Señor Moreno to find him.'

'There's more than just the caravans,' Merrivale said. 'Peruzzi has to ship the gold across the sea to Castile, at a time when Murrākush and Castile are at war.'

'Leave that to me. I have friends in the ports on the African coast. You find out whether Peruzzi is selling salt, and more importantly, where he is keeping the gold.' Fra Moriale paused. 'I will lend you Ficaris, to be your eyes and ears. He has a good head on his shoulders, and he can be useful in a fight, too.'

'Am I allowed a say in this?' asked Ficaris.

'Of course not. This is a ship of war, not the college of cardinals. Señor Moreno! I am sending you ashore with Master Merrivale. Tell your crew they may return home.'

Moreno bowed. 'Thank you, *señor*,' he said, and he called down to the crew of the other vessel. The little ship turned, its sail gradually filling once more, and made its way back out into the strait towards Africa. On board the galley, the *padrun* called orders to the crew and the oarsmen leaned back and dug their oars into the water. Merrivale looked at the ring of blue mountains and the gleaming white city of al-Jazīra, and felt the hairs rise slowly on the back of his neck. *Ficaris is right*, he thought. *This is a different world.*

2

7th of September, 1343

A small boat carried Merrivale, Ficaris, Warin and Moreno ashore to the Castilian camp, landing them not far from the beached galleys. It was after midday now, and the heat was rising. Merrivale stood for a moment in the strong sunlight, looking towards al-Jazīra. High double walls crowned with towers faced a broad water moat; massive fortified gatehouses had fighting platforms with stone throwers and cannon. A little island offshore was fortified with its own ring of walls. Behind the ramparts, white minarets rose finger-slim against the hazy blue sky.

Outside the walls lay all of the familiar detritus of siege warfare: barricades, trenches, fire pits, abandoned ladders from a failed escalade, the charred skeleton of a siege tower opposite one of the gatehouses. Further back was a row of gaunt wooden trebuchets. Men laboured around them and, as Merrivale watched, one of the trebuchets was released, its arm rising to the vertical and releasing a stone projectile against the walls, where it broke in a shower of fragments. Cannon on the ramparts boomed in reply, belching clouds of sulphurous smoke.

Most of the camp lay on rising ground west of the city, rows of tents and pavilions with a few larger wooden buildings. Standards and banners flapped gently in the light air. To the north was a marshy plain with a shallow river running down to the sea; beyond the river was a jumble of ruined buildings with a watchtower rising from the summit of a low hill. Away in the distance was the camp of the army of Garnāta, half-hidden in the haze.

Merrivale looked at the Castilian camp. He saw the great square standard of the king of Castile, red lions on white quartered with gold castles on red and banners in bright colours, red and silver, blue and ermine, green and gold. He paused for a moment in surprise. Some of these banners were familiar. Those white leopards on red with a black bend, surely that was the coat of arms of the Earl of Derby, and that gold lion belonged to the earl of Arundel. And there was absolutely no mistaking the red and ermine bars of Sir John Sully of Iddesleigh, one of Merrivale's oldest friends.

He glanced at Warin, and saw the groom was smiling; he too had recognised Sully's colours. 'Serendipity,' Merrivale said. 'Let us go.'

—

Over time, siege camps acquired a sense of permanence and began to resemble small towns. This camp, unlike many in Merrivale's experience, was orderly and reasonably clean. Walking uphill towards the English banners, they passed women doing laundry in a stream that splashed down the hill, pounding clothes on the pale stones and hanging sheets to dry on lines. An open-air shrine to the Virgin stood by the riverbank, candle flames flickering pale in the sunlight. Moreno stopped for a moment, uncovering his head and bowing to the shrine.

Music sounded through the lanes between the huts, guitarras and tabors, rebecs and tambourines and voices singing strange, ululating rhythms. Smells drifted in the air, some strange, some familiar: charcoal smoke, horse dung, latrines, pitch, tallow, vinegar, the smell of roasting meat perfumed with cinnamon and cumin and the sharp tang of pepper. Drainage ditches had been cut through the camp at intervals; in one of these, a woman lifted her skirts and squatted down to urinate.

Beyond the ditch was a market, busy with people. They saw stalls and booths selling bundles of firewood, bags of flour, stone jars of wine, piles of fruit buzzing with wasps, strings of onions, baskets of almonds and pistachios, poultry clucking in cages, cured hams sweating in the sun. A voice shouted and people scattered out of the way as a company of men-at-arms rode through the market, lances at the upright, glittering with mail and plate armour. All wore the same device: red floretty crosses on white surcoats. Their leader had raised the visor of his bascinet, revealing a dark-bearded face with deep-set eyes. He glanced at Moreno as they passed, and his eyes widened a little. For a moment Merrivale thought he was going to pull up, but instead he turned in the saddle, calling to his men. They rode on, cantering down the hill towards the siege lines.

'Knights of Calatrava,' Ficaris said.

Moreno nodded. 'I recognise their leader. His name is Pero de Garcíez.'

'He recognised you, too,' said Merrivale. 'Where did you meet him?'

'At Prado del Rey, when I tried to discover what had happened to my family. The Knights have a castle nearby, and Garcíez was the commander there. I asked if he knew anything about the raid, but he refused to answer my questions. He ordered me to leave at once.'

'Arrogant bastard,' said Ficaris. 'Mind you, all of the military orders are. Consider Fra Moriale, for example.'

Merrivale looked at him. 'Moriale was quite offhand with you. Are you certain that you are happy serving with me?'

Ficaris smiled. A friendly man, he spoke fourteen languages and seemed to call everywhere and nowhere home. 'Of course I am. I could use a run ashore, if nothing else. I just like to remind Fra Moriale that his officers are human beings, not automatons who dance to his tune.'

'Does he listen?'

'No, but I feel better for trying. As Saint Augustine once said, free will was given to us by God so that we could make our own moral choices.' Ficaris paused. 'Mind you, he also said that free will gives us the ability to commit sinful acts against the wishes of God, so there you are.'

Merrivale could almost hear Warin rolling his eyes.

A row of mules stood tethered to a wooden rail, swishing their tails at flies. The mule seller was arguing in Castilian with an older man, white-bearded and white-haired in a grey Franciscan friar's habit. The friar was holding the reins of another mule, and clearly was not happy.

'You lied to me!' he shouted. 'You told me that this animal was fit and healthy, but when I set out for Sevilla, it went lame before I even reached Tarifa! I had to walk all the way back to Algeciras! Take this mule back and provide me with another, at once!'

'Nothing to do with me, *señor*,' snapped the mule seller. 'You bought this mule, and whatever happened afterwards is on your head. Now, go away, or I shall call the constables!'

'Call them, by God! Let us take this matter to the law! I am ready!' The other man stabbed his finger at the mule-seller's chest. 'I warn you, *señor*, I have access to unlimited legal resources! I will fight this case all the way to the Cortes if I must!'

The mule seller shook his head in disbelief and turned his back. Muttering, the older man led his mule away. He glanced once at Merrivale before disappearing into the crowded market.

'I think *he* recognised *you*,' said Moreno.

'I've never seen him before,' said Merrivale. 'Warin, did he look familiar to you?'

'No, sir.' Warin paused. 'But he's wearing some very fine leather boots for a Franciscan.'

They climbed the hill past a row of picketed horses and came to a row of tents where lean men in green and russet coats and hose sat playing dice. Longbows lay unstrung on the grass along with quivers of arrows. Merrivale heard the homely accents of Devon and smiled a little. This might be a different world, but just for a moment he was home again.

The pavilion with Sir John Sully's banner was straight ahead. A man walked out of it, snapping his fingers to a dog that trotted at his heels. He stopped suddenly, eyes widening in surprise. 'Simon Merrivale, by all that's holy! What are you doing here, boy?'

Merrivale laughed. 'I might ask you the same question, John. Don't tell me you've turned crusader.'

'This is diplomacy, boy. King Edward sent Derby and Arundel as ambassadors to King Alfonso of Castile, and appointed me captain of their escort.' Sully caught Merrivale by the arms, holding him for a moment. He was sixty years old; his hair was white and his face was lined, but his grip was strong as iron and his blue eyes were bright with youth. 'It's good to see you, boy,' he said quietly.

'You also, John.' Merrivale hesitated for a moment. 'How is my father? Have you seen him?'

'I called on him in the spring, before we came away.' It was Sully's turn to pause. 'Physically he grows frailer. His mind wanders far astray, but you already know that.'

'Yes.' The last time Merrivale had seen his father, the old man no longer remembered his son's name. 'But he is well cared for?'

'The canons at Frithelstock are kind men. They look after him very well.' Sully released him, clapping him on the arm. 'I sense there is a story behind why you are here. Tell it to me over a glass of wine.'

'I should report to my lord of Derby first.' Merrivale introduced Ficaris and Moreno, who bowed. Sully grinned at Warin. 'And I remember Warin of Hexworthy very well. How are you, boy? Still following Simon around, I see. Not tempted to go back to a quiet life in the mines?'

Warin, who came from a tin-mining village on Dartmoor, grinned back. He was a groom and Sully was a knight banneret, but both were from Devon and that levelled the ground between them. 'I'd be bored there, sir. Whatever else you might say, service with Master Merrivale is never dull.'

Sully chuckled. 'Come along, Simon, I'll take you to see Henry. Your companions can wait here until we return. My servants will bring them wine.'

'I don't suppose there is any beer, sir?' asked Warin.

'You're not in Devon now, boy. I haven't seen ale since we crossed the Pyrenees. But the wine here is good, better than those sour, murky vintages we get at home. Try it, boy. You'll see.'

Henry of Grosmont, Earl of Derby and leader of the English embassy to Castile, was playing chess in his pavilion. In his early thirties, big and broad-shouldered with a mane of blond hair and piercing blue eyes, Derby was a cousin of the king of England and one of the most prominent men at the English court. He and Merrivale had known and respected each other for many years.

His opponent, a little older, wore a white robe patterned with red saltires. Merrivale recognised him at once, even though it had been several years since they had met: Philippe d'Évreux, ruler of the little mountain kingdom of Navarre in the far north of Spain. He and his wife were both blood relations to the king of France, and England and France were at war. Yet here he was now, playing chess and drinking wine with Derby like they were old friends.

Well, Merrivale thought, they probably were. The kings of England and France were also closely related, which meant that Derby and Philippe were distant cousins. War in Europe was usually a family affair.

'Simon Merrivale!' Derby said, smiling and rising to his feet. 'By God, now we know the storm clouds are coming! Trouble is never far away when you are around. How are you, my friend? What brings you here?'

The heat of the day was intense now, and the painted canvas sides of the pavilion had been rolled up to let in the breeze. 'It's a long story,' Merrivale said. 'How fares your embassy, my lord?'

'We were just discussing it when you arrived. Philippe, I present to you Simon Merrivale, one of England's most trusted servants.'

Merrivale bowed. 'We have met already,' said Philippe. 'During the truce negotiations in Flanders, three years ago, if you recall?'

'I remember well, Your Grace,' Merrivale said. His eyes were still watchful. Philippe had been at the right hand of the king of France that day, while he himself had been in King Edward's service.

'Be seated, Simon,' Derby said, motioning to a servant to bring more wine. Sully sat down too, uninvited. Sir John Sully of Iddesleigh had been leading men into battle since Derby and Philippe were in swaddling clothes; seniority had its privileges. The dog, who had followed them into the pavilion, curled up at Sully's feet and went to sleep.

'When did you arrive, my lord?' Merrivale asked.

'Three months ago,' Derby said. 'Three long, hot, weary months, with not a damned thing to show for it. Our mission is to persuade King Alfonso to form an alliance with England and join us in our war against France, but quite frankly, it feels like we are banging our heads against a wall.'

'Has the king received you?'

'We see him every week, but he doesn't listen to anything we say. "I am too busy with affairs of state," he says, or "I am too preoccupied with the conduct of the siege. Come back next week." And next week, it is more of the same.'

The wine arrived, a dark rich malvasia, well-watered. 'You have nothing that King Alfonso wants,' Philippe said. 'Had you brought ten thousand of your famous English longbowmen, you might have commanded his attention. Rightly or wrongly, the only thing that matters to him at the moment is al-Jazīra.'

'How is the siege progressing?' Merrivale asked.

'Not well,' said Derby. He looked down at the city at the foot of the hill, its walls wreathed in smoke. 'The sultan of

Murrākush has sent his best troops to hold the city, and every assault so far has been beaten back. Alfonso can't commit the whole of his army to attacking the city, lest the army of Garnāta sally out from its own camp and attack him in the flank.'

'Why have they not done so already?'

'An excellent question. Garnāta and Murrākush are uneasy allies, we are told, and the sultan of Garnāta is unlikely to risk his own army to save the sultan of Murrākush's city. But we also hear that Murrākush is sending reinforcements. When those arrive, the picture will change. The king needs to take al-Jazīra, and quickly.'

'King Alfonso made a cardinal error,' said Sully. 'He should have seized the Jebel Tāriq first, to deny the enemy a base. That would have left al-Jazīra unsupported, and the city would have fallen straight into his hands.'

Philippe sipped his wine. 'Sir John speaks truly,' he said. 'Alfonso also lacks power at sea. Most of his own fleet was destroyed by the Moors three years ago, and he is reliant on Aragón and Genoa for galleys. But he has quarrelled with the king of Aragón, and the Genoese crews have not been paid for weeks and are on the brink of mutiny. The sultan of Murrākush can run supplies into the city without hindrance.'

'Is King Alfonso short of money?' Merrivale asked.

Derby's face was wry. 'Is the pope a Frenchman? The vaults of Alfonso's treasury contain nothing but dust and cobwebs. But he has a new banker now, who has promised to deliver him a fortune.'

'Donato de' Peruzzi,' Merrivale said.

The others looked surprised. 'How did you know?' Sully asked.

'Peruzzi is the reason why I am here,' Merrivale said.

Around them the camp baked with heat. Flies buzzed in the distance. The rock of Jebel Tāriq was burnished with sunlight. On the far side of the strait, its companion the Jebel Musa had disappeared into the haze. Merrivale looked out over the azure sea, wondering how much to say in front of Philippe of Navarre.

'You may speak freely,' Philippe said, reading his thoughts. 'I am no longer in the service of the king of France. Navarre is neutral in the conflict between yourselves and the French.'

Merrivale's eyebrows rose. 'I did not know this, sire,' he said.

'Donato de' Peruzzi was one of the reasons for my rupture with France. I discovered that he was coining false money and lending it to the crown, which is of course an act of treason. I reported this to the king of France, but he refused to believe me and accused *me* of betraying France. I departed from the French court, and will not return. Later, inevitably, Peruzzi's crimes were exposed and he was forced to flee France. But he has not forgotten that I tried to expose him.'

'Peruzzi does not forget or forgive,' Merrivale said slowly. 'If he recoups his wealth and rebuilds his bank, he will be a threat to England.'

'He will be a threat to all of us,' Philippe said, 'but King Alfonso is too blind to see it. He thinks only of the gold Peruzzi has promised him.'

'What are your orders from King Edward?' asked Derby.

'I have none at the moment, my lord. I sent word back to England before I left Florence, but it will be many weeks before I receive a reply. I decided not to wait for orders. Before I left Florence I was given the name of a man who might be able to help me with information about Peruzzi. Dámaso Reyes, the king's physician.'

Derby's looked surprised. 'A physician?'

'He also practises alchemy, my lord, and alchemists spend their lives studying gold. They know where it comes from and who handles it. Peruzzi is obtaining gold from Africa. I am hopeful that Señor Reyes can tell me more.'

Philippe nodded slowly. 'Dámaso Reyes is not in the king's household, but my own physician, Lorenço de Alameda, may know of him. Lorenço also has some skill in alchemy. Please feel free to call upon his services.'

'Thank you, sire. I am grateful.'

Philippe's face was serious. 'I do not know what your intentions are, Master Merrivale, but go carefully. The king has made a favourite of his new banker, and will not hear a word against him. And Peruzzi has also given lavish gifts to the king's mistress, Leonor de Guzmán, to buy her support. Anyone who has Leonor's favour is untouchable.'

He drained his wine glass and rose to his feet. The others rose with him; Sully's dog raised its head briefly and went back to sleep. 'Henry, dear friend, I must go,' Philippe said. 'Master Merrivale, be welcome. If there is anything I can do to assist you, please let me know.'

3

7th of September, 1343

After Philippe departed, Merrivale looked at Derby. 'I really had no idea that His Grace had broken with France,' he said. 'Exile must be hard for him.'

Derby smiled. 'You would never know it. He's been keeping himself busy in Navarre, reforming the laws, building roads, improving agriculture. You know, the sort of things kings ought to do, but seldom get around to doing.'

'Do you trust him, my lord?'

'Philippe of Navarre is an honourable man. Even when he was fighting against us, I trusted him.'

John Sully leaned forward. 'Why do you think Peruzzi is here, Simon? You know him better than anyone. What are his intentions, do you think?'

Merrivale stared out across the camp towards the distant city shimmering in the sunlight. Broad-shouldered and strongly built, he had a plain, unremarkable face; he had once been told that he was the sort of person people would walk past in a crowd, which, in his line of work, could be taken as a compliment. Now in his early thirties, he had spent the last fifteen years as a messenger in the service of King Edward III of England. Officially, his duty was to carry messages from the king to royal agents in the field. His real responsibilities, as Derby and Sully both knew, were more complex and more dangerous.

'You know Peruzzi's history, my lord,' he said. 'While serving as banker to King Edward, he suborned some of the king's senior officials, including some of His Grace's close friends, and used them to plunder our treasury of hundreds of thousands of pounds, meaning that we could not pay our army or defend our coasts from pirates. Earlier, in Savoy, he promised to support our plan to create a new kingdom allied to England against France, and then betrayed our plans to the enemy. Good men died there. I was nearly one of them.'

'Thank God you escaped,' Sully said.

Merrivale looked down at his hands. 'I escaped,' he said. 'But I left part of my soul behind.' Derby and Sully waited. 'We foiled Peruzzi's plots,' Merrivale continued. 'We prevented him from stealing the great crown of England, and drove him back to Florence. Last year I followed him there and succeeded, finally, in driving him into bankruptcy. When his bank collapsed, I thought we had finished with him. But nothing of the sort.'

'What happened?'

'In Rome, I discovered that Peruzzi has a secret source of gold. I could learn very little, only that the gold came from Africa, but it was clear that he intends to rebuild his power, and that he is starting here in Castile. His influence over the king and his mistress disturbs me, but of course this is only the beginning. Peruzzi desires power more than he desires life itself, and he will try to gather as much power as possible into his own hands.'

'Castile is the largest kingdom in Europe,' Derby said soberly. 'If Peruzzi gains control of it, he is indeed a threat to us all.' He paused for a moment, regarding Merrivale. 'You have no commission from King Edward. That means you have no status here. Peruzzi could use his newfound influence to have you expelled, or even arrested.'

'What do you suggest, my lord?'

'Come into my service,' said Derby. 'Are you familiar with the duties of a herald?'

A herald advised his master on matters of heraldry and coats of arms, but more importantly he was also an ambassador. By law, no one was allowed to hinder him or use violence against him, not even an enemy. In token of this immunity, heralds did not carry swords. This suited Merrivale, who had abandoned his own sword some time ago.

'Yes, my lord,' he said.

'It seems the perfect solution, don't you think? As my herald, you would have freedom to move around the camp and talk to anyone you wish. If anyone questions your authority, tell them that you are acting on my behalf.'

'That is very generous of you, my lord. I am in your debt.'

Another man walked into the pavilion, pulling off his gloves and throwing them onto the wooden table beside the chessboard. Slender and dark-haired with chiselled cheekbones and hazel eyes, he was in a state of barely suppressed fury. 'Wine,' he snapped, and a servant hurried forward with a goblet. Arundel drank half of it in a gulp, and slumped down in a chair.

Derby watched him, pursing his lips a little. 'Richard, dear friend,' he said. 'Let me guess. You have had another quarrel with Eleanor.'

Richard Fitzalan, the Earl of Arundel, drank the rest of his wine and held the goblet out to be refilled. 'I'm sorry, Henry,' he said abruptly. 'I know she's your sister, but she is also the most damned unreasonable creature in God's creation. I've seen oxen that were less stubborn.'

'Don't expect me to contradict you,' Derby said. 'Where is Eleanor?'

'Out hunting in the hills.'

'Did she take an escort?'

'That's what we quarrelled about. I told her it was too dangerous to go alone, and she told me to mind my own business. I am paraphrasing, of course. Her exact words were rather different.'

Derby sighed. 'You're right, it really is too risky. I'll have a quiet word with her when she returns. Richard, you will remember Simon Merrivale from Flanders.'

Arundel grunted. 'I do. What's he doing here?'

'I'll let him explain,' said Derby.

Merrivale paused. He and Arundel had met several times in the king's service, and they had not always got along. Arrogance and petulance were two of the earl's least attractive qualities, but King Edward thought highly of him; highly enough to send him on this embassy to Castile. He explained about Peruzzi and the African gold in a little more detail than he had given Derby, and by the end of the story Arundel had forgotten his own problems and was sitting forward a little, looking interested. 'Who is this Fra Moriale?'

'His real name is Jean de Montréal, and he is a Knight of Saint John, at least in theory. At some point in the past he gave up on crusading and became a mercenary captain instead. He served with Carlo Grimaldi's corsairs in Monaco, and later with the Great Company.'

'Is he reliable?' asked Sully.

'So long as his own interests are being served, yes.'

'And you think Peruzzi is getting the gold from Timbuktu?' Arundel said. 'It sounds plausible. But where is he acquiring the salt?'

'That's one of the things I need to discover.' Merrivale explained about Juan Moreno, and his missing nephew Mauro. 'We know this young man served on the caravans,' he said. 'If we can find him, he may be able to tell us more about Peruzzi's scheme.'

'It should be easy enough to find Mauro. If Kāsim's ship was captured in the strait, it's likely that the captives were brought here. There's a slave market in the camp.'

Merrivale was startled. 'Slaves are sold here?'

'Everything is sold here,' Arundel said. 'This is not so much a siege camp as a Michaelmas fair.'

'Thank you, my lord,' Merrivale said. 'I will investigate this.'

'Let's hope you are able to find the poor fellow,' Derby said, and he turned to Sully. 'John, be so good as to find my steward, will you? Tell him to assign accommodation to Master Merrivale. We tend to follow the Spanish custom and rest during the afternoon heat, apart from my mad sister, who has chosen to go out and shoot birds with her crossbow.'

'Not mad,' growled Arundel. 'Mad*dening*, yes, along with intransigent, infuriating and a host of other adjectives. But not mad.'

'That's your opinion,' said Derby. 'Welcome again, Simon, it is good to see you. We dine at sunset.'

Derby's steward was, like his master, a pleasant, easy-going man who welcomed Merrivale to the household and promised that a pavilion would be made ready as soon as possible. 'Come and have another glass of wine while we wait,' Sully said. 'A friend sent me a flask of bastard wine from Portugal. A bit lighter than that syrup Henry insists on drinking.'

They sat in the shade of Sully's pavilion, sipping wine in the heat. The dog rolled over onto its back at Merrivale's feet, hoping to have its belly scratched. Sully glanced over at Merrivale. 'How have you been, boy?' he asked quietly.

'What do you mean?'

'You know what I mean.' Sully studied him for a moment. 'You've changed,' he said. 'You're quieter, not so restless. Who did that to you?'

'I did it to myself.' Merrivale looked into his wineglass. 'I threw away my sword, John.'

'Did you? In this violent and godless world, that seems like a reckless thing to do.'

'Yes, and it will probably get me killed. So be it. My time will come when it comes. But I realised that every time I killed a man, a part of my humanity died with him. I had to stop.'

'Don't tell me you're going to become a monk, boy. I doubt you'll find peace in the cloister.'

Merrivale smiled a little. 'Becoming a herald is good enough for me.'

'And that fair maid in Savoy, Yolande of Bohemia. You still think of her?'

'I will think of her until I die.' Merrivale raised his head, looking up at the sky. 'You're right, John, I am not so restless. My soul is at least partly at peace. But it is not a happy peace.'

Silence fell. Sully cleared his throat, changing the subject. 'Your problem seems simple enough. Go to the slave market, find out what happened to this lad and track him down. If he is a Christian, they will surely have set him free once his identity was known.'

'It won't be that easy,' Merrivale said. 'It never is.'

'You're a pessimist, boy.'

'I'm a realist.'

Another silence descended. 'Pardon me if I am intruding on something which is not my business,' Merrivale said, 'but when I left England eighteen months ago, both the Earl of Arundel and Derby's sister Eleanor were married to other people.'

Sully leaned back in his chair. 'Eleanor's husband was killed in a tournament accident last year. My lord of Arundel's wife is back in England, and still very much alive. He left her to live with Eleanor.'

'Derby makes no objection to this?'

'His lordship is broad-minded, as you know, and he dotes on his sister. She can do no wrong in his eyes. He thinks Arundel is a good man, too.'

'Then he must see something in Arundel that the rest of us are missing,' Merrivale said. 'Come to that, so must she.'

'Eleanor thinks with her heart, not her head.'

'Yes.' Three years ago, during a hard, bitter winter in Flanders, Eleanor of Lancaster had been lady-in-waiting to Queen Philippa of England, while he was a King's Messenger unravelling Donato de' Peruzzi's plot against England. He remembered her well: tall, fair and slender as a sylph with warm expressive eyes, unhappily married and bitter about the lot that fortune had cast for her. She had raged against fate a great deal.

So, for that matter, had he. By spring they had become unlikely friends.

'John, could Peruzzi be using his influence with King Alfonso to stop him from listening to our embassy's proposals?'

'It seems likely, doesn't it? All the more reason to put Peruzzi out of the way. We could find an assassin,' Sully said thoughtfully.

'I thought of that in Florence, but he was always too well protected. I suspect it will be the same here. Tell me more about the king's mistress.'

'Leonor de Guzmán? She's the real power in the kingdom. Alfonso makes no decision without consulting her.'

'What hold does she have over him?'

Sully chuckled. 'The usual one. Alfonso is what you might call a passionate man. Have you heard of the old Castilian hero, El Çid Campeador, my lord the champion? In the army they refer to Alfonso as El Çid Fornicador. You don't need me to translate that, I'm sure.'

'Alfonso is married, is he not? Where is his queen?'

'The spurned woman? Queen María is in Córdoba, plotting her revenge.' Sully pondered for a moment. 'I am concerned, Simon. I think Philippe of Navarre is in danger, too. Leonor dislikes him intensely, and Peruzzi must surely see him as a threat.'

Merrivale leaned forward a little. 'Why? Because of the accusations he made in France?'

'Partly,' Sully said. 'But partly because he is a peacemaker. He's friendly with the kings of Aragón and Portugal, who have both fallen out with Alfonso. He is also negotiating with the sultan of Garnāta about concluding peace with Castile.'

'Does Alfonso know this?'

'He does. Peace with Garnāta would be to Castile's advantage, of course, because if the sultan withdraws from the war, Murrākush will be left high and dry and al-Jazīra will fall. But Philippe's objective is different. He wants to see all of the kingdoms of Iberia live in peace with their neighbours.'

'And that would not suit Peruzzi,' Merrivale said. 'He thrives on chaos. How has Philippe offended Leonor?'

'He's popular, not just with his own men but with the Castilians too. When he first arrived back in the spring, the whole camp was covered in muck and filth, half the troops were down with runny bellies or the flux, and there was hardly any food. Philippe arranged for regular provisioning of the camp, ordered drainage ditches to be dug and ensured there was a supply of clean water from the rivers. That won him respect, so much that Leonor now sees him as a rival.'

'Why didn't the Castilian captains clean up the camp themselves?'

Sully smiled. 'This is Spain, boy. Things are different down here. Among the nobility, it's every man or woman for themselves, grab as much power as you can at the expense of the others. They're like cats in a sack. No one works together unless it benefits them personally.'

'And the king doesn't put a stop to this?'

'He couldn't if he tried. The Castilian nobles are as fractious and unruly a tribe as you will ever see. Have you heard the oath of allegiance the nobles swear when a new king is anointed? *We, who are as good as you, say to you, who are no better than us, that we will obey you so long as you respect our rules and customs; and if you do not, we will not.* Every *fidalgo* in the army thinks they are as good as the king, if not better. They obey him so long as it serves their own interests.'

'And that too will serve Peruzzi's ends,' Merrivale said soberly. He looked out across the camp, baking in the afternoon sun. 'This is the kind of atmosphere in which he thrives. I only hope I have not arrived too late.'

Further up the hill, at the highest point of the siege camp, a cluster of newly built wooden buildings huddled around a stone watchtower. The Castilian royal standard flew from a mast on the tower's roof. Behind it was a row of stables, built for the pampered palfreys of the royal household so that they should not have to endure the same heat and dust as the ordinary horses of the army.

Sunset was casting long shadows across the camp. The smells of roasting meat and spices wafted between the pavilions. Somewhere down the hill, a bagpipe sang a dolorous farewell to the day; further away, the long mellow chants of the muezzins drifted from the minarets of al-Jazīra, calling the faithful to evening prayer. Inside the stable, the horses stood nodding in their stalls, paying no attention to the three people standing in the gathering shadows. Two were men: one thin and ascetic with a long, aquiline nose, the other dark-haired and bearded with deep-set eyes. The third was a woman, full-figured and wrapped in a black cloak despite the heat, a veil covering her face.

'Juan Moreno is here,' said Pero de Garcíez, the bearded man.

Donato de' Peruzzi, the man with the long nose, looked impatient. 'Why are you and your friends in the Order of Calatrava interested in Juan Moreno?'

'He is the uncle of Kāsim's man, Mauro. He came to Prado del Rey looking for his sister and her son. I drove him off, but the bastard has carried on searching for his nephew. He arrived today with the Englishman, Merrivale.'

'Is he a threat?' asked the veiled woman.

'To you, perhaps,' said Peruzzi. 'Not to me.'

'Do not be so sure of this,' said Garcíez. 'Merrivale has already spoken to the English delegation, and to your enemy Philippe of Navarre. If Moreno finds his nephew, he and Merrivale will have a weapon to use against us.'

Peruzzi sneered at him. 'And whose fault is that? If you had obeyed orders, all would be well. But no, you were greedy, and you wanted to placate your allies. In the future, you will follow my orders to the letter. Is that understood?'

'Yes,' Garcíez said sullenly. 'How much longer must we wait?'

'Until we are ready. My arrangements are not yet complete. When they are, we will proceed. Wait for my orders, both of you.'

'You are arrogant, Peruzzi,' snapped Leonor de Guzmán. She pulled her veil aside, revealing a round face with full lips and vivid dark eyes. 'You have power by the king's favour, remember? He can withdraw that favour at a snap of his fingers.'

Peruzzi gazed at her. 'Was the last gift I gave you too insubstantial? Do you desire more?'

'You are also presumptuous.'

'And you are forgetful, *mi çaida*. I have what the king needs. Gold. I can supply him with all the gold maravedís he desires; enough, even, to buy a replacement for you.'

Her eyes glinted. 'You go too far, banker.'

'Mother of God, let us not fall out,' Garcíez pleaded. 'Believe me, if Moreno discovers our secret, we are all undone!'

'Then ensure that he does not discover it,' Peruzzi said. 'Do whatever you must. But do not touch Merrivale, is that understood? If anything happens to him here in the camp, fingers will point at me. I cannot afford that, not yet.'

'Do not fail, either of you,' said Leonor de Guzmán. She was still angry. 'A kingdom is at stake, *señores*. Make no mistakes, or I personally will see to it that both of your heads are on the block. Do you understand me?'

Both men bowed. Leonor drew her veil back across her face and swept out of the stable. Garcíez stood for a moment, waiting until she had gone. 'Does she know?' he murmured.

'Know what you are planning to do to your own grand master? Of course not. If she did, you would be dead by now. Do not fear, your secret is safe with me.'

Garcíez departed too. Donato de' Peruzzi stood for a moment longer, listening to the soft breathing of the horses close at hand and the murmur of the camp beyond. A rare smile crossed his shadowy face.

'A kingdom?' he murmured. 'Oh, my dear lady, there is so much more. More than you could possibly dream of.'

Dinner at Derby's pavilion was a quiet affair. The embassy was a small one, and the households of the two earls numbered only about thirty people; the archers of their escort ate separately. Roast pork and roast capon, mutton pies and venison all with highly flavoured sauces were accompanied by Derby's favourite malvasia. Juan Moreno thought the wine was excellent; Ficaris tasted his and made a face.

Eleanor of Lancaster did not come to dinner. Arundel sat brooding in silence, and partway through the meal he rose and left.

'My archers are taking bets,' Sully murmured to Merrivale. 'Half – the romantic ones – think they will sort out their problems and be married soon. The other half reckon she'll leave him before we get home.'

'How can they marry when he still has a wife?'

'He can get an annulment. It'll cost money, but that's no obstacle for the richest man in England. But there would be a stigma for his wife, and his son would be made a bastard. Other men would think nothing of that, of course. But say what you want about Arundel, he has a conscience.'

After the meal, Merrivale returned to his own pavilion. Ficaris, Moreno and Warin went to bed, but Merrivale, restless and unable to sleep, went back outside. The moon, just past full, cast a path of silver across the bay and shone bright on the hills around it. Watchfires glowed in the siege lines and on the ramparts of al-Jazīra, and sparkled in the camp of the army of Garnāta across the bay. A dog barked nearby; he heard Sully's voice, hushing it.

Arundel's pavilion showed no lights, but in Merrivale's imagination the canvas walls seemed to quiver with tension. From inside came the sound of two soft voices, a man and a woman; murmuring, sometimes dropping to an agonised whisper, always too faint to make out the words. After a few minutes the voices stopped, and a heavy silence fell.

Merrivale studied the shadows on the face of the moon. His own blunt features were suddenly weary. *Poor troubled souls*, he thought. He knew what it was like to love someone who was unattainable; he remembered sitting in a garden in Turin, holding the hand of another fair, beautiful woman, gazing at the same moon. The time he had spent with Yolande was bittersweet, full of dreams of a future they both knew could never come to pass. He felt a moment of sympathy for Eleanor, and even for Arundel.

Enough, he told himself. *Concentrate on Peruzzi. Concentrate on the mission. Time will take care of the rest.* He gave the moon one last searching glance, and went back into his pavilion.

4

8th of September, 1343

The pavilion allocated to Merrivale and his companions came with some plain wooden furniture, a stray tabby cat attracted by the leavings from a nearby kitchen, and a Castilian servant who greeted Merrivale, Ficaris and Moreno with respect and Warin with insulting indifference. In the morning the servant brought flatbread, dishes of green olives and salted almonds, lemon juice sweetened with honey and some weak white wine, setting these ostentatiously in front of three wooden stools around the table and indicating that Warin should fetch his own food. Warin said nothing.

Moreno was hesitant. 'It is kind of you to help me find my nephew, but he was only a slave in Kāsim's service. He may know nothing that can assist you.'

'Or he may know a great deal,' Merrivale said. 'If he served on those caravans, he must know something about them, and at this point any information is of value. But also, Señor Moreno, an injustice has been done to Mauro. I want to put that right.'

'You are a good man,' Moreno said quietly.

'Not everyone would agree.' Merrivale turned to Warin, sitting on a bench in the corner. 'While we are at the slave market, find out where Peruzzi is quartered and anything you can about his household.'

'Already done, sir,' said Warin, spitting an olive stone into his hand. 'I went for a walk while you were at dinner last evening.'

'Did you meet anyone interesting?' asked Ficaris, feeding a piece of bread to the cat. 'A pretty *señorita*, perhaps? Or two?'

Warin eyed him. 'If you are accusing me of neglecting my duty, Master Ficaris, come out and say it.'

'I was joking,' Ficaris said. 'Have I done something to offend you, Warin?'

'No,' Warin said. 'I just don't trust you, that's all.'

Servants were not usually this forthright, but Ficaris already knew that Warin was no ordinary servant. 'I am sorry to hear it,' he said regretfully. 'I shall do my best to earn your trust.'

Warin looked sceptical. 'Peruzzi has a proper house, sir, not a tent. A big wooden one not far from the king's house, with more servants than you can count. There are guards at the main gate and the postern, and they're not just ordinary foot soldiers. They're serving brothers from the Knights of Calatrava.'

Knights of the military orders were required to be of gentle birth; serving brothers were men from the lower orders of society, recruited as spearmen or crossbowmen. They were usually highly professional, veteran fighters. 'Could we get inside the house?' Merrivale asked.

Warin shook his head. 'There's an old wives' tale that says if you put beans in your mouth while looking at your reflection in a mirror, you become invisible. We could try that, I suppose, but otherwise, sir, I don't give much for our chances.' He paused. 'We'd have to kill a cat first. That's part of the ritual.'

'No one is killing any cats,' Ficaris said firmly, reaching down to stroke the tabby rubbing around his legs. 'So, Peruzzi has hired the Order of Calatrava to guard him. Why?'

'I have heard of the Order of Calatrava, but no more,' Merrivale asked. 'Tell me about them.'

'They are the most powerful military order in Spain,' said Moreno. 'Monks, but also seasoned warriors. They have thousands of men at their command, knights and lay brothers, and vast landholdings. Their grand master is a sovereign prince in his own right, who answers only to the pope.'

'They also have an alliance with the Knights of Saint John,' said Ficaris. 'I don't know if that means anything.'

'It might,' said Merrivale. 'Peruzzi was in Rhodes before he came to Spain. When are we expecting Fra Moriale to return?'

'Four or five days,' said Ficaris.

'I'm betting he knows more about the Knights of Calatrava.' Merrivale rose to his feet. 'Warin, Master Moreno, Master Ficaris—'

'Call me Jac,' said Ficaris.

Moreno nodded, smiling suddenly. 'I am Juan,' he said.

'Very well. Juan, Jac, let us go and pay a call at the slave market.'

The servant entered the pavilion, bowing to Merrivale and holding out a cloth bundle. 'This has just arrived for you, sir.'

Merrivale unfolded the bundle. Inside was an open-sided silk tabard, painted with the Earl of Derby's coat of arms, three white leopards on a field of red with a black bend. Wrapped in the tabard was a slender wooden wand, painted white: his sign of office. Merrivale pulled the tabard over his head, smoothing it over his worn travelling clothes. It was curious to be so visible, he thought. In his previous service with King Edward he had usually tried quite hard to avoid being noticed. That was how one survived.

The others rose to their feet. Warin turned to Merrivale. 'Sir, might I have a word in private?'

Warin had been in Merrivale's service for many years, and Merrivale trusted him as he trusted few others. 'Of course,' he said.

Ficaris and Moreno went outside. 'Is this about the servant?' Merrivale asked.

'I can deal with him. It's about Master Ficaris, sir. You do know he is spying on us for Fra Moriale?'

Merrivale looked surprised. 'Of course. Why else would Moriale have sent him?'

'That doesn't worry you, sir?'

'Not at all. At the moment, our interests and Moriale's coincide. There is no need to conceal anything from him.'

'At the moment,' Warin repeated. 'I understand, sir.'

Outside, the air was hazy with smoke from thousands of charcoal fires. The morning sun hung red over the rock of the Jebel Tāriq. Already, the heat was rising. The camp was busy; today was the feast day of the Nativity of the Blessed Virgin Mary, and the processions and parades of relics through the camp had already begun. The chants of priests and monks echoed through the lanes between the tents, '*Benedicta tu in mulieribus, et benedictus fructus ventris tui. Kyrie eleison.*' Ignoring the chants, a *juglar* sat on a wooden stool strumming a *guitarra* and singing a song about King Alfonso.

El Çid Fornicador is a mighty hero
He has the strength of Hercules
He mates with anything that has legs
Last week, he impregnated a table

Hawkers cried their wares, importuning Merrivale and his companions to buy flatbread wheels strung on long poles, bunches of rosemary, baskets of hazelnuts and almonds, amulets to cure warts, sausages tied with string; a Michaelmas fair, Arundel had called the camp. Most of the hawkers moved swiftly on once they were rebuffed, but one of the amulet sellers turned after they had passed, and followed them.

The slave market was at the southern end of the camp, where the hills came down to the sea, and was as shabby and despairing as its name implied. A couple of open wooden pens with no shelter or relief from the blazing sun stood on one side of a dusty yard. A weather-beaten stone hut that might once have been a stable stood opposite the pens. Guards stood outside the hut, leaning on long spears. The air smelled of dust and sweat and stale urine, and despair.

One of the pens was full of tall lean men with brown skins and hard-planed faces. Most wore long dark robes and loose turbans, but some were stripped to the waist and a few were naked apart from leather sandals. Many had tattoos, rows of deep blue geometric symbols on their faces and arms. Some bore the long red lines of sword wounds on their bodies; others had round punctures from crossbow bolts on their arms or legs. All of the wounds were untreated and crusted with blood. Flies buzzed in the air. The men stared at Merrivale and his companions with dark, hostile eyes.

'Dear God,' Ficaris said under his breath. His usual good humour had vanished.

Warin moved up beside Merrivale. 'Did you see the amulet seller, sir?' he asked quietly.

'Keep an eye on him. Jac, can you talk to the slaves?'

Ficaris swallowed and walked towards the slave pens, moving slowly like a man pushing through an invisible barrier. '*Salaam*,' he said quietly in Arabic. 'Where do you come from?'

Silence, apart from the droning of the flies. Ficaris tried again in a different language, one that Merrivale did not recognise. '*Sslam. Ansa-k?*'

The door of the hut opened and a man walked out into the yard. His coat was blazoned with the arms of Castile, and a sword was girdled at his bulbous waist. The pommel of the sword was dirty and the leather scabbard was scuffed and scarred. 'Welcome, *señor*,' he said cheerfully. 'The sale isn't until tomorrow morning, but you are welcome to view the merchandise.' He waved a hand at the men in the slave pen. 'We took this lot a couple of days ago during a sortie from the city. Fresh meat, you might say.'

Merrivale inclined his head. 'Permit me to introduce myself. My name is Merrivale, and I am herald to the Earl of Derby. I am here to make inquiries about some slaves that were sold in February of this year. Can you assist me?'

'Of course, of course! I am the *alcalde*, I keep the records. Come with me.'

'Talk to the slaves,' Merrivale murmured to Ficaris. 'Find out whatever you can.'

He followed the *alcalde* into the hut, the interior dim after the harsh sunlight outside. A row of tables ran down the centre of the room, with benches pushed up behind them. Rolls of parchment rested in pigeonholes on the wall behind.

'You are fortunate to find me here,' the *alcalde* said. 'Except on market days, there's usually no one here but the guards. I only came down to check on our new arrivals and make sure they aren't causing any trouble. Now, which consignment are you looking for?'

'They were taken at sea,' Merrivale said. 'Members of the household of a merchant from Marrakesh, Kāsim al-'Aswad.'

'Kāsim al-'Aswad,' the *alcalde* repeated thoughtfully. 'I remember now. A good big consignment, a hundred heads or more. The Lord was bountiful that day.' He pulled one of the parchment rolls out of its pigeonhole, untying the red ribbon and unrolling it. 'Yes, here we go. Kāsim al-'Aswad of Marrakesh, two wives, several children, forty-two members of his *casa*, then some other passengers and the crew of the ship. One hundred and two in all. The women weren't much to look at, so they were sold off cheap, but Kāsim and his men were in prime condition. They fetched a good price.'

'Kāsim was sold? I heard that he was killed when the ship was captured.'

The *alcalde* shook his head. 'The record is quite definite. *Kasim de Marrakech venditus inemptis pro sexaginta maravedis.* It's all here.'

'Do you have the names of the other members of the household?' Merrivale asked.

'Oh, no, our records aren't that detailed. We record the names of the quality, in case anyone from the other side should be interested in ransoming them back. The rest are just Moors. Merchandise, as I said.'

Merrivale fought down his anger. 'Is it possible that one of the household could have been a Christian? A slave owned by Kāsim?'

The *alcalde* frowned. 'A Christian? Seems unlikely.'

'Why?'

'Well, if he was a Christian, he would have identified himself, wouldn't he? He'd hardly let himself be sold into slavery again, he'd have to be mad. No, all the people sold here are Moors. You can take my word for it.'

Merrivale nodded curtly. 'Two more questions, if I may. Who brought the crew and passengers to the market?'

The *alcalde* consulted the parchment. 'Here it is. The Order of Calatrava. No name, just an officer of the order, it says.'

'And can you tell me who purchased them?'

'The steward of the manor of La Algaba, it says here. No idea where that is, I'm afraid. What is your master's interest?'

'He might be interested in buying some of them,' Merrivale said.

'Well, if he wants slaves, take a look at the stock in the yard. Some of them are a bit damaged, but they're good strong workers.'

Merrivale gripped his wand of office until his knuckles were white. 'I will be sure to do so,' he said. 'Thank you for your time, *señor*.'

Back out in the dust and heat, Merrivale motioned to his companions and they walked away from the slave pens. The brown-skinned men watched them go, the silence of death draped around them.

'What happened to the amulet seller?' Merrivale asked Warin.

'He left just after you went inside, sir. I haven't seen him since.' Warin looked back at the men in the pens. 'What will be their fate?'

'They will be sold as labourers, in the fields or in the mines,' Ficaris said. He looked as if he wanted to be sick. 'They will be treated badly and fed worse. In a few years' time, unless their families offer to ransom them – which is very unlikely – they will be dead.'

'Why is it unlikely?' demanded Warin.

'Those men are Imazighen,' said Moreno. 'Amazigh, in the singular. The outside world calls them Berbers, but never call them that to their faces. I met many of them when I was in Marrakesh. They are proud, but they are also poor. There is little money in the high mountains where their families live, certainly not enough to pay for ransoms.'

'Did you discover anything?' Merrivale asked. A tight knot of rage still burned in the pit if his stomach. *Those men are human beings. God's creations, just like ourselves. And he called them merchandise.*

'None of them would talk at first,' said Moreno, 'but later one man came and spoke to us alone.' He hesitated. 'His name is Ghilas. He offered information in exchange for liberty.'

'And you promised it to him?'

'I have seen enough of slavery,' Ficaris said abruptly. 'To save even one man is better than nothing.'

'Ghilas served with a company called the Warriors of the Faithful in the army of Granada,' Moreno said. 'He knew nothing of Kāsim or his household, but he has heard rumours that some Castilians are colluding with the Moors in the slave trade. They weaken the defences along our *frontera*, the frontier with Granada, so that the Moors can raid our villages without opposition. The Moors sell the slaves they take, and share the profits with the corrupt officials.'

'Who are these officials?' demanded Merrivale. 'How long has this been going on?'

'Ghilas did not know the details, but he said this has been happening for many years.' Moreno's fists clenched. 'People like my sister and her husband are being sold into slavery so that other men may profit. I hope that God strikes them down.'

'He hasn't so far,' said Ficaris. He looked at Merrivale. 'Can we free Ghilas?'

'I'll speak to Derby,' Merrivale said. 'If he consents, we'll buy Ghilas at the auction tomorrow, and hear his story. Jac, Juan, can I leave this to you?'

They were passing another set of horse lines, rows of heavy warhorses picketed and munching straw from feed boxes. Ficaris said nothing. 'Jac?' said Merrivale. 'What is wrong?'

'I said I had seen enough of slavery,' Ficaris said quietly. 'I was a slave myself once, in Egypt, a few years ago. I wasn't harshly treated, at least not often, and in the end I managed to escape. But seeing those poor devils made me remember.'

Moreno touched him on the arm. 'I will go alone to the auction, Jac. You need not come with me.'

'No,' Ficaris said. 'No, I will go. It's all in the past, time I got over it—' He looked up sharply. '*Christ! Behind you!*'

Merrivale turned. Men were running out from behind the picketed horses, men in dark coats with no badges, knives and short swords glittering in their hands. *Six of them*, Merrivale thought, *always establish the odds*, and he moved sideways as the first man sprang at him, knife upraised. Merrivale hit the man with his herald's wand, which snapped. Dropping the broken wood, he grabbed his assailant's arm and dragged it down, twisting his arm to force the knife from his hand, and punched him hard in the stomach. The man doubled up and staggered backwards. He saw Ficaris stab another with his dagger, Moreno on his back wrestling with a third, Warin cornered by two more, swiping with his own knife to keep them at bay. Moreno's assailant had the saffron grower by the throat, but Merrivale grabbed the man's hair and pulled him back, remembering just in time not to break the man's neck, and hit him a sweeping blow across the side of his head, rolling him over in the dust, and kicking him hard as he tried to get to his feet. Ficaris ran towards Warin and stabbed one of his attackers in the arm; the man howled with pain and bolted back through the horse lines. The others followed, two of them bleeding heavily.

Moreno rose to his feet, brushing the dust off his clothes. Another man stood next to the horses, watching them for a moment. His eyes met Merrivale and he turned away, walking quickly back into the camp and disappearing.

'Did you see him?' Merrivale asked quietly.

'Yes,' said Moreno. There was confusion in his dark eyes. 'It was Pero de Garcíez.'

Ficaris bent over, resting his hands on his knees, panting and trying to catch his breath. 'Well?' he said finally to Warin. 'Do you trust me now?'

Warin sheathed his knife, gasping too. 'I'm prepared to admit you have your uses, Master Ficaris,' he said.

Ficaris grinned and straightened, clapping Warin on the arm. 'Call me Jac,' he said.

5

8th of September, 1343

Merrivale reported to Derby, and described the morning's events. The earl frowned. 'I'll pay for this man's freedom myself, of course. This attack on you. Is this Peruzzi's work?'

'Possibly,' said Merrivale. 'Peruzzi has not troubled to conceal his links to the Order of Calatrava. But the involvement of the Knights in the capture of Kāsim and his people troubles me. Why did they intercept Kāsim's ship?'

'Coincidence. One of their galleys was in the right place at the right time.'

'I don't like coincidences, my lord. And further, why was Juan Moreno told that Kāsim was dead?'

Derby puffed out his cheeks. 'Perhaps someone wanted Kāsim to disappear. The rumour of his death was put about to discourage anyone from trying to find him or ransom him.'

Merrivale nodded. 'Which makes it all the more important that we find him. He was a merchant and caravan master, and he will certainly know who was trading with Timbuktu and where the salt came from. We need, urgently, to find out whether Peruzzi has access to the royal salt mines.'

Derby nodded. 'We are invited to dine with the king to celebrate the feast of the Nativity, so perhaps that will give us a chance to ask some questions. Meanwhile, we must give thought to your protection.'

'I'm not convinced those men really meant to kill us, my lord. I think their intention was to frighten us off.'

'Perhaps, but let's not take chances. I'll ask John Sully to assign some of his men to keep watch on you.'

'Thank you, my lord.'

Merrivale returned to his pavilion, where the servant brought him a cup of wine. There was a fresh bruise on the man's cheek, and he treated Warin with respect. 'What happened to him?' Merrivale asked after the servant had withdrawn.

'Not sure, sir,' Warin said. 'I think he may have tripped over the cat.'

'And accidentally landed on your fist?' Ficaris asked.

Warin shook his head. 'There's no witnesses to prove it,' he said. 'Jac.'

'We must discover where La Algaba is so we can find Mauro and Kāsim,' Merrivale said. 'Ask everyone you meet, buy them as many drinks as they want, but find out.'

'Where are you going, Simon?' Ficaris asked.

'To join Derby and his household at the king's banquet,' Merrivale said. 'For my sins.'

Changing into fresh clothes and pulling on his tabard once more, Merrivale joined Derby, Arundel and their esquires. Eleanor of Lancaster was there too, tall and fair in a red gown shot with silver, her hand on Arundel's arm. Her eyes lit up with genuine pleasure. 'Simon Merrivale! It is good to see a familiar face so far from home.'

'I could say likewise,' said Merrivale. 'How are you, my lady?'

'I am well, thank you.' Merrivale wondered how true this was. She was thinner than he remembered, and there were shadows under her eyes.

Philippe of Navarre joined them with his own entourage, including the captain of his escort, Guilhem-Arnaut de Irunberri, tall and broad-shouldered with long brown hair and a drooping moustache, and the royal physician Lorenço de Alameda, a pleasant-faced man in a long red robe. They walked up the hill together, Philippe and Derby chatting pleasantly like old friends.

King Alfonso's house stood on high ground near the old watchtower, a low timber structure surrounding a stone-flagged courtyard. An altar had been set up at one end of the courtyard and priests in glittering robes stood in front of it, sweating in the afternoon heat. The *fidalgos* of Castile and their wives – at least, Merrivale thought, one assumes they are wives – gathered in the courtyard, the men robed in brilliant colours and the women all in white with veils covering most of their faces. None of the nobles appeared to be talking to each other, or even looking at each other, and their hands were never far from the hilts of their swords. The hot air vibrated with tension and hostility.

A thin, vulpine man robed in black stood next to a big, balding, grey-bearded man-at-arms in a white surcoat blazoned with the red floretty cross of Calatrava. The thin man looked up suddenly, and his gaze met Merrivale's. Six years of hostility and hate flared invisible in the air between them before Peruzzi's face changed to a cold mask of indifference. Merrivale stared back at him, mastering his own anger. Their eyes locked for a few moments before Peruzzi turned deliberately away.

'Donato de' Peruzzi,' John Sully murmured to Merrivale. 'Look at him standing there, like he owns the place.'

'Let's hope he doesn't already,' Merrivale said. 'Who is that with him?'

Peruzzi was talking behind his hand to the balding man, who nodded and looked at Merrivale. 'That is Brother Juan Núñez, grand master of the Order of Calatrava,' Sully said. 'A prince of the church, and the veriest hypocrite you will ever meet.'

'What do you mean?'

'Like all of his order, he took vows of poverty, chastity and obedience. He obeys no law but his own, he is far from chaste and his greed is legendary. I don't like the idea of him getting too familiar with Peruzzi.'

A chamberlain stepped into the courtyard and rapped his staff on the flagstones for silence. 'His Grace, the king!' he announced.

Everyone bowed, some more reluctantly than others, Merrivale saw. One older man with a white beard barely inclined his head. The king, a short, stocky man robed in white, red and gold, stamped into the courtyard. He looked discontented; Merrivale wondered if something had displeased him, or whether that was his usual expression. A woman followed him, full-figured in an expensive black gown, a gold wire cap set with citrines and amethysts holding her veil in place over her hair.

'Leonor de Guzmán,' Sully whispered.

One of the priests raised his arms and began to intone in Latin. Mass began, and went on, and on still longer. Hymns and chants succeeded each other in monotonous succession. Clouds of incense filled the courtyard, stinging everyone's throats. The king and his mistress knelt to take communion, which was not offered to anyone else. 'Just as well,' Sully murmured, 'or we'd be here all night.' The sun swam down into the west, turning orange as it reached the shrouds of haze hanging over the hills. Finally, the celebration ended, ironically just as the lilting call to evening prayer drifted up the hill from the mosques of al-Jazīra.

Dinner was served in the great hall, lit with banks of candles that wavered a little in the evening breeze. The walls were hung with tapestries depicting scenes from the life of the legendary hero Rodrigo de Vivar, El Çid Campeador himself, dispensing justice to his subjects and slaughtering his enemies. The king took his seat in a gilded chair, with Leonor de Guzmán at his right hand. To his left was his new best friend, the banker Donato de' Peruzzi. Grand Master Núñez was on Leonor's other side. Merrivale saw Philippe of Navarre at the high table too, watching the scene with sombre eyes.

The king's mistress, the Order of Calatrava. Peruzzi was gathering his allies. *This is how it always begins*, Merrivale thought. *This is how Peruzzi plays the game.*

Philippe's household and the English delegation were seated partway down the hall, below the Castilian nobles and just above the court officials and minor clergy; a snub, as John Sully remarked under his breath. Merrivale sat next to Alameda the physician, watching while servants laid out dishes of roast pork with cumin, pepper and raisins, pigeon pie with almonds and saffron, puddings of lamb's brains with pepper and sugar, green salad with fresh pungent herbs and pastries with rosewater syrup. Red wine, dark and rich, splashed into goblets and cups. Merrivale turned to his companion.

'May I ask where you studied medicine, *señor*? Did you attend the medical school in Salerno?'

Alameda smiled. 'Alas, I could never afford to travel to Italy. I studied at the university in Salamanca, but some of our professors had been to Salerno. Why do you ask?'

'A friend of mine once taught at Salerno. Her name is Mercuriade. Do you know her?'

There was respect in Alameda's eyes. 'I know her reputation, of course. The queen of apothecaries, they call her. How did you come to make her acquaintance?'

'It's a long story... When I last saw Mercuriade, she suggested that I speak to Dámaso Reyes, the king's physician. Is he here at court?'

Alameda shook his head. 'Señor Reyes now serves Queen María. I understand from His Grace that you wanted to talk to Señor Reyes about alchemy? If so, I have made some study of the subject. I am at your disposal.'

'Thank you,' Merrivale said. 'I am grateful. How much do you know about the importation of gold from Africa?'

Alameda looked surprised by the question. 'Officially, no African gold has entered the kingdom since the war with Marrakesh began. I imagine there is still some smuggling, but the quantities would be quite small to avoid detection. Perhaps a few thousand maravedís come in each year, no more.'

'Where else is gold found?'

'Hungary and Transylvania, primarily, but the quality is not as good. By the time it gets to us, Hungarian gold has usually been alloyed with other metals. African gold is extremely pure, and therefore more expensive.' Alameda smiled. 'Which is why we alchemists are so keen to discover the secret of making it.'

'May I ask another question, which has nothing to do with alchemy? I understand that salt is a royal monopoly in Castile. Has that monopoly been farmed out?'

The smile this time was wry. 'You mean, to Italian bankers who promise the king that they can raise money? Oh, there has been plenty of speculation about what reward Donato de' Peruzzi is receiving. Bankers always want something, don't they? But I have heard no rumours about salt.' Alameda hesitated for a moment. 'Why do you ask?'

'It was just an idea,' Merrivale said. He looked up at the high table. The king was talking to Leonor, smiling, his hand on her arm, and she was laughing. Peruzzi, on the king's other side, was once again looking straight at Merrivale. Suddenly, for all the heat of a summer evening, the air felt cold.

Dinner finished and the boards were cleared in preparation for dancing. Alfonso and Leonor remained seated while the rest of the guests moved around the hall, wine goblets in hand. A page arrived, requesting that the Earls of Derby and Arundel attend on the king. Derby looked at Philippe of Navarre, who had come to join them. 'Perhaps he is ready to receive us at last,' he said hopefully.

'Good fortune, cousin,' said Philippe.

But fortune, it seemed, had other ideas. Derby and Arundel were back in a few minutes, the former looking exasperated, the latter's face flushed with anger. 'He summoned us into his presence to tell us that he didn't have time to summon us into his presence,' Derby said. 'He has ordered a new attack on the city six days from now, and will not be able to see us before then. All of his attention is on the siege.'

'That, and humping Guzmán,' Arundel said sourly.

Eleanor of Lancaster rolled her eyes. 'Don't be crude.'

'I daresay Richard has a point,' Philippe said dryly. 'Have patience, my friends. Sooner or later, Alfonso will run out of excuses.'

'We could all be old and grey by then,' Derby said wryly. 'Simon? Anything?'

Merrivale shook his head. 'Nothing definite. But I am beginning to have suspicions about the Knights of Calatrava.'

'Which is interesting,' said Eleanor, suddenly eager. 'Because I think at least one of the Knights is in league with the enemy.' Everyone looked at her. 'When I go riding in the hills – no, Richard, not now – I sometimes see others riding out too. Usually it's just noblemen out hawking, or huntsmen looking for deer. But on at least three occasions I have seen a Knight of Calatrava ride up into the hills and, once he was out of sight of our lines, turn east towards the sultan of Garnāta's camp.'

'For God's sake, I told you it was dangerous to go alone!' Arundel exploded. 'What if he had spotted you?'

'I said, *not now*!' Eleanor snapped.

Silence fell for a moment. Music drifted down from the gallery, overlaid with the hum of voices in conversation. Merrivale spotted John Sully on the far side of the room, talking with the white-bearded *fidalgo*. They were looking back at him as they spoke.

'The Knights have a watch post at the Torre de Cartagena, on the far side of the river,' Philippe said finally. 'Perhaps he was going there, and not to the enemy camp.'

'Then why did he not ride directly there?' Eleanor demanded. 'Why did he disappear into the hills before changing course?'

'My lady, was it the same man every time?' Merrivale asked.

'Yes. I would recognise him again if I saw him.'

Merrivale nodded. 'My lords, have we learned anything further about the salt monopoly?'

'I've spoken to everyone I know at court,' Derby said. 'There is no word of a farm. That doesn't mean there isn't a clandestine arrangement, of course.'

Someone coughed discreetly behind them. They turned to see Donato de' Peruzzi, corvid-like in his black robes, standing with his hands clasped in front of him. Seen close up, his face was thinner than Merrivale remembered, but his eyes were as dark and cold as ever.

'Pardon me for intruding upon your conversation,' Peruzzi said, inclining his head. 'My lord of Derby, my lord of Arundel, you must forgive the king for his perfunctory dismissal of you. He is preoccupied with the siege, of course, but that does not excuse his rudeness.'

'What do you want?' Derby asked directly.

'I wish to help you. Tell me your proposals for an alliance against France, and I will raise them with the king myself. He will listen to me, I assure you.'

'Why would you do that?'

'Ask your herald,' Peruzzi said. 'He will tell you.'

'Because he wants to ingratiate himself still further with King Alfonso,' Merrivale said. 'Brokering an alliance between Castile and England would demonstrate how valuable he is, and increase King Alfonso's dependence on him.'

Philippe of Navarre looked sceptical. 'Peruzzi, you have betrayed us all, time and again. Why should we trust you?'

Slowly, almost insultingly, Peruzzi bowed to him. 'What happened is in the past, Your Grace. Now, everything is new, everything is being remade. I have put my past resentments and animosities behind me. I invite you to do the same.'

'That does not answer my question,' said Philippe.

'It does, but not in a way that you would understand. My lord of Derby, ask your herald to send to me tomorrow morning. I will tell him then where and when we will meet. Your Grace, my lords, my lady, I wish you a good evening.'

Peruzzi bowed again and walked away through the candlelight. 'Don't go, Simon,' Eleanor said abruptly. 'In Flanders, he tried twice to kill you. Remember?'

'He *failed* twice to kill me,' Merrivale corrected. He touched his tabard. 'And now, I am protected. Even Peruzzi will not dare to harm me here in the camp, before witnesses.' He paused. 'What happens outside of the camp is, of course, quite another matter.'

Up in the gallery the musicians began to play and the bright, sullen figures of the *fidalgos* and their ladies began weaving through the patterns of dances, the carola and estampida, seguidilla and murciana. The king watched, caressing Leonor de Guzmán's hand, breaking off occasionally to applaud. To the relief of everyone else, both he and Leonor rose and retired early, leaving the other guests free to escape each other's company. The English and Navarrese parties walked back down the hill through the torchlit night, with John Sully mopping his forehead. 'I'm relieved that's over. I told you they're like cats in a sack, but tonight was even worse. Have you ever felt tension like that?'

'Yes,' said Merrivale. 'Turin, five years ago, just before the axe fell. Peruzzi was there, too. Your friend with the white beard, the one you were talking to after dinner. Why was he interested in me?'

Sully's face was in shadow, but Merrivale could hear the smile in his voice. 'He asked who you were, and I told him. That's all I know.'

'Who is he?'

'His name is Don Juan Manuel, and he is the oldest, wealthiest and most powerful *fidalgo* in the army. He is King Alfonso's cousin.'

'He is not fond of the king,' Merrivale said, remembering how the old man had given the merest hint of a bow in Alfonso's direction.

'He led a rebellion against the king for ten years. For a time, he and his fellow rebels were forced into exile in Garnāta. He was reconciled with Alfonso a few years back, but I'm not sure how deep that reconciliation is.'

'How well do you know him, John?'

'We play chess together,' Sully said non-committally. 'He could be useful to you, I reckon.'

'How do I contact him?'

Sully clapped him on the shoulder. 'He'll contact you.'

'Does everyone in this army have secrets, John?'

'Yes,' said Sully. 'Surely that should be evident by now.'

—

The heat of the day began to abate. Lamps twinkled on the walls of Algeciras, and a dim haze of firelight shone from the enemy camp below the Jebel Tāriq. The moon had risen, shining once again across the waters of the bay. Walking out of his pavilion Merrivale heard music in the distance: the plucked plangency of a guitarra, the click and rattle of a tambourine, the soft floating notes of a reed dulzaina. From closer at hand came the sound of a lute being played, very well, and a man's voice singing. The sound was coming from Arundel's pavilion, and he realised that the voice was Arundel's too, a fine tenor, soft and warm with love.

Sweet the song is, fair the tale,
And no one living under the sun,
No matter how full of sorrow or care,
No matter what sickness of the soul

They suffer, but they will be healed
And their hearts will be made glad again,
So sweet is the song.

Merrivale knew the words well. They came from a work called *Aucassin et Nicolette*, part-chanson and part-fable, the tale of two thwarted lovers seeking happiness together. For a moment his mind drifted and he was back again in Turin, in the sunlit garden of the Count of Savoy's palace watching Yolande sitting beside a fountain and playing a lute. He remembered how the light sparkled off the rings on her fingers and the pale gold of her hair, and the smile in her eyes when she looked up and saw him.

Who suffers the most? he wondered. *Those who never find the love they are looking for? Or those who do find it, like Aucassin and Nicolette, only to have it cruelly torn away from them?* He knew how the bereaved felt, the echoing empty hole in his life that only one person could ever fill, and that person was gone. He thought suddenly, not of Eleanor and Arundel, but of Arundel's wife alone in England, and wondered if she felt the same.

> *Nicolette, how fair you are, how sweet your eyes,*
> *Sweet is the sound of your footsteps coming and going,*
> *Sweet is the sound of your laughter, so full of joy,*
> *Sweet is your face, your lips, your eyes, your brow,*
> *And ah, how sweet is the touch of your embrace!*
> *How deep is my sorrow to see you captive in an evil place,*
> *And I am unable to set you free.*
> *Ah, how sweet you are, my friend!*

The music stopped abruptly. The silence that followed was full of unspoken passion. Merrivale looked once more at the moon rising through the clouds of stars, and went back into his own pavilion.

6

9th of September, 1343

Morning brought heat and golden haze, the morning call to prayer interrupted by the thump of cannon fire. Merrivale's servant entered the pavilion and bowed, holding out a small parchment roll.

'A message has arrived for you, *señor*.'

The bruise around the man's eye was turning purple. Merrivale broke the seal, unrolled the parchment and read it.

> *And when the people complained, it displeased the Lord, and the Lord heard it, and his anger was kindled. The fire of the Lord burned among them, and consumed them that were in the uttermost parts of the camp.*

He recognised the words, a verse from the Book of Numbers.

'What is it, Simon?' asked Ficaris.

'A threat,' said Merrivale. 'Someone is calling the fire of God down on our heads.'

Moreno was concerned. 'Who is it?'

'There is no signature, and the seal is plain and has no device.' Merrivale looked at Ficaris and Moreno. 'When you go to the slave auction, take a couple of Sir John's archers with you.'

Ficaris nodded, tucking his knife into his belt. 'We're leaving now.'

Merrivale's writing set was laid out on a plain oak table at one side of the pavilion. Spreading out a piece of parchment, he dipped his pen in the inkwell and wrote a quick message of his own.

> *To the most esteemed Signor Donato di Pacino de' Peruzzi, greeting. I am available to meet with you at a time and place of your choosing. Your most humble servant, Simon Merrivale, heraldus.*

He sealed the letter with his own signet and handed the roll to Warin.

'Deliver this Peruzzi's house, if you please. And ask two more of Sir John's archers to accompany you, at a discreet distance. If anyone follows you, tell the archers to watch them and find out where they come from. I want to know who sent that note.'

Warin departed, and Merrivale walked out into the smoky air. The cat followed him, rubbing against his leg. He looked down at the animal, who gazed trustingly up at him. 'Not me,' he said. 'Jac is the one who feeds you.'

The cat swished its tail and walked away. He stood, thumbs hooked through his belt, watching the sun climb into the sky and listening to the murmur of the camp around him. The rippling sea shivered with fractal reflections; the minarets of al-Jazīra were blurry in the heat. He was reminded again of what Ficaris had said, about this being a different world. He was beginning to feel that difference, very keenly. Peruzzi was a Florentine rather than a Castilian, but he was on home ground. *And I am a long way from Dartmoor*, Merrivale thought.

Warin returned half an hour later with another letter:

> *Signor Peruzzi will be pleased to receive Master Merrivale at his house, at terce.*

Simple and straightforward, Merrivale thought, giving nothing away. 'Anything to report?' he asked.

'I was followed, sir, just as you suspected. It was Garcíez. He followed me to Peruzzi's house and waited until I came out, and then made off. The boys are tracking him now.'

The archers returned not long after. 'Garcíez didn't go far, sir,' said one of them. 'He went straight to the plum pudding's house.'

'The plum pudding?'

The archer shifted a little on his feet. 'Sorry, sir. I meant the king's lady. Señora Guzmán. Some folk call her the plum pudding. They reckon if you open her up, she's sticky and—'

'I understand the allusion,' Merrivale said, handing over some coins.

He walked across to Derby's pavilion and entered to find Derby, Arundel and Guilhem-Arnaut de Irunberri, Philippe of Navarre's captain, talking together. 'We've all received these,' said Derby, holding up a parchment with the same verse from the Book of Numbers. 'Philippe, Richard and myself. Is this Peruzzi's work?'

Arundel shook his head. 'Peruzzi would hardly send a threat of this nature when he has already invited Simon to negotiate.'

'Presumably, he intends to deliver his threats in person,' Merrivale said. 'I have just been summoned to meet him.'

'For God's sake, be careful,' Derby said.

From outside came Ficaris's voice, demanding to speak to the Earl of Derby's herald. He and Moreno were shown in a moment later. Ficaris's fists were clenched, and the normally quiet Moreno was grim-faced with anger.

'You know the slave we were meant to buy?' Ficaris asked. 'Ghilas? Well, he's dead.'

Merrivale's heart sank. 'What happened?'

'The guards wouldn't let us see the *alcalde*. Our archers tried to start a fight, but the guards called up reinforcements and we had to back down. Juan managed to speak to some of the prisoners before we departed.' Ficaris drew an angry breath. 'The guards took Ghilas out of the slave pens last night. They brought his body back this morning. His throat had been cut.'

Back at their own pavilion, Merrivale turned to his companions. 'Ask around. Be discreet, don't draw attention to yourselves, but talk to everyone who might have been near the slave pens last night, and whether they saw or heard anything. In particular, ask whether anyone saw Garcíez.'

'What will you do, Simon?' asked Ficaris.

Merrivale glanced up at the sun. 'It's time to see Peruzzi.'

'Take me with you, sir,' said Warin.

Merrivale shook his head. 'Help the others. I will do this alone.'

'Wait a moment, sir.' Warin hurried into the pavilion, returning a moment later carrying a sturdy white wooden staff. He bowed, presenting it to Merrivale.

'What is this?' Merrivale asked.

'A herald's staff, sir. I painted it myself last night. I thought it might be more useful than that wispy little wand. If you take my meaning, sir.'

'Thank you.' Merrivale took the staff and hefted it in his hands, feeling its weight. He smiled a little. 'Yes,' he said. 'This is far better than a sword.'

—

Guards in the red and white livery of the Order of Calatrava stood outside the doors of Peruzzi's house. They bowed and admitted Merrivale with a silent courtesy that he had not been expecting. A steward in black robes appeared, bowing too.

'Señor Merrivale, the master is waiting to receive you. Your escort may wait here.'

Inside, the hall was plastered and painted in Peruzzi's own colours, a field of blue adorned with golden pears. High windows admitted shafts of sunlight; motes of dust danced in the currents of air. The steward bowed again and withdrew. An interior door opened and Donato de' Peruzzi entered the room, dressed in blue robes exactly the same shade as the walls. When he stopped moving, robes and wall seemed to merge together, making his head and hands seem almost disembodied.

'Simon Merrivale,' Peruzzi said. 'I would offer you wine, but I suspect you would not drink it.'

Merrivale paused for a moment. Was this Peruzzi's attempt at humour? A few years earlier in Flanders, a good friend of Merrivale's had been killed by poisoned wine provided by Peruzzi's agents; shortly thereafter, Merrivale himself had been poisoned and nearly died. He looked up to see Peruzzi studying him, his own face expressionless. *He knows what I am thinking*, Merrivale thought.

'Do you wish to discuss the terms of the English alliance?' Merrivale asked directly.

'There is no point. Castile has always been a friend to France, and King Alfonso will not deviate from that path.'

'What might persuade him to change his mind?'

Peruzzi considered this briefly. 'Money, of course, but you may put that out of your mind. The amount required would bankrupt England.'

'Then why does the king keep the embassy here? Why not send them away?'

'Have you not worked it out yet?' asked Peruzzi. 'The king of France knows the English embassy is here, and so does his puppet, Pope Clement. So long as the embassy remains, so too remains the fear that Castile might change its mind and ally with England. The French are determined to keep Castile close, which improves King Alfonso's bargaining position. Money is already on its way from the papal treasury in Avignon, and more will follow.'

'Was that your doing?' asked Merrivale.

'You know better than to ask such questions. The real question, the one you are *not* asking, is, why did I summon you here?' Merrivale waited. 'You have made enemies in the Order of Calatrava,' Peruzzi said. 'That was unwise.'

'Are you referring to Pero de Garcíez?'

'I advise you to keep away from him. Above all, do not get caught between him and Núñez, the grand master.'

Merrivale considered the last sentence. He glanced towards the door. 'Soldiers from the Order guard your house,' he said. 'Perhaps you should follow your own advice, and stay away from them.'

'Unlike you, Merrivale, I am subtle enough to navigate my way between the rock and the whirlpool. As I am sure your friend Fra Moriale told you, I have the patronage of the Knights of Saint John, who in turn wield influence over the Order of Calatrava. I cannot be harmed.'

Merrivale touched his tabard. 'Neither can I.'

'Painted silk and a white stick? Those will not protect you. Let me give you another piece of advice. I know you are seeking Kāsim al-'Aswad, and also a slave named Mauro. Drop this matter, if you wish to live.'

He knows Mauro's name? How, and why? 'I cannot do that,' said Merrivale.

'Then pray to God for mercy,' said Peruzzi. 'This audience is at an end. You may go.'

—

'He wasn't serious about negotiating,' Merrivale said to Derby a little later. 'He warned me away from the Order of Calatrava and told me to stop searching for Mauro. He did not say so in so many words, but the clear inference was that we should pack up and go home.'

Derby shook his head. 'He may get his wish. A letter from England arrived by courier while you were out. King Edward is demanding to know what progress we have made. If we tell the king we have failed, he will recall the embassy.'

'Which would play into Peruzzi's hands,' Merrivale said. 'Can you persuade King Edward to wait a little longer, my lord?'

'I will try.'

Back at his own pavilion, Merrivale found Ficaris, Moreno and Warin seated around the table, examining a deck of painted Egyptian playing cards. 'The rules of *kanjifah* are very simple,' Ficaris was saying. 'There are four suits: coins, batons, cups and swords. Each suit has pip cards with values from one to ten. Then there's the court cards: the under-vizier is worth eleven, the vizier is valued at twelve and the malik is worth thirteen. Highest card in the lead suit takes the round.'

Warin looked up and saw Merrivale, and his face filled with relief. 'Good to see you back, sir. What did he say?'

'He threatened me, which is no surprise, but he let one thing slip. He knows who Mauro is.'

'How?' Moreno asked slowly. 'Mauro was only a slave.'

'He must have been somewhat more than that. Don't you see? Fra Moriale was right. Mauro does know something important, very probably something about Kāsim's caravans. That's why they have taken an interest in him.'

'Which makes it all the more important that we find him,' Ficaris said.

'What about yourselves?' Merrivale asked. 'Anything?'

Moreno looked up. 'I did hear one thing, Simon. I don't think it helps us, but...'

'Go on,' said Merrivale.

Moreno sighed. He looked downcast, and Merrivale understood his disappointment. All of them had hoped that Ghilas would help them solve the mystery and find Mauro.

'I spoke to a slave working in the horse lines,' Moreno said. 'He was an Amazigh like Ghilas. He knew nothing about the killing, but he had heard of Kāsim and knew a little about him. He told me that Kāsim had been rich, a man of consequence in Marrakesh before the revolt. He also had connections in Granada. One of them is the *amir*, the commander of the Warriors of the Faithful, the same company where Ghilas served. Another is a senior royal official in Granada named al-Rumani, who is said to have invested in Kāsim's business. It might have been him that Kāsim was trying to reach when he fled from Marrakesh. But, as I say, I don't think this helps us very much.'

Ficaris scooped up the cards and arranged them in a deck. 'Al-Rumani might know more about what happened to Kāsim and Mauro, and why. Is there any way of reaching him?'

'Not in Granada,' said Moreno. 'He might as well be on the moon.'

Merrivale pondered for a moment. 'There might be a way,' he said finally.

Moreno did not appear to have heard him. He rose to his feet, his face full of sudden pain. 'It is hopeless,' he said quietly. 'I have spent four years on this quest, and all the money I have in the world, yet I am as far from finding Mauro as I ever was. Every time I think I am getting close, something happens and my hope is torn away from me. I don't think I will ever see him again.'

'No!' Ficaris said. He stood up abruptly, facing Moreno. 'Never, ever give up hope, Juan. Never, do you hear me?'

Moreno swallowed, unable to speak. Ficaris gripped him by the shoulders, shaking him gently. 'Remember I said that I was once a slave?' Ficaris asked. 'Three years in Egypt, in the household of a Mamlūk official. Unlike Mauro, I knew that no one was coming to rescue me, because none of my friends or family even knew I had been taken. But I never gave up hope, Juan, no matter how much my captivity oppressed me. And my hope was rewarded, because there came a day when God smiled on me and show me the way to escape.'

He paused. Merrivale and Warin watched them. 'This is my oath,' Ficaris said. 'I swear to you, Juan, that we will find Mauro together, you and I. It will be done. Do you hear me? We *will* find him.'

'Thank you,' Moreno said, in a voice close to tears. 'You are a good friend, Jac.'

'What will Fra Moriale think of this?' Merrivale asked quietly.

Ficaris released his grip on Moreno and turned. 'Fra Moriale's orders were to inform him if you should find the gold,' he said calmly. 'I will do so. And whatever else I choose to do is none of Fra Moriale's business.'

A pageboy appeared in the doorway of the pavilion, bowing. He wore a short tabard brilliant with a complex coat of arms, a gold and red chequerboard on a field of blue quartered with ermine on silver. 'I bring greetings from my lady of Guzmán,' he said, his voice squeaking a little. 'She wishes to speak to the herald, Señor Merrivale. Be pleased to come with me, *señor*.'

—

Leonor de Guzmán's residence was next to the king's house, built in the same fashion with wooden buildings around a stone-paved courtyard full of flowering shrubs and plants: lemons glossy in the midday heat, bay trees with shimmering dark leaves, oleanders flowering white and pink, white climbing roses all growing in profusion. More flowers bloomed in the hall whose windows had been fitted with expensive coloured glass. This was a military camp, but the siege of Algeciras had already lasted for more than a year; some of the besiegers, at least, had settled in.

Leonor was seated at one end of the hall, in a high-backed chair made comfortable with cushions. She wore a light embroidered robe that emphasised rather than concealed the unfashionable curves of her body, and another gold wire cap set with garnets that glistened like drops of blood. Dark curling hair framed a face with high cheekbones, full lips and almond eyes hard with suspicion. Undeniably sensuous, Merrivale thought, yet full of latent power; steel encased in silk, sugar dusting the razor's edge.

He bowed. 'You met with Donato de' Peruzzi this morning,' she said directly. 'What did you talk about?'

Merrivale wondered what had prompted the question. 'I conveyed the terms of the proposed alliance between England and Castile, my lady. I did so at Señor Peruzzi's invitation.'

Leonor shifted a little. 'Do not play games with me. You know who I am, and you know what power I have.'

'I am well aware,' said Merrivale. 'May I ask what prompts your ladyship's question?'

'May *I* ask if heralds in your country are always so impertinent?'

Merrivale bowed again. 'On the whole, I believe they are,' he said.

There is a moment of silence. 'Why are you searching for Kāsim al-'Aswad?' she asked.

'Actually, I am searching for someone from his household. A Christian named Enrique Cavador, who goes by the name of Mauro. We think he was sent to a place called La Algaba. Have you heard of it?'

'No. Why are you interested in him?'

'Because I wish to see justice done,' said Merrivale.

'Justice?' She pretended astonishment, as if she had never heard of the word. 'This is Castile, not England.'

'I made a promise,' Merrivale said.

'To whom? To this Mauro? He is a commoner, a slave. You owe him nothing. No, the truth is that you are searching for Kāsim. Why?'

It was clear from her demeanour that she too knew who Mauro was. 'Because he trafficked in salt and gold,' Merrivale said. 'Need I say more, *mi çaida*?'

There was another short pause. 'How much do you know?' she asked.

'Why are you afraid of Peruzzi?' he countered.

Leonor's lips compressed. 'I am afraid of no man, Señor Merrivale.'

'The king relies on Peruzzi, and trusts him. With Peruzzi suddenly so prominent, you must fear that your own influence over the king will weaken.' Merrivale bowed again. 'My apologies, *mi çaida*. I fear I am being impertinent once more.'

Her mood had changed. She studied him, stroking her cheek with a richly ringed finger. Cabochon gemstones flashed in the sunlight.

'Work for me,' she said finally.

Merrivale considered this. 'You think Peruzzi might betray you, and you wish for me to deal with him? Break his power before he breaks yours?'

'Never mind my reasons. Work for me. Name any sum you like. I will pay it.'

Slowly, Merrivale shook his head. 'I am sorry, my lady, but I cannot accommodate you. I have promised to serve the Earl of Derby.'

The gemstones flashed again as Leonor pointed towards the door. 'Get out,' she said.

Merrivale turned and walked out into the courtyard, where the smells of lemon blossom and roses filled the air. Full of thought, he walked through the gate and away down the hill, watching the minarets of al-Jazīra shiver in the waves of heat.

—

Another fiery sunset, and once again three people met in the stables by the tower as the shadows began to fall. 'Why have you summoned us?' demanded Donato de' Peruzzi.

'Because we are working at cross-purposes,' said Leonor de Guzmán. 'This must stop. Either we work together, or we die separately. Is that clear?'

'I was under the impression that we were already working together, *mi çaida*. We all desire power in Castile.'

'Yes,' said Pero de Garcíez. 'But at whose expense?'

Leonor stamped her foot. 'Listen to me, both of you! This is more serious than you can begin to imagine. At this very moment, Queen María is preparing a coup that will overthrow the king and place her son on the throne, with herself as regent.

If she succeeds, *señores*, she will kill me and my children, and then take her revenge on everyone who was close to the king. You, Señor Peruzzi, will find yourself hanging from a gibbet with crows pecking at your eyes.'

A cannon boomed, its harsh report echoing off the hills behind them. A horse whickered in the stalls.

'Queen María's revolt will fail,' Peruzzi said.

'How do you know?'

'Because that is how I have planned it. She will fail, and in the vacuum that follows her failure, you will step forward. Your son will sit on the throne, not María's.'

'So you have said before. But to overthrow María, I need money, Peruzzi. I need gold.'

'And you shall have it,' Peruzzi said. 'It is coming.'

'When?' she demanded.

'When we are ready. Until then, you will wait.'

'Wait until Merrivale finds Mauro and brings us all down?' demanded Garcíez.

Peruzzi sighed, the weary sigh of a man constantly confronted by inferior minds. 'Today, I warned Merrivale to cease his quest to find Mauro, knowing that his obstinacy and stupidity would make him more determined to carry on. The more obstacles we place in his path, the more determined he will become. Eventually, he will walk into my trap.'

'What trap?' asked Garcíez.

Peruzzi explained briefly. 'You, Garcíez, will be the bait. It is the least you can do to atone for your blunder.'

'What about me?' asked Leonor.

'Keep Grand Master Núñez distracted. Keep his attention away from Garcíez and his friends.'

'Distract him? How?'

'You will think of something,' Peruzzi said. 'I am certain of it.'

7

10th of September, 1343

The next morning dawned bright with a breeze that blew the smoke and dust away; the hills around the bay were clear and sharp, and the Jebel Musa was like a whale's back on the far side of the strait. Arundel came to Merrivale's pavilion just as he and his companions were finishing their morning meal. 'Simon,' the earl said without preamble. 'Can you sing?'

'Emphatically not, my lord. Why do you ask?'

Arundel hesitated, his handsome face embarrassed. 'It is Eleanor's birthday tomorrow,' he said. 'I have written a verse for her, but I want someone else to sing it. I don't want her to know it is mine until I know if she likes it.'

'She loves you, my lord. If she knows you wrote it, she will like it.'

Arundel looked even more uncomfortable. 'I'm not so certain of that. I don't know where to turn. The local *juglares* are happy to warble away in Spanish, but I can't trust them to sing in English.'

Moreno looked up. 'Forgive me, my lord. I speak English, and I have been told I have some skill at music. I used to play in tavernas when I was young.'

Arundel's eyes opened wide. 'By God, *señor*, you are my salvation! Have you a lute? No? My servant will bring one over to you. Here are the words, see that you have learned them by tomorrow. Thank you, *señor*, I am in your debt.'

He hurried out of the pavilion, a much happier man than when he entered. Ficaris started to laugh. 'Juan! I knew you were a man of many parts, but I never dreamed you were a *trovador*.'

Warin nodded. 'Lucky fellow. You get to play for a princess.'

Merrivale looked at his groom. 'What are you talking about?'

'Lady Eleanor's great-grandfather was a king,' Warin said stubbornly. 'That makes her a princess.'

'Given the mating habits of kings, most of us probably have a royal great-grandfather,' said Ficaris. 'That doesn't make us all princes. Juan, my friend, I look forward to this. The notes will flow like silver from your lute, and your singing will make Tannhäuser himself weep with jealousy.'

'I doubt this,' Moreno said. He looked worried. 'I wish I had kept my mouth shut.'

'By tomorrow, we all may be wishing that,' said Warin.

Ficaris cuffed him on the arm, lightly. 'Come along, tin miner. Let's leave Juan to learn his song and go ask some more questions about La Algaba. We've asked half the camp already, but you never know, we might get lucky with the other half. How hard can this cursed place be to find?'

They departed. 'That was good of you,' Merrivale said.

Moreno smiled a little. 'I hope I don't regret it. What will you do, Simon?'

'I have been thinking about al-Rumani. There may be a way I can get into the Garnāta camp and ask some questions. It won't help us find La Algaba, but we might learn something more about Kāsim and al-Rumani. It's not much of a chance, but it's better than nothing.'

Philippe of Navarre was in his pavilion, scanning a parchment roll while Irunberri stood waiting. Alameda the red-robed physician was there too, mixing mustard and honey in a jar with wine and saffron. Merrivale saw that Philippe was sweating and his eyes were red. 'Are you unwell, sire?'

'A touch of influenza, or so Lorenço tells me. It will soon pass. How goes your quest?'

'We are still searching for La Algaba,' Merrivale said. 'However, we have another prospect. I would like to follow it, sire, but I need your help.'

'Go on.'

'You mentioned that you have been conducting negotiations with the sultan of Garnāta. Do you meet with the sultan himself?'

'Rarely. Usually we are received by Abū Nu'aym Ridwan, the *hajib*. The chancellor, you might say, and Sultan Yūsuf's right-hand man.'

'Who accompanies you during the negotiations?'

'Guilhem-Arnaut, and often Lorenço. The Moors respect physicians and hold them in high esteem.'

Alameda dipped a spoon into the mixture and tasted it. 'Quite right, too,' he said. 'Wise people, the Moors.'

'Would you be willing to help me gain an audience with Ridwan, sire?' Merrivale asked.

'Of course. Guilhem-Arnaut, will you send a messenger to Ridwan under a flag of truce? Ask if he will receive the English ambassador's herald.'

Irunberri bowed and went out. 'I had an interesting meeting with Leonor de Guzmán yesterday,' Merrivale said. 'She thinks Peruzzi intends to betray her, and tried to hire me to work for her. Beneath the façade, I think she is quite frightened.'

'She has cause to be,' Philippe said after a moment.

'Sire,' said Alameda, a note of warning in his voice.

'We can trust Simon, Lorenço, and he needs to know. When the king first became... enamoured of Leonor, he imprisoned his wife. She escaped and fled to her family in Portugal, but a few months ago she returned and set up her court in Córdoba, where she began corresponding with the king's numerous enemies. It is my belief that she is plotting a revolt.'

'And Leonor thinks Peruzzi might be secretly supporting María,' Merrivale said reflectively. 'Which, of course, he may well be doing. Playing both sides against each other is one of his favourite games.'

'If María triumphs, Leonor could lose everything,' Philippe said. 'Her lands, her power, her life, even the lives of her children by the king. María is a bitter and vengeful woman and her hatred of her rival runs strong. One can understand why, of course.'

'And Leonor has allied with Peruzzi in hopes of mounting a coup of her own,' said Merrivale. 'Both she and María are playing into Peruzzi's hands. Is there any way of dissuading them, sire?'

'Leonor dislikes me,' Philippe said. 'I have no influence over her... I know María a little, and I know her father quite well. I might be able to persuade her. I would need to go to Córdoba.'

'Sire, you are not well enough to travel,' Alameda warned.

'I know. I shall give this some thought. But I warn you, Lorenço, if I think I can do more good in Córdoba than here, I shall go, even if I must be carried on a litter.'

11th of September, 1343

Warin held the horse's head while Merrivale stepped up into the saddle. The bright colours of his tabard glowed in the morning light. Warin handed up the white staff, to which a large white flag had been tied. 'Good luck, sir,' he said.

'Let us hope I don't need it.'

A message had come back the previous evening that Abū Nu'aym Ridwan, *hajib* of Garnāta, would be pleased to grant an audience to the English herald, and Derby had given his consent. Merrivale rode slowly through the camp, watching the sun climb higher above the Jebel Tāriq, as he reached the palisades at the northern edge of the camp. The sentries opened the gates without speaking and let him pass.

Outside the gate was the burial ground, long mounds of earth in rows and a couple of empty trenches waiting to be filled whenever the next assault on the city took place. The ground sloped down to the river, which he now knew was called the Río Palmones. It was late summer and the water was low; he forded the river without difficulty and crossed the meadows on the far side, skirting a low hill scattered with ruined houses and the pale broken pillars of a Roman temple. A watchtower stood on the crest of the hill, the red cross banner of Calatrava fluttering in the breeze; this, he realised, was the Torre de Cartagena that Philippe had mentioned. Ahead lay open fields and, two miles away, the camp of the army of Garnāta, which the Castilians called Granada.

Movement to his left, puffs of dust; a column of men on small, wiry horses trotting towards him. They wore chainmail coats and high-crested helmets, and carried leather shields and lances held at the upright. Merrivale reined in, holding up his staff so that the white flag fluttered in the breeze. The horsemen halted in front of him, watching him in silence. He had learned some Arabic from Ficaris on the voyage from Genoa, and now he summoned the phrases they had rehearsed that morning. 'I am the herald of the Earl of Derby. The *hajib*, His Excellency Abū Nu'aym Ridwan who is favoured by God, awaits me.'

The leader of the horsemen raised a gloved hand in salute. '*Marhaban, saīdi.* Be pleased to follow me.'

Inside the palisades, the camp was neat and orderly. Drums thudded in the air, and he heard the faint skirl of a flute. In some ways, the camp was very much like the one he had just left, but there were differences too; there were no tavernas, and the dark-faced men and veiled women who watched him ride past were grave and quiet, speaking only in low voices. The banners overhead were bright with colour but their heraldry was unknown to him, stars and scimitars and bright elegant calligraphy embroidered in silver and gold. Again, he remembered Ficaris's words: *You will find yourself in a place beyond anything you have experienced before.*

Ahead lay another enclosure, guarded by men in red robes with gold turbans wrapped around their helmets, armed with heavy swords and long spears. Beyond the gates was an open courtyard, surrounded by red silk pavilions. An immense crimson banner flew overhead, flapping in the breeze. Merrivale read the golden letters, translating slowly in his mind. *Wa-lā ghāliba illā Allāh*: only God is victorious.

He dismounted. The horsemen turned and rode back through the gates. Four of the red-robed guards formed up around Merrivale and marched him across the courtyard and into one of the larger pavilions. Inside, rows of low wooden benches were arranged on the carpeted floor. Men in long robes and turbans or skullcaps sat on cushions behind them, writing on sheets of paper or rolls of parchment in elegant, flowing scripts. At the far end of the chamber another man sat alone behind an ornately carved wooden table, studying another parchment roll and making occasional notes with a brass pen. His robes were black, trimmed with silver braid at the neck and sleeves, and his black turban was shot with silver thread. He was about fifty, Merrivale guessed; his black beard was streaked with grey. His eyes were dark and expressionless.

The guards halted. The man in black motioned with his hand and they withdrew to the rear of the pavilion. Merrivale bowed, and waited.

'Come forward,' the man said in Castilian Spanish. 'Be seated.'

The only seat was a silk cushion on the carpet. Merrivale sat down on it, crossing his legs. 'Have I the honour of addressing His Excellency Abū Nu'aym Ridwan, *hajib* of Garnāta?'

'I am he,' said the bearded man. 'You come from his lordship, the Earl of Derby, may God grant him peace. Do you bring a message from him?'

'His lordship wishes that peace be upon you, and God grant you his mercy and blessings. On his behalf, I apologise for troubling you, but I have a great favour to ask. Men's freedom, even their very lives, are at stake.'

'What is it that you wish, Señor Merrivale?'

'Excellency, I seek information about a subject of the sultan of Garnāta, a man named al-Rumani. He had dealings with a merchant of Murrākush, Kāsim al-'Aswad.'

There was the briefest of pauses. Ridwan's dark eyes stared at Merrivale. 'What is your concern with them?'

'I am trying to trace a young Christian man who was once a slave in Kāsim's household. I hope that al-Rumani can tell me something about him.' Not the exact truth, Merrivale thought, but near enough.

'You desire to ransom this slave?'

'It is more complex than that,' said Merrivale.

This time the silence was longer. Merrivale watched Ridwan, and sensed that the other man was choosing his words. 'I know of Kāsim,' he said finally. 'He was a rebel against the sultan of Murrākush, whom my lord Sultan Yūsuf esteems like a brother. He would not have been welcome in Garnāta.'

'Excellency, Kāsim is no threat to you,' Merrivale said. 'He and his household were captured and were sold as slaves by the Knights of Calatrava.'

'Then why are you here?' demanded Ridwan. 'This matter is nothing to do with us. Find whomever bought the slaves and set your friend free.'

'It is more complex than that,' Merrivale repeated.

Ridwan leaned forward a little. 'Enlighten me.'

'Excellency, I believe Kāsim would indeed have been welcome in Garnāta. Al-Rumani had invested in Kāsim's business, and al-Rumani himself is a royal official in an important post. Presumably he has influence at court. Kāsim also had connections with the *amir* of the Warriors of the Faithful. I would like to speak with either al-Rumani or the *amir*, if they are present.'

'The Warriors of the Faithful guard the frontiers of Garnāta,' said Ridwan. 'Their *amir*, may God reward him, is Hamou Ou Akka ibn Zayani, and he is in Runda on the far side of the mountains. To my knowledge, he has no connection with Kāsim. I have never heard of al-Rumani.'

Merrivale gazed at Ridwan, watching his eyes. *He is lying*, Merrivale thought. *And he knows that I know he is lying.*

'Are there salt mines in Garnāta, excellency?' he asked.

'Why do you wish to know?'

'Did Kāsim's caravans carry salt from Garnāta south to Mali? To Timbuktu? Did they bring gold back north to Garnāta?'

'I would imagine that this is common knowledge,' said Ridwan.

'Do they carry gold to Castile also?'

'We are at war with Castile, *señor*. There is no traffic between our kingdoms.'

Merrivale thought about the Knight of Calatrava that Eleanor had seen. 'Does the name Donato de' Peruzzi mean anything to you?'

Suddenly, there was danger in the air. 'You ask a great many questions, *señor*. I have answered them out of respect for your master, and also for King Philippe, whom I hold in high esteem. But my patience is not endless.'

Merrivale inclined his head. 'Forgive me, excellency. My zeal to find my friend has betrayed me, and I have been presumptuous. With your permission, I will withdraw.'

'You may go,' said Ridwan, and he motioned the guards forward.

After Merrivale had departed, Ridwan sat in silence for a while, toying with the inlaid brass inkwell on the table in front of him. Finally, he beckoned to one of the men working nearby. The man came forward and knelt in front of him.

'Merrivale knows,' Ridwan said. 'Or at least, he suspects. Send word to Ibn al-Rāzī in Garnāta. Tell him to be prepared.'

'And Saīda Rīm, *saīdi*?' the man asked. 'Do we warn her?'

After a long moment Ridwan shook his head. 'Let God's will be done,' he said.

'Al-Rumani is a highly placed official in the court of the sultan of Garnāta, and yet Garnāta's own chancellor pretended not to have heard of him,' said Merrivale. 'Why?'

'Perhaps he was telling the truth,' said Ficaris. 'Perhaps Juan's source was wrong.'

Merrivale shook his head. 'Ridwan was lying. He wasn't even particularly subtle about it. He answered my other questions, mostly, until I mentioned Peruzzi. Then he warned me off. Which means that whatever plot is going on, Ridwan is involved in it.'

'And he wanted you to know it,' said Ficaris. 'He wants you to go looking for al-Rumani.'

'It could be a ruse,' said Moreno.

'It could be a trap,' Warin said sharply. 'Sir, please say you are not thinking of going to Garnāta. The Moors kill enemy spies by skinning them alive.'

'And we kill spies by burning them,' Merrivale said. 'There's not much to choose between us. No, Warin, I am not intending to go to Garnāta. However, it is more urgent than ever now that we find La Algaba. Have you heard anything more?'

The others shook their heads. Merrivale sighed. 'Once again, we are stymied,' he said. 'Every time we discover a new prospect, our enemies block the road.'

Ficaris held up one finger. 'Simon, remember what I said to Juan. Never give up hope.'

'No.' Merrivale smiled a little. 'No, of course not.'

'And there is nothing more we can do today,' Warin pointed out. 'It's nearly time for Princess Eleanor's birthday celebration.'

'Once again, Warin, she is not a princess.'

'Maybe not to you, sir. But she is in my eyes.'

Merrivale stared at his groom. 'What do you mean?'

Warin's lips compressed. Ficaris chuckled. 'She was having trouble with her horse yesterday morning, and Warin helped her gentle the animal. He also found a burr under its girth that was causing it to act up. She was so grateful that she gave him a silver real.'

Merrivale looked back at Warin. 'A real makes her a princess? What would she be if she gave you a gold maravedí? An angel?'

'With respect, sir, that is absurd,' Warin said stiffly. 'Everyone knows that angels only use English money.'

—

The entertainment hosted by Richard Fitzalan, Earl of Arundel, in honour of the lady Eleanor of Lancaster would have graced any royal palace in Europe. A silk canopy decked with garlands of roses covered the space in front of Arundel's pavilion, providing shade for the guests. Merrivale counted more than a hundred people, including Philippe of Navarre and his household and some of the Castilian nobles and their veiled wives. The Castilians were on friendly terms with the English and Navarrese, although they continued to glare at each other. The old white-haired *fidalgo*, Don Juan Manuel, was one of the guests.

At other times there might have been a tournament where men showed off their knightly skills to entertain the guests, but given that Eleanor's husband had broken his neck in a tournament not long before, that would have been in poor taste. Instead there were quarterstaff fights and wrestling bouts, and some of John Sully's archers engaged in a shooting contest that made the Spanish onlookers stare in disbelief at their speed and accuracy. The martial contests were followed by acrobats and jugglers, and later everyone moved out into the open to watch a display of falconry where men flew tiercels and merlins and a great golden eagle at pigeons released for them to hunt. Eleanor, sitting enthroned like a queen in a white gown shot with gold, watched smiling as the birds soared into the lapis-blue sky. Merrivale thought that her smile was a little wistful.

Dancing came next, brightly dressed men and women dancing to the thudding, wailing music of flute and dulzaina and tambor, rebec and castanet and guitarra. Last of all, just as the sun set, Juan Moreno came and took a seat on a stool before Eleanor, clutching a lute with white-knuckled hands. Eleanor was puzzled at first; she gave Merrivale a quizzical look, wondering if this was his doing, but he shook his head. Moreno touched the strings of the lute, and music flowed like cool water beneath the silk and roses.

I hear the nightingale's voice
And my heart is full of joy
I see the clear streams in the meadows
And my heart is bright as the sun
But the happiness I see in my love's eyes
Is greater than all of these
The gift of her love is wondrous to me
I do not know if I am awake or asleep
For she has enchanted me wholly
Willingly I fall under her spell
And will remain her devoted servant for all time
If only she is constant in her love for me

It did not take long for Eleanor to work out who the author was. At the end of the song she rose and embraced Arundel, and Merrivale could see the tears in the eyes of both of them. He felt a stab of pain in his chest. *One day*, he thought, *I will reach a point where watching the happiness of others does not remind me of what I myself have lost. Not soon, though.*

Moreno sat down beside him. His hands were shaking a little. 'I think I want to be sick,' he murmured.

'Oh, come,' said Ficaris. 'The poetry wasn't *that* bad.'

The sun set in crimson fire, touching the hills around the bay with points of flame. Silver lamps were lit on every table. The guests sat down to dine on roast lamb flavoured with pepper and ginger, chicken baked with garlic and coated with ground almonds, minced meat with cumin and rose petals, saffron eggs with cloves and lavender, pigeons fried in oil with cinnamon, roast hare basted with vinegar and almond oil and an immense array of sweetmeats, some made with cane sugar.

'I must apologise to our Castilian friends,' said Arundel, presenting Eleanor with a candied plum. 'The sugar comes from Granada, I fear.'

Don Juan Manuel smiled. 'Many good things come from Granada, my lord. We need to remember that the sultan and his subjects are neighbours, not just enemies.'

Merrivale looked up and met Philippe of Navarre's eyes. Neither spoke, but both were clearly thinking the same thing.

Much later, after the guests had departed and the lamps had gone dark, Merrivale sat outside his own tent drinking a glass of wine and eating sweet pastries with pistachios. Two of John Sully's archers stood guard nearby. Arundel and Eleanor's pavilion was dark; a murmur of low voices came from within, once again too faint to hear clearly. Lights glowed inside Derby's pavilion, where he and Philippe were drinking wine and playing a game of tabula. Alameda had tried to persuade Philippe to retire after dinner, but Philippe had declared that his health was much improved.

Philippe was an interesting man, Merrivale thought. He did not behave very much like a king. Even Edward of England, who rarely stood on ceremony, still demanded respect and due attention to his rank, but Philippe never did. He treated his household, Irunberri, Alameda and the others, like they were his friends rather than his servants, and they responded with willing loyalty. Perhaps that is his secret, Merrivale thought. By laying his rank aside, he captures men's hearts and makes them even more ready to join him. There is a leader that men seem happy to follow.

It was hard not to contrast Philippe with the bombastic, libidinous King Alfonso. What a pity Navarre is so small, he thought. If Philippe had Castile in his hands, he could change the world... But on the other hand, if he *was* more powerful, perhaps Philippe himself might be different. He had seen the corrupting influence of power; in Savoy, he had paid its price.

The door of Arundel's pavilion opened and Eleanor walked out, still in her white gown. Her fists were clenched and Merrivale saw the shining tracks of tears on her face as she strode away through the camp. He rose quickly, picking up his staff, and followed her.

The camp was mostly quiet now. Men lay snoring in their tents while horses whickered in the lines. A group of Castilian soldiers sat in an open-air taverna, drinking wine and playing dice. They watched the lone woman walking through the camp and one of them stood up, but a powerful hand on his shoulder pressed him hard down onto his bench again. 'No,' Merrivale said quietly. 'Not unless you wish to hang.'

The man remained seated. Merrivale followed Eleanor uphill. She had, he realised, no destination in mind; she was walking aimlessly, trying to work off a storm of emotion. He recognised this because he had done it himself, many times. Finally, she stopped on a high point of ground and turned, tall and slender and pale in the starlight, and only then did she notice Merrivale.

'I did not ask you to follow me,' she said abruptly.

'I know,' he said, and waited. Below them, torches flickered in the camp and the lights of the besieged city glimmered like fireflies.

Several minutes passed. Eleanor reached up and used the tippet of her silk sleeve to wipe her eyes. 'Have you ever been in love, Simon?'

'Yes.'

'Did it hurt? Did it make you feel bitter and angry, like you wanted to rip your heart out of your chest?'

'Yes.'

Silence fell again. Eleanor looked up at the night sky. 'What am I doing?' she asked the stars. 'I want Richard and myself to live the rest of our lives together, but that is clearly impossible. Why do I continue to delude myself into thinking that happiness can be made real?'

'Is that why you quarrelled, my lady? You want him to leave his wife, and he refuses?'

She did not answer directly. 'The fault is mine, Simon,' she said finally. 'I want so badly to be Richard's wife, and I know I cannot be, and I feel like I am being eaten alive. And when the pain becomes too much, I lash out.' She shook her head. 'All the things he did for me today, that beautiful song your friend sang, and I repaid him by saying terrible things to him. I did not mean those things, but I could not help myself.' She wiped her eyes again. 'You are so clever, Simon. Everyone says so. Tell me what to do.'

'No one can tell another how to be happy, my lady,' Merrivale said quietly. 'Each of us must find our own road.'

'And what if we never find it?'

'We weep,' Merrivale said.

The starlight shaded Eleanor's face, pulling an infinite sadness out of her soul. 'I must go back,' she said after a while. 'I must find some way to apologise, if he will listen. Will you escort me?'

'Of course.'

'I am sorry, Simon. I did not mean for you to become involved in my tragedies.'

'We all have tragedies, my lady,' Merrivale said quietly, and he thought of Juan Moreno and his family. 'It is a part of being human.'

They walked down through the silent camp. Watchfires burned here and there, and torches flickered on the palisades. A dark shape loomed in front of them, a man silhouetted against the flames. Merrivale motioned to Eleanor to move behind him. 'Who goes there?' he called sharply.

'Señor Merrivale,' the man said. His voice was deep, grating a little in his throat. 'You did not heed our warning.'

'It takes more than a passage from scripture to frighten me,' Merrivale said.

The other man stepped forward, and Merrivale gripped his staff. Firelight fell across the other man's face, revealing a dark beard and deep-set eyes. 'You are meddling in affairs that do not concern you,' he said.

'I am not answerable to you, Pero de Garcíez. Only to my lord of Derby, to my king and to God.'

'Give up your quest,' said Garcíez. 'Tell this to your masters also. You are facing powers far greater than you. If you persist, you will most certainly meet your death.'

'One of us will,' said Merrivale.

Garcíez looked into his eyes, holding his gaze. 'Go home, Señor Merrivale,' he said. 'Go back to England. There is nothing for you here except pain. Go.'

'Get out of my way,' said Merrivale.

A long moment passed before Garcíez nodded and stepped back. He bowed ironically to Eleanor. 'My felicitations, *mi çaida*. May God grant you a long and happy life.'

Garcíez turned and walked away into the shadows. Eleanor stood rigid, staring after him. 'That's the man,' she murmured. 'That's the Knight of Calatrava I saw riding to the enemy camp.'

Merrivale stood for a moment, thinking. 'My lady, you say he rode up into the hills, out of sight of our lines, before turning east towards the sultan's camp.'

'Yes, that's right.'

'I wonder why he didn't simply ride directly to the camp under a flag of truce, as I did?'

'I don't know,' Eleanor said. Her unhappiness was forgotten, at least for the moment; there was something almost eager in her face. 'Could he have been meeting someone else before going to the camp?'

'Perhaps,' Merrivale said. 'Tomorrow, will you show me the route that he took?'

'Of course.' She smiled a little. 'And if you are with me, Richard cannot complain about my lack of escort.'

8

12th of September, 1343

Another hot morning, the weather unvarying. Clouds hung over the African shore, but the sky above al-Jazīra was a flawless blue.

'Warin, fetch two horses,' Merrivale said. 'You are coming with me. Jac, Juan, keep asking questions about La Algaba.'

'I have prayed to the Virgin Mary to help us find it,' Moreno said. He held up the rock salt crucifix that had once belonged to his sister. 'I have asked her to show us the way.'

Merrivale touched him lightly on the shoulder and went out. Eleanor was already mounted, with a crossbow and a quiver of bolts slung from the pommel of her saddle. The crossbow itself was finely made, with a steel bow and wooden stock inlaid with nacre.

'Do you know how to use that, my lady?' Merrivale asked.

She smiled a little. 'I'll wager that I am a better shot than you.'

Warin led the horses around and they both mounted. 'I have asked Warin to come with us, my lady,' Merrivale said. 'I believe we need to take Garcíez's threats seriously.'

He had thought of taking some of Sully's archers, too, but a larger party was more likely to attract notice. They rode to the western gate in the palisades, next to a little river that tumbled down from the hills; the Río de la Miel, Eleanor said, the river of honey. She pointed uphill. 'There's an old watchtower about three miles away. That's where I first saw him.'

The hills were steep and stony, forested with gnarled oak trees and wild olives. Clumps of dry golden grass grew in the open spaces. The sounds of the camp were soon lost behind them, absorbed by the trees. They picked their way along narrow tracks, hearing nothing but the clink of their own horseshoes and harness and the gentle warble of birdsong coming from the trees.

'I apologise for my behaviour last evening,' Eleanor said after a while.

'There is no need, my lady.'

'There is. My behaviour was unbecoming.'

'You needed to unburden yourself,' Merrivale said. 'I understand entirely.'

'I wish Richard did.' There was a long pause. 'Sometimes I think he and I are too much alike,' she said finally.

Sensing that she wanted to talk, Merrivale waited.

'When we were young, we both read and listened to poetry,' she said. 'Lancelot, Galahad, Chaitivel, Bisclavret, Tristan and Iseult, all of those bright figures of romance and tragedy. We wanted to live like them, and to die like them. Instead, we were both married to people we barely knew. I was married to John at the age of twelve, and Richard married Isabel when he was only eight. We both dreamed of love, but we never found it until we met each other.'

'*Aucassin and Nicolette*,' Merrivale said. 'I heard him singing the other night. He has a very fine voice.'

'One could fall in love with that voice alone... Aucassin swore to love Nicolette, and he let nothing stand in his way. He defied his family, even went to prison for her sake. But, Aucassin wasn't already married.'

'He too faced the wrath of his father,' Merrivale pointed out. 'When Aucassin escaped from his prison at Beaucaire, he and Nicolette fled to the land of Tora Lora. But when they were captured by pirates and separated, it was Nicolette who went searching for Aucassin.' He paused and looked at Eleanor. 'She never gave up on her own love.'

'It is only a fable,' she said after a while. 'It isn't real.'

'Of course not,' Merrivale said. 'In Tora Lora, the men give birth to children while women go off to war, firing apples and cheeses from their catapults. I have always assumed that this is how the poet thought the world should be, not how it really is. The point is, we don't have to accept what fate gives us. We can make our own destiny.'

'Some of us can,' said Eleanor.

'I was five when my mother died,' Merrivale said. 'My father lost his lands soon after and became destitute. I was forced to make my own future, and I did. I have few virtues, my lady, but I do not surrender meekly to fate. I don't think you do, either.' He glanced again at the crossbow. 'Where did you learn to shoot?'

She seemed relieved by the change of subject. 'At Lancaster, where I spent much of my youth. I grew up in troubled times, and my father was determined that I should be self-reliant. I learned to ride and shoot, and to use a dagger. Richard doesn't understand that I am quite capable of defending myself.'

'Who taught you? Your brother?'

Eleanor shook her head. 'He was already away at court. My mother died when I was young, and my father was often away too. My father's huntsman taught me to shoot. As a child, I saw more of him and his wife than I did of my own family.'

The Lancasters, Merrivale knew, had sometimes been on the wrong side during the turbulent years of the last English king's reign. Leaving Eleanor at home was probably the best way of protecting her. Ahead, to the west, the ground rose steeply and they saw the ruins of a stone watchtower on the crest of a hill.

'Sir!' Warin hissed. 'There's someone up ahead of us.'

Merrivale held up a hand and all three halted. 'Where?' Merrivale asked, staring through the trees.

'Climbing the hill. I caught a glimpse of him just now. Man in a white coat on a sorrel horse.'

'Garcíez rides a sorrel,' Eleanor whispered.

Silence fell, the air buzzing with heat. To their right lay the valley of the Río Palmones, full of charcoal smoke and haze, behind them, glimpsed through the trees, was the shimmering sea. Warin dismounted and slipped away through the trees. From up ahead came a rattle of horseshoes on stone. Two horsemen came into view, riding away from them and climbing the bare slopes of the hill. Both wore white surcoats with a splash of red; it was too far to see clearly, but Merrivale was quite certain that the device was the red floretty cross of Calatrava. 'Did Garcíez ride alone?' he asked Eleanor.

'Always when I saw him.'

The riders reached the crest of the hill and dismounted. A third man walked out from behind the tower, leading a horse. He wore long black robes, with a sparkling mail coat and helmet. The three men spoke for a few minutes before all of them mounted again. The man in black rode away to the north and was quickly lost to view. One of the men in white rode back down the hill and disappeared among the trees. The third turned his horse to the northeast, riding towards the river and the sultan's camp just visible through the heat waves in the distance.

Warin returned, perspiring a little. 'Two of them were Knights of Calatrava. One of them was Garcíez. He's the one that rode off towards the river. The other was a big fellow, balding with a grey beard.'

Merrivale slapped his hand against his thigh. 'Núñez,' he said. 'The grand master himself. So much for Peruzzi's story about dissension within the Order. What about the man in black?'

'I didn't recognise him, sir, but I'm guessing he was a Moor.'

'You were right, my lady,' Merrivale said finally. 'Garcíez rode into the hills because he was meeting someone from Garnāta before going to the sultan's camp. But why would they meet out here, rather than at the camp? And why did Núñez come with him?' He frowned. 'Did you see which way Núñez went?'

'Deeper into the hills, sir. Maybe he has another meeting somewhere else.'

'He might be heading for the Río de la Miel,' Eleanor said. 'He can water his horse there.'

'Lead the way, my lady.'

They rode south through the heat, down into a dry water-course, up another steep stony slope to the crest of a ridge and down again to another valley. The oaks gave way to leafy thickets of ash and willow along the banks of another river. Water poured over a ledge of rock into a deep green pool before cascading down the hill towards Al-Jazīra. Eleanor dismounted, leading her horse to the pool to let it drink.

Merrivale scanned the ground looking for footprints or hoofprints. 'You have been here before?' he asked Eleanor.

'This is my place of peace. I hate the confinement of the camp, I feel like a prisoner there. Here, I can breathe.'

A faint noise came to Merrivale's ear, a splash of water that did not come from the waterfall. He motioned for silence. The noise came again, a little louder. He motioned with his hand, telling the others to remain silent, and quietly skirted the pool and climbed up the slope beside the waterfall.

Above was another pool, fed by the river bubbling down through the trees. Two horses were tethered beside the pool, both in plain harness without livery. Clothing lay discarded on the rocks, including a white and red surcoat.

A black-haired woman crouched on all fours in the pool, head down and gasping for breath. Her back glistened with water. A balding, grey-bearded man knelt behind her, holding her by the waist and humping her hard from behind, grunting with effort, sending little ripples through the pool around them. Even as Merrivale saw them, the man began to shudder, closing his eyes and slowly sitting back in the water. The woman rolled over in the pool and sat up, splashing water on her breasts. She looked up at the man, smiling, and Merrivale saw her face.

It was Leonor de Guzmán.

He slid back down the slope to join the others. Eleanor was kneeling by the water's edge, cupping her hands in the water. 'You won't want to drink that,' Merrivale said quickly. 'Come, my lady, we must go. Now.'

13th of September, 1343

The following day, a big galley flying the banner of the Knights of Saint John entered the bay and ran gently up onto the beach next to the Genoese ships, and half an hour later Fra Moriale walked into Merrivale's pavilion.

'I hear you are a herald now,' he said to Merrivale. 'Congratulations.'

'Thank you. What news do you bring?'

Fra Moriale sat down next to Moreno and Ficaris, and Merrivale signalled to the servant to bring wine. 'I went first to Sebta and made inquiries among certain friends of mine,' Fra Moriale said. 'Kāsim al-'Aswad was indeed shipping African gold across the strait, but not to Castile. The shipments went to a port called Suhayl, in the lands of the sultan of Garnāta. I made a reconnaissance of the place. The port is in ruins, all except for a castle nearby which is guarded by the Warriors of the Faithful.'

Merrivale nodded slowly. 'Kāsim had a connection with their *amir*. Who exactly are they?'

'Exiles from Murrākush,' said Ficaris, 'who incurred the displeasure of its sultan and fled across the straits to take service in Garnāta. They are *ghāzīs*, holy warriors, not unlike the Knights of Calatrava in some ways. The Warriors fight for their own faith just as the Knights fight for theirs. But, again like the Knights of Calatrava, they are not always humble servants. There is friction between them and the sultan of Garnāta, and their *amir*, a man named Zayani, seized power after murdering his predecessor. As I said before, they are ruthless.'

'Again, not unlike the Knights,' Merrivale said. 'Would I be correct in assuming that there is dissension within the Order of Calatrava as well?'

'Of course,' said Fra Moriale. 'Just like Zayani, Juan Núñez rebelled against the previous grand master and overthrew him, but the result was a civil war that nearly tore the Order apart. Núñez still has his rivals. Pero de Garcíez is said to be one of them.'

'Anything else?' Merrivale asked.

'I considered attacking Suhayl, but the defences are strong and well-manned. I went next to the port of Alicante, which has the largest *salina* in Castile. Officials there confirmed that the salt monopoly remains in royal control and has not been farmed.'

'That confirms what I have been told,' Merrivale said. 'This leaves us with a problem. There is no evidence that Peruzzi is dealing in either salt or gold.'

Fra Moriale sipped his wine. 'Is it possible that we are wrong? That there is no plot?'

'There are many plots,' Merrivale said. 'The queen and the king's mistress are about to start a civil war, and Peruzzi and the Knights of Calatrava are backing Leonor de Guzmán.'

'Ah, yes, the queen. I also called again on my friend the prior of Portugal. According to him, Queen María is acquiring gold. A great deal of gold.'

'Where is she getting it from?' Ficaris asked.

'That, my friend did not know,' said Fra Moriale. 'What about you, Simó? Any progress?'

'It appears that Kāsim was not killed after all. He and his entire household, presumably including Mauro, were sold to the steward of the manor of La Algaba. Have you heard of it?'

'No, but I have made no great study of the geography of Castile. Why didn't Mauro identify himself as a Christian and ask for his freedom?'

'We do not know,' said Moreno.

'So, which man are you trying to find, Simó? Kāsim? Or Mauro?'

'Both,' said Merrivale. 'If we can establish a connection between Kāsim and Peruzzi, we can get to the heart of Peruzzi's scheme. But Mauro is important too. We have been threatened and warned three times to stop looking for him, which means that you were right. He knows something important, something that threatens Peruzzi, Garcíez and Leonor. We will not stop until we find him.'

Fra Moriale smiled. 'You are like a terrier,' he said. 'I am intrigued, Simó. Peruzzi is supporting Leonor de Guzmán, you say. Could he in fact be playing both sides against the middle?'

'The thought had occurred to me,' said Merrivale.

'I will investigate a little further. First, I shall call at Sevilla, where I have some useful friends. They may be able to tell us where La Algaba is. Thank you, Simó, for the wine.'

Fra Moriale departed. 'He has a lot of friends in a lot of places,' Warin said suspiciously.

'He has contacts in every port on both sides of the Middle Sea,' said Ficaris. 'He relies on them for information. That is how he stays alive.'

'If he finds La Algaba,' Warin said, 'he'll go straight there, take Kāsim and Mauro and wring them both dry. He'll use that information to grab the gold for himself.'

'He is welcome to it,' said Merrivale. 'So long as he gives us Mauro.'

By afternoon the heat was intense. Towers of cloud began building over the hills, vivid white against the sky. As time passed the clouds spread, their underbellies dark and threatening. Sir John Sully came to see Merrivale.

'Don Juan Manuel sends his compliments, Simon. He asks that you attend on him.'

Despite being a cousin of King Alfonso, Don Juan Manuel did not live in a wooden house like the king or his mistress, but in a simple canvas pavilion more like that of the common soldiers. A banner showing his unusual device, a golden winged hand holding a sword on a field of red, was the only sign of his rank.

Juan Manuel wore a simple black robe, contrasting with the snowy white of his beard and hair. He received Merrivale alone. 'Unlike the other *fidalgos*, I do not see why I should subject my wife to the rigours of life in camp,' he said. 'She looks after our estates while I do my duty to the king. Please, be seated.'

He sat down in a carved wooden chair. Merrivale pulled up a bench opposite him. 'How may I serve you, *mio çid*?' Merrivale asked.

Thunder rumbled in the air, echoing off the hills. 'I wanted to meet you,' Juan Manuel said. 'My friend Sir John has told me much about you. I find you interesting.'

'I shall take that as a compliment, *mio çid*.' Merrivale thought for a moment. 'Will you permit me to ask a question? Your estates are vast and are scattered across Castile, so you will know the country well. I am searching for a manor called La Algaba, so obscure that no one seems to have heard of it. Do you perchance know where it is?'

The white beard moved a little, and Merrivale realised the other man was smiling. 'You must allow me to ask some questions first,' he said. 'How did the feud between you and Donato de' Peruzzi begin?'

The rain came suddenly, drumming on the canvas and pouring down the outside of the pavilion. 'Peruzzi defrauded my government and put my country and my king in peril. He is still a threat, and I intend to remove him. I also wish to see justice done.'

'Ah, justice. Is this why you are also pursuing this young man who was wrongfully enslaved?'

'Yes.'

'Your concern for justice is laudable, *señor*, but you are putting yourself and your friends in danger.'

Peruzzi and Garcíez had said the same thing, but Juan Manuel's tone was one of warning rather than threat. 'Danger, *mio çid*? From whom?'

'From all sides. You must know by now that a crisis is coming in Castile. Queen María is in Córdoba, plotting against the king. But in Leonor de Guzmán she possesses a formidable foe, one who understands well the art of war. Leonor will not wait for María to make the first move. Already she is planning her own first strike. You would do well to cultivate her, and stay on her good side.'

The rain increased in force. Watching the other man's face, Merrivale realised that Juan Manuel knew that Leonor had tried to recruit him, and was testing him. 'She is allied with Peruzzi, my lord. That means she is no friend of mine.'

'We cannot always choose our allies,' Juan Manuel said.

'Do you support her?' Merrivale asked directly. 'Or are you backing Queen María?'

The older man smiled again, steepling his hands. 'Let me tell you a story,' he said. 'One day, a swallow saw men sowing flax in a field. He perceived at once that they would harvest the flax and weave it into nets for catching birds. The swallow assembled the other birds and said to them, we must eat the flax seed, or pull up the plants and destroy them, so that the men cannot make nets. Then we shall be safe. But the birds refused to listen, and so the swallow went to the men and placed himself under their protection. The men made the nets and caught many other birds, but the swallow was always safe. Do you understand the meaning?'

'If danger threatens, root it out,' Merrivale said. 'Or if you cannot, make sure you are on the winning side.'

'That is more or less the point,' agreed Juan Manuel. 'Be careful, my young friend. As you said, I find you interesting, and I would hate to lose you too soon. I believe you were asking questions about a man named al-Rumani.'

'Yes,' Merrivale said, wondering where this was going.

'I met him during my last journey to Garnāta. He is the *musharaf*, the controller of the salt works.'

As suddenly as it had arrived, the rain began to die away. 'I see,' Merrivale said slowly. 'And La Algaba? I think you do know where it is.'

'You are right, it is a small manor and very obscure. I am unsurprised that no one had heard of it. La Algaba, or al-Ghaba as the Moors called it, lies in the valley of the Río Guadalquivir, thirty miles west of the city of Córdoba Alyana, the City of Paradise. The current lord of the manor is the king's lady, Leonor de Guzmán. I will not advise you against going there, because I know you will not listen. But tread carefully, my young friend. Your enemies know your intentions, and will be waiting.'

Merrivale rose to his feet and bowed. 'Isn't that always the way?' he asked.

'I shall pray that you find your friend's nephew and bring him home. It is the least that I can do.'

'Thank you, *mio çid*. I appreciate it.'

Outside the rain had ceased and the clouds were already blowing away. Shafts of sunlight sparkled brilliantly off the sea. A prickling on Merrivale's neck told him someone was watching him. He turned, expecting to find Garcíez. Instead, a white-bearded man in the grey habit of a Franciscan friar stood looking back at him. The man turned away, but not before Merrivale recognised the man he had seen arguing with the mule-seller the day he arrived at the camp.

Ficaris and Moreno were playing cards when Merrivale returned to the pavilion. 'Juan has something to tell you,' Ficaris said.

Moreno nodded. 'We were wondering which of the Knights of Calatrava captured Kāsim and his household, and suddenly I realised who might know. I asked the Genoese shipmasters, thinking that they would know about the movement of ships, and they confirmed my guess. The master of the galley that took Kāsim and my nephew was Pero de Garcíez.'

Merrivale sat down. The servant brought them glasses of wine, a rich dark malvasia. 'There is more,' Ficaris said.

Moreno nodded. 'Garcíez boasted of his capture. He had known exactly where and when to intercept Kāsim, he said, because a spy in Granada had told him. This spy's name was al-Rumani.'

'Christ in Heaven,' Merrivale said.

'Garcíez was in his cups, which explains why he talked so freely. He talked of the money he could make from the sale, and how it would help his brother's wife and family. I don't understand the last part, but I gather Garcíez spoke of the lady a great deal. Before he passed out on the taverna floor, that is.'

Ficaris frowned. 'Capturing Kāsim was a legitimate act of war,' he said finally. 'But... if so, why are they trying so hard to stop us from finding him? Why threaten us?'

'I don't know,' Merrivale said, 'but we shall find out. I know where La Algaba is.'

He related what Juan Manuel had said. Moreno closed his eyes and Merrivale saw his lips move in prayer. 'I have probably passed by it,' Ficaris said. 'I sailed upriver to Córdoba once, a long time ago. How do we get there?'

'I have an idea,' Merrivale said. 'The next assault on the city goes in tomorrow. When it is over, I shall speak to Philippe of Navarre.'

14th of September, 1343

Trumpets sounded at first light the following morning, summoning the camp to arms. Merrivale went to Derby's tent to find the earl and his esquires pulling on arming doublets and mail coats and buckling on plate armour. 'Alfonso is assaulting the Tarifa Gate,' Derby said. 'He is worried that the sultan of Garnāta might attack the camp while he is concentrating on the city. Philippe offered to guard the river crossing, and we're supporting him.' He smiled a little. 'Anything to help a friend.'

'Shall I come with you?' Merrivale asked.

'You're a herald now, Simon, not a fighting man. If there is any negotiating to be done, I will send for you.'

Merrivale nodded. Just for a moment, his sword hand had twitched again.

The Navarrese men-at-arms were already moving away through the camp. John Sully's archers followed, sunburnt men in russet and green moving in file with longbows resting over their shoulders. Horses were brought around and Derby and his esquires mounted. Arundel rode up alongside them, his face white, his eyes furious. 'What is wrong?' Derby asked.

'Nothing,' Arundel said shortly.

'Ah, you've had another quarrel with Eleanor. Leave it behind, Richard. We have work to do.'

The two earls rode away after their men. The sound of horses and men moving into position was a distant murmur in the air; the camp itself had fallen eerily silent.

A groom appeared outside Arundel's pavilion, leading another horse. The door opened and Eleanor strode out, dressed for riding and carrying her crossbow and quiver. Before Merrivale could reach her, she had mounted and picked up the reins.

'My lady,' Merrivale said quickly. 'Where are you going?'

Her face was wild with anger. 'Get out of my way, Simon,' she snapped. 'I am not in a mood to be trifled with.'

'My lady, it is too dangerous. A battle is about to begin.'

'The battle is around the city. I am going in the other direction, as far as I can. Get out of my way, Simon, and do not try to follow me.'

There was no arguing with her in this mood. He stepped back, and Eleanor spurred the horse and cantered away through the lines of tents. Merrivale turned to the groom. 'Do you have another horse?'

'No, sir. His lordship's men have taken them all. We're desperately short of horses at the moment.'

Derby's grooms had no horses remaining either. Merrivale returned to his own pavilion where two of Sully's archers remained on guard, grumbling about missing the fighting. Ficaris, Moreno and Warin were playing *kanjifah*, and Merrivale beckoned to Warin. 'Find me a mount. Horse, mule, jennet, it doesn't matter. Anything I can ride.'

Ficaris laid down his cards. 'I'll come with you, Warin. You'll need a translator.'

'I speak some Castilian.'

'You know how to order wine in Castilian. You don't know how to haggle for a horse.'

Warin and Ficaris departed. Moreno laid down his own cards and sat staring into space; dreaming, Merrivale thought, of seeing his nephew once more, yet fearing for him at the same time. He thought of the incredible courage Moreno had shown, venturing alone into a hostile land, persevering for years in his quest. A lesser man would have given up long ago, but beneath Moreno's pious, quiet exterior there was a will of steel.

Restless, Merrivale went back outside. There was a vantage point next to Arundel's pavilion where he could look out over the camp and see the siege lines and the city. He watched the assault beginning to unfold, trebuchet arms swinging as they pounded the walls with stone shot, crossbowmen moving forward to sweep the ramparts, pressing on despite the arrows raining down on them, while behind them siege towers rolled slowly into position. Cannon boomed, belching yellow smoke, and a cannon shot cut a swathe through the dismounted men-at-arms massing behind the siege towers. Armoured men staggered and fell.

Another cannon hit one of the towers. It staggered drunkenly and the hides that protected it from fire fell to the ground. Fire arrows soared from the walls, trailing gossamer lines of smoke. Within a few minutes the siege tower was burning like a torch, and Merrivale saw men jumping from its platforms to escape the flames.

In Tora Lora they make war with eggs and cheeses, he thought. *We could do with following their example.*

Eventually Warin appeared, red-faced and sweating, leading a reluctant horse. 'It's the best we could do, sir. Not much to look at, but at least it has four legs.'

'Thank God for that.' Eleanor had a long start now, but he thought he knew where she would go. Hopefully her anger would have cooled a little by the time he caught up with her.

Ficaris ran up to them. 'Simon, come quickly! Something is wrong with Juan.'

They hurried into the pavilion. Juan Moreno lay on the floor, his face contorted, eyes staring blankly. A pool of fresh vomit spread out beside his head. His hands were cold, and even as Merrivale touched his neck, his pulse flickered and stopped.

9

14th of September, 1343

A cask of wine stood on the table next to the playing cards. It had been opened and a small, abstemious cup had been poured. Not much had been drunk; the poison that killed Moreno must have been a powerful one. Merrivale picked up the cup and sniffed it. A faint smell rose to his nostrils, bitter and sweet at the same time.

A parchment letter lay on the table. Merrivale picked it up, seeing the arms of the house of Lancaster on the broken seal.

> *My thanks to you, Señor Moreno, for singing and playing so beautifully on my birthday. My lord of Arundel will have rewarded you generously, of course. But please accept this gift of malvasia from my own hands, as an expression of my thanks.*
> *Eleanor de Lancastria, domina*

Ficaris was silent with shock. Merrivale went outside. 'Did anyone come to the pavilion within the last hour?' he asked the two archers.

'Yes, sir,' said one of them. 'A pageboy came only a few minutes ago. He brought a cask of wine, a gift from the lady Eleanor.'

'When did this boy leave? Which way did he go?'

The archer scratched his ear. 'I couldn't rightly say, sir. He didn't go to my lord of Arundel's pavilion.'

'Body of Christ!' Merrivale turned, and stopped suddenly like he had been punched in the stomach. At the far end of one of the lanes of tents, seated on the back of a warhorse and clad in full armour and a white and red surcoat, was Pero de Garcíez. Merrivale ran towards him. Garcíez raised one hand in ironic salute, pulled down the visor of his bascinet and galloped away through the camp.

'*Warin!*' Merrivale shouted. 'Fetch the horse! *Now!*'

Warin came running, leading the horse. 'What is it, sir?'

'Juan is dead. I'm going after Garcíez.'

Silent with shock, Warin held the horse's head as Merrivale mounted, clutching his staff, and kicked the horse into motion. He had expected Garcíez to ride west and go up into the hills again, but hoofprints still damp from yesterday's rain showed that he was heading north towards the Río Palmones. Merrivale's own horse kept lurching to the left, and he had to haul on the reins to bring it back on course. He kicked the animal again, trying to make it go faster, without noticeable effect. Off to the right, fighting still raged along the city walls; the stink of sulphur and burning wood drifted up the hill, accompanied by the sounds of clashing metal and screams.

Ahead was the palisade, the gate shut and barred. Merrivale pulled his horse to a halt and called out to the sentinels. 'Did a Knight of Calatrava pass through here, not long ago?'

'Yes, *señor.*'

'Open the gate. Now.'

They looked at his tabard, and opened the gate. Merrivale kicked the horse again and rode down past the burial ground, searching for his quarry. Ahead lay the river, with the Navarrese and English companies lined up on its bank; beyond, a lone rider splashed through the water, heading towards the ruined village and the Torre de Cartagena on its low hill.

Derby turned as Merrivale rode up. 'Simon? What are you doing here?'

Merrivale pointed at the fleeing horseman. 'That's Garcíez. He has just murdered Juan Moreno.'

Derby's handsome face was shocked. Arundel was the first to react. 'Come on, after him! *Philippe!*' he shouted across to the Navarrese company. 'We must stop that horseman!'

A trumpet sounded. The men-at-arms spurred their horses, thirty English with white-haired Sir John Sully in the vanguard and a hundred Navarrese, racing across the shallows of the Río Palmones, kicking up sheets of spray. Garcíez was over the river now, galloping towards the tower. There will be no refuge for him there, Merrivale thought grimly. If the garrison won't hand him over, we'll smash the door down and take him anyway.

They raced across the meadows towards the tower. Philippe of Navarre and Irunberri were out in front, reeling in the distance between themselves and Garcíez. The latter looked back, seeing the pursuit, and suddenly reined in his horse, slowing to a walk. Sully raised a clenched fist. 'His mount has gone lame! We've got him!'

Out from behind the low hill came a solid wedge of fast-moving horsemen with lances and leather shields. Spired helmets and chainmail coats glittered like silver in the sun; red and gold banners proclaiming the name of God the victorious fluttered above their heads. Along the shore from the direction of the sultan's camp came another column, moving at speed.

'Mother of God!' Sully yelled. 'Ambush!'

Derby stood up in his stirrups, raising his voice. 'Richard! Philippe! Everyone, *back to the river!*'

Garcíez turned in the saddle. Once again he raised an arm in mocking salute, and spurred his horse away towards the tower. Furious, Merrivale hauled his horse around with the others and they fled back the way they had come, hooves thundering over the flat fields and kicking up clods of earth.

'Come on, boys!' Sully roared. 'Ride like hell itself is after you! *Come on!*'

But, fast as they rode, the enemy were faster still. Turning his head, Merrivale saw that the foremost riders were already probing at the Navarrese rearguard with their lances. Arrows whirred around them. Irunberri's horse was down, the captain tumbling to the ground. Merrivale hauled on the reins again, and for once his horse obeyed. Galloping hard, he reached Irunberri just as an enemy horseman rode at him, lance levelled for the kill. Ducking under the lance, Merrivale closed in, raised his herald's staff and hit the other rider a two-handed blow across the side of the head. The man fell unconscious to the ground, and Merrivale seized the reins of the other horse, halting it.

Irunberri was on his feet, groggy but moving. 'Quickly!' Merrivale shouted, throwing him the reins, and the captain climbed into the saddle. Philippe of Navarre was not far away, fighting two men who hacked at him with long swords. Merrivale kicked his horse into motion once more, couching his staff like a lance and using the blunt end to knock one of the assailants out of his saddle. Philippe raised his own sword and cut the other man down, and he and Merrivale rode hard for the river.

They reached the Río Palmones and splashed into the water, the enemy yelling behind them. On the far bank the English archers stood in a long line, longbows raised. Grey-feathered arrows rushed overhead, hissing like venomous snakes. The shouts behind them turned to screams as men and horses crashed down into the shallow water. The archers reached for fresh arrows, nocked, drew and released, over and over again, and the arrows flew like rain.

No one could stand in the face of an arrow storm for long. The enemy horsemen pulled back out of range, and after a moment turned and began riding towards their own camp. Merrivale turned to Irunberri. 'Are you all right, captain?'

'My head is ringing like a bell,' Irunberri said, 'but I will survive.' He gasped suddenly. 'The king! He is wounded!'

Blood stained Philippe's surcoat and his bright armour. He held up a gauntleted hand, which dripped more blood. 'It's nothing,' he said. 'A mere scratch.'

'All the same, cousin, we shall take you back to the camp,' Derby said. He looked at the sun, now past its zenith. 'The enemy are retreating, and the assault on the city seems to have ended. We have no more purpose here.'

They returned to the camp, the archers and the Navarrese foot soldiers following the horsemen. Despite his words, Philippe was obviously in pain, and when they reached his pavilion he needed Irunberri's help to dismount. Merrivale, Derby and Sully followed them inside while Arundel, anxious now to make up his quarrel with Eleanor, rode back to his own pavilion. Merrivale realised he had not told the earl that Eleanor had ridden out. With luck, she would have returned by now, and he would never know.

Philippe's attendants stripped off his cuirass and arming doublet, revealing a deep gash in his shoulder where a sword blade had found a gap in his armour. Alameda knelt beside the king and began cleaning the wound. 'You are very handy with that quarterstaff, Simon,' Philippe said, wincing a little. 'Where did you learn to fight?'

'On Dartmoor, when I was a child,' Merrivale said. 'During the famine, we fought to survive.'

Philippe nodded a little. 'What happened to Señor Moreno?'

'Someone claiming to be the lady Eleanor sent him a cask of malvasia which had been poisoned with laurel water. It's an unusual poison, largely undetectable except for a very faint smell, but the effects are immediate and deadly.'

'Who really sent it?' Philippe asked. 'Garcíez?'

'I am certain of it. He sent a messenger to deliver the wine to Juan, waited to make certain that I spotted him, and led myself and the rest of us into a trap.'

'But why kill Señor Moreno?' asked Derby.

'Because we have found La Algaba, and because Juan had also discovered that Garcíez had captained the galley that captured Kāsim and Juan's nephew. Garcíez is also colluding with some of the sultan of Garnāta's men. For whatever reason, he is desperate to ensure that we do not find Juan's nephew. Or rather, Peruzzi is desperate.'

'He is behind the killing?'

'I believe so, my lord.' Merrivale turned to Philippe and bowed. 'Sire, I have a proposition to put to you.'

Alameda picked up a roll of cloth and began bandaging Philippe's wound. 'Go on,' the king said.

'La Algaba is only a little way from Córdoba. I need to go there, quietly and without attracting attention. If you are still intending to go to Córdoba and intercede with Queen María, may I travel as part of your household? If my lord of Derby gives me leave, that is.'

Derby nodded. 'Do you need to go that far?' asked Sully. 'Garcíez went to the Torre de Cartagena. Why not lay what we already know before King Alfonso and Grand Master Núñez, and ask them to hand him over? Put him to the question, and extract a confession implicating Peruzzi.'

'Alfonso is powerless in this matter,' Merrivale said. 'Núñez answers only to the pope, remember? And Núñez is colluding with the enemy, too. He and Garcíez met an officer from the army of Garnāta two days ago. I reckon that's when today's plot was set up and the plans for the ambush were laid.'

Philippe nodded slowly. 'Then to Córdoba we shall go,' he said. 'We can kill two birds with one stone.'

'Not immediately, sire,' Alameda said. 'Your wound is deep, and you must not over-exert yourself. Wait a few days.'

'Two days,' said Philippe. 'No more. Guilhem-Arnaut? Pass the word to the men, and tell them to make ready to travel.'

The door to the pavilion opened and Arundel hurried in, breathless and sweating. 'Eleanor is missing,' he said. 'She went out riding again this morning, just after we marched. She hasn't returned.'

Philippe was growing dizzy from loss of blood. Reluctantly, he listened to his physician and remained behind. The others rode out, Merrivale and Sully, Derby and Arundel with their horsemen, Irunberri and the Navarrese men-at-arms; Don Juan

Manuel and some of his men joined them too, the old *fidalgo* expressing his shock at the news of Eleanor's disappearance.

Merrivale himself, with Ficaris and Warin, rode straight up the valley of the Río de la Miel to the little pool that she had described as her place of peace. She was not there, nor were there any tracks to indicate that she had passed through recently.

All through the afternoon they searched the hills, until the shadows grew long and veils of dusk began drifting in from the east. Wearily, they rode through the sweltering heat back to the camp. Arundel, too distraught to speak, went into his pavilion. Derby, Irunberri, Merrivale, Sully and Don Juan Manuel conferred.

'Nothing,' Sully said. 'Not a sign of her or the horse. Not even so much as a hoofprint in the ground.'

'Could the Moors have captured her?' Juan Manuel asked. 'She might have encountered a wandering patrol and been taken.'

'We saw no sign of them either,' said Irunberri. He stroked his long moustache. 'Mind you, these hills are hard ground, even after yesterday's rain. There's a lot of bare stone where a hoofprint would leave no indent. A rider could pass through them without leaving tracks, if they were careful.'

'I will go to the sultan's camp tomorrow and make inquiries,' Merrivale said. He shook his head. 'This is my fault. I saw her riding out this morning, and tried to stop her.'

Derby put a hand on his shoulder. 'Simon, if you can prevent my sister from doing what she wants to do, you're a better man than all of us. Do not reproach yourself. Go to the Moors tomorrow, and we will continue the search.'

Arundel did not join them for dinner. The meal was eaten mostly in silence. Once, Ficaris looked over at Merrivale. 'We have prepared him,' he said simply. 'A priest will be waiting in the morning.'

Merrivale nodded. It was urgent that they find Eleanor, but it was equally important that they say farewell to a friend.

15th of September, 1343

Dawn was an arch of gold in the east. The hills around the city were funereal with shadow. A waning moon hung in the dark western sky.

Juan Moreno had been a humble man, and his funeral was humble too. A grave had been dug for him; Merrivale had insisted he not be consigned to the burial pits where the common soldiers lay. His body had been wrapped in white linen, and a wooden handcart was his catafalque. Merrivale, Ficaris and Warin were the only mourners. Merrivale wondered if Eleanor would have attended, had she still been here.

The priest, a black-robed Dominican friar, looked at Merrivale. 'Now?' he asked.

'No,' Merrivale said. 'Wait.'

They waited. The light grew stronger. A blaze of fire touched the horizon, the rim of the sun climbing over the edge of the world. Merrivale held up the rock salt crucifix, watching the cross and the figure of Christ fill with light.

'Now,' he said.

'*Requiem aeternam dona eis, Domine. Et lux perpetua luceat eis...*' Merrivale listened to the flowing words of the service. He had heard it many times before, but the first time was still the one that echoed in his mind: the service in the little church on Dartmoor where his mother and sisters had been laid to rest, victims of the famine that still raged outside. His father, leaning on a stick, was gaunt and weak; his own stomach was cramped with hunger. He was only a boy and had not yet learned Latin, but he had never forgotten the words.

'*Kyrie eleison. Christe eleison. Kyrie eleison.*' God have mercy on us. But what mercy was shown to Juan Moreno? he thought bleakly. He looked at the light flowing through the crucifix, and made his own silent vow. *There will be justice*, he told himself. *There will be blood.*

The mass ended. Merrivale paid the friar, who walked away counting his coins. 'What now?' asked Ficaris.

'"*Dies irae, dies illa, solvet saeclum in favilla,*" Merrivale said, quoting the requiem. '"This day, this day of wrath shall consume the world in ashes." I am going to speak to Abū Nu'aym Ridwan. Both of you, join the search. We will find the lady Eleanor, and then we will find Mauro. And when we have done so, we shall hunt Pero de Garcíez to the ends of the earth.'

The Torre de Cartagena was silent, but as he passed, the banner on its roof turret was suddenly lowered and raised again. A signal, Merrivale thought. To whom?

He did not have to wait for long. A cloud of dust erupted ahead of him; out of it came a company of horsemen all wearing the same white robes with chainmail and spiked helmets. He pulled his horse to halt beside the row of broken Roman columns and waited while the riders surrounded him. They were considerably less friendly than on his previous visit.

'*Mani auntu?*' Lances jabbed at him, threateningly. '*Madha turidu?*'

Merrivale gripped his staff. 'I am the herald of the English earl of Derby, and I have immunity as an ambassador. Take me to His Excellency the *hajib*.'

There was a long moment of silence before the leader motioned with his hand. 'Come.'

In Ridwan's scarlet pavilion, nothing had changed; the same turbaned men sat cross-legged in rows at their low desks. Ridwan himself was dictating to one of his secretaries. His expression did not alter when Merrivale was escorted in.

'Señor herald. To what do I owe the pleasure of your company?'

'Forgive me for arriving unannounced, excellency,' Merrivale said, folding his hands and bowing. 'One of our people has gone missing. The lady Eleanor of Lancaster, sister of the Earl of Derby, went riding in the hills yesterday and has not returned.'

Ridwan motioned to the secretary, who bowed and withdrew. 'Riding in the hills, without an escort? That was reckless of her.'

'The lady has a mind of her own,' Merrivale said. 'Excellency, it occurred to us that she might have been found by a scouting party of your men. If she is a prisoner, my lord of Derby will gladly pay her ransom.'

A long silence followed. Merrivale could almost hear the calculations running through Ridwan's mind.

Finally, unexpectedly, the chancellor rose to his feet. 'If the lady Eleanor is in this camp, she will be restored to you at once. There will be no question of a ransom.'

'Thank you, excellency. You are gracious and generous.'

'I serve God, who esteems it a sin to make war upon women. Remain here while I make inquiries. My servants will bring refreshments while you wait.'

Merrivale waited. Servants brought refreshments, little dishes of almonds and olives and thick fermented milk called *zabadi* scattered with pomegranate seeds, accompanied by a sweet drink flavoured with rose water. The clerks working behind their desks paid him no attention. The camp murmured around him, horses moving restlessly, men talking in low voices, the distant beat of drums. Outside the shadows moved as the sun tracked across the sky. At midday the long, solemn chant of the call to prayer drifted through the camp. Merrivale found his Arabic had improved to the point where he could recognise some of the words. *Come to prayer, come to the best of deeds. There is nothing worthy of worship except God.*

It was late afternoon before Ridwan finally returned. His face, as always, was devoid of expression. 'The lady Eleanor is not in this camp. However, I have questioned our scouts. Late yesterday morning they saw a lone rider going over the hills to the northwest. There is a track there that leads through the mountains to Xerez, and ultimately to Sevilla.'

'Thank you,' Merrivale said slowly. 'We will investigate. Excellency, may I ask one question before I take my leave? We know that a Knight of Calatrava, a man named Pero de Garcíez, has visited this camp several times in the past few months. Did he come here yesterday, after the skirmish along the river?'

Ridwan's expression did not change. 'I do not know this name.'

'Thank you, excellency.' Merrivale folded his hands and bowed. 'It is kind of you to take so much trouble, and his lordship is grateful for your help. We shall continue to search for the lady, and hope to find her.'

'If God desires it, she will be found,' said Ridwan, and he too bowed his head.

—

Sunset was burning orange behind the hills when Merrivale returned to the camp. The search parties had just returned. Arundel, stoop-shouldered with weariness, red-rimmed eyes burning in his pale face, turned as Merrivale dismounted. 'Well?'

'Ridwan says they don't have her, and I believe him. But his scouts saw someone going across the hills, riding in the direction of Sevilla.'

'Sevilla?' Arundel stared at him. 'Why would Eleanor be going to Sevilla?' Merrivale said nothing. 'They must have seen someone else,' Arundel said abruptly. 'We will continue the search tomorrow.'

He turned and strode into his pavilion. Don Juan Manuel smoothed his white beard. 'Could this lone rider have been the lady?' he asked.

Derby shook his head. 'If so, she took nothing with her. No baggage, not even her jewels, Richard says.'

'It may have been a spur of the moment decision, my lord,' Merrivale said. 'She intended to return as usual, but while she was out in the hills she changed her mind. If she did reach Sevilla, could she find a ship to take her to England?'

'Yes, although she might need to wait a few days, or weeks,' said Don Juan Manuel. 'But the road to Sevilla is not without danger. I fear for the beautiful lady.'

The old man bowed and departed. 'He is not the only one who is fearful,' Derby said tiredly. 'Why is Don Juan Manuel being so helpful, do you think?'

'I asked him,' said Sir John Sully. 'He gave what I can only describe as a gnomic answer. "God wills all things," he said, "but man is too often the author of his own misfortunes." The same, he added, applies to women.'

'I'm too tired to think what that means,' Derby said.

Merrivale went into his own pavilion to find Ficaris and Warin waiting. The relief on both their faces clear to see. 'We had begun to wonder if you were coming back,' Ficaris said.

Merrivale related what had happened. Ficaris frowned a little. 'Ridwan also went out of his way to be helpful, did he? I wonder why?'

'Come, Jac, the answer is obvious. He did it to throw me off the scent.'

'Oh? The scent of what?'

'It would be interesting to know, wouldn't it? Ridwan never gives anything away.'

'What do we do about the runaway princess, sir?' Warin asked.

Ficaris shook his head. 'Runaway princesses only exist in fabliaux, Warin.'

'Ordinarily I would agree with you,' Merrivale said. 'But this time, I think Warin may be right.' He heard Eleanor's voice in his mind. *The camp is so confined, I sometimes feel like a prisoner there.* And, with a sob in her voice, *I feel like I am being eaten alive. And when the pain becomes too much, I lash out at him.*

'We'll search again tomorrow,' he said. 'But if we don't find her in the hills, we shall have to assume that she has fled. If

Philippe of Navarre is ready to travel, we will join him as planned and go to Sevilla. If she is there, we shall find her.'

'Then what?' asked Warin.

'That rather depends on her,' Merrivale said.

—

They searched again the following day, probing deeper into the hills, and finally in the heat of the afternoon they found what they had been looking for: the tracks of a single horse in a patch of dust, moving northwest towards Sevilla. The tracks, said Irunberri, were a couple of days old. It was too late in the day to follow them.

Merrivale looked at Irunberri. 'Is King Philippe still resolved to depart tomorrow?'

'Yes.' Irunberri stroked his moustache, his usual habit when thinking. 'It will take us a week to reach Sevilla, I think. Five days to the town of Xerez, and two more to the city.'

They had no choice but to go overland; the Genoese crews had still not been paid and were refusing to put to sea, and Fra Moriale and the *Santa Creu* were already in Sevilla. Back in the camp that evening Merrivale turned to Derby and Arundel.

'My lords, I am sorry. But it appears increasingly likely that the lady Eleanor is attempting to return to England.'

Arundel's fists clenched. 'The road to Sevilla is dangerous. And even if she does find a ship, it won't be over. The seas are full of pirates.' Suddenly his eyes were full of tears. 'God help me, Eleanor! Why did I drive you away?'

'You didn't drive her away,' Derby said sharply. 'Don't blame yourself, Richard.'

'Who else is there to blame? I failed her. She wanted marriage, and I refused. I could not break my oath to my wife, I said. I could not imperil my immortal soul.'

'I will find her for you,' Merrivale said.

'No. Tomorrow, I will ride with you and Philippe.'

'No, Richard,' Derby said gently.

Arundel raised his hands to his head. 'I cannot remain here!'

'You can, and you must. You have many skills, Richard, but tracking fugitives is not one of them. This is Simon's world. If anyone can find Eleanor, he will.'

'And I will find her,' Merrivale repeated. 'When I do, what do you wish me to tell her?'

'Tell her... Oh, God. Tell her that when she smiles, the stars cease turning in their circles. Tell her that when I look into her eyes, I see the light of a hundred sunrises.' Arundel rubbed his own eyes. 'Tell her that I have made my choice,' he said. 'Remind her of what Aucassin said: "What use have I for Paradise? I have no wish to enter there. To Hell I will gladly go." I will give her everything I have. Including my soul.'

Merrivale said nothing. 'Tell her I am desperate to see her again,' Arundel said finally. 'But also... if she has made her own choice, she should not return unless she wishes it. I want to know that she is alive, and safe... and happy. I can be content with that.'

How much it cost Arundel to utter those last words was impossible to guess. Merrivale nodded. 'I will tell her, my lord,' he said. 'You have my word that she will be safe.'

City of Paradise

10

17th of September, 1343

They departed the camp at dawn the next day. The men-at-arms of Philippe's escort rode ahead, sending scouts out into the stony hills. The baggage wagons followed and the foot soldiers, a mixture of spearmen and crossbowmen, tramped along behind them. The sun rose, and the heat rose with it. The hills became higher and steeper, their crests crowned with old watchtowers. Oak forests gave way to pine, and the hot air was pungent with resin and the scent of wild roses.

Philippe turned in his saddle. 'Ride with me, Simon?'

'Of course, sire.' Leaving Warin and Ficaris behind, Merrivale eased his horse up alongside the king's.

'You come from Dartmoor,' Philippe said. 'I imagine it was an idyllic place, until the famine came.'

'I remember very little before that time, sire. I am afraid I have no pleasant memories of home.'

'Did you remain there after the famine?'

Merrivale shook his head. 'My father and I were the only survivors of our family. The experience had broken him, and he was no longer able to care for his lands or pay his rents. His overlord dispossessed him a few years later. Had not Sir John Sully and his wife taken us in, we would have been destitute.'

'Sully. That good old man. Sometimes I envy cousin Edward the quality of his retainers. Men like Henry of Derby, and Sully, and you of course... How did you come into the king's service?'

'That was Sir John's doing. He procured a position for me at court, where I was educated. When I was fifteen I was appointed a King's Messenger, and have held that post ever since.'

'From what I hear, Simon, you have been much more than a messenger. The king relies on you.'

'It is an honour to serve him, sire.'

Philippe winced a little, and Merrivale could see that his wound was paining him. 'And you?' the king asked. 'Your whole life is service? You have never dreamed of taking a wife, having a son to inherit your name?'

Merrivale pushed the thought of Yolande out of his mind. He smiled a little. 'I have been rather busy, sire.'

They camped that night in a high valley that Alameda said was called the Val de Infierno, which reminded Merrivale of the poems of Dante. The road here was comparatively safe, as the Castilian garrisons at Tarifa and Vejer de la Frontera patrolled the hills frequently, and the big enemy strongholds of Runda and Zahara were further away to the northeast. All the same, a strong guard was posted. As dusk fell, one of Irunberri's officers came and saluted.

'*Kapitaina*, a Castilian wishes to ride with us as far as Sevilla. He says his name is Buscador.'

'Does he have a weapon?'

'Yes, *kapitaina*, he is a crossbowman.'

Irunberri stroked his moustache. 'If we run into trouble, we could use another man. Tell him he can ride along.'

Merrivale turned to Alameda. 'How is the king's health, Lorenço?'

Alameda frowned. 'Not the best. He has yet to fully recover from the influenza, and the wound took more out of him than he realised. He will need to rest when we reach Sevilla, possibly even before then.'

'You must tell me if you think he is too weak to travel,' Merrivale said. 'I will seek permission to ride on ahead and try to find the lady Eleanor.'

'Of course.'

Night fell. Merrivale stood for a few moments, looking up at the stars over the hills. *We seem to be aiming at many different targets*, he thought. Bringing Moreno's killer to justice, finding and rescuing his nephew, bringing down Peruzzi, and now finding – yes, Warin was right – the runaway princess... He studied the stars, finding the invisible lines that connected them and formed them into constellations: the Harp, Arthur's Wain, the Archer with his bright glittering belt. *No*, he thought, *all of our aims are connected. All are part of the same thing.*

–

The next day took them over rough mountain tracks where the foot soldiers had to lay aside their weapons and put their shoulders behind the baggage wagons to heave them up and over the stony hills, and then hold onto drag ropes to keep them from plunging down the inclines on the far side. The air was less humid away from the coast, but the heat was no less intense. Buzzards circled in the air above them, but otherwise the land was still. Occasionally they passed ruined villages, crumbling stone walls and the remains of charred roof timbers, burned out in raids long ago; raids by which side, it was impossible to tell.

At midday they halted beside a dry riverbed to rest. Horses and men were both sweating. Irunberri waved a gauntleted hand to the left. 'Just over there is the valley of the Río Salado, the Salt River. Three years ago, the Marrakeshis came over the straits in force and laid siege to Tarifa, and Sultan Yūsuf's army came down and joined them. If they'd taken Tarifa, the way would have been open to Cádiz and Sevilla, and nothing would have stopped them.'

'What happened?' Merrivale asked.

'For once, the kings stopped fighting each other and united. We sent troops to aid Alfonso, and so did Portugal and Aragón. We advised Alfonso to remain on the defensive, but... he doesn't really understand what *defensive* means. He attacked, and by the grace of God we broke the Moorish line and slaughtered them. Granada and Marrakesh both lost thousands of men.' Irunberri took a long drink of water from his skin. 'It shows what can happen when we are able to work together,' he said.

Merrivale glanced at Philippe, seated nearby while a page held a sunshade over his head. 'Is that what he wants? For everyone to work together?'

'For all the kingdoms to work together for the common good,' said Irunberri. 'He wants an end to strife. He has a vision of peace, he says.' The captain's voice was full of sudden admiration. 'There are few men like him in the world.'

'Yes,' Merrivale said slowly. 'When you say all of the kingdoms, do you mean Granada also?'

'Of course. Faith apart, Granada has more in common with Castile than it does with Marrakesh.'

'That won't make Philippe popular with the crusading orders. The Knights of Calatrava, for instance.'

Irunberri smiled. 'Kings do not need to be liked, he says. Only to be respected.'

The column moved on. Evening found them deep in the mountains, making camp at the bottom of a valley where springs fed a small bubbling stream, enough to provide water for horses and men. Buscador, the crossbowman who had joined them the previous evening, led his mount down to the stream and dismounted, holding the reins while the horse bent its neck to drink. Merrivale moved up quietly behind the horse and studied the crossbow hanging from the pommel. It was a beautiful weapon, with a steel bow and a polished wooden stock inlaid with nacre; exactly the same bow that Eleanor of Lancaster had carried with her when she rode out of the camp at al-Jazīra.

Quietly, before Buscador noticed him, he turned and walked away.

Dusk fell and campfires were lit. As the shadows deepened Merrivale saw Buscador slip away from the camp, heading up the pine-clad slopes. Merrivale followed him, his boots almost silent on the carpet of pine needles. Fifty yards from the camp he stopped, moving into the darkness under the trees. He listened for a few minutes, hearing nothing at first, but then came the soft sound of footsteps coming back down the slope. Merrivale waited until Buscador was only a few feet away, and stepped out into the open.

'Good evening, my lady,' Merrivale said.

Buscador went rigid with shock. 'Damn you,' a woman's voice said finally, and she pulled back her hood. 'I thought my disguise was good.'

'Your disguise was excellent.' It was; Eleanor of Lancaster was naturally tall and slim, and the ragged brown cloak and shapeless grey cote and hose concealed any traces of femininity. She had cut her hair short and dyed it black, and had used walnut juice to stain her face and hands a deep brown.

'The crossbow, on the other hand, was easy to recognise,' Merrivale said. 'It's a rather elegant weapon, isn't it? How do you explain it to your fellow soldiers?'

'I told them I took it from a dead Moor. Are you going to expose my identity?'

'Not unless you wish me to,' said Merrivale. There was a long silence. He cleared his throat. 'You took a chance, my lady. Despite your disguise, Philippe might have recognised you, or Irunberri.'

'There are four hundred soldiers in this company, plus cooks and servants and grooms. There are plenty of places to hide. What *are* you going to do?'

Merrivale did not answer the question. 'Juan Moreno was murdered,' he said.

Her lips parted. 'Mother of God! What happened?'

He told her in a few words. 'Garcíez has disappeared. I strongly suspect he has gone over to the enemy. Now I am going to La Algaba to rescue Juan's nephew. It is the least I can do.'

'The least you can do,' she repeated softly. 'I did not know him well. But he sang so beautifully, and I admired him for that.'

'Juan was a fine man, and the world is a poorer place without him.'

Something changed in her face. 'Richard. What did he say after I left?'

'Aucassin in his prison cell did not suffer as much as he is suffering now. He asked me to tell you that he has made his choice, and he wants you back. But if you choose not to return, he will understand, he says. If you are safe and happy, that is enough for him.'

'Happy,' she said bitterly. 'When or where will I ever be happy?'

'I told you once before, my lady. We must make our own happiness. You yourself must decide, Nicolette, whether you will sail over the sea to Tora Lora, or whether you will turn back to Beaucaire.'

They gazed at each other for a long time in the faint glow of firelight. Far away in the mountains, a wolf howled at the stars.

'I must get back to the camp,' Eleanor said abruptly.

'I shall have to tell Jac and Warin. They might recognise you, Warin especially.'

'And Philippe?'

'He is a good man, but he entertains strong notions of duty. He would probably feel it incumbent upon him to send you back to al-Jazīra with an escort. I shall keep my counsel.'

'Thank you.' She brushed past him, walking swiftly back towards the camp.

—

Ficaris and Warin took the news calmly. 'At least she's safe, sir,' said Warin.

'Yes. Keep an eye on her, both of you, until we reach Sevilla.'

On the following day, the 19th, the road led out of the hills onto a high rolling plain stretching away to the west. A line of jagged mountains, dark and threatening, barred the horizon to the east. This was dangerous country now, well within reach of Garnāta's raiders, and the column moved quickly with scouts deployed in all directions. Evening brought them to Medina-Sidonia, a white town and castle perched on the crest of a steep hill jutting up from the plain. The governor agreed to give them shelter for the night, and the Navarrese troops crowded into the courtyard of the castle.

Merrivale glanced around for Eleanor and saw her spreading out a blanket in a corner of the courtyard. No one around her seemed to question her identity. Perhaps, he thought, they already knew she was a woman, and did not care. It was unusual but by no means unknown for women to disguise themselves as men and join companies of soldiers, for any of a variety of reasons: running away from a husband or lover, in need of money to pay a debt, wanting to serve their king or simply because they liked fighting. He had seen women among the Welsh archers fighting in Scotland, and in Flanders the city militias welcomed women volunteers without question.

He had promised Arundel and her brother that she would be safe, and she was. But when they reached Sevilla, some hard choices would need to be made.

Philippe and his entourage were given chambers in one of the towers. The rooms were cramped and uncomfortable and the beds hard, but Medina-Sidonia was a fortress, not a palace. Food was brought, grilled meat, bread, figs with honey, and they ate hungrily. A tall lancet window looked down into the narrow lamplit streets of the town. Dogs barked in the gathering dusk. Philippe smiled a little. 'This could be in any mountain town in Navarre,' he said. 'Am I not right, Guilhem-Arnaut?'

Irunberri smiled too, wiping honey from his moustache. 'All of Navarre is mountains,' he said. 'Our cattle have legs shorter on one side than the other, to enable them to stand up on the slopes without falling over.'

The others chuckled. 'Have you ever been to Navarre, Simon?' Philippe asked.

Merrivale, who had just discovered that he had a hole in one of his boots, looked up. 'No, sire. My travels have not yet taken me there.'

'Then you must visit us one day,' said Irunberri. 'We would welcome you.'

'We would indeed,' said Philippe. 'Some people, the ignorant or foolish ones, account Navarre a poor place. True, we have no great wealth, and the language of the people bears no resemblance to any other language you have heard before, but we have pride in ourselves and our kingdom. Navarre is a land of possibilities. We can make of it whatever we wish to make.'

'Navarre is also beautiful,' said Irunberri. 'The mountains and the rivers are glorious, and teem with life. In summer, the fields are like gardens, and you can go hunting in the high forests and never fail to come home with a good bag of venison or boar. In winter the snow shrouds the high peaks in white majesty. I tell you, Simon, I am proud to go abroad in His Grace's service, but my heart sings when I see home again.'

Alameda the physician looked up, smiling. 'You sound like a poet, Guilhem-Arnaut.'

Philippe chuckled. 'That is Navarre,' he said. 'It brings out the poet in all of us. And now to bed, my friends. We march at dawn.'

—

The next day found them crossing an empty plain, passing more abandoned villages with roofless houses collapsing into ruins. 'These were Moorish villages once,' Philippe said. 'Castile occupied this land three generations ago, and at first the Moors were left to live in peace, so long as they paid their tribute. The sultans of Granada urged them to rebel, promising support, but the support never came and the rebels were defeated and driven out. These lands have been abandoned ever since.'

'Why don't the Castilians resettle them?' Merrivale asked.

'They have tried,' said Philippe. 'Successive kings have offered free land and maravedís to anyone who will come and live here, but there are Moorish strongholds in those mountains to the east, and it is too dangerous. This is the *frontera*, Simon, where every man fears to dwell.'

The king gestured at the barren plains around him. 'This could be a rich country,' he said. 'You could grow corn here, grapes, olives, mulberries to feed the silkworms. These villages should be populated, men working in the fields and groves, women going to market, children playing in the streets. Instead, we have this. See what war brings, Simon? Desolation and waste.'

'I know,' Merrivale said quietly. 'I have seen its consequences, in Scotland and in Flanders.'

'Then you know what I am talking about.' Philippe was silent for a moment. 'You are very loyal to my cousin Edward,' he said finally.

'I owe him a great deal, sire.'

'Are there any circumstances under which you would consider leaving his service? With his consent, of course.'

Merrivale wondered where the questions were leading. 'I am not certain, sire. I don't know where else I would go. With whom would I take service?'

'I was thinking of myself,' said Philippe.

Merrivale did not reply. 'My chamberlain in Navarre is my right hand,' the king said. 'He advises me in all things. He is wise and far-sighted, but he is also old. He dreams of retiring to sit by the fire, drinking wine and bouncing his grandchildren on his knee. I have been loath to let him go because I did not know where I would find a replacement. Until now.'

Merrivale was not often startled, but he was now. 'Sire, I know nothing of—'

'You understand people,' Philippe said. 'You see what is in their minds, in their hearts. You believe in justice and in truth, and you follow them with the tenacity of a wolfhound. You are upright and honest. That is what I need. Everything else, you can learn. Come and work with me, Simon. Help me turn Navarre into a garden of peace and plenty. What do you say?'

For a moment Merrivale's heart was so full he could not speak. 'There is Peruzzi,' he said finally.

'Of course. Peruzzi is my enemy too, remember. I will help you to destroy him.'

'First, I must go to La Algaba.'

'What will you do when you get there? Mauro is bound to be guarded.'

'An associate of mine, Fra Moriale, is in Sevilla with his ship, the *Santa Creu*. If we sail upriver, we could arrive at La Algaba at night, overpower the guards and take the place by stealth. I have directed this sort of operation before, and I know what to do. So does Fra Moriale.' Merrivale paused. 'Of course, even if we do find Kāsim and Mauro, that may not be the end of it. It will take time to unravel Peruzzi's schemes.'

'I understand, and I am content to wait.' Philippe smiled. 'Patience is one of my virtues.'

Merrivale drew a deep breath. He thought about fields like gardens, and mountains shrouded in snow. He thought about the opportunity to put the past behind him, to start life anew in the company of men he liked and respected. *Navarre is a land of possibilities. We can make of it whatever we wish to make. It brings out the poet in all of us.*

'When this is over, sire, I will apply to King Edward,' he said. 'And if the king grants me leave, I will serve you most willingly. There is nothing in this world that I would rather do.'

11

21st of September, 1343

Late the following morning they reached inhabited lands once more, villages with olive groves and fruit trees and cattle grazing in the fields, and in the middle of the afternoon they crossed a range of low hills and found a shallow river and the walls and towers of a town on the far side. 'Xerez de la Frontera,' Irunberri said. 'Hopefully the governor will offer us a comfortable bed for the night.'

The threatening mountains were far away now, but the high walls were still well guarded. Square towers protected a massive gatehouse. The captain of the guard recognised the colours of Navarre and bowed deeply. 'I shall send a message to the *alcázar*, Your Grace, and inform the governor. He will wish to arrange a suitable ceremony of welcome.'

Philippe smiled. 'I have no need of ceremonies,' he said. 'I shall announce myself, captain.'

All the same, word had reached the *alcázar* before they arrived, and the governor himself was at the gate, still tying the points on the sleeves of his best coat. There was a great deal of bowing, and the beginnings of a flowery speech of welcome which Philippe politely cut short. 'My entourage and I need rest, *señor*. Would you be so kind as to show us to the guest quarters?'

Dismounting, they led their horses through the gate. The *alcázar* was a little town in its own right; another curtain of walls surrounded a plaza flanked with flat-roofed houses built of brick and stone. An ancient church stood in one corner, with a cluster of buildings behind it. Smoke drifted from the chimneys of a bathhouse. Red roses bloomed in gardens part shaded by orange trees, their fruit glowing like jewels amid the dark green leaves.

The guesthouse was in one corner of the enclosure, facing another garden with a long ornamental pool. A fountain bubbled in its centre. Philippe, looking weary, retired to his own chamber. Alameda followed him. Irunberri was outside, arranging billets for his men. Merrivale looked for Eleanor but could not see her. It had to be admitted, he thought, that she did blend in well… He considered again what to do when they reached Sevilla, and pushed the matter out of his mind. *We'll deal with the future when it comes*, he thought.

The hole in his boot was growing larger. 'Make yourselves comfortable,' he said to Ficaris and Warin. 'I am going to find a cobbler.'

'I can take your boots to be repaired, sir,' Warin said.

'I'm stiff as a board from riding. I need to stretch my legs.'

The cobbled streets of Xerez were narrow and quiet. Tall houses faced the streets, with gates giving onto courtyards. There were few people about; most were probably still indoors, resting in the heat. He saw a couple of merchants in sober black, an old man leading a mule, a woman in white with her face veiled to the eyes accompanied by a maidservant and two broad-shouldered guards with hands resting on the hilts of their knives. He passed a blacksmith's forge, an empty marketplace, a baker's oven silent in the heat.

Someone was watching him.

He spun around. Pero de Garcíez was standing twenty yards away. He was unarmoured, but he still wore the white surcoat and cross of Calatrava. A sword and dagger were belted at his waist.

'I could kill you now,' Garcíez said.

Merrivale hefted his staff. 'I wouldn't advise you to try. Why did you kill Juan Moreno?'

The other man's eyes flickered. 'I killed no one.'

'I don't believe you,' Merrivale said after a moment.

'It is true. As God is my witness, I did not kill Moreno.'

'If not, you know who did.' Slowly, with measured steps, Merrivale began to walk towards Garcíez. 'Come with me to the *alcázar*, and make a full confession in front of the king of Navarre. If you really are innocent, as you claim, you will have nothing to fear.'

'No one is innocent,' Garcíez said. 'All of us should be afraid. Especially you, Merrivale.'

'What are you doing here?' Merrivale demanded.

'My business is my own. Remember what I said. You should be afraid.'

Garcíez turned and walked away. 'Stop!' Merrivale commanded, but the other man paid no heed. Merrivale began to run. Garcíez glanced over his shoulder and dodged into an alley. Cursing, Merrivale followed him, but the alley twisted and turned and within moments he had lost sight of his quarry. By the time he reached the far end of the alley even the sound of Garcíez's running footsteps had disappeared.

The lanes of the old town were like a maze. Sometimes they broadened out into little plazas, at other times they shrank into narrow *carrils* barely wider than his shoulders; sometimes, too, they ended in blank walls, forcing him to retrace his steps. The hot air reeked of charcoal, lemons, rotten vegetables, urine, spices. Gradually he noticed that the houses had become smaller, and some had six-pointed stars engraved in the stone over their gates. There was no sign of Garcíez.

A gate opened and a bearded man in black robes with a skullcap perched on the back of his head stepped into the street, carrying a book in one hand. When he saw Merrivale, he stopped and bowed. '*Buen día, señor*. Are you lost?'

'I fear so,' Merrivale said. 'Can you tell me where I am?'

'This is the *judería, señor*. The Jewish quarter.'

'I am searching for a man, about forty years old, black-bearded with deep-set eyes. He wears a sword. Did he come past here?'

'I do not know, *señor*.' The other man held up the book. 'I have been absorbed in reading. I did not see who passed in the street.' He glanced at Merrivale's feet. 'You have a hole in your boot.'

'Yes,' Merrivale said. 'I came from the *alcázar* looking for a cobbler.'

'I will take you to one. If you will permit me to introduce myself, my name is Asach de Sharīsh. A Castilian would call me Isaac of Xerez. I am a scholar and a *qadi*, a magistrate.'

'I am Simon Merrivale.'

The cobbler's workshop was in another courtyard not far away. The cobbler bowed to Asach, whom he clearly reverenced, and took Merrivale's boot away to be repaired. The older man sat down on a bench in the shade, and gestured to Merrivale to sit beside him. 'Who is this man you seek?' he asked.

'A Knight of Calatrava named Pero de Garcíez. I believe that he killed a friend of mine.'

'And you seek revenge, Señor Merrivale?'

'No. I seek justice.'

'Justice? Ah. A very different and altogether more complex thing. Revenge is a property of the spirit, but justice is a property of intellect, and that brings it nearer to God. And once we perceive the hand of God, of course, we are in a very different realm.'

'I beg your pardon?' Merrivale said after a moment.

Asach held up the book. Its wooden front board was incised with flowing Arabic script. 'The *Ghāyat al-Hakīm*,' he said. '*The Goal of the Sage*. According to its tenets, the first of all things in the world is God, the creator and shaper of all. After God comes consciousness, or intellect, because without intellect there can be no understanding of God. After the intellect comes the spirit.

And finally, after the spirit comes matter, the base material from which all of the world is made.'

'What do you mean, *señor*?'

'The spirit is simple. It does not think, it merely acts. The intellect thinks and acts, and it does so with reference to God. We appeal to God to show us what justice is, but God does not always answer. We are left to struggle on our own, to understand His design and chart a course of action for ourselves. It is rarely easy.'

'You are saying that I would be better off seeking revenge?'

Unexpectedly, the other man's eyes twinkled. 'It would be easier, yes.'

'I am sure that you are right,' Merrivale said. 'Unfortunately, I seldom choose the easy path.'

Asach stroked his beard. 'Perhaps that is what God has ordained for you. I have influence in the *judería*, and in other parts of the city too. I will make inquiries about this Garcíez. When do you depart?'

'In the morning, I hope. We travel to Sevilla, and thence to Córdoba.'

'Come and see me before you go. I will tell you what I have learned.'

The repaired boot was returned; the cobbler refused to take payment. Merrivale pressed a silver real into his hand anyway, and the cobbler called to his son to guide Merrivale back to the *alcázar*. Ficaris was waiting, his face serious. 'Philippe is ill again. Lorenço says that his influenza has returned. He has advised the king to remain here tomorrow and rest.'

Merrivale shook his head. 'I don't like this, Jac. Garcíez is here.' He told Ficaris what had happened. 'I would like to get Philippe as far away as possible.'

'Perhaps he will be feeling better in the morning,' Ficaris said hopefully.

'Perhaps. I'll tell Irunberri, too. We must ensure that the king is guarded at all times.'

'Should we search for Garcíez?'

Merrivale looked up at the sun. 'It will be evening soon, and the streets are like Porsena's labyrinth. You could wander in there for years, and not come out. We'll wait until morning and see what Asach has to say.'

A trumpet called them to dinner in the governor's hall. The governor was put out to learn that his guest of honour was ill. 'This is most disappointing. I had hoped to have the honour of conversing with His Grace.' He pulled up his chair at the head of the table and sat down. 'No point in waiting. Be seated, *señores*, and my servants will bring us food.'

Dinner passed largely in silence. Afterwards Merrivale called at Philippe's chamber and was met by Alameda, wearing his red robe and carrying a wooden chest full of medicines. 'He is resting comfortably,' the physician said, 'but certainly he will be unfit to travel tomorrow. In the morning I shall prescribe a visit to the bathhouse. Perhaps we can sweat the illness out of him.'

'May I see him?'

Alameda frowned. 'Only if you must. He is resting now, but any excitement could worsen his fever.'

Merrivale shook his head. 'I will return in the morning.'

Restless, he wandered through the gardens where the scent of roses hung heavy in the evening mist. The little church glowed faintly from within; someone had lit candles, perhaps as a prayer for the king's health. Two of Irunberri's men were patrolling the garden, and they saluted him. '*Gau on, jauna*,' one said politely. 'Good night, sir.'

'Good night.'

He walked into the quiet church. White plastered octagonal walls were topped with a high brick dome. Candles burned steadily, clear flames tapering to a point, and the air smelled of wax and incense. Merrivale bowed to the statue of the Virgin above the altar and folded his arms, gazing up at her.

'Was Asach right?' he asked aloud. 'Does the intellect bring us nearer to God? Or would life indeed be easier if we had no intellect, no comprehension of God?'

The Virgin looked back at him, unmoving. Merrivale waited for inspiration, for some inkling of what was about to happen, something that would ease his dark forebodings. Nothing came. We are indeed sometimes left to struggle on our own, he thought.

22nd of September, 1343

In the morning he went to the king's chamber again. 'He woke with a fever in the night,' Alameda said. 'I gave him a sleeping draught and he is resting now. In a little while, I shall wake him and take him to the bathhouse.'

Church bells rang as the morning mists burned away and golden shafts of sun reached down into the narrow streets. Outside the *alcázar* the town was busy this morning, men on their way to work, servants going to market, old women going to the churches to light candles. The tavernas were busy, too. Merrivale nodded towards one of these, on the far side of the square in front of the cathedral. 'Jac, you and Warin ask about Garcíez. I'll talk to the magistrate, and we'll meet back here at terce.'

Merrivale retraced his steps to the *judería*. He found Asach the *qadi* seated on a stone bench in a quiet courtyard filled with flowering plants and trees in earthenware pots. Another fountain gurgled quietly in the background.

Merrivale bowed as Asach rose to his feet. 'A Knight of Calatrava matching your description was seen coming out of the cathedral yesterday evening,' Asach said. 'My informant noticed him because members of the Order are rarely seen in Xerez. They do not have a convent or property here.'

'Did your informant see where he went?'

'I fear not. I am sorry not to be of more help to you.'

'Please, do not apologise. I am grateful for your help.'

Asach was silent for a moment. 'I observe that you do not carry a weapon,' he said. 'But I have seen the callouses on your hands, and I think that you were once a man of the sword. May I ask why you gave up that life?'

The simple answer was that heralds did not carry weapons, but that was not what Asach was asking. 'I abandoned my sword in hopes of finding peace,' Merrivale said. 'Not in the world around me, that is too much to hope for, but within myself.'

Asach smiled a little. '"Peace that comes from fear is the opposite of peace. True peace comes from the heart."'

Merrivale nodded. 'Those are the words of Levi ben Gershon, I think.'

The magistrate was surprised. 'You have read the great rabbi's works?'

'No, but I had the honour to meet him. He is a wise man.'

'One of the wisest,' Asach agreed. 'If you are going to Córdoba Alyana, perhaps you will meet him again. I had word from him last week. He is in Córdoba now, staying at the house of his nephew.'

'Thank you,' Merrivale said slowly, thinking of La Algaba. 'If my duties permit, I shall call on him.'

'Hear again the words of the *Ghāyat al-Hakīm*. The wise know that enlightenment comes in unexpected places. "When I wished to find knowledge of the secrets of Creation, I came upon a dark vault within the depths of the earth, filled with blowing winds. There appeared to me in my sleep a shape of most wondrous beauty. I said to him, "Who are you?" And he answered, "I am your perfected nature."'

Merrivale smiled a little. 'I take this to mean that perfection comes only in dreams. Not in the real world.'

'Who knows what is real, and what is dreaming? The great alchemist Ibn al-Rāzī of Garnāta argues that the world we see around us is a simulacrum, a poor representation of the real world that exists in dreams.'

'I hope he is right,' Merrivale said. 'If he isn't, we are all in a great deal of trouble.'

Asach smiled in response. 'If I hear further word of Garcíez, I will send a message to you in Córdoba. May God, the king of the universe and the just judge, watch over you, Simon Merrivale. He knows your destiny, even if you do not.'

In the square before the cathedral, the market was underway. The cries of hawkers touting their wares blended with barking dogs, squawking chickens, banging drums, the braying of a mule. Merrivale pushed his way through the crowd towards the taverna, frowning. Why did Garcíez come here? He had been certain that Garcíez had gone over to the enemy, but now here he was in Christian lands once more. It did not make sense.

He waved away a peddler selling holy relics and magical amulets from the same tray and walked on towards the taverna. The mule brayed again, startlingly loud. Merrivale turned to find the animal only a few feet away, a white-bearded man leading it by a halter. He realised it was the same man he had seen yesterday afternoon; and suddenly, Merrivale recognised him. It was also the man he had seen in the camp at al-Jazīra, arguing with the mule seller, and later outside Don Juan Manuel's pavilion.

'Put no faith in physicians,' the man said in Castilian.

Merrivale caught him by the arm before he could turn away. 'Who are you?'

'Put no faith in physicians,' the man repeated. 'That is all I have to say to you, Señor Merrivale.' With surprising strength, he pulled his arm free and led the mule away through the crowds.

Ficaris and Warin were standing outside the taverna. 'No sign of him,' Ficaris said. 'Did the magistrate have anything to say?'

'Garcíez is still here. We need to get back into the *alcázar*. Something is wrong.'

They hurried to the *alcázar* and crossed the garden to the guesthouse. One of Philippe's servants met them. 'His Grace is not here, *jauna*. Maisua Alameda took him to the bathhouse.'

The bathhouse was quiet and calm. An attendant appeared, bowing gravely, but Merrivale brushed past him, walking through the warm room and into the hot room beyond. Sunlight coming through the star-shaped apertures in the roof reflected off brilliant tiles on the floor and walls, patterned intricately in azure blue and rich green, black and white. Steam hissed gently from apertures in the floor.

The same sunlight showed him King Philippe of Navarre, sitting on a stone bench clad only in a light robe, leaning back against the tiled wall. A silver cup of wine sat on the bench beside him. His eyes were closed, but his mouth was open and his lips had a bluish tinge. A thin trickle of vomit, still wet, ran down his chin and dripped onto his robe. Merrivale touched his neck and felt the skin cold and clammy with steam. There was no pulse.

12

22nd of September, 1343

Ficaris came into the hot room and stopped in his tracks. 'Mother of God,' he said, staring. 'Is he dead?'

'Yes.' Merrivale picked up the cup and sniffed it. The bitter almond smell of laurel water rose at once to his nostrils. 'Where is Alameda?'

'I assumed he would be here with the king.'

'Come with me,' Merrivale said.

Back at the guesthouse Merrivale hurried into the physician's chamber, next to the king's. Alameda was not there. The wooden medicine chest stood open next to the bed. Merrivale knelt beside it and began pulling out pots and jars. All were labelled neatly in Latin, except for one small stone crock with a string around its neck, attached to a paper tag with faded Arabic script. Merrivale pulled out the stopper. This time the smell of laurel water was so strong that he jerked his head back, quickly replacing the stopper.

Ficaris was staring again. 'I don't believe it! *Lorenço* killed the king? *Why?*'

'Fetch Irunberri, Jac. As quickly as you can.'

Rage glowed like a hot ember. He rose to his feet and walked into the king's chamber, where he summoned the servants. 'His Grace is dead,' he said, as calmly as he could. 'You will find his body in the bathhouse. Attend to him with all due reverence.'

The servants gaped in shock. One man broke down in tears. Unable to watch as their pain and loss mirrored his own,

Merrivale walked outside. Irunberri hurried across the garden, Ficaris and two men-at-arms behind him. The captain's eyes were wide with horror. 'Dear God, what happened?'

Merrivale told him. 'We must find Alameda, quickly. I'll ask the governor for permission to search the town.'

'My king is dead,' Irunberri snapped. 'I need no permission to search for his murderers.' He turned to the men-at-arms. 'Sifredo, Peiro, rouse the others. We shall turn the town upside down if we must, but we will find that bastard Alameda.'

Angry and grief-stricken, the Navarrese poured out of the *alcázar* into the town. Irunberri led them, dividing the men into search parties as they went. Warin ran up to join Merrivale and Ficaris, his own face full of shock. 'What shall we do, sir?'

'Come with me. We're going to the *judería*.'

'Why there?' asked Ficaris.

'Because Alameda will reckon that the last place we will look for a Christian fugitive is the Jewish quarter. And because if he is hiding there, we need to drag him out before anyone accuses the Jews of colluding with a regicide. We don't want a massacre on top of everything else.'

Irunberri, a humane man, would not dream of blaming the Jews. What the governor of Xerez might do, facing the humiliation of the death of his royal guest, was beyond knowing.

Asach de Sharīsh was sitting on the same bench in the courtyard of his house, a book in his hands. He rose quickly when Merrivale entered, his face full of surprise. 'Señor Merrivale. I assumed you were on your way to Córdoba.'

Merrivale told him what had happened. 'We need your help, *señor*. We need to find this man before anyone else does.'

Asach's eyes closed for a moment. 'The death of a king,' he said softly. 'A wise and good king. Many people's hopes will have ended with him.'

Including mine, Merrivale thought. He watched Asach fold his hands and softly intone a prayer.

Man is like a breath; his days are like a passing shadow.

In the morning it blossoms and is reborn,
In the evening it is nought but a passing shade.
Thus the dust returns to the ground as it was,
And the spirit returns to God who gave it.

Asach opened his eyes again. 'Come. We shall find the man you seek.'

They walked through the streets of the *judería*, Merrivale and Ficaris angry and heartsick, Warin still blank-faced with shock. Asach stopped everyone who passed, speaking in a language that was part Castilian Spanish and part Hebrew, asking if they had seen anyone who matched Alameda's description. At first the answer was negative, but a porter carrying a basket of melons pointed down a side street. 'I saw him, the man in the red robe. He was walking slowly, like he was in no hurry, but he kept looking over his shoulder.'

'Wait here, *señor*,' Merrivale said to Asach.

They hurried down the street. A woman in a first-floor window, hanging laundry on a line, called down to them in Castilian. 'Are you lost, *señores*?'

'We're looking for someone,' Merrivale said. 'A man in a physician's robe.'

She pointed along the street. 'Down there you will find a *carril* running to the right. He went there a little while ago. I don't know why, there is no one sick down there.'

'I'll follow him,' Ficaris said. 'You and Warin go ahead and see if you can cut him off.'

Ficaris disappeared into the *carril*. Merrivale and Warin hurried along the street, but they had not gone more than twenty paces before Ficaris shouted, his voice echoing off stone walls.

'Simon! Come quickly!'

The *carril* ended in a high wall, but a staircase ran up to the rooftops beyond. Lorenço de Alameda lay at the foot of the stair. He seemed smaller than in real life, as if death had somehow diminished him. Dark blood stained his red robe and pooled on the stones around his chest. There were more bloodstains on the skirts of the robe, where the killer had wiped the blade of his weapon clean.

Ficaris knelt beside the body. 'Stabbed in the chest,' he said. His voice was suddenly hoarse. 'He's not been gone for more than a few minutes.'

Gripping his staff, Merrivale hurried up the stairs to the top of the wall. There was nothing to see but empty flat roofs stretching away towards the ramparts. Tracking anyone across those stone roofs would be impossible. Merrivale called down to Warin.

'Fetch Irunberri and tell him to bring some of his men, quickly. Jac, guard the body.'

Irunberri arrived a quarter of an hour later, mopping his brow in the heat. Several of his men-at-arms followed him. Merrivale, who had been watching the rooftops on the remote chance that the killer might reappear, came back down the stairs. 'We need to get the body out of here as soon as possible, Guilhem-Arnaut.'

Irunberri's face was grim. 'Any idea who killed him?'

'No, but I'm willing to bet it was someone he knew. This was a pre-arranged rendezvous.'

'If the killer came into the *judería*, someone will have seen him,' Irunberri said, his voice bitter with anger. 'We need to start knocking on doors.'

'No. The fewer people who know about this, the better. Leave this to me.'

Asach was still waiting where Merrivale had left him. Another man waited with him; the cobbler who had mended Merrivale's boots. 'We have news,' said Asach. 'Not good news, I fear.'

The cobbler bowed. 'I have seen the man you seek, the Knight of Calatrava, here in the *judería* not more than an hour ago. A bearded man with eyes that looked like they had been punched into his head.'

Merrivale shook his head in anger. They would never know, now, what had led Alameda to betray the master who trusted him. The physician had already been given his instructions, first to incapacitate Philippe and then, when he was ill and isolated, to kill him and make his escape. He had probably been told to meet Garcíez here so that the two of them could escape over the rooftops. Instead, Garcíez had stabbed him and left him to die.

Another man hurried up, bowing to Asach and speaking quickly. Asach turned to Merrivale, his face grave. 'Garcíez rode out of the Puerto Real a few minutes ago. He took the road towards Arcos de la Frontera.'

'I am going after him,' Merrivale said.

Back at the *alcázar*, Merrivale had a short dispute with Irunberri. 'You cannot follow Garcíez alone, Simon,' the captain said. 'I have four hundred men at my back, and every one of them loved their king. They want justice for him.'

'I'm not going alone,' Merrivale said. 'I am taking Jac and Warin.'

Irunberri shook his head. 'You could be walking into an ambush.'

'I could. But equally, so could you and your entire company. You are needed back in Navarre, Guilhem-Arnaut. Take your king's body home and bury him with honour, and help his heir to rule the country. That is your duty now.'

'His heir is eleven years old, and is being educated in Normandy.'

'All the more reason for you to return, my friend. Someone must govern the kingdom.' Merrivale paused. 'Swear your men to secrecy about what happened here. Let it be known that Philippe died after his wound had become infected. The rest of the world is not ready for the truth.'

Irunberri nodded. 'Take some men with you, at least. You will need more protection than a secretary and a groom can give you.'

'I will take two men,' Merrivale said. 'If this is an ambush, a larger party will be easily spotted. A small group should be able to slip through.' He remembered Derby's words back at al-Jazīra. 'This is my world, Guilhem-Arnaut. I know what I am doing. Leave this to me.'

—

It was still only late morning and Arcos de la Frontera was less than twenty miles away. Irunberri introduced two of his men-at-arms, Peiro d'Iguna, a young man who looked like he knew exactly how handsome he was, and Sifredo de Berriz, quieter and a little older, who carried a carved wooden crucifix that he often touched, as if offering a prayer. Merrivale was reminded of Moreno's rock salt crucifix that he himself still carried inside his coat.

'I will remain here for a few days,' Irunberri said to Merrivale. 'It will take some time to prepare His Grace's body.' The captain swallowed suddenly, choking back emotion. 'If you do not return by Thursday, and I have received no message from you, I will come searching for you.'

'Hopefully it will not take that long,' Merrivale said.

Horses were brought into the courtyard. Waterskins and bags of food were strapped to the saddles. Merrivale, Ficaris, Warin, Peiro and Sifredo all mounted. Irunberri rested a hand on the pommel of Merrivale's saddle. '*Jainkoa zurekin egon dadila*,' he said quietly. 'May God be with you. I know how much you have lost today.'

'We have all lost,' Merrivale said.

'Come to Navarre when all is done. We will always have a home for you.'

'Thank you.' Merrivale turned his horse. He would never go to Navarre, not now; the experience would be too bitter. But he did not want Irunberri, who was a good man, to see this in his face.

They rode out of Xerez and turned east towards Arcos de la Frontera. Fields and groves bounded by stone walls gradually gave way to dry pastures where herds of cattle and goats grazed. Kites and buzzards circled in the air overhead. They rode in silence at first, Merrivale shading his eyes and scanning the horizon. Fresh hoofprints in the dusty road showed that their quarry was still ahead of them.

A sudden tap of hoofbeats, coming up fast from behind. Merrivale turned to see a lone horseman riding hard, trailing clouds of dust. 'Who is it?' asked Ficaris.

'I think it's that crossbowman,' Peiro said. 'The one that joined us a while back. Buscador, that's his name.'

Ficaris and Warin both looked at Merrivale. 'Wait here,' the latter said grimly, and he turned his horse and rode back to meet the oncoming rider. Eleanor of Lancaster pulled her own horse to a halt and waited for him.

'What do you think you are doing, my lady?' Merrivale demanded.

Expressive eyes looked out of a brown-stained face with a fringe of untidy black hair. 'Philippe was my cousin. I have every right to be here.'

'You have no right whatever to be here. Go back and wait with Irunberri.'

'You do not give me orders,' she snapped.

'Yes,' Merrivale said. 'I do.'

'As God is my witness, Simon, if you don't let me join you, I will follow you anyway. And don't you think I'd be safer travelling with you, rather than on my own? That's what Henry would say, if he was here,' she added.

'He isn't here. Why, my lady?'

Her horse stirred a little, and she gentled it. 'Because I can ride and I can shoot,' she said. 'And because you are not the only one who believes in justice.'

'Body of Christ,' Merrivale said explosively. He turned his horse and rode back to the others. Ficaris and Warin watched him, apprehension in their faces. Merrivale turned to the two Navarrese. 'Peiro, Sifredo, allow me to present a runaway princess, the lady Eleanor of Lancaster. She will explain herself why she is here, because frankly, I don't have the words.' He looked up at the sun. 'Ride on. We must reach Arcos before nightfall.'

They reached Arcos de la Frontera in the light of an enormous orange sun sliding down through streaky bars of haze towards the horizon. Sawtooth mountains, blue with dusk, walled off the eastern horizon.

The castle was perched on the edge of a high cliff, overlooking a river far below. One end of the courtyard had been walled off to create a pen, into which were crammed several hundred frightened-looking men, women and children. The captain of the garrison had a bandaged hand and a fresh sword cut running down his cheek and lips to his chin, but he greeted Merrivale and his companions cheerfully.

'Brought them in fresh this morning from a raid around Ubrique,' he said, indicating the captives. 'We had some trouble with the Warriors of the Faithful, but Christ was watching over us and he saw us through. The Warriors hate us, you see. We don't pay them off, like some do.'

Merrivale paused. Juan Moreno had mentioned corrupt officials were colluding in the slave trade, sharing the profits of slavery with their erstwhile enemies; was this what the captain meant? 'What are you doing with these people?' he demanded.

'Selling them, of course. Tomorrow morning. The men will go to the fields and mines, the women will be domestic servants. Except for the pretty ones.' The captain grinned, revealing bloody gums and two missing teeth in line with the sword cut. 'You can guess what happens to the pretty ones.'

The ride from Xerez through the afternoon heat had done nothing to abate Merrivale's anger. Once again he fought it down. 'Did a Knight of Calatrava come to Arcos this afternoon?' he demanded. 'A man named Pero de Garcíez?'

'A Knight passed through, but he didn't stop. He rode on east. I didn't ask his name.'

Some of the captives were calling out, stretching their hands up towards their captors and pleading for mercy, *Saīdi, saīdi! Airhamni ya, saīdi!*

'What lies east of here?' Merrivale asked.

'Not much, *señor*. This is the *frontera*. There's Prado del Rey, or what remains of it. The Knights had a castle nearby, but they no longer keep a garrison there. After that, it's the mountains and the Moors.'

The sword cut had opened and was weeping blood down the captain's face. Merrivale hoped he would bleed to death. 'How far to Prado del Rey?'

'About fifteen miles. You're not thinking of going there, are you? The Warriors of the Faithful are all over that country. They come down through the mountains from Zahara and ride out to raid our villages.'

'Do you not stop them?' Ficaris asked sharply.

'We try, if we're not too busy raiding the other way. Like I said, this is the *frontera*. We enslave their people, they enslave ours.'

'And both sides grow rich,' Merrivale said.

The captain's bloody face hardened. 'That's how it is. No one asked you to come here, *señor*.'

They left the castle as soon as possible, and found a guest room over a taverna with a window that looked out from the clifftop over a vast gulf of air towards the mountains. Dusk was falling, and it would be impossible to track Garcíez by night. 'Not to mention the chances of running into the Warriors of the Faithful,' said Ficaris. He paused for a moment. 'May I ask a question, Simon? Why are we here? What about La Algaba, and Mauro? Shouldn't we be going up the river to find him?'

'We will,' Merrivale said. 'But there is a score to settle with Garcíez first.'

'What makes you think he is going to Prado del Rey? Juan's sister and her family lived there, but that was a long time ago.'

'You heard the captain. The Knights of Calatrava have a castle nearby. Garcíez may be going there.'

Ficaris shook his head. Merrivale turned on him in sudden anger. 'Go back to Xerez if you don't like it, Jac.'

'I was only asking a question,' Ficaris protested.

'I know what you were doing. Go back, anyway, all of you. This is too dangerous. You in particular, my lady.'

Eleanor lifted her crossbow. 'I told you, Philippe was my cousin. And Juan Moreno sang for me. I am not going anywhere.'

'If the princess stays, I stay,' said Warin.

Ficaris sighed. 'So do I... My lady, what do we tell the Earl of Arundel if you don't come back?'

'Tell him whatever you like, Master Ficaris. It will hardly matter to me, will it?'

Ficaris smiled suddenly. 'Please,' he said. 'Call me Jac.'

—

The loss of Moreno had been painful; Merrivale had respected him for his piety and integrity, for his willingness to sacrifice everything to save his family. The death of Philippe of Navarre was something else. The difference in rank between them had never mattered; Philippe himself had made that clear from the start. A bond had developed between them. It was not the loss of his future prospects that tore at Merrivale's heart; it was the death of a friend.

At sunrise they ate a little of the food they had brought with them, pepper sausage and olives and roasted almonds. 'You do realise that we are doing exactly what Garcíez wants us to do,' Ficaris said.

'Yes,' said Merrivale. 'But we need to find him.'

The road to Prado del Rey was little more than a track through rolling low hills dotted with olive trees and fields full of dry stubble. The hoofprints of a single horse were plain to see in the dust. Merrivale scanned the ground as they rode, following the trail; the others watched the horizon, Ficaris and Warin shading their eyes, Eleanor with the crossbow resting on the pommel of her saddle, Sifredo holding his little wooden crucifix, Peiro whistling a tune, the same little fragment over and over. Finally, Ficaris reached over and tapped him on the arm.

'Is that the only tune you know, *anaia*?'

'It's the only one I can whistle,' Peiro said.

Merrivale held up a hand. 'Quiet, both of you.' Something was moving far ahead of them, a tremor in the ground, felt rather than heard. After a moment it died away, and silence fell. They rode on through an empty land, seeing fields full of scrub and weeds, a few buildings roofless and deserted, stone walls of cattle pens reduced to tumbled heaps. The jagged blue mountains drew nearer.

Around mid-morning they came to an abandoned farm. A well stood in the shade of an oak tree, its bucket and crank surprisingly intact. Sifredo dismounted, drew up a bucket of water and sniffed it. 'Clear,' he said. 'Some of these wells go brackish over time, but this is safe to drink.'

The others dismounted too, watering the horses and eating olives and raisins from their provision bags. A red kite perched on the wall of the roofless farmhouse, regarding them with a malevolent yellow eye.

Out in the haunted distance there was movement again, a low murmur of sound. Merrivale pulled his eating knife from its sheath and drove it hard into the trunk of the oak tree. Resting his hand on its hilt, he felt the faint vibrations. 'Horsemen,' he said quietly. 'Hard to know how many.'

Sifredo knelt and put his ear to the ground. 'Moving north,' he said, pointing towards the mountains.

They waited. Slowly, the murmur died away. The air crackled with heat and tension. Merrivale withdrew his knife and the six of them mounted their horses. 'At the first sign of trouble,' Merrivale said to the others, 'turn around and ride like the wind towards Arcos. Don't stop until you get there.'

Silently, they rode on towards the mountains.

13

23rd of September, 1343

Once in the past, Merrivale thought, Prado del Rey would have been a place of peace and beauty. Nestled into a green valley at the foot of the mountains, it would have had a church and a marketplace and some fine houses, the latter probably owned by the masters of the *salina* at the mouth of the valley. Cattle and goats would have grazed in the pastures, and the surrounding hills would have been covered by olive and fig and almond trees. The castle on the hill to the north would have been a friendly, protecting presence.

Now, all was gone. The houses were ruins, their interiors full of charred wood, weeds and dust. The church was a roofless shell, and the market cross had been pulled down and lay broken on the ground. The fruit trees had been cut down too, their grey withered trunks scattered across the hillsides, and at the *salina* the salt pans had been broken and the well filled with stones.

'Body of Christ,' Peiro whispered. 'Why did they destroy everything?'

'To ensure that no one could ever come back and settle here,' Ficaris said. 'The equivalent of ploughing the earth with salt.'

Only the castle was still intact but it was empty and, by the looks of it, had been for some time. There were no hoofprints in the dusty courtyard. Garcíez had not come here.

Behind the church was a long low heap of stones. Merrivale did not need the wooden cross standing at one end to tell him that this was a burial pit, but that was not what caught his attention. A horse, saddled and bridled, was tethered just outside the vestry entrance. Gripping his staff, he walked forward. 'Who is there?' he called in Castilian. 'Come out and show yourself.'

After a moment a man walked out of the vestry. He was a small man with a weather-beaten face and bristling grey hair. His friar's robe was grey too, emblazoned with an unusual eight-pointed cross; the vertical arm of the cross was red, while the horizontal arm was blue. He stared for a moment at Merrivale's tabard and staff. 'Who are you, stranger?'

The others, hearing voices, hurried to join them. Sifredo and Peiro had drawn their swords, but at the sight of the friar they sheathed their weapons. 'I am Simon Merrivale, herald to the Earl of Derby,' Merrivale said.

The friar bowed. 'I am Brother Sebastián of the Order of Santísima Trinidad,' he said. 'You are a long way from England, señor.'

'We are searching for a Knight of Calatrava who rode this way from Arcos. Have you seen anyone?'

'No, señor, but I did not come by the Arcos road. I travelled south from Sevilla.'

Warin scratched his head. 'Garcíez must know he is a fugitive. Do you suppose he really has gone over to the enemy this time?'

Brother Sebastián looked at them in astonishment. 'Garcíez? You are seeking Pero de Garcíez?'

'Do you know him?' asked Ficaris.

'No, but I know his name, all too well.' The friar waved his hand around the desolate village. 'He is responsible for this.'

'What do you mean, brother?'

The friar pointed at the castle. 'Garcíez was the garrison commander here for many years. When the Warriors of the Faithful attacked the town, he made no move to stop them. He and his men remained behind their walls while the enemy slaughtered our people, destroyed the town and took away many captives. Garcíez did nothing to save them.'

'Why not?' asked Merrivale.

'Because Garcíez was in league with the Warriors of the Faithful,' the friar said. 'He allowed the Moors to take our own people as captives and sell them, in exchange for a share of the profits. Many of the Knights do the same. Even the grand master profits from the sale of Christian slaves. And, of course, it goes the other way. When the Knights sell Moorish slaves, they send part of the profits to the Warriors.'

Merrivale remembered the words of the captain at Arcos. *They hate us because we don't pay them off, like some do.*

'Mother of God!' Sifredo said, his face shocked. 'Why have you not put a stop to this?'

'What can we do? Our own Order is small and poor, and the Knights of Calatrava are rich and powerful. They are untouchable.' Brother Sebastián looked at the heap of stones. 'Our Order's mission is to ransom back Christians who have been enslaved. We tried to rescue the captives from Prado del Rey, and we sent an emissary to the Warriors of the Faithful in Runda and offered to pay their ransoms, but they refused to deal with us. All we could do was bury the dead. One of our people comes down from Sevilla every month, to check that graves like this one have not been defiled.'

'Are there many graves like this?' asked Peiro.

A black arrow whistled through the air and hit Brother Sebastián in the chest. Before anyone could move, he fell to his knees and collapsed onto his side, blood pouring from his mouth. One hand clutched at the dust before relaxing into death.

Men came running around the church, men in black with mail tunics and spired helmets with chainmail lappets. Some carried bows with arrows on the nock; others had spears and long straight swords. In a moment, Merrivale's party were surrounded, cut off from their horses. Sifredo and Peiro reached for their weapons. 'No!' Merrivale snapped.

They were outnumbered by five or six to one; resistance was futile. Reluctantly, the Navarrese let their hands fall from their hilts. Sick with self-directed anger, Merrivale leaned on his staff and waited.

One of the men stepped forward. Taller than the others with a hard planed face, he wore a breastplate inlaid with yellow metal in simple geometric patterns, square and circles. Three of the fingers of his left hand were missing. '*Iqjan ikafriyen!*' he commanded. '*Ssers imrigen-ik!*'

'He is telling us to lay down our weapons,' Ficaris said quietly.

'Obey him,' Merrivale said.

The others laid their weapons on the ground and stepped away. The man with the breastplate pointed at Merrivale's staff. 'Tell him it is my badge of office,' Merrivale said.

Ficaris repeated this in Tamazight. 'He says he doesn't care. Hand over your staff, or he will kill you.'

Merrivale dropped his staff. 'Tell him we come in peace,' he said. 'We are part of the English embassy, and have no part in this war. We are on our way to Córdoba.'

Ficaris started to speak, and the man stepped forward and hit him a back-handed blow across the face. Blood flowed from a split lip; Ficaris reached up to wipe it away, and the man hit him again. '*Awi-d ikjan-a!*' he shouted, and the black-clad men swarmed around them, seizing their arms and tying their hands. Roughly, they were dragged away from the church, leaving the small, forlorn body of Brother Sebastián on the ground, and hoisted into the saddles of their horses. Their feet were bound to their stirrups, making escape impossible. Still feeling sick, Merrivale glanced at Eleanor. She sat upright, stiff-backed, not looking around. *God help her if they find out she is a woman*, he thought. *God help us all.*

Around them, the black-clad warriors were mounting their own horses. '*Anda ara ten-nawi a, Aksal?*'

'*Zahara*,' said the man in the breastplate.

There was still one chance. Irunberri had promised that if he did not receive a message by the end of tomorrow, he would come looking for them; and Irunberri was a man of his word, with four hundred armed men at his back. The Imazighen who surrounded them numbered forty riders at most. Gripping the pommel of his saddle with his bound hands, Merrivale forced himself to be calm, and to think.

The secret that Garcíez and the Knights of Calatrava were trying to protect was clear now. The corrupt officials that Moreno had mentioned were Knights, and if it could be proven that a crusading military order, sworn to the defence of Christendom, was conniving at the selling of Christians into slavery, the entire future of their Order would be in jeopardy; not even the pope could save them, or would even be willing to try. Garcíez, and his masters, must have realised that if Moreno was reunited with his nephew, or any of the other captives from Prado del Rey, the truth would soon be exposed. It was only thirty years since the last of the Knights Templar were burned alive for heresy and treason. The Knights of Calatrava would be anxious to avoid the same fate.

Ahead, the ground was rising. They climbed through narrow steep valleys full of stones and pine trees, surrounded by mountain walls. Glancing up at the sun, Merrivale saw that they were heading roughly northeast. He hoped Irunberri would be able to pick up the trail, and reassured himself. The passage of more than forty men and horses would leave obvious tracks.

They rounded a corner of the hills and rode out into another, broader valley. Ahead lay another, steeper hill with cliffs rising to its summit. Clustered around the base of the hill was a village of flat-roofed houses, their whitewashed walls glowing with sunlight. A stubby minaret jutted up, surrounded by dark green pines. High above the cliffs stood a castle with a square tower. Its walls too were snowy white, brilliant against the aching deep blue of the sky.

The men around them were talking excitedly, some laughing and chuckling. Ficaris leaned towards Merrivale, dried blood crusted on his split lip. 'That is Zahara,' he murmured. 'That is where they are taking us.'

Merrivale looked up at the cliffs and the castle far above. Suddenly he felt sick again. 'Christ have mercy on us,' he said.

A steep narrow track led to the castle gates, guarded by more archers and a couple of stone-throwing machines. In the courtyard, their bonds were cut and they were herded down a flight of stairs into a musty chamber with high windows letting in shafts of sunlight. The heavy door of the chamber was slammed and bolted from the outside.

They stood for a few moments, flexing numbed fingers and wincing with pain as blood began to flow again. 'What happens now?' asked Sifredo.

'At least they didn't kill us outright,' said Ficaris.

'Perhaps they are intending to sell us,' said Warin.

Ficaris shuddered. Peiro wandered around the walls, tapping the whitewashed stone as if looking for weak points, but it was hopeless; the walls were several feet thick. Sifredo knelt on the floor and closed his eyes, holding the little wooden crucifix while his lips moved in silent prayer.

Jac was right, Merrivale thought. *We should have carried on to La Algaba... But he killed Philippe. He didn't administer the poison, but he was the guiding hand. How could I let him go?*

He looked at Eleanor. 'I am sorry,' he said quietly.

'I knew the risks.'

'I should be able to procure your freedom. Before we left I spoke to Ridwan, the chancellor of Garnāta. He said that if his people had taken you, you would be set free at once. I shall ask our captors to honour Ridwan's word.'

'It is too dangerous. You would have to expose my identity, and what if these men refuse to honour Ridwan's pledge? I have no wish to end up as Sultan Yūsuf's concubine. Or worse.' She paused. 'What about the Navarrese? Will Irunberri rescue us?'

Merrivale shook his head. 'There is only one way into the castle, and it is heavily guarded. Irunberri has four hundred men. Even if he had four thousand, I wouldn't give much for his chances.'

'Can we get a message to al-Jazīra through some other route? Henry would pay our ransoms.'

'Possibly. Let me think on it.'

Peiro was staring up the windows, perhaps wondering if he could climb the wall. *What it is to be young*, Merrivale thought, *and never know the meaning of defeat...* 'How did they know where to find us?' Warin asked.

'Yes,' Ficaris said. 'I'd like to know that too.'

Sifredo stood up, putting the crucifix back inside his tunic. 'The captain at Arcos warned us it would be dangerous. Perhaps we were just in the wrong place at the wrong time, and bumped into a patrol.'

'No,' Ficaris said. 'They were waiting for us.' He shuddered. 'I hope to God they either ransom us or kill us. I will not be a slave again.'

'What happened the last time?' Warin asked.

Ficaris looked wry. 'Back then, I really *was* in the wrong place at the wrong time. I had spent most of my life drifting, looking for a place to fit in and never quite finding it... I ran away from my home in Catalunya and joined a Catalan mercenary company in Athens for a while, but ended up poorer than when I signed on. I served the Knights of Saint John in Rhodes, but I didn't fit in there either. Eventually I went up to Constantinople and took service with the Greek empire, and ended up in the garrison at Nicomedia. I was captured by the Osmanli Turks when the city fell.'

He looked down at his hands for a moment. 'I was luckier than most, because I was educated and a polyglot. After the usual beatings, I was sold to a Mamlūk *amir* in Egypt where I served as a scribe. I was well-fed and mostly well-treated, but... It's an evil thing, slavery. It corrodes your soul. After a while you start to forget what freedom feels like. Being a slave is the only thing you know. I knew I had to escape while I still could.'

'How did you get away?' asked Peiro.

'My master trusted me enough to send me out of the house on errands. One day I didn't return. I went down to the harbour and stowed away on a Genoese trading ship. By the time they found me, we were far away at sea, and I persuaded them to put me ashore in Cyprus.'

Ficaris reached into his tunic and pulled out the little leather bag that held his playing cards. 'The only good thing was that I learned to play *kanjifah*,' he said.

Peiro looked around. 'What is *kanjifah*?'

Ficaris brightened a little. 'A game, my friend,' he said with a sudden smile. 'The best game in the world. Come, I will teach you to play. You too, Sifredo. We need to pass the time somehow.'

Warin joined the others to play cards. Eleanor sat on the floor, knees drawn up under her chin, staring into space. Merrivale leaned against the wall, looking up at the shafts of sunlight, thinking about what might happen next and how he would deal with it when the time came.

The sunlight through the high windows turned golden, then orange. The evening call to prayer drifted up from the village, reverberating off the cliffs: *Come to prayer, come to prayer, come to salvation, come to salvation. There is no god except the one God.* As the echoes died away, the door was unbolted and two men entered carrying a large brass dish full of steaming food and a waterskin. They set both down on the floor at the foot of the stair, and closed the door and bolted it again. The dish contained rice and a few pieces of tough, stringy mutton. Merrivale looked at Eleanor. 'Do you want food?'

She spoke without moving. 'I'm not hungry.'

The others ate with their hands, rolling the rice into balls. Night fell. They lay down on the stone floor and slept as best they could, trying not to think about what the morning would bring.

24th of September, 1343

Sunrise, soft light stealing through the windows overhead. The muezzin's call to prayer echoed across the valley, and shortly after the guards brought a basket of bread and some wrinkled olives. Ficaris, Warin and the two Navarrese resumed their card game. Peiro had mastered the game quickly, but Sifredo complained that he could not understand the rules.

'Look, it's simple,' Ficaris said. 'The highest card in the lead suit takes the game.'

'But you said that in coins, the ten-card is only worth one.'

'Yes, in coins and cups, the values run backwards. Ten is worth one, nine is worth two and so on. It's really very easy, Sifredo.'

'Señor de Ficaris, I think you are making up the rules as we go along.'

Ficaris looked pained. 'Would I do that? And please, call me Jac.'

Eleanor leaned against the wall, looking up at the shafts of sunlight. Merrivale moved over to join her. 'This is an absurd question,' he said. 'But are you all right, my lady?'

She smiled a little. 'I'm thinking about Aucassin at Beaucaire. I've never been a prisoner in a dungeon before.'

'For me, it is not a new experience,' Merrivale said wryly. 'I think I know how to get a message to your brother at al-Jazīra.'

Eleanor looked sharply at him. 'How?'

'They are holding us here for a reason,' Merrivale said. 'Sooner or later, they will interrogate me. The chance will come then.'

Time passed, achingly slow. At midday the call to prayer sounded again. The other four had stopped playing cards and lay on the stone floor, dozing in the heat.

The door opened. Everyone sat up. A man with a drawn sword stood in the doorway, pointing at Merrivale. '*Kell. As-d yid-i.*'

'He wants you to go with him,' Ficaris said.

Silently, Merrivale rose to his feet. Two more guards waited beyond the door. He was escorted upstairs and across the courtyard to another stair, which led to a high chamber with windows looking out across the sunlit valley. Fields and olive groves lay far below. Pine-covered mountains towered up to the sky.

The man with the missing fingers stood leaning against the wall, his good hand caressing his sword hilt. His high cheekbones and sharp nose reminded Merrivale of a hawk. Another man, broad-shouldered and strongly built, stood by the window with his arms folded across his chest. Both wore long black robes over loose trousers and loose black turbans on their heads.

The guards who had escorted Merrivale remained standing just inside the door. '*Salaam aleikum,*' said the man by the window. 'Do you understand Arabic?'

'Some,' said Merrivale.

'I speak Castilian, but my brother-in-arms does not. He refuses to speak the tongue of pig-eaters and idolaters. I am Mouha ben Tirga and this is Aksal ben Mellal. We are officers of the Warriors of the Faithful.'

Merrivale folded his hands and bowed. 'I am Simon Merrivale, herald to the Earl of Derby. As I told your friend yesterday, I am an ambassador and I come in peace. Those who travel with me are under my protection.'

'And what was an English ambassador doing in Prado del Rey?' Mouha asked.

'I am searching for a man named Pero de Garcíez. He murdered three men, including the king of Navarre, and has taken refuge in the sultanate of Garnāta. I formally request that you hand him over to me and allow me to continue on my way.'

'Who are you to make demands?' Aksal spat.

'I have not yet perfected my study of your language,' Merrivale said. 'But I have learned a little of your laws and customs. "Oh, you who believe, stand firm in your faith in God and be witnesses to justice, and do not let the hatred of a people prevent you from being just. Be just; that is nearer to righteousness." Justice demands that Garcíez be punished.'

Aksal took a step towards Merrivale, hand tightening on his sword. Mouha held up a hand. 'Enough. The man you seek is not here.'

'Then allow me to find him. If it is ransoms you desire, send word to my master at al-Jazīra and he will pay you. Let it be done quickly, so that I may continue my quest.'

'My friend is right,' said Mouha. 'You make many demands. Why do you carry no sword?'

'Because I am a herald,' Merrivale said. 'I am protected by God.'

'A man who rides through a dangerous land with no weapon to defend himself is either an imbecile or a madman, and I judge that you are neither. What is your real purpose? Are you a spy?'

Merrivale spread his hands. 'What is there to spy on? There is nothing in Prado del Rey but death and ruin. I can find those anywhere.'

'Then why did you go there?'

There were times when the truth was a better probe than even the most expert lie. 'When Prado del Rey was destroyed, many of its people were taken away and sold as slaves. I am searching for one of them, a young man named Mauro.'

There was a long silence. 'You yourself would make an excellent slave,' Mouha said. 'You are strong, and would fetch a good price. You might last three or four years in the mines. On the other hand, you are also disrespectful and arrogant. Your overseer would probably beat you to death as an example to the other slaves, to teach them their place.'

'You would sell me,' Merrivale mused. 'With all the African gold you have in your castle at Suhayl, you still desire more? My faith teaches that greed is a sin.'

Mouha's face hardened. 'He is dangerous,' said Aksal. 'Kill him.'

'Not yet,' said Mouha. 'One of your party understands Tamazight. Who is he?'

'Jacme de Ficaris. He is my secretary, and I repeat, he is under my protection.'

Mouha motioned to the guards. '*Kkes-it*. Return him to the *zinzana*, and bring the other one.'

—

In the dungeon they waited in silence. Once, the sound of hooves in the cobbled courtyard echoed through the windows; a lone horseman arriving from the valley below. The horse halted, and silence fell again.

An hour later the guards opened the door and pushed Ficaris through it. He was breathing hard; the cut on his lip had opened up again, and there was a fresh bruise on his cheek. Warin handed him the waterskin. 'Are you all right, Jac?'

'I've had worse.' Ficaris wiped the blood from his mouth and drank some water. 'They wanted to know why we are here,' he said. 'I told them about Juan and his nephew, but they didn't believe me.'

'Did you say anything about Kāsim?'

'I thought it best not to, but I reckon they knew I was concealing something. That's when their fists started doing the talking. That Aksal is a bastard.'

'Put *me* in a room alone with him,' said Peiro. 'I'd pay him back for the killing of that old friar.'

'Unfortunately, my brave friend, I was not alone with him, and neither will you be. If you start a fight, the guards will have your guts out and cut them into tripes before you can say *kanjifah*. Simon, I told them we were a peaceful embassy and asked them to send a message to al-Jazīra. They refused.'

'They refused me as well,' said Merrivale. 'Anything else?'

'Yes, a courier came in while we were... discussing matters. He had orders for Aksal and the other fellow, Mouha. They are taking us to Runda tomorrow.'

'Runda,' Merrivale said quietly. 'According to Ridwan, that is where the *amir* of the Warriors of the Faithful has his headquarters. And Zayani, the *amir*, was a friend of Kāsim al-'Aswad.'

'So they do know why we are looking for Mauro,' Eleanor said.

'If they knew everything, we would be dead already,' Merrivale said. 'Very well. Let us play the game, and see where it takes us.'

14

25th of September, 1343

In the morning they were taken up to the courtyard again. Horses awaited them; they were instructed to mount and their hands and feet were bound once more. An escort of thirty riders assembled, with Mouha and Aksal at their head. They rode through the gates and down the steep road through the village, passing a watchtower that guarded the road on the village's northern flank.

Someone hailed them from the roof turret of the tower, speaking in Tamazight. Ficaris listened for a moment. 'Our people are coming up the valley from the west,' he said. 'At least a hundred. Their leader has a red banner bearing a tower on a blue shield.'

Irunberri's device. Guilhem-Arnaut had kept his word. 'If only we could escape,' Peiro murmured. 'I think I can get my hands free.'

'Be careful,' Merrivale said quietly. 'Don't do anything foolish.'

'But if I can get away and find the captain—'

'We could all be killed,' Eleanor said in a fierce whisper. 'Do as Simon says.'

Mouha turned his horse, calling to Aksal. Leaving the main road behind, the Warriors of the Faithful and their captives followed a narrow path below the castle, riding single file with the cliffs to their left and a steep slope covered in scree to their right. Beyond the cliff was a high ridge; they climbed through forests of scrub oak and carob trees, hooves scrabbling and sliding on the stony ground. By the time they reached the crest of the ridge, horses and riders were both sweating.

The descent on the other side was even more perilous. The Warriors were superb horsemen, and they needed to be; sometimes their horses were down on their haunches struggling for balance, and once Peiro was pitched backwards out of his saddle and dangled for a moment over his horse's rump, suspended by the leather bonds tying his boots to his stirrups. One of the Warriors hauled him upright and back into the saddle again and he hunched over, breathing hard.

'Are you all right?' Merrivale asked him.

'I've managed to free my hands, *jauna*,' Peiro whispered.

At the foot of the ridge was a green valley with a little whitewashed village tucked into the lee of the hills. Merrivale looked down the valley and saw specks of bright colour moving towards them. He knew a brief moment of hope. Had Irunberri and his men somehow picked up the trail?

Mouha rode alongside him. 'There will be no rescue,' he said. 'If your friends come too close, we will slit your throats. Aksal intends to do it himself.'

'Then you had better get moving before they spot us,' Merrivale said. 'Someone in Runda wants us kept alive, don't they? They won't be very pleased if you bring in our corpses.'

Mouha raised one gauntleted hand. His fist did not travel far, but it hit Merrivale on the side of the head with a force that made his head ring. Half-stunned, he slumped in his saddle. Dimly, he heard Mouha and Aksal calling orders and then they were moving again, climbing up another steep forested slope in the blazing sun. There had been nothing to drink apart from a little water that morning, and his throat was rasping and dry, his tongue thick in his mouth. Flies whined around him, drinking the sweat from his skin; his hands were still bound, and he could not brush them away.

Behind him, Sifredo's voice murmured. 'Where is the captain?'

'I've lost sight of him,' Peiro whispered. 'We have to get word to him, Sifredo. We have to break out.'

'My hands aren't free.'

'It doesn't matter. Just hold onto the bridle and ride. You go left, I'll go right.'

'No!' Merrivale hissed. 'Not now! Wait your chance!'

He was too late. Peiro was already moving, kicking his horse into a gallop and flying through the trees. Merrivale and Sifredo both screamed at him to stop, but Peiro did not waver.

'*Qerres!*' Mouha shouted. A dozen bows twanged and black arrows hissed away through the trees. Some hit tree trunks or were deflected by low-hanging branches, but two found their mark. Peiro went limp and rolled out of the saddle, his body bouncing a little as it hit the ground.

'Oh, dear God,' said Sifredo. His face had gone pale. 'I should have gone too. I might have distracted them long enough for him to get away.'

'Then you too would be dead,' said Merrivale.

Aksal had ridden after Peiro. Reaching the body, he dismounted and drew his sword. Sunlight glinted on the steel blade as it rose and fell. Aksal looked down at the body for a moment, and remounted and rode back, halting beside Merrivale and raising his bloody sword. His eyes were dark with violence. *I must have looked like that, once*, Merrivale thought. *I too enjoyed killing.*

'Now for the rest of them,' Aksal said in Arabic.

'No,' Mouha said sharply. 'You heard the orders. We take them to Runda.'

—

The ramparts of Runda rose from the top of sheer cliffs towering four hundred feet above the surrounding plain. Only to the south did the ground slope away more gently, and here the place was protected by high double walls and a turreted gatehouse. Black-robed guards hailed Mouha and Aksal and stepped aside to allow passage through the gates. Inside was a town of whitewashed houses and narrow streets that sloped steeply uphill.

The *qasaba*, the citadel, was on the northern side of the town, perched on the edge of a deep narrow gorge that cut through the cliffs. Inside the curtain walls, gardens bloomed with roses and dark green cypresses marched in rows. Stone pavilions stood behind the trees; beyond them was a larger building that looked like a palace, flanked by the domes of a bathhouse and the tall minaret of a mosque. The Warriors dismounted and untied their captives, and at direction from Mouha, escorted them to a stair turret next to one of the pavilions. A door opened and they were pushed down a stone stairway, through a second door and into another dungeon. The lower door slammed behind them and they heard the bolts on the outside being pushed into their barrels.

They stood for a moment, weary from the long ride, looking around. The room was long and narrow; a high barred window on the north wall admitted the only light. A heap of straw lay in one corner, and a wooden bucket with a metal handle sat on the floor beneath the window. Eleanor pointed at the bucket. 'Is that what I think it is for?'

Warin picked it up and smelled it. 'Yes,' he said. 'Is there any way out of this place?'

Sifredo, still grieving for the death of his friend, said nothing. Ficaris tested the iron bars on the window, which did not budge. 'Solid as a rock,' he said.

Warin was examining the door. 'Oak planks at least four inches thick and bound with iron. I heard three bolts being shot home.' He looked at the hinges. 'Something might be made of these, though. The stone feels pretty soft. Remember Burstwick, sir?'

'Yes,' said Merrivale. Four years earlier, Warin had freed Merrivale from captivity in the castle of Burstwick in England by digging the hinges of his cell door out of the walls.

Ficaris shook his head. 'Even if we do manage to get the door open, what then? We still have to get out of the *qasaba*, and even if we do *that*, the only gate into the town is swarming with guards. I hate to say it, but I think we're stuck fast.'

Merrivale looked out of the window. The walls of the gorge plunged down hundreds of feet. Craning his neck, he saw a glint of sunlight on a little river at the bottom. To his right, a stone tower extended down the face of the cliff. It looked like a fortified passage or stair, and he wondered if there might be another gate at the bottom.

A few small houses stood on the far side of the gorge. Beyond these, pastures extended away into the distance; he saw horses grazing there. He looked again at the walls of the gorge. The wind-eroded walls were vertical and impossible to climb without ropes, but off to his left there was a gap, a kind of natural chimney carved by the passage of water. Merrivale studied this, the seed of a plan beginning to germinate in his mind.

The sun was moving into the west. There was no hope of rescue now. Irunberri was a practical man, and he had already been deep in enemy territory; he would, with a heavy heart, have returned to Xerez to do his duty by his king. *I would have done the same, my friend*, Merrivale said silently.

'Once again, we may as well pass the time,' Ficaris said. '*Kanjifah*, anyone?'

'I don't have any money to lose,' Warin said.

'Never mind. You can owe me.'

They sat cross-legged on the floor, playing cards. Eleanor watched them. Sifredo sat too, knees drawn up and head bowed, the wooden crucifix in his hand, and Merrivale heard him murmuring softly to himself, '*Agur Maria graziaz betea, Jauna zurekin dago. Bedeinkatua zu emakume artean eta bedeinkatua zure sabeleko fruitua.*'

'Is that a prayer?' Merrivale asked quietly.

Sifredo raised his head. 'The Gospel of Saint Luke. "Hail Mary, full of grace, the Lord is with you. Blessed are you among women and blessed is the fruit of your womb." I translated it myself into the Basque language. I've always heard it in Latin, but it feels more comforting in my own tongue.' He paused. 'I hope it will ease Peiro's soul into heaven.'

'Did he leave any family behind?'

'His mother is a widow. His brother is a timber merchant, and will care for her.'

'And you?' Merrivale asked. 'Any family?'

'My parents are both with God. There is a girl back in Iruña whom I intend to marry. I am saving money for her dowry.' Another pause. 'If we ever get out of this place.'

'We will,' Merrivale said. 'You have my promise.'

Sunset, the muezzin's call echoing once more, bouncing off the stone walls of the gorge. They heard the bolts being drawn back and the door opened. A man shuffled into the room, carrying a goatskin waterskin over his shoulder. He was barefoot and dirty, clad in nothing but a stained breechcloth, and so emaciated that his bones threatened to burst through his skin.

'Water,' he said, his voice creaking with strain, and he lowered the waterskin to the floor.

'Who are you?' Merrivale asked.

The man shook his head in fear and stumbled back through the door. Merrivale saw the whip marks on his back, old scars and fresher marks still crusted with dried blood. One of the Warriors came in carrying a dish of rice and meat. '*Kečini d imasihiyen?*' he demanded.

'He wants to know if we are Christians,' Ficaris said.

'Yes,' said Merrivale.

The man tipped the food onto the floor. 'You eat the flesh of pigs,' he said. 'Now, you can eat like pigs yourselves.'

The door slammed behind him and was bolted once more. Reluctantly, they ate some of the food and drank from the waterskin. They considered making beds out of the straw, but thought about what might be living inside it. Night fell, lit by a pale glow of moonlight washing through the gorge from the west. Wearily, they stretched out on the stone floor and fell asleep.

26th of September, 1343

They woke shivering in the morning, for Runda was high in the mountains and the night air was cool. 'I had forgotten what it was like to be cold,' Eleanor said.

A flash of gold lit the gorge outside as the sun rose. Another Warrior came with a bowl of rice, which he placed on the floor in contemptuous silence and departed. Merrivale waited until the door had been bolted. 'How many of them are out there?' he asked quietly.

Warin listened at the door. 'I can't hear anyone,' he said. 'Unless they are being very, very quiet.'

Ficaris shook his head. 'They may not bother putting guards on the door. As I said yesterday, even if we did manage to get out of the dungeon, where would we go?'

'What now?' asked Sifredo.

'They are keeping us waiting,' Merrivale said. 'They hope that as time passes, our resolve will weaken and we will begin to crack.'

Eleanor looked at him. 'Have you done this to people yourself?'

'Of course,' Merrivale said quietly. 'Many times.'

They waited. The sun rose higher, and with it came the heat once more. Warin and Sifredo grew weary of *kanjifah*, so Ficaris dealt two hands and began playing against himself. Merrivale gazed out of the window, watching birds fly through the gorge below him, studying the stone cliffs and examining the chimney. The first half, he thought, was straightforward; near the top the chimney became narrower and steeper, but could still be climbed.

Now all they had to do was work out how to get there, undetected.

Midday came, the sun shining straight down into the gorge. The call to prayer sounded once more. A little later the bolts were drawn and the door opened. Two Warriors stood in the doorway with drawn swords. One pointed at Merrivale and then at Eleanor. 'Both of you. Come.'

Eleanor looked at Merrivale, her eyes wide with sudden fear. Merrivale forced a smile. 'It will be all right,' he said.

The Warriors took them upstairs and out into the garden. Three men stood in the sunlight, waiting for them. Two of them were Mouha and Aksal. The third was a tall man with black hair and a close-cropped beard frosted with grey and the dark, far-seeing eyes of a man who had ridden across deserts and fought a hundred battles. He surveyed them in silence, hands clasped in front of him.

'Peace be upon you, and the mercy and blessings of God,' the man said finally. 'I am told that you speak Arabic.'

'I am far from fluent,' Merrivale said. 'Whom have I the honour of addressing, *saīdi*?'

'I am Hamou Ou Akka ibn Zayani, *amir* of the Warriors of the Faithful. And you are Simon Merrivale.'

'I am the herald of noble Henry of Grosmont, Earl of Derby. I claim protection for myself and all who travel with me.'

'Mm.' Zayani pointed at Eleanor. 'And who is this?'

'This is Buscador, a crossbowman in my service.'

'You lie, ambassador. This is the lady Eleanor of Lancaster, the sister of your master. Take her away.'

The guards seized Eleanor by the arms. She fought them in bright-eyed silence, twisting and trying to break their grip; one of them put his arm across her face and she bit him savagely on the hand, drawing blood. The guard winced and drew back. Zayani stepped forward and hit Eleanor on the jaw, snapping her head back. Her eyes rolled and she fell forward onto the tiles, unconscious.

'Take her away,' Zayani repeated.

'Wait!' said Merrivale. 'The *hajib* of Garnāta, Abū Nu'aym Ridwan, has given his word that the lady Eleanor will be returned to her brother.'

Zayani stared at him. 'I do not believe you.'

'Send a messenger to al-Jazīra and ask for confirmation.'

'I think not.' Zayani motioned to the guards, who picked Eleanor up and carried her out. 'An English noblewoman will be an interesting novelty in the slave markets of Murrākush,' he said.

'Whatever price you might receive for her, her brother will pay more,' Merrivale said. There was no need to mention Arundel, who would probably do the paying. 'Send word, and he will arrange her ransom.'

'You need to think about saving yourself, herald. Using the pretext of making inquiries about a man called Mauro, you have been asking some dangerous questions. About Kāsim al-'Aswad for example, and about La Algaba. And what do you know about Suhayl?'

'It is a port, or so I understand. It plays a part in Garnāta's trade in salt and gold with Murrākush.'

'And how do you know this? What business is this of yours?'

The truth could be a sword, but sometimes lies were a valuable shield. 'It is none of my business,' Merrivale said. 'I heard it in passing from a man called Fra Moriale, a mercenary who is very interested in gold. But my interest is in men, not money.'

Zayani reached into his robe and held up Moreno's little rock salt crucifix. It had been in Merrivale's saddlebag, and presumably one of the Warriors at Zahara had found it. 'Is this one of your *kāfir* idols?' he asked.

'It belongs to Mauro, the man I am looking for,' Merrivale said. 'It was bequeathed to him by his mother.' He held out his hand. 'Please return it to me.'

Zayani hesitated for a moment. To Merrivale's surprise, he placed the crucifix in Merrivale's palm. 'Take it. I have no use for it.'

'Thank you,' said Merrivale. He paused, again choosing his words with care. 'A Knight of Calatrava named Pero de Garcíez is responsible for Mauro's disappearance. Do you know of him?'

Zayani stepped forward until he was almost touching Merrivale, his face only inches away. 'Why do you ask?'

Time for another lie, Merrivale thought. 'I believe that Garcíez's men captured Mauro and sold him by mistake, not realising that he was a Christian.'

'And what do I care whether you Christians enslave each other?'

'I didn't ask if you cared,' Merrivale said. 'I asked what you know of Garcíez.'

Zayani's eyes flickered. 'You are insolent. I could have you executed at any moment.'

'Then you would be breaking God's law, *saīdi*,' Merrivale said. 'I told you, I am a herald and ambassador, and I am unarmed. Killing me would be an act of murder and a stain on the honour of the *amir*.'

There was a long pause. Zayani spoke without turning his head. 'Mouha. Return this prisoner to the *zinzana*.'

Mouha took Merrivale's arm and propelled him back down the stairs. Aksal turned to Zayani. 'He knows too much. Kill him.'

'Mouha is right. We must wait. This is a delicate moment, and there is no room for false steps. It would be folly to throw away everything we have worked for.'

'What about Garnāta?'

'Our ambitions remain unchanged. Saīda Buthayna will be the key that unlocks the door for us. We shall continue to cultivate her support.'

Aksal shook his head. 'I am not convinced that Buthayna is the right horse to bet on, *saīdi*. Rīm has the support of the Grandmother.'

'The Grandmother will support whoever comes out on top. She always has. But until we are ready to move, it is important that she and Abū Nu'aym Ridwan suspect nothing.'

'Abū Nu'aym is our ally.'

'Abū Nu'aym knows only what we have told him. We have drawn a veil over his eyes, and it must remain there until all is done. Bring the lady to this pavilion and put some of the women to guard her. See that she has everything she needs.'

'You will ransom her to her brother?'

Zayani smiled. 'I think Saīdi Peruzzi would pay a higher price.'

'They took Eleanor,' Merrivale said bleakly.

'God in heaven,' Ficaris said softly.

Sifredo touched his crucifix, his lips moving silently. Warin's fists clenched until his knuckles were white. 'What will they do with the princess?'

'The *amir* threatened to sell her as a slave, but that was a ploy to get me to talk. I think it much more likely that they will use her as a bargaining counter.'

Ficaris frowned. 'With whom are they bargaining?'

'An excellent question. I am beginning to see the nature of the game, but I don't yet know who all of the other players are.'

The rest of the day passed with painful slowness. Merrivale stood by the window, staring out over the gorge, desperately worried for Eleanor. The logical part of his mind told him that if Zayani and the Warriors of the Faithful wanted to kill them, they would all be dead by now; on the other hand, it was difficult to work out exactly why they were still alive.

His question about Garcíez had hit the mark; confirmation, if it was needed, that Garcíez was working with the enemy. *Ghāzīs* and crusaders, he thought in sudden anger, working together to sell people as slaves. One expected such behaviour of bandit gangs, but not of men who professed to be servants of God. Or was that simply naive?

Evening came. The door bolts rattled again; the door opened and the same slave shuffled in, this time carrying two waterskins. He knelt and laid one of them on the floor, and as he did so Merrivale seized his wrist. 'Who are you?' he whispered.

The man's voice was low. 'My name is Diago.'

'Where are you from?'

'Near Arcos. I was captured six years ago. I have been working in the water mine ever since.'

'The water mine?'

'There is a tower on the face of the cliff. At its base is a water wheel. We work it to draw water from the river, and carry it up to the *qasaba*. We call it the water mine because it is like working in a mine shaft.'

One of the Warriors appeared in the doorway, sword in hand. '*Aydi! Aegel!* Hurry up!'

Diago scrambled to his feet. 'The lady who was here,' Merrivale whispered quickly. 'Find out where they are holding her.'

Diago did not reply. He stumbled to his feet, carrying the other waterskin, and ran out of the room. The Warrior slammed the door and bolted it behind him.

Ficaris looked at Merrivale. 'What do you have in mind?'

'I'm not certain, yet,' Merrivale said. 'I'll let you know when I am.'

–

Eleanor's jaw hurt and her head ached, but she supposed it could have been far worse. The accommodation they had given her was rather more pleasant than the dungeon, a stone pavilion with an interior chamber surrounded on three sides by lattice screens; the fourth was a solid wall hung with bright tapestries, with a high arched window looking out over the gorge. Carved and painted pillars supported a vaulted roof. There were rugs on the floor and a couch for sleeping, and a brazier to keep her warm when the nights were cool.

There were also two attendants, veiled women who brought her a brass bowl of rice and meat and another smaller bowl of *zabadi*, sharp-flavoured fermented milk. Once she got used to the taste it was not unpleasant. The two women spoke no Castilian and did not respond to her few halting words of Arabic. She wondered if they were servants, or guards. Both, probably.

She looked out the window, staring into the depths the gorge and wondering what fate Zayani had planned for her. They might sell her, of course, and the prospect made her shiver. They might, indeed, agree to let Simon send a message to her brother, but she doubted whether it would be as simple as letting her go free in exchange for paying a ransom. They must realise that she too knew about Mauro and therefore, like Simon, she was dangerous. They all were.

This is entirely your own fault, she told herself. *You are the one who had the emotional storm and decided to leave Richard and return to England. You are the one who bolted into the hills without telling anyone where you were going. And you are the one who could have remained safely in Xerez but decided to follow Simon and the others to Prado del Rey.*

Why? Why the latter, especially? She was still not entirely clear. She had been horrified to learn of Moreno's death, but there was more to it than that. *Perhaps I really have read too much poetry,* she thought bitterly. *Perhaps I wanted to plunge myself into mortal peril, to force Richard to go on a quest to rescue me.*

But she herself might well die in this place, and if Richard tried to follow her, he too would die. She straightened, looking at the fields on the far side of the gorge and watching the horses graze. *No,* she thought. *My salvation, if it exists, lies in my own hands. Mine, and Simon's.*

A man shuffled into the pavilion, carrying a waterskin over one shoulder. He was barefoot and naked apart from a filthy breechcloth, and his back was scarred with whip marks. He knelt, laying the waterskin on the floor. The two attendants watched in silence from behind their veils. Suddenly understanding, Eleanor knelt too, picking up the waterskin. The man spoke in a whisper from the corner of his mouth.

'Your friends are in the dungeon directly beneath this place.'

'Are they guarded?' Eleanor whispered.

'No guards, but the doors are securely locked. I must go.'

He rose and shuffled out. Eleanor stood up, looking at the waterskin and thinking. She wondered what Simon intended to do, and realised she could probably guess. The beginnings of a plan came into her mind, and with it, a spark of hope.

—

At al-Jazīra the wind blew in from the sea, rippling the canvas pavilions and stretching the bright banners on their lanyards. Henry of Derby strode into the earl of Arundel's pavilion, his face grim.

'There is bad news,' he said.

Arundel, who had been sitting and staring into space, looked up. 'How bad?'

'A letter has come from Xerez. Philippe of Navarre has died of poison. Simon went after his killers, and has been taken prisoner by the Warriors of the Faithful. Irunberri followed him, but was too late to save Simon. And there is no sign of Eleanor.'

'Merrivale didn't find her,' Arundel said. His voice was dull with defeat.

'It seems not.' Derby drew a deep breath. 'There's more. A dispatch arrived this morning from King Edward's chancery. If we cannot conclude an alliance with Castile by the end of October, we are summoned home.'

'You go,' said Arundel. 'I will wait here until there is definite news of Eleanor.'

'The summons names us both. We must go, Richard. The orders are direct from the king.'

'I will wait,' Arundel repeated. 'I will wait until the Last Judgement if need be, but I am not returning without her. The king can do what he likes.'

Derby turned and walked outside, where he stopped and took another deep breath. He looked up at the sky for a moment, and then closed his eyes. *Eleanor, little sister, where are you? Why did you have to go?*

—

'Garcíez has done well,' said Donato de' Peruzzi. 'He set the trap, and Merrivale fell straight into it. Even better, he has dragged Eleanor of Lancaster down with him. I am leaving immediately, and will be away for several days.'

'When does my gold arrive?' Leonor demanded.

'It will arrive when it arrives. Why are you so anxious? Is Grand Master Núñez not satisfied with what you are already giving him?'

'He wants money. Everyone wants money. Why must you go at this delicate stage? Are you so keen to witness Merrivale's death?'

'That will be entertaining,' Peruzzi admitted, 'but I am more interested in what he can tell me about how much he knows of our plans, and whom he has told. Even more importantly, I want Eleanor of Lancaster in my hands. She is of royal blood, and while I control her, King Edward of England will be forced to listen to me. I have not yet finished with him or his miserable little country. This may give me my opening, sooner than I expected.'

'Isn't Castile enough for you?' Leonor demanded.

Peruzzi looked at her as if she were an idiot. 'Of course not,' he said. 'How did you ever imagine that it would be?'

15

27th of September, 1343

Another cold uncomfortable night passed; another day dawned. Ficaris, Warin and Sifredo played cards, game after game. Merrivale waited, feeling time flow past him. As he had said to Eleanor, he had been in this situation before. Over the past fifteen years he had learned when to act, and when to be patient.

Diago returned that evening with a fresh waterskin. He seemed to have more confidence; perhaps talking to Merrivale had given him a new resolve. 'The lady is in the pavilion directly above you.'

'Is she guarded?'

'Two women keep watch on her at all times. The palace across the garden is full of Warriors.'

The door closed after him. 'Thank God the princess is alive,' Warin said after a moment.

That night Merrivale found it impossible to sleep. Memories washed over him in waves, of his childhood, of fighting for scraps of food during the famine, of watching the white-shrouded corpses of his mother and sisters lowered into their graves, dead of hunger. Memories of the roads he had travelled in England and Scotland, Flanders and Savoy, Gascony and Tuscany. Memories of Yolande, sitting in a garden robed in blue, playing a lute and watching him with eyes of love.

Sweet is your laughter, sweet your face,

Sweet are your lips and sweet your brow,
And sweet is the touch of your embrace.
Now I, for love of you, am bound
Here in this dungeon underground,
All for loving you, I lie
Here, and for you, I daily cry.
Here, for loving you, I must die.

And he nearly had, because Yolande's father the king of Bohemia had discovered their secret and imprisoned them both before dragging Merrivale out, tying him in a sack and throwing him into a freezing river. The details of his escape were seared forever into his mind.

Nicolette had found Aucassin and freed him, and their love had a happy ending. But Merrivale did not know where Yolande was now, or even if she was still alive.

28th of September, 1343

The next day brought a strong wind from the mountains, whistling through the rocks of the gorge. Shortly after midday the door to the dungeon opened again and Mouha walked in. He pointed at Merrivale and Ficaris. 'Come with me.'

They climbed the steps to the garden. Zayani and Aksal were there, and with them was a man in a plain brown tunic and dark hose with riding boots, his bright surcoat with the floretty cross nowhere to be seen: Garcíez.

'What do you know?' Garcíez demanded. He spoke good Arabic. That was unsurprising, Merrivale thought.

'I know many things,' Merrivale said. 'Among them, I know that you are a murderer. You are responsible for the deaths of Juan Moreno, Lorenço de Alameda and King Philippe of Navarre. For that last, a place awaits you in the ninth circle of hell.'

'I killed no one,' said Garcíez. 'Tell me the truth. Why are you really searching for Mauro?'

'Because he is a Christian, and you sold him into slavery in Christian hands. That is against the law of God and man.'

Zayani pointed at Ficaris. Mouha and Aksal pinned Ficaris's arms behind his back and dragged him towards the gorge, pulling up him up until he was standing on top of the narrow curtain wall, looking down at the rocks hundreds of feet below. Ficaris staggered, trying to keep his balance. Merrivale could not see his face, but he could imagine the terror in his mind.

'Tell the truth,' said Zayani, 'or we throw him down onto the rocks.'

'You have a friend in Garnāta named al-Rumani,' Merrivale said to Garcíez. 'He is the superintendent of the royal salt works. He told you where and when to intercept Kāsim al-'Aswad and his household. Juan Moreno learned of this. Is that why you killed him, Garcíez?'

A gust of wind whistled down the gorge and Ficaris staggered again. 'For the love of God,' he said, his voice full of panic.

'I am telling you, I killed no one,' Garcíez said. 'Why are you so interested in Kāsim?'

'I do not care about Kāsim. I only want to find Mauro. Let Ficaris go. He has done you no harm.'

Garcíez looked at Zayani, who motioned to his two lieutenants. Aksal's fists clenched, and for a terrible moment Merrivale thought he was going to push Ficaris over the edge, but Mouha took Ficaris's arm and pulled him down. White-faced and shaking, Ficaris walked back to stand beside Merrivale. Garcíez turned to Zayani again.

'*Saīdi*, may I have a word with the captives in private?'

'No,' said Aksal.

Zayani looked irritated. 'Do not be discourteous, Aksal. Come.'

The three Warriors walked out of the pavilion into the garden. Garcíez glared at Merrivale. 'As God is my witness, I have not murdered anyone,' he said in Castilian. 'Not King

Philippe, not his physician and not your friend. I don't know who did kill them, but it wasn't me.'

Some of this was true, Merrivale thought. He wondered how much. 'You were seen several times riding to the sultan of Granada's camp, including the day that Moreno died. Why?'

'For the love of Christ!' Garcíez hissed. 'Isn't it obvious?'

'Apparently not,' Merrivale said after a moment. 'Go on.'

Garcíez reached into his coat and pulled out a piece of parchment, and handed it to Merrivale. It was a safe-conduct, written in Castilian and Arabic, and sealed with the floretty cross of the Order of Calatrava. Merrivale handed it back. 'Grand Master Núñez is negotiating with the sultan,' he said, 'and you are his agent. Does King Alfonso know?'

'You would have to ask the grand master.'

'And what is Donato de' Peruzzi's role in all of this?'

'Peruzzi is aware that Queen María is preparing to launch a rebellion against the king. He is determined to forestall her, and has thrown his support behind Leonor de Guzmán's faction, which includes our Order.' Garcíez leaned forward a little, lowering his voice. 'We are trying to negotiate a truce with the sultan, to give us time to deal with María. We cannot fight two enemies at once.'

'Why are you telling me this now?'

'I am trying to save your lives,' Garcíez said. 'Tell me the truth about why you are searching for Mauro. If you do, I can persuade Zayani to spare your lives.'

If I tell you the truth, you will throw all of us into the gorge. 'Perhaps you didn't murder anyone,' Merrivale said. 'But you sold Mauro into slavery, and probably other Christians along with him. I will give you the benefit of the doubt, and assume you made a mistake, that you didn't realise some of Kāsim's household were Christian slaves. But an injustice had been done, and that must be put right. I will find Mauro, Garcíez. I will not rest until I have done so.'

'That is your story?' Garcíez asked.

'That is the truth.'

Garcíez shook his head. 'I can do no more. Prepare your souls for death, *señores*. You have sealed your fate.'

Back in the dungeon Ficaris slumped down onto the floor. 'By God,' he said, his voice shaky. 'I thought they were going to do it. I thought they were going to throw me into the abyss.'

Sifredo passed him the waterskin and Ficaris took a long draught. 'Do you think anything Garcíez said was true?'

'He could have been telling the literal truth about the murders, in that he didn't kill anyone with his own hands. The rest is plausible, but there is no proof.'

'What do you think he wanted to know?'

'Whether we knew that he and Zayani's men are conniving in the slave trade, for a start. I would imagine that he and Zayani want to keep that secret at all costs, even from Peruzzi. I can't see that the destruction of the Knights of Calatrava would be part of Peruzzi's plan.'

'Nor would the Warriors of the Faithful come out smelling like roses,' said Warin.

'Indeed. We, however, are running out of time. Garcíez told us to prepare for death. We need to get out of this place before they come for us.'

'How?' demanded Ficaris.

'When?' asked Warin in the same breath.

'Tonight,' Merrivale said. 'Warin, can you get those door hinges off the wall?'

'I reckon so, sir. The handle of that bucket is made of iron. I can detach it and use it as a file.'

'How long?'

'There's three hinges, so two or three hours for each. I can't do it quickly, sir, or I'll make too much noise.'

The door opened inward; any of the Warriors who entered the room would not see that the hinges had been tampered with unless they closed the door behind them. 'Make a start,' Merrivale said.

'What if they come before Warin is finished?' Ficaris asked.

Merrivale looked at him. 'I assume that is a rhetorical question,' he said.

Evening came, the wind blowing in gusts through the gorge. Footsteps sounded on the stairs and Warin stepped quickly back, hiding the makeshift file in his coat. The door opened and Diago came in with their daily ration of water. Kneeling on the floor, his back to the Warrior in the doorway, he began to whisper.

'Someone is coming for you tomorrow. The guards at the water mine call him *tibexsisin*. It translates as "pears", I think. Perhaps that is not his real name.'

Pears.

Peruzzi. So that was when they would die. A night of grace had been given to them, and they had to use it.

'How many guards are there in the water mine?' Merrivale murmured.

'Six are on watch. Some sleep during the night, but some are always awake.'

The Warrior took a step forward. 'Quickly!' he snarled at Diago.

Diago began to cough. Merrivale looked sharply at the Warrior. 'Let him be,' he snapped. 'Can't you see he is not well?'

'When a dog is sick, we put it out of its misery. Quickly!'

With a slowness that was not entirely feigned, Diago struggled to his feet. 'Is the lady back in the pavilion above?' Merrivale murmured.

'They returned her there this afternoon.'

'Midnight,' Merrivale whispered. 'Do you understand?'

There was a glow in the slave's dark eyes. 'I understand, *señor*.'

Diago staggered towards the door. Another Warrior appeared with a bowl of food, placed it on the floor and slammed the door behind him. Merrivale waited until he heard the other door at the top of the stair open and close before turning to the others. 'Warin, back to work,' he said quietly. 'The rest of you, get some rest. I will wake you just before midnight.'

The sunset glow faded quickly, replaced by moonlight that flooded the gorge. The moon would set just before midnight, Merrivale calculated, giving them the darkness they needed. The wind continued to blow in fitful gusts.

Ficaris and Sifredo were dark motionless shapes on the floor. It was impossible to know if they were sleeping. Merrivale listened to the soft scrape of metal on stone, ears pricked for any sound of footsteps beyond the door. The wind outside should hopefully mask any noise that Warin might make; *hopefully*, he thought, being the operative word.

'Any progress?' he whispered.

'The top hinge is loose, sir, and the bottom one is nearly there. I'll leave the middle until last.'

The muezzin's call to prayer sounded once more: *God is Great. God is Great. There is no god except the one God.* The wind distorted the words, swirling them around the cliffs outside. Silence fell again, apart from the whistle of the wind. The shadows on the cliffs moved and lengthened as the half-moon descended into the west. Time dragged slowly onwards, reaching towards midnight.

'I think we're ready, sir,' Warin said finally. 'We'll have to pull the door sideways until the bolts are out of their chambers. It won't be easy.'

Merrivale knelt beside Sifredo and Ficaris and shook them gently. Both sat up, instantly awake. 'I've thought of a problem,' Ficaris said. 'That other door, at the top of the stairs. What if it is bolted too?'

'Eleanor will take care of it,' Merrivale said. 'Wait until the moon sets. Just a few more minutes.'

Ficaris blinked. 'Eleanor?'

'Yes. Wait.'

Sifredo raised the wooden crucifix to his lips and kissed it, and handed it to Merrivale. 'This was given to me by the girl I wish to marry,' he said quietly. 'Her name is Arrosa, the daughter of Erlantz Gebara, merchant of the San Nikolas quarter in the city of Iruña. Please return it to her, and tell her I am sorry.'

'What are you talking about?' demanded Ficaris.

'While I was sleeping just now, the Virgin Mary came to me in a dream. She told me that I would die here. These are my last hours in this world.'

There was a moment of silence. Ficaris laughed a little. 'God above, Sifredo. If I believed everything women told me in my dreams, I'd be...'

His voice trailed off. Merrivale took the crucifix. 'I will carry it for you,' he said. 'Tomorrow, when we reach safety, I will return it to you.' Outside the moonlight was fading in the gorge. 'Now, both of you, to the door. Follow Warin's direction.'

Quietly, feeling their way through the glimmer of starlight coming through the window, they took hold of the door. Warin has been right; it wasn't easy. The door was monstrously heavy, and they had to get it clear of the jamb before they could pull it sideways. Merrivale braced his feet and pulled until pain shot through his arms and shoulders and lights flashed before his eyes, and slowly the door began to move.

'Clear,' Warin gasped. 'Now, heave it sideways.'

Metal rasped as the bolts scraped in their chambers and drew free. The door lurched and slid sideways. A gust of wind came down the stairs. Warin pushed the door carefully against the wall and looked up. No light could be seen from above. Merrivale tapped Warin on the shoulder, then Ficaris and Sifredo, and sensed rather than saw them nod in the darkness. Slowly, planting his feet carefully, he climbed the stairs, the others behind him.

His outstretched fingers touched the door at the top of the stair. He felt for the latch, lifted it and pushed gently. The door opened, and he heard the wind rushing in the cypresses and smelled the bloom of roses in the night.

'Simon?' It was Eleanor, a shadow in the blue wash of starlight, whispering.

'Where are your attendants?' he whispered back.

'They were foolish enough to fall asleep. The slave had passed your message to be ready at midnight, I hit them over the head with my eating bowl, and unbolted the door.'

'Did you kill them?'

'I didn't stop to check. How do you propose we get out of here? Fly?'

Merrivale shook his head. 'Come.'

Torches fluttered in the wind outside the palace at the far end of the *qasaba*, where Diago had said the Warriors were quartered. The rest of the garden was dark. Keeping low, they skirted a row of cypresses and came to a tower on the curtain wall. Merrivale had spent most of the afternoon studying the water mine, and he was certain that this tower was above it.

There would be sentinels on the ramparts, of course, but they would be watching the outside world for threats, not the *qasaba* itself. Feeling his way along the wall, Merrivale came to another wooden door. Slowly, making as little noise as possible, he eased the bolts open and groped forward in the inky blackness inside the tower. His hands caressed stone, and he felt the curve of the stair turret. Another door opened onto a spiral stairway leading down.

The stairs were steep, and in places slippery with moss. They could hear the gurgle of water far below. The walls were pierced with small windows that let in the occasional glimmer of starlight, but for the most part they groped downwards in blackness, clinging to the wall for safety, aware that any slip could lead them tumbling down into the void below. Sifredo's voice whispered again: "*Agur Maria graziaz betea, Jauna zurekin dago…*"

Gradually the darkness melted a little. A dim orange light came from below, flickering a little; torches, Merrivale assumed, lit by the guards at the water wheel. The light brightened and he could see the stairs beneath his feet more clearly now. The bubbling of the water grew louder, drowning any small sounds they might make on the stairs. Inching downwards, he came to a place where the tower wall gave way to a large chamber lit by half a dozen torches. In its centre was a wooden mill wheel, turning slowly with a creak of metal gears. Guards – Warriors in black – sat against the wall. Two of them were awake, watching the slaves; the other four were dozing, one of them snoring a little. The room stank of damp and sweat and ordure.

The slaves lay chained together on a wooden platform, lying absolutely still. Merrivale spotted Diago just as the latter opened his eyes. Merrivale pointed at the guards. Diago nodded a little. Merrivale turned to his companions and motioned sharply downwards.

Abandoning concealment, they ran down the last few stairs into the chamber. The two guards who were awake ran towards them, drawing their swords; as they passed the platform Diago and the other slaves jumped on them, dragging the guards' sword arms down and wrapping them in chains. A whispered chant began, venomous and full of rage, '*Santiago matamoros, Santiago matamoros, Santiago matamoros*': Saint James the Moor-killer, the centuries-old battle chant of the Christian armies in Spain.

The other guards were climbing to their feet. Diago pulled a Warrior's sword from his hand and threw it to Merrivale, who caught it and tossed it to Sifredo. A whip hung from a hook on the wall; Merrivale pulled it down, turning and lashing one of the guards across the face. The man stumbled, blood pouring from his cheek, and Merrivale seized his arm and ripped his sword away, passing it to Ficaris, who promptly ran the guard through the body. Sifredo had already dispatched a second man and was fighting with a third; Warin ran to his aid, dragging the man down to the floor, and Sifredo raised his sword and brought it down hard across the guard's head. The fourth guard rushed at Eleanor. Merrivale swung his whip again and the lash coiled around the man's neck; he stopped, trying to tear the whip away, and Eleanor stepped forward, pulled the guard's knife from his belt and stabbed him in the belly.

As suddenly as it had begun, the melee was over. Six Warriors of the Faithful and two slaves lay dead or dying on the floor; the rest of the slaves had cuts and bruises. One knelt by the body of one of the guards they had strangled, taking a bunch of keys from the dead man's belt and unlocking their chains. 'There are more guards at each end of the gorge,' Diago said. 'You will not get past them.'

'I have found a place where we can climb. Come with us.'

Diago shook his head. 'We are too weak. We would only slow you down.'

'We will help you. Come, quickly. You can be free.'

'Free to do what?' asked Diago. 'Our homes are destroyed, our families enslaved and dispersed. We have nothing to return to. Far better to stay here and die like men.'

High above a door slammed in the tower, voices calling urgently down. Booted feet sounded on the stair. 'You are out of time, *señor*,' Diago said. 'We will hold them as long as we can.'

'God grant you grace,' Merrivale said quietly. 'Jac, Sifredo, give them your swords.'

A few more steps led to the foot of the tower. Sifredo went first, followed by Warin, Eleanor and Ficaris. Merrivale looked back to see the slaves crouching and preparing to meet the men coming down from above. Feeling sick, he turned and followed the others.

They reached the bottom of the tower and opened the door. The river splashed over rough rocks covered in moss. Stars and the torches on the battlements allowed a surprising amount of dim light to reach the bottom of the gorge, more than Merrivale had bargained for. Turning left, he followed the bank of the stream until he reached a place that looked shallow enough to ford. Quietly, they crossed the stream and continued on, the wall of the gorge now on their right. Behind them, shouts and screams and the clash of metal echoed from the water mine.

'How long do you think Diago and the others can last?' Ficaris asked.

Frail, emaciated men, even if burning for vengeance, would be no match for the Warriors of the Faithful. 'Not long,' Merrivale said grimly.

'Did you say something about climbing?'

'Yes. There is something at the top of these cliffs that we need.'

'What's that?'

'Horses,' said Merrivale.

The cliff to their right folded sharply. Turning, they saw the chimney Merrivale had observed from the dungeon, a deep carved channel where, in winter and spring, water rushed down from above. Now it was dry, a steep slope of scree covered with weeds and wiry scrub. As the chimney rose it became narrower, its top a dark shadow impossibly high above. Eleanor sucked in her breath, but said nothing.

A shout from the ramparts of Runda. '*Dinna llan! Dinna llan! Ruh deffir-sen!*'

'They've spotted us,' said Ficaris.

Merrivale nodded towards the clifftop. 'Time to go,' he said.

The first part of the climb was comparatively easy. The slope was so steep that they had to scramble up on their hands and knees, but broken rocks and scrub gave purchase for their hands and feet. Slipping and stumbling at times, they had climbed the first two hundred feet before the first Warriors reached the foot of the chimney.

Arrows rose, wavering in the wind; a few whickered around them, skipping and bouncing off the stones. Light flooded the gorge from below; he glanced down to see men running up with torches in hand, flames wavering in the wind. The light also showed that some of the Warriors were climbing after them. There was no way back, now.

The chimney began to narrow. The slope grew steeper still. The scree here was thin and treacherous under foot, and once Eleanor slipped and began to slide back down the slope, but Warin caught her arm in a powerful grip and held her fast. 'Get over to the sides of the chimney,' Merrivale said. 'Find solid rock, and look for handholds and footholds. Don't move until you are set, and don't rush. Haste is not our friend.'

'Tell that to the fellows coming after us,' Ficaris gasped.

The gorge was a swimming void now, the torches blossoming hundreds of feet below. The wind tugged at them, threatening to pull them off balance. Merrivale glanced down again and saw that their pursuers had fallen back a little. The Warriors were mountaineers from Murrākush, but they would be hampered by their robes and weapons. He looked up at the stars over the rim of the gorge. A hundred feet to go.

'Keep going,' he said.

Now the slope was only a few degrees off vertical. Wind and water had eroded the stone in horizontal layers, meaning that footholds and handholds were plentiful, but the soft stone often crumbled to the touch. Merrivale, searching for a safe handhold, heard a sudden crunch of stone and a hiss of indrawn breath. Both of Ficaris's footholds had broken at the same time, leaving him clinging by his fingertips while his boots sought for purchase. Merrivale heard him gasping for effort, and knew he could only hold on for a few more seconds.

'Jac,' he said quietly, keeping his voice calm. 'To your left. There is a stone ledge there, wider than the others. It should bear your weight. Feel for it with your foot.'

Groping, Ficaris found the ledge. Inching across the rock with his fingers, he managed to transfer his weight onto one foot, then two. The ledge held. 'How much further to go?' he asked in a voice full of pain.

'Fifty feet.'

They climbed on. Merrivale looked for Eleanor and found her off to his right. Lighter than the others, she found the soft stone footholds easier to manage and was climbing with something like confidence. Sifredo laboured below him, his breath coming in tortured gasps.

Twenty feet, the top agonisingly close. Merrivale's tabard snagged on a spur of stone; he forced himself upwards, hearing the cloth tear as it yielded. He felt for a fingerhold and tested it. Once again, the stone snapped away. Fragments tumbled down the slope, followed by larger chunks of stone as the rest of the ledge crumbled. Beneath him, Sifredo shouted with pain. '*Agur Maria!* Mary Mother, I cannot see! My eyes!'

The falling debris had hit him in the face. 'Keep moving,' Merrivale said urgently. 'Let your hands and feet be your senses. I will guide you.'

'I will do my best. *Ai, Jainkoa!* God aid me!'

Merrivale looked down between his feet, trying to ignore the dizzying gulf of air below. One of Sifredo's eyes was closed and there was blood around the other. 'Just above you,' Merrivale said. 'There are two good handholds. Reach for them.'

Sifredo stretched out a hand and caught one of the handholds, but he missed the other. His fingers clawed at the stone as he began to slip. 'Hold on!' Merrivale shouted, but it was too late. Sifredo lost his grip and his body slid back down the slope. One boot caught on a larger ledge and he pitched out into space, tumbling through the air and hitting the wall a hundred feet below, his body cartwheeling until it fell hard into the scrub, slid a little and lay still. In the gorge and up on the towers of Runda the Warriors waved their torches in the air, roaring with exultation.

16

29th of September, 1343

Merrivale hauled himself over the lip of the gorge and lay flat, reaching down to pull the others up one by one. Panting, aching with bloody hands, they lay still for a moment, trying to recover their breath.

Merrivale pulled himself to his feet. 'It's not over yet,' he said.

Still gasping for air, they rose and followed him past the scattered houses into the windswept fields beyond. The horses stood in the starlight, dozing uneasily, but they did not spook when Merrivale walked up to them. 'Have you ever ridden without a saddle or bridle?' he asked Eleanor.

'Not since I was child,' she said. 'But I can do it.'

Warin, like Merrivale himself, had grown up riding ponies on Dartmoor that were not much smaller than the Imazighen horses. Ficaris, as usual, would be able to look after himself. Merrivale approached one of the horses, caressing its mane and rubbing its forehead to hold it steady while Eleanor climbed onto it. Warin and Ficaris were already mounted, and Merrivale caught another horse and leaned over its neck, swinging his leg across its back. Seating himself, he looked up at the stars to get his bearings, trying not to think about Sifredo or Diago and the others. The time for mourning would come.

'Do we go west?' asked Ficaris. To the west lay Arcos and Xerez, and safety.

'West is the first direction they will search. We're going north.'

'To La Algaba,' said Ficaris. 'You really never do give up, do you?'

Forbidding mountains rose black against the stars, but to the northeast there was a gap of sorts, a narrow valley. Merrivale glanced out at the plains to the west and saw the sparks of torches moving slowly across the fields, hunting for them. Zayani would realise soon enough which direction they had taken, but darkness would hamper the pursuit. They had to put as many miles as possible between themselves and Runda before dawn.

Once again, though, haste would not be their friend. The riders had nothing to hold onto apart from the horses themselves; a single stumble or slip in the dark could send them to a bone-breaking fall on the hard ground. They picked their way across the pastures, Merrivale leading the way, resting his hands on his horse's neck and navigating as much by sound and feel as by sight. Runda's torches faded to specks in the distance. So far, there was no sign of pursuit.

In the glow of starlight Merrivale picked up the faint outlines of a caravan track leading across the fields. Following this was risky, because come daylight their hoofprints would be plain to see in the dust, but the track also allowed them to make more speed. They urged their horses to a canter and rode on until Runda was out of sight. Around them the dark mountains rose steadily, swallowing the stars.

Far in the distance a wolf howled. Closer to hand, another answered. Merrivale's horse balked, and he kicked it into motion again. 'What do we do if the wolves come?' Eleanor asked.

'Abandon the horses,' Merrivale said. 'The wolves will go after them rather than us.'

'Are you certain of this?'

'No.'

The ground rose more steeply. Cliffs rose black to their left and the ground was full of stones as they groped their way up into a narrow pass. Starshine showed them a notch in the mountains, a valley leading gently down to the northeast. By now it must be nearly matins, Merrivale thought, three hours after midnight. Another three hours of darkness remained. The wolves howled again, and again, voices keening through the windy night, and the horses whickered with anxiety.

Ficaris spoke quietly, his voice hoarse with thirst and fatigue. 'No sign of pursuit.'

'Zayani will have called off the hunt until morning,' Merrivale said. 'He will rest his men and horses and wait for daylight.' He looked at Eleanor, a shadowy shape beside him. 'That's what we did when hunting for you, after you disappeared at al-Jazīra.'

Exhausted though she was, her voice was full of irony. 'I am pleased that you took the trouble. How long did you search?'

'For all I know, they are still searching. The Earl of Arundel has his faults, but lack of perseverance is not one of them. And your brother is an exceptionally stubborn man.'

'You would know,' she said.

They pressed on. Cold air swirled around them. The hillcrests above them were crowned with watchtowers, spikes against the night sky. It was impossible to tell if anyone was manning them. The caravan track twisted and turned through the mountains and began to climb again, up to another watershed. Behind them, the wolves had fallen silent.

A faint light began to soften the eastern sky. By the time they reached the top of the pass the east was glowing yellow and orange. Ahead lay more mountains but beyond them the ground fell away to a broad plain.

'We are back on the *frontera*,' Ficaris said. 'That plain is the valley of the Río Guadalquivir, which leads to Córdoba.' He looked up at the watchtowers. 'Those towers could be garrisoned by Moors, or they could be in the hands of our people. There is no way of telling.'

Even as he spoke the turret of the watchtower bloomed with firelight. 'A beacon,' Eleanor said. 'But who are they warning?'

They did not have to wait long for the answer. To the south-west, back the way they had come, another beacon sparked into life, and another, passing a message back towards Runda. 'We've been spotted,' said Ficaris.

Eleanor looked at him, and the irony was back in her voice. 'Really? Do you think so?'

'Ride hard,' Merrivale said.

They rode, cantering along the track and clinging on as best they could, gasping with effort, the light around them growing all the time. Once, on a rise in the ground, Merrivale slowed a little and looked behind him. He saw what he had hoped not to see: a cloud of dust, moving fast along the track behind them.

Zayani had not waited for morning. His men had found their tracks near Runda and had followed them through the darkness, trusting that the watchtowers would spot their prey once daylight came, and guide them to the kill.

'How far are they?' asked Ficaris.

'About a mile back. Ride like hell, Jac.'

'You don't have to tell me.' Ficaris kicked his horse in the ribs and it lurched forward, so suddenly that Ficaris lost his grip and fell shouting over the animal's rump. He hit the ground hard, rolled over and lay still.

Merrivale pulled on his horse's mane, dragging it to a halt. Ficaris's own horse had also come to a stop and was standing with its head down. Merrivale reached over and grabbed a fistful of its mane, and looked back to see Ficaris struggling to his feet. 'Jac! Can you walk?'

'Just about.' Slowly, Ficaris limped towards his horse and, wincing, managed to get his leg over its back and mount. The approaching dust cloud was much closer now.

'Sir!' called Warin. 'There's a castle over to the left!'

A couple of miles away another high hill rose towards the morning sky. Whitewashed walls and towers surrounded its crest, with a tall keep behind them. 'Theirs or ours?' Eleanor asked.

'Pray to God it is ours,' Merrivale said grimly. 'Ride! And for Christ's sake, hold on this time!'

Leaving the track, they fled across fields of cropped stubble towards the foot of the hills. Another track ran away to the right and what looked like the main gatehouse of the castle. Riding without spurs or reins, they would not be able to force their exhausted horses up the steep road. Merrivale pointed straight ahead. 'Get as close as you can, abandon the horses and climb. See that barbican protruding out from the main wall? There will be a postern gate there. Make for that!'

'Mother of God,' he heard Eleanor say under her breath. 'Not more climbing.'

The sun came flaming over the eastern mountains. They reached the base of the hill below the castle, slid off their horses and scrambled up the steep slope. Cliffs lay straight ahead, but off to the left the slope was less severe and there were tufts of grass to cling onto. Hauling himself up, Merrivale realised his hands were bleeding again. Below, Zayani's riders were racing across the fields, each trailing his own long streamer of dust. He spotted Zayani himself, and another man carrying a black banner with red calligraphy, fluttering in the wind. Eleanor climbed swiftly behind him; below, Ficaris was labouring.

'Go on,' Merrivale said to Eleanor and he started to slide back down the slope to help Ficaris, but Warin was already there. Tin miners were strong, and none stronger than Warin; he pulled Ficaris to his feet, lifted him and slung him across his own shoulders like a sack of flour, and staggered up the slope. Merrivale took his arm, and between them they finally reached the base of the barbican. A wooden postern gate was set into the stone. He pushed on the gate, but it was firmly barred.

Zayani's men had reached the foot of the hill and were climbing after them. Ficaris slid off Warin's shoulders and sat shuddering on the ground. Turbaned heads looked down from the ramparts, some holding bows or crossbows trained on them. '*Anwa-k?*' someone shouted. '*Ansi i d-tusid?*'

'Oh, Jesus,' Ficaris said wearily. 'They're speaking Tamazight. Those are Imazighen, the same people as the Warriors.'

But the voice from above had been a woman's. There was only one hope left, and Merrivale seized upon it. 'Help us!' he called in Castilian. 'We are pursued by the Warriors of the Faithful! In God's name, aid us!'

Another woman's voice, deeper than the first, spoke words of command. '*Ldi tawwurt.* Open the gate and let them in.'

A moment later the postern rattled and opened. Merrivale pushed Eleanor through, then Ficaris and Warin. He looked down to see Zayani perhaps fifty feet below him, and stumbled through the gate himself. Figures in white slammed the postern shut, bolted and barred it. One, a big, broad-shouldered young woman with tattooed black symbols on her wrists, held out her hand. 'Surrender your weapons,' she said in Arabic. 'All of them, even your eating knives.'

'We have nothing,' Merrivale said. 'The Warriors took them from us.'

The woman looked dubious, but motioned with her hand. They followed her up a narrow stair to the roof of the barbican. More women stood behind the ramparts, bows and crossbows levelled. At their centre was another woman, tall and lean, robed all in white with a veil covering her hair.

Even in his exhausted state, Merrivale thought she had one of the most extraordinary faces he had ever seen. She might have been forty, or sixty; she looked ageless. Brown skin stretched over high cheekbones framed piercing deep green eyes. A tattoo ran across her forehead И Ѳ Е ФФО, and more tattoos flowed in vertical lines along her wrists and the backs of her hands. She wore elaborate five-branched earrings made of silver and turquoise beads, and a necklace of silver plates engraved with the same geometric symbols as her tattoos.

The Warriors were shouting below the ramparts, and the women above were calling back to them. Merrivale could not understand the words, but by their tone of voice they were not exchanging compliments. He realised that his tabard was torn in several places and stained with blood where he'd touched it with his shredded fingertips. He folded his hands and bowed to the woman in front of him.

'*Salaam*,' he said in Arabic. 'I am Simon Merrivale, herald to the Earl of Derby from England, and these are my companions. I beg you to take us under your protection.'

The woman did not move. 'I am Kahina, the lady of the Hisn al-Nājmi. What have you done to offend the Warriors of the Faithful?'

Merrivale groped for the words. 'It is a long story,' he said.

'It can wait,' Kahina said. 'First, let us rid ourselves of these vermin.'

She strode up onto the ramparts and looked down. 'Zayani!' she shouted in Arabic. 'You have no right to be here! Go!'

Zayani shouted back at her in Tamazight, but she cut him off with a swift motion of her hand. 'Do not use our speech! You are no true Amazigh, you foresworn pig! I will not hear our language sullied by your black tongue. Depart!'

'Return my prisoners to me!' Zayani snarled. 'They killed some of my men!'

'Then they have merit in my eyes, Zayani. Have you forgotten that *you* took something that was *mine*? The life of my husband, your own *amir*, whom you betrayed?'

Silence. The woman raised her voice again. 'My patience is at an end, Zayani. You are trespassing on *my* ground. Leave now, or I shall order my soldiers to shoot.'

The other women raised their bows. Zayani snapped an order and his men retreated back down the hill to their waiting horses. Everyone watched in silence as they rode back towards the mountain passes. Kahina came back into the courtyard and Merrivale bowed to her. 'Thank you, Saīda Kahina. We are in your debt.'

'Just Kahina,' she said. 'Why are you here?'

As briefly as possible, Merrivale told her about their capture at Prado del Rey and imprisonment at Zahara and Runda, and their escape. Kahina heard the story without moving. 'I am unsurprised that Zayani and his followers refused to recognise you as an ambassador,' she said at the end. 'They profess piety, but they practise its opposite. These days, vultures have more honour than the Warriors of the Faithful.' She paused. 'There is more to your story, I am certain, but it can wait. You need food and water, and rest.'

She turned to another woman, smaller and neat with a heart-shaped face and dark eyes with beautiful long lashes. 'Jidji, you and Yufayyur will see that our guests have everything that they need. Take them to the bathhouse, and afterwards, send food to them.'

Eleanor made a sudden movement. 'My apologies,' Merrivale said, bowing again. 'I should have explained that one of my companions is a woman. May I present the lady Eleanor, sister of my master, the Earl of Derby.'

Kahina's mouth curved in a hard smile. 'There really is much more to your story,' she said. '*Salaam, saīda.* Jidji will care for you. Welcome, all of you, to the Hisn al-Nājmi. The Castle of the Stars.'

—

The Hisn al-Nājmi was not just a castle; it was a small town, set within strong walls with its own little fortified *qasaba* and the great keep at its heart. Within the *qasaba* was a bathhouse which Eleanor visited first, followed by the three men. When they emerged from the bath they found that their clothes, dirty and torn, had been taken away and replaced by soft robes and trousers of light wool and soft leather shoes.

'Your garments will be cleaned and mended,' said Yufayyur, the young woman who had admitted them to the postern. 'Meanwhile you must eat and rest.'

The guesthouse to which she conducted them was next to the tower. Servants brought food, olives and raisins and almonds, flatbread sizzling from the fire and cubes of grilled mutton, with a pitcher of clear cold water. Merrivale glanced down at the plain far below, and thought about the water mine at Runda. 'Who brings the water up from below?' he asked.

'No one,' said Yufayyur. 'We have a well here in the *qasaba*. God provides for those who have faith.'

'Where is the lady Eleanor?'

'She has been given her own quarters. Rest now. You will see her again this evening.'

Too exhausted to object, they slept through the heat of the day. As evening fell, the call to prayer seeped into Merrivale's dreams; for a moment he thought he was back in Runda, until he awoke fully and looked around. His clothes were folded neatly beside his cot, laundered and mended; the rents in his surcoat had been repaired so skilfully that he could barely find them. Ficaris and Warin were still sleeping in the next room. He dressed and pulled on his boots and stepped outside.

The western sky flamed like a furnace. Dusk, bat-like, moved in silently from the east. Vesper, the evening star, glimmered in the west, waiting to greet the half-moon drifting across the sky. Two lemon trees stood on the far side of the courtyard, perfuming the air. The soft chants of prayer drifted through the *qasaba*. Up on the walls the sentinels knelt too, bowing their heads. All of them, so far as he could see, were women.

The prayers finished, and the sentinels resumed their posts. Yufayyur walked into the courtyard. 'Kahina wishes to speak with you. Come.'

She led the way into the keep and upstairs to a big chamber with high, horseshoe-arched windows facing north across the plain. Silver oil lamps cast a mellow light across the room. Bright tapestries in patterns of red and blue and black hung on the walls.

Kahina sat cross-legged on a cushion. To Merrivale's mild surprise, Eleanor was already there, dressed in an ankle-length white robe with a veil across her hair. Jidji sat beside her.

Merrivale folded his hands and bowed. '*Salaam*,' said Kahina. 'Be seated.'

Still stiff from riding without a saddle, Merrivale sat on another cushion and folded his legs.

'I am curious,' he said. 'Are there only women in this place?'

'There are a few men,' said Kahina. 'Old men, or boys, or those crippled in war. Our muezzin is one of those. But most are women, yes, and they do most of the work, including fighting. Does this surprise you?'

'A little,' Merrivale admitted. 'Women do sometimes command armies in the nations of the north, but it is not usual.'

'Unlike the Arabs, we Imazighen hold women in high esteem. Some of our people are like Yufayyur, whose husband is in the sultan's army near the Jebel Tāriq. Others are widows like Jidji, whose husband was killed three years ago at the battle of the Salt River, the Río Salado. Now, they are warriors too.'

Eleanor looked at Jidji. 'I am sorry about your husband,' she said.

Jidji bowed her head for a moment. 'He is in God's hands.'

'I established Teba as a place of refuge,' said Kahina. 'I first came here ten years go, after my husband's murder.'

'Teba?' Merrivale asked.

'Teba is the name of the town outside. The *qasaba* is known as the Castle of the Stars.'

'And who is it that you seek refuge from?'

Kahina smiled a little. 'I too have a long story,' she said. 'My full name is Damya bint Hamou Tin Mal, and I come from an ancient and noble clan of the Imazighen. In the past our family, the Miknasi, were very powerful. We ruled Sijilmasa for two hundred years, and had our own mosque in Tamurrakušt. But my father's generation rebelled against the sultan, and we were forced to flee to Garnāta.'

Juan Moreno had mentioned Sijilmasa; the caravans passed through there. 'Just like the Warriors of the Faithful,' Merrivale said.

Again, the hint of a smile. 'Saīdi Merrivale, we *were* the Warriors of the Faithful. My husband's father, Uthman ben Abi al-Ula, commanded the Imazighen in the service of the sultan of Garnāta, here at Teba. Down at the bottom of the hill they killed one of the greatest of your Christian knights, the Saīdi Jims Duhglas of Skutlanda, who was fighting for Castile. Do you know of him?'

'Sir James Douglas? The Black Douglas? I met him once,' Merrivale said. 'That is to say, I fought with him once.'

He saw the respect in her green eyes. 'You crossed swords with Duhglas? That is honour indeed.'

'It was very brief,' Merrivale said. It was, in fact, one of the images that haunted his dreams: himself as a young man attending on an equally young King Edward during a disastrous campaign against Scotland; midnight when all of the camp was asleep, the canvas wall of the royal pavilion slashed open and a big man in armour with a red heart on his surcoat, striding in with upraised sword. Merrivale had jumped in front of the king, raising his own sword in defence, and Douglas had struck him a blow so powerful that it knocked him to the other side of the pavilion and stretched him winded on the floor. His intervention had bought enough time for the guards to come rushing in and drive Douglas back, but it had been a near thing.

'Duhglas fought like a lion, and died a hero's death,' Kahina said. 'My husband and his father were so impressed that they sent his body back to his own people, to be buried with honour. In the end, the Castilians took Teba and the Castle of the Stars but they could not hold them, and the place became deserted. Uthman also died not long after the siege and my husband, Musa ben Uthman, became *amir*. But there was bad blood between him and Zayani, and three years later Zayani killed him and proclaimed himself *amir*. I fled here to save my own life. Over time, hundreds of others have joined me.'

'Has Zayani attacked you?' asked Eleanor.

'Several times, but his men shed fountains of their own blood, and he could not prevail. He knows better now than to plunge his hand into this hornet's nest. He cannot harm us, but equally, the Warriors of the Faithful are too strong for us to harm them. Zayani has many men at his command, and some say he aspires to be more powerful than Sultan Yūsuf. He professes to be a man of faith, but he is inflamed with pride and ambition.'

'Yes.' Merrivale thought for a moment. 'Kahina… May I ask what that name means?'

'Kahina was a queen of the Imazighen, centuries ago, who fought for our independence. The people called me by this name when they chose me as their leader. I accepted it as God's will.'

'Kahina, I know little of the will of God, but I do recognise the hand of man at work when I see it. Are you aware that the Warriors of the Faithful are in league with the Knights of Calatrava?'

Slowly, ominously, Kahina crossed her arms over her chest. 'Tell me what you know,' she said.

Merrivale did so. 'I swear that this is the truth,' he said at the end.

'Once, we were true to our sultan and to God,' Kahina said. 'But by selling his own people into slavery, by betraying Garnāta and making common cause with the scavengers of Calatrava, Zayani has profaned the name of the Warriors of the Faithful forever.'

'We will kill him,' said Yufayyur.

'I swore to kill Zayani to avenge my husband,' Kahina said. 'Ten years have passed, and I am no nearer the mark. But now, I perceive it is written. The time has come to send Zayani into the abyss, where he will burn forever.' She rose to her feet. 'Go now. I must pray to God for guidance. We will speak of this again tomorrow.'

–

Thirty miles away in Runda, Hamou Ou Akka ibn Zayani stood in the garden of the *qasaba*, arms folded across his chest and face rigid with anger. Pero de Garcíez and Donato de' Peruzzi faced him.

'They are gone beyond my reach,' Zayani said. 'That hellspawn in Teba has defied me again, and I am powerless to stop her.'

'Powerless?' demanded Peruzzi. 'The great *amir* of the Warriors of the Faithful, powerless to stop a woman? You have failed me, Zayani. Now Merrivale is free and doubtless on his way to al-Ghaba.'

'Let him go,' Zayani snapped. 'He will find nothing. I cleared up your mess, Garcíez, several months ago.'

'What do you mean?' Garcíez demanded.

'You were supposed to kill Kāsim and all of his followers, but instead you decided you needed the money, and sold them. When I discovered this, I made sure the original orders were carried out. The evidence has been erased from the earth. Merrivale will find nothing because there is nothing to find.'

'You do not know Merrivale,' Peruzzi said. 'Not even he would expend so much time and energy to rescue a slave. He knows more about our plans than you think, and you, Zayani, let him escape.'

There was a moment of silence. 'Both of you have failed me,' Peruzzi said. 'How will you rectify this situation?'

'I will send men to find Merrivale,' Zayani said sullenly. 'And I will give orders for the next caravan. Ibn al-Rāzī will make the preparations.'

'Ibn al-Rāzī can be trusted?'

'We are paying him very well.'

'Good. Inform me when the caravan has departed. Garcíez, the time is come for the next stage of the plan. Ride to Córdoba and make yourself known to Queen María. Tell her the story we agreed, and win her over to our side. This is of the utmost importance.'

Garcíez bowed his head. 'It shall be done,' he said. 'I will not fail you again.'

17

30th of September, 1343

Comatose with exhaustion, Merrivale had slept heavily during the previous day, but that night he could not sleep. His back ached and his lacerated fingers throbbed faintly. He lay staring into the darkness, trying not to force himself to sleep, and failing.

In the small hours he rose and walked out into the courtyard and went up onto the walls. The sentinels recognised him and did not disturb him. He leaned on the ramparts, breathing in the cold air of the mountains. The wind had died away; all was still. The plain to the north was steeped in blackness.

Overhead the stars bloomed in their thousands, sharp and clear, so close that in his imagination he could reach out and touch them. Teba seemed to hang suspended in the air, with the rest of the world far below. Brilliant as the breath of God, the Milky Way spanned the sky with an arch of pale fire. He gazed at it for a long time, not feeling the cold, trying to clear his mind.

Someone had once told him that the spirits who guide souls to heaven dwelt among those clustered stars. He hoped that those spirits had taken good care of Sifredo de Berriz and Juan Moreno. They had been two of a kind, Sifredo and Juan: pious, selfless, determined. The world was poorer without them. Peiro d'Iguna had been a good man too. And then, there was Philippe…

He reached into his coat and took out the two little crucifixes, resting them in the palm of his hand. The wooden one was dark, inert. The rock salt crystals in the other caught the starlight and twinkled in dim reflection. Hag-ridden, hallucinating a little with lack of sleep, he imagined for a moment that it was alive.

A motion caught the corner of his eye and he turned to see Eleanor climbing up onto the ramparts, wrapped in a cloak. She stood for a moment, looking at the majesty of the night sky. 'It is easy to see why it is called the Castle of the Stars,' she said after a while. 'This is probably as close to heaven as I will ever get.'

Merrivale smiled a little. She turned to him. 'I see you couldn't sleep either.'

'No.'

'I don't need to ask why. You are reproaching yourself for the death of Sifredo.'

'I dislodged the stone that blinded him and killed him.'

'Sifredo was Navarrese, and knew his way around the mountains. He should have known that you never climb directly beneath someone else. I learned as much on Clougha Pike when I was a girl.'

Merrivale did not answer at first. Light was growing in the east, cold and grey at first, quickly brightening to a smoky rose. 'That does not absolve me of responsibility,' he said finally.

'Perhaps not. Yes, Sifredo died because of your actions. But Jac, Warin and myself are alive, also because of your actions. Had you not led us up those cliffs, we would all be dead.'

'It was I who put you in danger in the first place,' Merrivale said. 'I led you into the trap, because I thought I could outwit Garcíez. It's not just Sifredo, it is young Peiro too, and Diago and the other slaves in the water mine. If I had never been born, they would be alive.'

'That is too metaphysical for me, especially at this hour of the morning,' Eleanor said. 'You took risks, Simon. You had to, and you must continue to do so.'

The rosy light was turning to orange, bright as fire behind the mountains. The air around them stirred with sound; the muezzin in the mosque behind them, calling people to the Fajr, the dawn prayer. *Come to prayer, come to prayer. Prayer is better than sleep.* Merrivale looked down at the crucifixes in his hand. 'What do I do with these?'

'What you promised to do,' she said. 'Find Mauro, and give him what is rightfully his. Return Sifredo's crucifix to his lover, and hope that it gives her consolation. "Now make no more lament, but come away with me and I will show you the thing in the world that you love best."'

The quote was from *Aucassin and Nicolette*; it was both ridiculous and apposite. Despite his mood he could not help but laugh a little. 'And what is that thing?'

'Your duty, of course,' she said a little impatiently. 'It is what you live for. I remember you very well from Flanders, my friend. You would walk through hell, if your duty commanded it.'

Merrivale looked at the crucifixes again. 'Perhaps it does,' he said. 'You are right, or rather, Nicolette was right. We cannot remake the past. All we can do is live through the present, and hope that the future does not require too much in terms of atonement.'

Eleanor said nothing. The east was brilliant with gold. Land and sky were all hushed, as if waiting for some mighty event. It came; in Merrivale's imagination a trumpet called and the sun burst over the rim of the world, sharp rays shining between the mountains to light up the keep and ramparts and minaret. A few moments longer and light flooded over the plains far below, pushing the twilight back and making the plain itself glow like gold.

He put the crucifixes back into his coat and turned to Eleanor. 'Enough of my travails,' he said. 'What about you? Have you had time to think about what you want to do?'

She pursed her lips a little. 'I had plenty of time to think, while we were in Runda. About what I wanted to do if we survived… And in truth, I never doubted that we *would* survive. I had faith in you, even if you have so little in yourself.'

'Thank you,' he said bleakly. 'Have you come to any conclusions?'

'No,' she said, and there was a world of bitter meaning in that syllable.

He did not press the matter. The sun climbed higher, its warmth glowing on his skin. Ficaris climbed up onto the ramparts, scratching his head and yawning. 'There you are. Warin is looking for you.' He grinned a little. 'He doesn't like letting either of you out of his sight.'

'He is right,' Eleanor said. 'I'm not sure we are safe to be let out on our own.'

'Also, Kahina has sent a message. She wants to speak with us later this morning. Can we trust her, Simon?'

'We must,' Merrivale said. 'We have no one else. The real question is, can she trust us?'

The night's cold had been burned away and heat haze was blurring the horizon by the time Kahina's servants showed them up to her room in the tower. Buzzards circled slowly overhead, wheeling in the dry, exalted air.

As before, Kahina sat cross-legged on a cushion. Jidji and Yufayyur were with her. 'Tell me more about this collusion between the Warriors of the Faithful and the Knights of Calatrava,' Kahina said.

'So far as I can tell, it started as a commercial transaction,' Merrivale said. 'Each side was allowed to raid each other's lands for slaves, and they divided the profit between them. However, things have since become more complex. We think Queen María is planning to overthrow her husband and kill her rival, Leonor de Guzmán. Leonor is gathering her own forces, and the Knights are supporting her. This makes me wonder if Zayani and the Warriors of the Faithful will also become involved.'

Kahina sat for a moment, green eyes full of thought. 'Perhaps,' she said finally. 'But I believe Zayani has other interests.'

'What do you mean?'

'Sultan Yūsuf's palace in Garnāta is called al-Qal'a al-Hamrā, the Red Fortress. The sultan has two favoured concubines, Rīm and Buthayna, and behind the walls of the al-Hamrā they are engaged in a struggle for power every bit as deadly as the one you have described in Castile. Rīm believes she has the support of the sultan himself. To counter her, Buthayna has turned to Zayani and the Warriors of the Faithful. With their support, she will attempt to take control of the palace and put her own son on the throne.' Her eyes were sombre. 'The last three sultans of Garnāta were assassinated. Yūsuf may soon be the fourth.'

'Do you know of Donato de' Peruzzi?' Merrivale asked.

She looked puzzled by the change of subject. 'I have heard the name. King Alfonso's new banker, it is said.'

'He is much more than that. I detect his hand behind both of these plots. He has influence over Leonor. And Pero de Garcíez, one of the Knights, is Peruzzi's creature and is also close to Zayani. He is deeply involved in the slave trade.'

Kahina's eyes were intent now. 'You know this man.'

'I know how dangerous he is. I intend to stop him.' Merrivale paused for a moment. 'You mentioned that your family had once been lords of Sijilmasa. That is where the caravans go, is it not?'

'Yes,' said Kahina. 'All of the caravans from south and north converge on Sijilmasa.'

'Do you know of a man named Kāsim al-'Aswad?'

'When I was younger I knew him well. We both come from the same clan, the Miknasi.'

'Will you tell me a little about him?'

'He values money more than honour, I think. He rose from a poor family in the mountains to become one of the lords of the caravans, a man of wealth and power. That was after my own family went into exile, but still we heard of him. For a time, he controlled much of the salt trade across the desert.'

'And he brought gold back to Murrākush,' Merrivale said. 'And at least some of that gold came to Garnāta, and into the hands of Zayani. He is keeping it at his castle of Suhayl. Could he be using this gold to finance Buthayna's revolt?'

'He could,' Kahina said finally. 'In which case, this situation is much more dangerous than I imagined.'

'Are the salt mines of Garnāta under royal control, like those of Castile?' Eleanor asked.

'Yes,' said Kahina. 'Which means that the gold belongs to the sultan. How is it ending up in Zayani's hands?'

'Peruzzi is behind this,' said Merrivale. 'I am certain of it. Kāsim, who ran the caravans, was captured by the Knights of Calatrava and sold as a slave, along with his household. One of them, a man called Mauro, knows some of the secrets of the trade. We know this because people have been trying desperately to stop us from finding him.'

'Where is this Mauro?'

'At La Algaba, near Córdoba.'

'Al-Ghaba. I know of it. My husband used to raid around there. But why do you need Mauro? If you find Kāsim, surely he will tell you everything.'

'But Mauro has been wrongfully enslaved,' Eleanor said, before Merrivale could speak. She recounted Moreno's story and the events that had happened since his murder. Kahina watched Merrivale's face as Eleanor spoke, her eyes full of respect. At the end she nodded.

'A tiny handful of you came to a foreign land, risking danger and death, to rescue a man you have never met? That is noble.'

'I made a promise,' Merrivale said.

'We all did,' said Eleanor.

Merrivale glanced at her for a moment. 'And, of course, everything leads to the same place,' he said. 'If we can set Mauro free, we hope he can give us evidence against Garcíez. And if we can find Garcíez and force him to confess his role in the plot, or plots, he in turn can help us to bring down Peruzzi.'

'You are what we call *imjahden yef teydemnt*, warriors for justice,' Kahina said. 'When do you depart for al-Ghaba?'

Merrivale looked out across the plain to the north. 'With your permission, we will rest today. Tomorrow morning, we will go.'

'Good,' said Kahina. 'As I said, I know where al-Ghaba is. I shall guide you there.'

Back downstairs, Eleanor turned to Merrivale. 'It seems we have won her trust,' she said.

'Yes. You made no promise to find Mauro.'

'Not to you,' she said. 'I told you, I had plenty of time to think at Runda. I did come to one conclusion.'

'This is not your fight.'

Eleanor looked down her nose at him. 'Peruzzi threatens England. May I remind you that I am of royal blood? I too have a responsibility, Simon. As I told you at Xerez, if you try to leave me behind, I will follow you.' She turned to Ficaris. 'We will need weapons. Ask the Imazighen if they can provide them.'

Kahina's warriors had plenty of weapons, and were more than willing to share them. Long straight cutting swords with razor-sharp blades were brought for Ficaris and Warin. Yufayyur presented Merrivale with another sword and a dagger with a cabochon turquoise in its pommel, but he shook his head.

'I need only a wooden staff,' he said. 'If you have any whitewash, I would be grateful if you would paint it.'

Yufayyur's heart-shaped face was blank with astonishment, but she folded her hands and went off to find a staff. A dagger was offered to Eleanor, too.

'*Tannemirt*,' she said. She looked at Ficaris. 'Tell them what I really want is a crossbow.'

The women stared at her, brown faces full of surprise. Jidji brought a crossbow and a leather quiver full of quarrels. 'Do you know how to use this, *saīda?*'

Eleanor put her foot in the stirrup and drew the bow. Cocking it, she fitted a quarrel into the groove, and reached up and pulled a green lemon from the tree above her, which she handed to Jidji. 'Throw it,' she said.

Jidji threw the lemon high into the air. Eleanor raised the crossbow, sighted briefly and squeezed the trigger. A black streak flew through the air and pierced the lemon. Lemon juice flashed in the sunlight, and bolt and lemon dropped with a thud onto the cobbles.

The women shouted with delight. Laughing, Jidji pointed at Eleanor's fair hair. 'We shall call you Tizemt,' she said. 'The lioness. If you wish, we can tattoo the name onto your body. Your hand, perhaps, or your face.'

'Thank you, Jidji,' Eleanor said gravely. 'Perhaps later, once I have earned this honour.'

The women dispersed, still bubbling with excitement. 'That was a very fine shot,' Merrivale said.

Eleanor smiled. 'Don't ask me to do it again,' she said.

1st of October, 1343

They departed at first light the following morning, Merrivale and his three companions, and Kahina, Jidji and Yufayyur armed with swords; Jidji and Yufayyur also had bows and quivers slung over their backs. They went on foot because, as Kahina explained, they would be travelling through wild lands and it was easier for a small company on foot to go unnoticed. It was harder to hide horses, and they also kicked up dust and left more noticeable tracks. They carried their own food and waterskins too, because many of the wells and streams were brackish.

Down on the plain, away from the mountain heights, the air was dry and hot. They covered their heads and faces with turbans and walked on through a desolate landscape, empty even of ruins. Kahina was certain that Zayani would have left watchers at Teba. She often turned to look behind them, checking for signs of pursuit, and sometimes Jidji or Yufayyur peeled off and circled around to see if anyone was following them, but they saw no one. The only other forms of life were the carrion birds circling overhead.

As evening drew down they halted beside a salt lagoon where flamingos stood in the shallows, feeding their young. Their honking cries filled the silence. 'Do we light a fire?' asked Ficaris.

'No,' said Kahina. 'Fires might attract Zayani's men, but they could also attract wolves. These plains are full of them.'

Dinner was a few handfuls of olives and raisins, washed down with water. As night fell they wrapped themselves in blankets and lay down on the hard ground. The moon, three-quarters full, hung above the horizon, and as it rose higher the wolves began to howl. Rolling over, Merrivale saw Ficaris rise to his feet. 'Jac?' he murmured. 'Where are you going?'

'Privy,' Ficaris whispered. 'I ate too many raisins.'

'Be careful.'

Ficaris picked up his sword. He was back five minutes later, lying down and beginning to snore almost at once. Merrivale lay in silence, watching the shadows on the silver face of the moon.

—

The next day they walked on through the heat, checking the ground behind them but seeing no one. Clouds of flies appeared, buzzing around them and landing on their hands and faces. Heat waves danced all around them.

Towards the end of the day the road skirted a clump of hills, slopes littered with the grey stumps of cut-down olive trees, and came to the ruins of a small town with crumbling walls and a larger, roofless building at the centre. Looking inside, they saw a tiled *mihrab* with a horseshoe arch, empty save for a smashed statue of the Virgin Mary; a mosque which had been converted into a church, and now was neither.

'Who desecrated this place?' Warin asked.

'It looks like both sides did,' said Ficaris.

A stone tower stood at the top of the hill. Hot sunlight glinted off the helmets of men on the battlements. They walked towards it cautiously, and someone hailed them from the battlements as they approached. 'That's close enough,' the voice said in Castilian. 'State your business.'

'I am Simon Merrivale, herald to the Earl of Derby,' Merrivale said. 'We seek shelter for the night.'

'Are those Moors with you?'

'They are.' The story he and Kahina agreed was close enough to the truth. 'They seek members of their family who have been enslaved. They wish to ransom them back.'

'Ransom?' The man on the battlements spat. 'No ransom for Moors! *All* Moors should be slaves. Take those filth away from here!'

They found shelter instead in the ruined mosque-turned-church. There was nothing with which to make a fire, but down here on the plains the nights were still warm; they ate and drank, and stretched out on the tiled floor to sleep.

—

In the morning as they prepared to depart, Ficaris walked over to the smashed statue and picked up a fragment of the Virgin's robes. He stood for a moment with his back to Merrivale, holding it in his hands. 'Why?' he asked.

'Why what?' asked Eleanor.

'Killing people, for greed or hate or religion or whatever reason, I understand. But why destroy statues? They do no harm.'

Kahina was listening, and Merrivale suddenly realised that she spoke good Castilian. 'In the eyes of our faith, that statue is an idol to be worshipped. It contradicts the belief that God is the only god.'

Ficaris laid the fragment on the floor. 'Three centuries ago, in Córdoba and Sevilla, Christians, Muslims and Jews lived together in harmony. They respected each other's customs, even adopted some of them. Muslims and Christians drank wine together in monastic refectories, and Muslim musicians played sacred music in Christian churches. Where did we go wrong, Kahina?'

'We started to think more about what separates us, and less about what we have in common,' Kahina said.

Eleanor frowned. 'Can we rediscover that sense of unity, do you think?'

'No,' said Kahina. 'The hourglass of time does not run backwards. Come, we must go.'

The others walked outside. Merrivale lingered a moment, looking down at the carved fragment. A small Σ symbol had been scratched into its surface. Thoughtfully, he followed the others out into the streets of the ruined town.

The mountains were dim shapes on the southern horizon now, and they walked on under an enormous pale sky devoid of clouds. The sun was a bronze ball, hammering them with heat. Finally, they came to more cultivated lands and saw fields of golden corn, unharvested, and groves of trees with fruit lying on the ground. Some of these groves had been cut down too, quite recently, judging by the colour of the hacked wood. They passed skeletons of cattle in the fields, and once or twice, the bones of people. A village had been levelled almost to the ground, its well filled with stones; wild dogs fought among the ruins. They walked on in grim silence.

Around midday, Jidji dropped back again to check to see if they were being followed. She did not reappear.

Late in the afternoon, white shapes appeared through the heat waves ahead, gradually resolving themselves into a deserted town beside a shallow river. They knelt on the riverbank, refilling their waterskins. Kahina stood looking south, the direction Jidji had gone. Her face had not changed expression, but Merrivale could tell she was worried.

'This place is called Istigga,' she said. 'Écija, the Castilians call it. My husband attacked this place once, many years ago.'

Merrivale looked at the devastation around them: felled olive trees, burned mills on the riverbank with their millstones broken beside them, broken walls streaked brown with old dried blood. 'Did your husband do this?' he asked.

Kahina did not answer. 'In old times, the Warriors of the Faithful plundered their enemies,' Yufayyur replied. 'They took slaves. But they did not destroy, not like this.'

'This is Zayani's work,' Kahina said finally. Her brown face was taut, the tattoo stretched across her forehead. 'Only he is capable of this kind of hatred.'

A shape came out of the heatwaves: Jidji, arriving on the run. 'We are being followed,' she panted. 'Fourteen Warriors of the Faithful, on foot, about two miles behind us.'

'Can we fight them?' asked Warin.

'Too many,' Kahina said. 'Let us lose them instead.'

'Get into the river,' said Merrivale.

The river was shallow, barely enough to wet their boots, but the water flowed fast over a stony bed and would obliterate any tracks they left behind. They splashed past the broken ramparts of the town, under an ancient stone bridge and on until they came to the confluence with a smaller stream tumbling out of a range of low hills to the east. They turned and followed this for another mile, climbing steadily over wet rocks, and scrambled up a steep slope covered in dry grass to the crest of the nearest hill. Here they lay flat, watching the fields to the south. Flies droned around them, looking for exposed skin.

After a long time, Jidji pointed. 'Here they come.'

Down on the plain, tiny black-robed figures emerged from the heat waves and moved cautiously towards the ruined town.

Reaching the river, they gathered for a moment and then divided, half of them moving in to search the town, the others following the course of the river. From the hilltop they watched as the Warriors moved on north and, once the enemy were out of sight, slid down the far side of the hill and rose cautiously to their feet.

'Is that all of them?' asked Warin.

Kahina shook her head. 'It is impossible to say. Like ourselves, Zayani's men will be relying on stealth rather than numbers, but... there may well be others out there in the haze.'

'They know we are going to La Algaba,' Merrivale said. He wiped the sweat from his face. 'My original plan was to approach by night, but now I fear an ambush.' He turned to Kahina. 'How much further?'

'Twenty miles,' she said. 'There is a town called Palma del Río on the banks of the Nahr al-Kebr, which the Castilians call the Guadalquivir. Al-Ghaba is on high ground east of the town.'

Merrivale looked at the sun swimming down into the west, burning red and streaked with dark bars of haze. 'We'll need to make camp soon,' he said. 'Tomorrow, let's circle around to the east and make camp again, close to La Algaba. We can scout during the night, and if it is safe, make our approach in the morning.'

'Good,' said Kahina. She chuckled a little. 'You are crafty, Simon Merrivale. You would make a good Amazigh warrior.'

'I used to be a King's Messenger,' Merrivale said. 'I imagine it is much the same thing.'

The sun set in fire, its afterglow fading quickly. An enormous full moon popped over the eastern horizon, gliding up through the blossoming stars. They made camp in an oak grove, still not risking a fire. The night was warm and humid, the air buzzing with the songs of cicadas. As he lay down to sleep, Merrivale put a hand inside his tunic and touched the two crucifixes he carried. He thought briefly about praying, and decided against it.

The following day, the fourth of October, brought them to a rolling plain cut across by watercourses running down to the west, many of them dry. During the morning they saw herds of goats in the distance and they gave these a wide berth, not wanting to attract the attention of the herdsmen. By midday the heat was intense once more, and sheets of shimmering mirage covered the horizon. The plain stretched around them, vast and empty and silent.

Late in the afternoon the heat waves and mirage subsided a little, revealing a low hill to the northwest. Shading his eyes against the sun, Merrivale thought he could make out the shapes of buildings on its crest. 'That is al-Ghaba,' Kahina said.

'This is close enough,' said Merrivale. He pointed to another watercourse. 'We will make camp down there.'

Down by the stream bed they found water gurgling among the rocks and refilled their waterskins again. The evening meal was, once again, olives and raisins with a few roasted almonds. Merrivale looked at Kahina. 'You say your husband raided around here. Is that how you know where La Algaba is?'

'Sometimes I came with him.' The corners of her mouth twitched a little. 'We were young, and in love.'

'I thought that until a few years ago Castile and Garnāta were at peace.'

'Peace has different definitions,' Kahina said.

That was certainly true; on England's borders with Scotland, even in times of truce men on both sides still tried to steal each other's cattle. 'If we find evidence that shows Zayani is colluding with your enemies, what will you do?'

Kahina watched the setting sun. 'I do not know,' she said finally. 'I have few allies in Garnāta. I have been on the frontier at Teba for so long that most people have forgotten me.'

'What about the *hajib*? Abū Nu'aym Ridwan?'

She wrinkled her nose. 'Abū Nu'aym is a subtle man who has served three sultans, and survived the murders of two of them. He always takes care to be on the winning side. Would he support me against someone so powerful as Zayani? I do not know.'

'There is the Grandmother,' Jidji suggested. 'She has no love for Zayani.'

'The Grandmother?' said Eleanor.

'Sultana Fātima bint Muhammad bint al-Ahmar,' Yufayyur said. 'The grandmother of Sultan Yūsuf. She and Abū Nu'aym were regents of Garnāta during the sultan's youth. She would not be pleased to learn that Zayani is plotting against her grandson.'

'Or that he is stealing gold that rightly belongs to the sultan,' Merrivale said.

'Do you know the Grandmother?' Eleanor asked Kahina.

'We were friends once,' Kahina said slowly. 'But it was a long time ago.'

—

Just before dawn, in the yellow light of the setting moon, Jidji and Yufayyur went out to scout. They returned at sunrise. 'The farm is deserted and in ruins. We saw no one save for a goatherd.'

There was a moment of silence. 'Let us go and see,' Merrivale said.

They stalked La Algaba like hunters, going forward slowly in a dispersed line with Jidji and Yufayyur on the wings with arrows on the nock and Eleanor in the centre with Merrivale, her crossbow raised. As they approached through the morning sun, Merrivale saw a familiar scene: a roofless manor house, barns with collapsed walls, the charred ruins of a windmill, the piled skeletons of cattle that had been slaughtered rather than driven away.

The goats were still there, grazing in the pasture beside the manor. There was no sign of the goatherd. Frowning, Merrivale walked through the ruins and saw the prints of sandalled feet in the dust. Entering the manor house, he found the man kneeling in what had been the chapel, hands over his head. 'Please! For the love of God, do not hurt me!'

'No one will hurt you,' Merrivale said, resting the butt of his staff on the ground.

'The Moors! You have brought Moors with you!'

'No one will hurt you,' Merrivale repeated. 'All I want is information. Do you know what happened here?' The man hesitated, shivering. 'Tell me what happened,' Merrivale said. 'Then you may go back to your flock.'

'The Moors came, a few months ago. They destroyed everything and took the people away.'

'Everyone? The slaves included?'

'Yes. They took them to Palma del Río.'

'And after that? They took their captives back to Granada?'

'They are at Palma del Río,' the man said, and he shivered again.

Back outside, Merrivale looked at the others 'Kahina and I will go,' he said. 'Jidji, Yufayyur, keep watch for Zayani's men. The rest of you wait here. The goatherd may depart in peace.'

Palma del Río was two miles away at the foot of the hill. The Río Guadalquivir, green and serene, flowed smoothly past its walls. The little town was blackened by fire, empty of signs of life; only ghosts lived here now. They walked through the marketplace and out of the western gate where groves of oranges stretched beside the river, and stopped.

'Mary, Mother of God,' Merrivale said under his breath.

Skeletons lay sprawled beneath the trees, scores of them – no, hundreds. Long grass grew around their bones and up through their ribcages. Oranges fallen from the trees overhead lay next to them, shining bright like grave goods. The bones were still very white and new, only recently picked clean by scavengers. Many showed signs of violence, missing arms or smashed skulls. A long trail of bones through the orange trees showing how some of the victims had tried to flee and been cut down.

At the end of the trail, a final skeleton lay on its back. It was impossible to tell the identity of the person who had died here, but the skull had been severed from the torso by a blow that had shattered the vertebrae in the neck. An orange had fallen into one of the skull's eye sockets. The skin of the orange had burst open, and wasps buzzed around the rotting fruit. A rictus of teeth grimaced up at the canopy of trees overhead.

A light breeze rustled the leaves, whispering of souls trapped in purgatory. Merrivale reached into his coat and touched the crucifixes, offering a silent prayer for the dead.

Movement in the trees, and Kahina drew her long sword, crouching into the fighting position; but it was Jidji and Yufayyur who came running towards them. 'Zayani's men are coming.'

Kahina turned to Merrivale. 'Take your friends to safety. The Castilians have a castle at al-Mudāwar, a little way upriver. We will draw Zayani's men away.'

'Come with us and be safe,' Merrivale said. 'You will be under my protection.'

Kahina smiled, a little bitterly. 'Your protection means nothing in Castile, not for our people. Go. We have been outwitting Zayani's men for many years, and we can do it again.' She paused for a moment. 'You say Zayani is gathering gold at Suhayl. I will try to learn more.'

'We will see each other again,' Merrivale said.

'Of course. Our work is not yet done. *Ddu d Rebbi*, Simon Merrivale. Walk with God.'

18

5th of October, 1343

Quietly, Merrivale retraced his own steps through the haunted grove, skirting the walls of Palma del Río and climbing up to the hilltop where Eleanor, Ficaris and Warin waited. They saw his face, and said nothing.

'We are going to al-Mudāwar,' he said.

Ficaris nodded. 'Almodóvar,' he said. 'I remember seeing it once from the river, when I was going up to Córdoba.'

They began to walk east, following the path of the winding green river. Compared with the plains to the south, this land was lush and green. They passed an abandoned village with storks' nests in the chimneys, and saw herons and egrets wading in the river. More herds of goats grazed in the meadows. 'At some point you will have to tell us what happened,' Eleanor said finally.

Merrivale told them. 'Zayani's men took the people from La Algaba, and by the looks of it everyone from Palma del Río too, and slaughtered them in the orange grove. Men, women, children, everyone.'

Her face was pale under her sunburn. 'Why kill everyone? Why not sell them as slaves?'

'Partly to make it look like an ordinary piece of butchery and disguise their real purpose,' Ficaris said grimly. 'They didn't want anyone asking questions about why Kāsim and his people had been singled out, so they killed the others too. And partly because they didn't know who else Kāsim might have talked to, or how much he had told them.'

Merrivale said nothing. The bones at Palma del Río were at least a month old; even if he had let Garcíez go and come straight here from Xerez, he would still have been too late. Mauro was already dead. *I am sorry, Juan. I tried.*

'What do we do now, sir?' Warin asked.

Merrivale roused a little. There was nothing he could do now; Mauro would become just another of the ghosts that haunted him. 'We're going to carry out Philippe of Navarre's mission. We'll go to Córdoba and persuade Queen María to abandon her plans for revolt. If she stands down, Leonor de Guzmán and Peruzzi will have no excuse to strike at her, and they will have to reset their own plans. Once Garcíez re-emerges, and I am sure he will, we will take him. We'll use thumbscrews and the rack, if we have to, but we will force him to divulge the details of the plot.'

'And the other plots?' asked Ficaris. 'The collusion between the Knights of Calatrava and the Warriors of the Faithful? The incipient revolt in Garnāta, which Kahina thinks Zayani may be supporting?'

'One thing at a time,' Merrivale said. 'When we reach Almodóvar, let me do the talking. I am the herald of the Earl of Derby and you are my household; Eleanor, you will become Buscador once again. We were travelling upriver from Sevilla, but our boat was wrecked and we lost all of our baggage. We will ask for an escort to take us to the queen in Córdoba.'

'I have a better idea,' said Eleanor.

'Let us hear it.'

Eleanor explained. Merrivale heard her out, and nodded. 'Good. Give your crossbow and quiver to Warin. Jac, how much further to Almodóvar?'

Ficaris pointed to a distant hilltop. 'That's it on the horizon.'

—

The castle of Almodóvar crouched on a spur of rock above the north bank of the river. High walls with four square stone towers surrounded a powerful donjon. A banner flew from the donjon, the lion and towers of Castile quartered with the arms of Portugal, five blue escutcheons on a field of white. Merrivale looked at this, his eyes thoughtful.

They crossed a stone bridge and walked through a small village at the foot of the hill. A cracked church bell rang, its notes harsh and strident in the heavy air. Climbing towards the castle, they came to an outer work manned by guards with long spears and crossbows, who barred their way and demanded to know who they were.

Merrivale tapped the butt of his staff on the ground. 'I am Simon Merrivale, herald to the Earl of Derby from England. I present to you the noble lady Eleanor of Lancaster, my master's sister and cousin to King Edward of England. Our boat was wrecked in the river and we have lost our baggage. Pray let us enter, and give us sanctuary.'

The guards gaped in astonishment at the brown-faced woman with a veil over her hair. 'Are you waiting for something?' she asked crossly.

Quickly they were escorted up to the main gate, and the castellan was summoned. 'My lady, what a terrible event. Thank God you were able to escape the wreck. Where are the boat's crew?'

'I assume they have all drowned,' said Eleanor, improvising. 'If so, it will be no more than they deserve. Find me some proper clothes, if you please, and an escort to take me to Córdoba.'

'Of course, of course.' Flustered, the castellan did not think to ask why the noble lady Eleanor was wearing the clothes of a common soldier. 'I fear there are no ladies of quality here, we can only offer you a servant's gown.'

'Anything is better than these rags,' Eleanor said. 'And the escort, please. Quickly.'

The castellan spread his hands. 'The bells have just rung nones, my lady, and you would never reach Córdoba before dark. It is rumoured that there are Moorish raiders in the area. It would be wise for you to wait until morning.'

Eleanor raised her eyebrows and looked at Merrivale. 'Thank you,' the herald said. '*Señor*, we are pleased to be your guests for the night.'

'Splendid, splendid.' There was a moment of hesitation. 'We would be most honoured, my lady, if you would dine with us.'

They gathered in the hall as the sun began to descend, Eleanor in a plain gown of grey undyed wool and a white wimple over her hair, the others in their travel-worn clothes made as presentable as possible, the captain and his officers in their best coats and hose along with a Dominican friar in a black cassock. The food was plain, roast pork with a pepper sauce, grilled capons with lemon and olives and some bowls of chopped herbs accompanied by a rough red wine, but after four days on the trail, no one in Merrivale's party minded.

Conversation was stilted; some of the younger officers ate in silence, eyes down and focused on their trenchers. 'You mentioned that there might be Moors nearby,' Merrivale said to the castellan. 'Surely we are a long way from the *frontera*.'

The castellan and the Dominican friar glanced at each other. 'You are correct,' the friar said. 'But a Moorish company known as the Warriors of the Faithful keeps breaking through our defences. They have raided all the way up to the river twice this year. Many Christian lives have been lost, and much damage has been done.'

'Can the defences along the *frontera* not stop them?'

The castellan made a discreet motion with his hand. The friar ignored him. 'The defences are manned by the Knights of Calatrava. If you wish an answer to your question, *señor*, I suggest you apply to their grand master.'

Eleanor looked disapproving. 'I was informed that travel along the Guadalquivir would be perfectly safe. I am sorry to hear that it is not. I shall take up the matter with Her Grace the queen when I reach Córdoba.'

The castellan winced a little. 'Speaking of Her Grace, I note you fly a banner with the arms of Castile and Portugal together,'

Merrivale said. 'As a herald, I am curious. Is that usual practice here in Spain?'

The younger officers stared even more fixedly at their trenchers. 'As Her Grace is present in Córdoba, we of course wish to honour her,' the castellan said stiffly. 'I know of nothing in the laws of arms that prevents this.'

Much later they gathered in Eleanor's room in one of the square towers overlooking the river. 'That was rather strained,' Ficaris observed. 'Why?'

'Because they support María,' Merrivale said. 'That banner is their declaration. She is already gathering her strength.'

'How do we persuade her to abandon her revolt?' Eleanor asked.

'I don't know,' Merrivale said. 'Not yet.'

He paused for a moment, still grieving for the death of a man he had never met. 'As a King's Messenger, our first rule was always this: study the board and see where the other pieces are, before you make your own move. Let us see what we find when we reach Córdoba.'

6th of October, 1343

In the morning, the castellan provided horses and a strong escort and – not without relief, Merrivale thought – wished them a safe journey to Córdoba. The sun was casting longer shadows now and autumn was on its way, but summer was not yet done; once again the valley of the Guadalquivir rippled with heat waves as they rode.

Mid-afternoon, and out of the heat, Córdoba began to emerge. First came the ruins of an ancient palace, broken columns standing in a field of stubble; then, ahead, high crenelated walls and a long bridge spanning the river. Water mills lined the bridge, wheels churning in the current. Church towers, pale and slender, rose beyond the ramparts. At the

Puerto de Almodóvar, double walls were connected by a gatehouse larger than many castles. A big standard of painted silk with the same arms – Castile quartered with Portugal – hung limp in the windless air.

A quay ran along the waterfront just below the city walls, and several ships were moored here. One of them, drawn up alongside the quay just below the bridge, was a big galley with a catapult on a turntable and a Greek fire projector up in the bows. Another banner, red with the white cross of the Knights of Saint John, hung from her masthead. Merrivale turned and looked at Ficaris. The latter shook his head.

Passing through the gates, they rode down through narrow winding streets faced by windowless white houses. Merrivale saw the six-pointed star carved in stone over some doorways, and realised this was the *judería*. The lanes gave way to a broad stone plaza, more walls and another gate, where they dismounted.

'Farewell, *mi çaida*,' said the captain of the escort from Almodóvar. 'May God watch over the remainder of your journey.'

The escort trotted back towards the western gate. Grooms took their horses and led them away. A grey-bearded man in a long black robe, carrying a staff of office, bowed to them. '*Mi çaida*, I am Queen María's chamberlain. Tell me how I may serve you.'

'I lost my baggage and my money when our boat sank,' Eleanor said in a voice of command. 'I require adequate clothing for myself and my servants. After that, be pleased to tell Her Grace the queen that I have arrived and desire an audience with her.'

Behind the gate was the *alcázar*, a palace far larger and grander than the one in Xerez. Long pools of mirror-smooth water with little gurgling fountains stretched away to the far walls. Roses bloomed in heavy banks, overshadowed by trees; oranges brilliant with fruit, tall tapering cypresses, palm trees with spreading canopies of fronds. White walls reflected light so brilliant that it made the eyes ache. The colours, green and white and red, contrasted with the unbroken blue of the sky overhead. This contrast, Merrivale guessed, was no accident; everything in this garden, even the birds that sang in the trees, was artifice, designed to capture all the beauty the world had within it, and lay it out for the pleasure of kings and queens.

The guesthouse lay next to the south wall of the *alcázar*, and had its own tiled courtyard full of flowers in clay pots, with another fountain in the centre. Bees hummed around the flowers. On the first floor, a small refectory overlooked the courtyard, with a richly carved dark wooden table and benches; a pearwood lute stood on a side table. Servants, friendly but respectful men in loose turbans, long white tunics and trousers, brought them dishes of olives and skewers of grilled meat and candied fruits, along with brass jugs containing wine and water. Others brought clothes and, for Eleanor, some jewels and a purse of money to cover her expenses. The chamberlain bowed again.

'Her Grace bids me tell you that she is sorry for the accident that befell you on the way here, but thanks God for delivering you safely. Today you must rest, she says, and in the morning she will be pleased to grant you audience.'

After the chamberlain had gone, Merrivale turned to Ficaris. 'Did you know Fra Moriale would be here?'

'I had no idea. He said he was going to Sevilla, but he said nothing about Córdoba.'

'That was his ship in the river?' Eleanor asked.

'The *Santa Creu*, yes. Shall I find him, Simon, and ask him to join us?'

'I would imagine he will find us,' Merrivale said. 'Quite soon, too.'

Twilight drew in, the church bells tolling vespers. Eleanor summoned a servant and asked to be taken to the bathhouse. Merrivale, Ficaris and Warin rose and followed her, walking across to the men's entrance. 'A bathhouse large enough to have separate rooms for men and women,' Ficaris said as they entered reception. 'This *is* civilised.'

Warin sniffed. 'Back in England we don't bother with this nonsense. Everyone bathes together.'

'Yes,' Ficaris said. 'I'm sure they do. As I said, here we are civilised.'

The bath attendants took their clothes, giving them towels to wrap around their waists and showing them where to wash. Afterwards they were guided into the warm room, a long chamber with marble columns and painted murals on the walls, and sat down on stone benches. Wine was brought; the attendants offered manicures, which they rejected, and shaves and haircuts which they readily accepted. Merrivale leaned back and closed his eyes, listening to the snip of scissors and trying to blot out the vision of the massacre at Palma del Río. Instead, a face with a black beard and deep-set eyes swam through his mind. Haunted eyes, perhaps? he wondered. The eyes of a murderer and a regicide? Garcíez had denied killing anyone, but why had he done so? Why not boast about how well he had carried out Donato de' Peruzzi's orders?

Someone else had entered the room. Merrivale opened his eyes and looked up to see a man sitting down opposite him, a big man with a hard face bronzed by sun and wind. For once, Fra Moriale was not wearing the regalia of the Knights of Saint John, only a towel around his waist like the rest of them. Merrivale looked over at Ficaris, who reclined on a bench while an attendant shaved his chin.

'You see? I told you he would find us.'

Fra Moriale looked at Ficaris too. 'Well met, Jac. It has been some time since I heard from you.'

'I know,' Ficaris said. 'Things have become somewhat complicated.'

'Tell me.'

'Unusually for me, I will let someone else do the talking. Simon can explain better than I.'

Merrivale's barber had finished; he bowed, folding his hands, and withdrew. Merrivale summarised what had happened over the past few weeks. 'We know that salt and gold are traded between Garnāta and Murrākush, which is not surprising. We believe that Zayani is siphoning off at least some of the gold to help finance a revolt against Sultan Yūsuf by one of his concubines, and we suspect that Donato de' Peruzzi is behind this revolt, in part because Peruzzi's agent Pero de Garcíez is on good terms with Zayani. What we don't know is how that revolt links to the troubles brewing in Castile. They *are* linked, I would stake my soul on it. But we need evidence.'

'What about Queen María?' asked Fra Moriale. 'I told you last month that she is gathering gold.'

'That is one of the reasons I am here. What about you?'

Fra Moriale sat back a little. 'In Sevilla, there were more rumours. I heard about the destruction of La Algaba and the slaughter at Palma del Río. I am sorry, by the way. I rather liked Moreno, and I wished him well on his quest.'

'We all liked him,' Ficaris said.

'But it's not only Moorish raiders who are coming north. At least one caravan has come north too. No one could tell me what goods it carried, but if María is having commerce with the sultan's men, we need to know more.'

'Forgive me, sir,' said Warin, 'but wouldn't it be dangerous for Her Grace to trade with the enemy? If her supporters found out that she was trafficking with the Moors, they would disown her.'

Fra Moriale shook his head. 'They wouldn't turn a hair. Most of the *fidalgos* who follow her now are former rebels, and many of them took refuge in Garnāta. Don Juan Manuel was one of them.'

Ficaris nodded. 'They'll all have friends and contacts at the sultan's court at the al-Hamrā palace. It's been like that for centuries.'

Warin looked exasperated. 'How does anyone know whose side anyone else is on?'

'They don't,' said Fra Moriale. 'That's what makes it interesting.' He looked at Merrivale. 'Peruzzi and his friends have clearly found a replacement for Kāsim, because gold is still being brought in from Africa. My friends in Sebta sent word that another shipment had arrived and was being loaded onto a big nef. Unfortunately, when it sailed it had an escort of Garnātan galleys. The Genoese at al-Jazīra still haven't been paid and won't put to sea, and I couldn't challenge them on my own. But they landed the gold at Suhayl. I'm certain of that.'

'I want to know what happens to the gold after it reaches Suhayl,' Merrivale said. 'Kahina is attempting to find out, but it will take time. What do you intend to do?'

'I'm staying in Córdoba for a few days. I want to know more about these caravans coming north. And you?'

'I'm going to try to persuade María to abandon her revolt.'

Fra Moriale laughed. 'Good luck. What are you going to do about the lady of Lancaster?'

'That is up to her,' Merrivale said.

'God preserve us all from noblewomen with minds of their own.' Fra Moriale rose and went through into the hot room, and they heard the hiss of steam. Merrivale looked at Ficaris. 'Aren't you going with him?'

'No, thank you,' Ficaris said. 'I am content where I am.'

Merrivale studied the other man for a moment. 'What do you mean by that?'

'I mean that I have no interest in returning to Fra Moriale's service.' Ficaris paused. 'I wondered if you would consider taking me on permanently.'

'Why?'

The question was blunt, and Ficaris looked a little surprised. 'I don't entirely know,' he said slowly. 'I told you once that I have drifted for most of my life, looking for a place where I could fit in. It feels like I might have found one.'

The silence that followed lasted for a long time. Merrivale was concious of Warin's steady gaze. 'At the moment the future is too uncertain,' he said finally. 'Ask me when this is all over, Jac. I will give you my answer then.'

He saw the hurt in Ficaris's eyes. 'Is that all you can offer me?'

'I don't think you will be disappointed,' Merrivale said.

7th of October, 1343

Slender, smooth-skinned, immaculate from the gold circlet resting on her coifed hair to the tip of her red leather shoes, Queen María sat in a gilded chair, hands resting on its arms. Her blue gown was the same shade as the robes of the statue of the Madonna standing behind her throne, but to Merrivale's eyes she looked less like the Virgin and more like Alecto, the Fury who symbolised eternal anger. If her coiled hair had turned into hissing snakes, he would not have been unduly surprised.

Her attendants, men and veiled women, stood on either side of the throne. He recognised two of them. The first was a man with white hair and a close-cropped beard. He did not know the man's name, but he had seen him three times before: once in the camp at al-Jazīra, arguing with a mule dealer, again in the camp near Don Juan Manuel's house, and finally in Xerez when he had warned Merrivale not to trust Lorenço de Alameda. What he was doing here now, dressed in a physician's red robe, was an intriguing question.

The second, and Merrivale realised that he really should not have been surprised by this, was Pero de Garcíez, attired once again in white surcoat with red floretty cross. He watched Merrivale follow Eleanor of Lancaster into the room, and he smiled a little.

A gentle afternoon breeze brought the scent of roses and oranges in from the garden. The audience chamber was intricately carved with geometric designs and arabesques, painted and gilded and hung with tapestries so that it resembled the casing of a jewel designed to frame the gem itself: the cold-faced queen who sat motionless and watched them approach.

Eleanor of Lancaster robed in red silk with a veil across her own hair and borrowed rings on her fingers, knelt. Merrivale and Ficaris did likewise. 'You may rise,' the queen said. 'Are these your only attendants?'

'Yes, Your Grace,' Eleanor said. 'We are all that escaped the shipwreck.'

'You were fortunate, my lady. Stella Maris, the star of the sea, watched over you. I understand that you come from the camp at Algeciras.'

'Yes, Your Grace.'

'And how is my loving husband, El Çid Fornicador? Has he worked out yet that he is besieging the wrong town?'

Eleanor kept her composure. 'I believe not, Your Grace, but others have begun to recognise the futility of the siege. There are growing concerns about the peace of the kingdom itself.'

'Concerns?' the queen asked. 'Who has expressed these concerns?'

'My brother, the Earl of Derby, the English ambassador, for one,' said Eleanor. 'His Grace the king of Navarre for another. Tragically, King Philippe died of wounds received while fighting the Moors. May God grant him rest,' she added.

Garcíez looked straight at Merrivale. Their eyes locked for a few moments before Garcíez looked deliberately away. 'Navarre's death was a tragedy,' said the queen. 'But the fact that Alfonso's nobles hate him is hardly new. It is indeed customary for the *fidalgos* of Castile to despise their sovereign. Why did your brother and King Philippe choose to become embroiled in our quarrels?'

'This is more serious than a few disgruntled nobles,' Eleanor said. 'There is a rumour that you yourself are not entirely on good terms with the king.'

'It is not a rumour,' said the queen. 'The fact that I intend to remove my husband's genitals with a rusty razor, throw his balls into the river and tan his scrotum for use as a jewellery bag is public knowledge. Come to the point, *mi çaida*.'

She knows exactly why we are here, Merrivale thought. *What she is trying to work out now is how much we know.* He cleared his throat. 'What my lady of Lancaster means is that some of the *fidalgos* – perhaps from a sense of loyalty to you, perhaps to further their own advantage – are threatening to rebel against your husband. Their plan is to replace him with your son, the Infante Pedro, with you as regent.'

'What a charming story,' said the queen. 'It has the air of a folk tale, does it not? Did you hear it in a taverna, perhaps, or from some *juglar* by the roadside?'

Merrivale bowed. 'So, we can assure my lord of Derby and the rest of the English embassy that there is no truth to this tale?'

'Tell them whatever you like,' said the queen.

'Very well, Your Grace. May I bring one more rumour to your attention? Fearing that your adherents are about to rise against the king, Leonor de Guzmán is preparing a coup of her own, and she has enlisted the support of the Order of Calatrava. Perhaps Brother Pero de Garcíez can confirm this?'

Garcíez started to speak, but the queen held up one manicured hand, silencing him. 'I am not concerned with the king's whore,' she said. 'She will not trouble me.'

Oh? Why not? Merrivale thought. 'Leonor is dangerous, Your Grace, whatever you might think. She may well decide to remove the king herself and place one of her own children on the throne, calling on the loyal *fidalgos* and the Knights of Calatrava to back her as regent. That would mean civil war.'

'In which case she will be condemned as a traitor, and will be burned alive. It will be a time of joy and celebration, I am sure. I will say it again. Come to the point.'

Merrivale glanced at Eleanor, who nodded to him to continue. 'Knowing that Your Grace will be concerned for the welfare of your subjects,' he said, 'we suggest that you take steps to preserve the peace of the kingdom. You could, for example, make a public declaration of loyalty to the king and the Cortes of Castile. You could also return to Portugal for a time, until the present tensions have subsided. If you do this, Leonor de Guzmán will have no excuse to mount her own coup. You will cut the ground from under her feet.'

'I *will* cut—' The queen stopped, biting her lower lip. Vexation, Merrivale thought, at having given herself away. He waited while she regained her composure.

'My lady of Lancaster,' she said coldly. 'I thank you for your good offices. You have leave, of course, to remain in Córdoba for as long as you wish. If there is anything you desire for your comfort, inform my chamberlain.'

She rose and swept out of the room, followed by her attendants including the physician. Garcíez waited until they had gone, and bowed to Eleanor. 'Congratulations on your escape from Runda,' he said. 'That was very daring. I confess I did not expect you to succeed.'

'Why are you here?' Merrivale demanded.

'Do you really not understand?'

'Mauro is dead.'

'I know. I tried to tell you that in Runda.'

'You still haven't explained why you are here,' Eleanor said sharply. 'Are you also trying to make peace between the queen and King Alfonso?'

Garcíez chuckled, and for a moment his face became almost animated. 'Of course not,' he said, and he turned and walked out of the room.

19

7th of October, 1343

'She has no intention of backing down,' Ficaris said.

They were sitting in the refectory of the guesthouse, looking out over the garden. 'She is so angry that she is not thinking straight,' Merrivale said. 'The only thing in her mind is revenge.'

'And Garcíez is clearly here to support her,' said Eleanor. 'But we thought the Knights of Calatrava were backing Leonor de Guzmán.'

Warin came in, holding a small parchment roll sealed with red wax. 'This has just arrived for you, sir.'

Merrivale glanced at the seal, but did not recognise it. He broke it and read the short letter.

> *To the esteemed Magister Simon Merrivale, heraldus, Magister Dámaso Reyes sends greeting. I believe there are matters between us that we need to discuss. Meet me at the altar of San Miguel in the Cathedral of Nuestra Señora at terce.*

–

The cathedral of Nuestra Señora in Córdoba, which once had been the Great Mosque of Qurtuba, lay to the east of the *alcázar*. From the outside it was unimpressive, a big flat-roofed building surrounded by a colonnade, approached through a courtyard lined with orange trees dazzling in the sun. The interior was quiet and cool, the air smoky with incense. Silver lamps hung from the ceiling glowed softly.

A forest of pillars surrounded Merrivale. Made of porphyry with ancient carved capitals, they supported intricate double arches of banded brick and white limestone. The rows of pillars stretched away into seeming infinity. Each time Merrivale took a step, the pattern of the pillars and arches changed, almost as if they themselves were floating across the marble floor. The effect was overwhelming and he halted for a moment, feeling a little dizzy.

A sweeper passed, a man in white robe and skullcap. Merrivale stopped him. 'Where is the altar of San Miguel?' he asked.

To his surprise, the man answered in Arabic. '*Hunaka ya, saīdi*,' he said, pointing towards the south wall.

'*Shukran*.' Merrivale slowly walked through the cathedral, and the pillars in front of him gave way as he approached while more closed in behind. Near the south wall the arches became more elaborate, scalloped and carved with fine interwoven lines. Ahead lay a *mihrab*, its entrance a much larger horseshoe arch surrounded by lines of elaborate golden Arabic letters inlaid on a field of lapis. An altar had been set up in front of the *mihrab*, a painted triptych showing the archangel Michael slaying a dragon flanked by the Virgin and John the Baptist. A white-haired man in a physician's robe lit a candle and bowed his head for a moment before turning to greet Merrivale.

'At last we meet properly, *señor*,' he said smiling. 'I am Dámaso Reyes, the queen's physician.'

'You recognised me the day I arrived at al-Jazīra,' Merrivale said.

'I had been given a description of you by our mutual friend, Mercuriade of Salerno. She and I taught together at the Salerno Medical School, many years ago. She said I should look out for a man, plain, non-descript, unremarkable in face, but with a powerful soul. I spotted you at once.'

'You can see my soul?'

'Everyone's soul is visible to those who can see. "Perfection dwells within you, and it is a light that will never fail. Open your spirit to the light, and receive its wisdom."'

'Mercuriade once said those words to me. They come from the Marcosian gospel, I think. Do you share her faith?'

'Not specifically, but I esteem knowledge wherever it is found. My old friend Asach de Sharīsh, for example, opened my eyes to the writings of Maimonides as well as the *Ghāyat al-Hakīm*, and Ibn al-Rāzī the great alchemist of Granada introduced me to the works of the Brethren of Purity. It is interesting to find that Islam has its heretics, just as we Christians do. But I sometimes wonder if the heretics, who question everything, are not actually closer to the truth than those who accept it without thinking.'

'Why were you in Xerez?' Merrivale asked.

'As you have probably guessed, Queen María employs me not only as her physician but as her go-between with her supporters in the army at Algeciras. Don Juan Manuel asked me to keep an eye on your party. He was aware that King Philippe was attempting to reconcile the queen and the king, or at least prevent the queen from rebelling. Needless to say, he was anxious that this should not happen.'

'Needless to say?'

'*Señor*, one thing you must understand is that both sides badly want to fight each other. Queen María and Leonor de Guzmán desire nothing more than to gouge each other's eyes out. The urge to power is strong, but bloodlust is stronger still.'

Merrivale shook his head. 'I had taken Don Juan Manuel to be an educated man, a philosopher. I am sorry to hear that he encourages civil war.'

'He does not encourage it,' said Reyes. 'He sees it as inevitable, and he believes that María would be a better ruler for Castile than la Guzmán. Therefore, he reasons, let us have things out in the open now, finish the conflict and move on. That is one of the things I wanted to say to you. Your embassy, no matter how well-intentioned, will fail.'

'And Garcíez? Is he one of the queen's councillors?'

'Of course. Years ago, when Juan Núñez rebelled against the grand master of Calatrava, Garcíez was one of his closest supporters. When Núñez became grand master himself, Garcíez expected to be rewarded. A commandery, perhaps, or a high post in the administration of the order. Instead, he received nothing. He seeks his own revenge on Núñez.'

Merrivale nodded slowly. 'Núñez has promised Guzmán the support of the Order, but Garcíez will split the Order apart and his faction will join the queen. Another civil war within the wider conflict… Tell me, *señor*, how does the queen expect to pay for her rebellion?'

Reyes spread his hands. 'Support has been promised. That is all I know.'

A suspicion was growing in Merrivale's mind. 'Support from whom?'

'Again, I do not know.'

Merrivale wondered if this was true. 'If you wanted to see King Philippe's embassy fail, why did you warn me about Alameda?'

Reyes looked shocked. 'We did not want the embassy to succeed, but we wished no ill to King Philippe. Don Juan Manuel greatly admired and esteemed him. I had no prior contact with the king or his household, and it was not until you arrived in Xerez that I discovered that Lorenço de Alameda was his physician.'

'You knew Alameda?'

'I taught him at Salerno. He was fascinated by toxins and poisons, although he always claimed that he was studying them to better understand the symptoms and antidotes. After he left Salerno, he took a post in the household of Leonor de Guzmán. Soon after he did so, her husband died. It was given out that he had died of a tumour in his belly, but everything I heard about the case pointed to poison.'

'Laurel water,' Merrivale said slowly.

'Exactly. Soon after, Leonor became the mistress of King Alfonso.'

'I hope the king is having his wine tasted... Señor Reyes, why are you telling me this?'

'Your intentions are honourable, I am certain,' Reyes said. 'For that reason, and for the sake of Mercuriade, whom I reverence, I wish to warn you. Do not linger in Córdoba. There are many secrets here, and if you try to uncover them you will put yourself in danger. I do not wish harm to come to you.'

'Thank you,' Merrivale said. 'In return, let me warn *you*. Do not trust Pero de Garcíez. Among other things, he has dealings with the Warriors of the Faithful.'

Dámaso Reyes smiled. 'Are you expecting me to be shocked? *Señor*, a hundred years ago the pope sent Christian mercenaries to Marrakesh, to help the sultan put down a rebellion among his own people. The great Çid Campeador served the Moors against his fellow Christians, and the scholar Giovanni di Napoli has argued that it is lawful for Christian kings to employ Muslim soldiers to defeat rebels. There is nothing new under the sun.'

Fra Moriale had also said this, the day they arrived at al-Jazīra. 'Queen María knows about Garcíez's connection with the Warriors?'

Reyes's eyes were watchful. 'I did not say that.'

'So, she does know. Which leads me to assume that she must also have her own contacts in Granada. Do you know who they are?'

'*Señor*, I advised you not to interfere in this matter.'

'And I listened to your advice,' Merrivale said. 'Very carefully. Now, I am ignoring it. How does the queen send messages to the court at Granada?'

Reyes smiled again, but his eyes were still uneasy. 'I have told you all that I can. God watch over you, *señor*.'

The streets were quiet now, as people moved indoors to avoid the afternoon heat. Despite his final words, Dámaso Reyes had very definitely not told him everything that he knew. In particular, whatever role Garcíez was playing seemed murkier than ever.

He was about to return to the *alcázar* when a thought struck him. He walked up the broad street past the palace walls and turned towards the *judería*. A short walk brought him to the heart of the district and he paused outside a little synagogue, looking around. There were no windows in the houses, but there were eyes on the street all the same; no more than a minute passed before a door creaked open and a muscular man who looked like he might have been a blacksmith, dressed in a long robe and skullcap, stepped out into the street.

'Can I help you, stranger?' he asked in Castilian.

'I am searching for the house of the nephew of Rabbi Levi ben Gershon. I am sorry, I do not know the nephew's name.'

'Why are you looking for him?' the man demanded.

'I was told that Rabbi Levi is in the city, and I wanted to pay my respects. My name is Simon Merrivale, and I am from England.'

After a moment the man nodded and pointed. 'The nephew's name is Duran ben Shlomo Catalan. He lives in the Plaza de Teberiades, third house from the left as you enter.'

The house in the Plaza de Teberiades had a strong oak door studded with nails. Merrivale knocked and waited. After a long moment the door opened and one of the largest men Merrivale had ever seen, with a thick muscular neck and bulging biceps, stood in the doorway. 'What is your business?' he demanded.

'I seek the Rabbi Levi ben Gershon. Please tell him that Simon Merrivale wishes to see him.'

The big man called into the interior of the house, speaking in Hebrew. Another voice answered, and the man relaxed and stood to one side, indicating that Merrivale should enter. 'My apologies,' he said. 'We have to be careful. I am Duran ben Shlomo. I shall take you to my uncle.'

They passed through a tiled courtyard full of flowers and up a stone staircase into a long room with a colonnade open onto the courtyard. The shelves were lined with books and rolls of parchment. Levi ben Gershon rose smiling from his seat, holding a codex in one hand. 'Simon Merrivale. You have not changed, my friend.'

'Nor you, master,' said Merrivale. It was true; Gershon's beard was a little greyer and his hairline had receded a little more, but he was still the same courteous scholar Merrivale had met four years earlier. 'But do I come at a bad time? Has there been trouble?'

'Not yet,' said the younger man. 'Qurtuba is a thousand years old, but the Castilians only conquered it a century ago.' He smiled a little. 'Such a short time, that we still call the city by its old name. I cannot get used to Córdoba.'

'Do the authorities treat you well?' Merrivale asked.

'The governor and his men are respectful, but there are only a handful of Castilians in the city, administrators and merchants. Most of the people are still *mudéjars*, Muslims who live under Christian rule, or Jews like myself. Among the Castilians there are some who covet our property, and others who believe that we are in correspondence with their enemies in Garnāta. They would like to drive us out, as happened in Sharīsh and Hims al-Andalus and many other cities. So, we are prepared to defend ourselves.'

'And you are one of the defenders?' Merrivale asked.

'If necessary, yes. I practise regularly with arms, and I compete in wrestling matches. If the time comes when we must fight, I will be ready.'

Merrivale paused for a moment. 'This rumour that some people in the city are in correspondence with Garnāta. Could it be true?'

Duran stiffened a little. Levi ben Gershon laid down the book he was holding and moved forward. 'You may trust this man, nephew,' he said gently.

'I would like to know why you ask this question,' Duran said.

Merrivale turned to Gershon. 'When we last met, I was trying to stop a Florentine banker named Donato de' Peruzzi from stealing the great crown of England. I succeeded, thanks in part to you and your friends, but Peruzzi is active once more. This time, he is attempting to foment a civil war in Castile.' He looked back at Duran. 'If that happens, you and your people will be caught in the middle, as has happened so many times before. Help me now, and I can put an end to Peruzzi's scheme and prevent this conflict.'

'I think we should do as he asks,' Gershon said gently.

Duran gestured around at the books and parchment rolls. 'Do you see all of this?' he asked.

'A collection many libraries would envy,' said Merrivale.

'Qurtuba was once one of the world's great centres of learning,' Duran said. 'Muslim, Christian and Jewish scholars worked side by side. Qurtuba Alyana it was called, the city of paradise, in part for its wealth of scholarship and learning. After Qurtuba fell, another great centre was created at Hims al-Andalus, but the Castilians took it and renamed it Sevilla. Now, only the libraries of Garnāta remain. So, yes, I have contacts in Garnāta, but they supply me with books, not secrets.'

'You collect these works to preserve them,' Merrivale said.

'And to disseminate them. Scholars from all over Europe, including your University of Oxford, pay me for translations from Arabic and Hebrew into Latin. I am not a spy, Señor Merrivale. I am trying to hold back the darkness.'

'And for that, I admire you,' Merrivale said. 'But I wonder if others have similar contacts. I am thinking in particular of Dámaso Reyes, the queen's physician.'

Duran looked out into the garden for a moment. 'I know Señor Reyes,' he said. 'And yes, he corresponds with a physician and alchemist in Garnāta named 'Ali ibn al-Rāzī. Like Señor Reyes, he once studied at the Salerno Medical School.'

'Just one more question,' Merrivale said. 'Have your correspondents mentioned trade caravans coming from Garnāta into Castile? Especially within the last few months?'

Duran looked surprised. 'I have heard nothing.' He glanced at his uncle. 'I can make inquiries, if you wish.'

'I would be grateful if you did,' Merrivale said. 'Be careful not to draw attention to yourself. In particular, be wary of a Knight of Calatrava named Pero de Garcíez. You know this man?'

'I know of him,' Duran said. 'His family comes from Jayyān, but his brother was executed three years ago for leading a revolt against King Alfonso. It is said that Garcíez bears a grudge for this.'

'Garcíez is made of grudges,' Merrivale said. 'Thank you, *señor*.' He bowed to Gershon. 'It is good to see you again, master.'

'You too, my friend.' Gershon studied him for a moment. 'I was wrong,' he said. 'You have changed. You are at peace with yourself now, I think.'

It was Merrivale's turn to be surprised. 'Does it show?' he asked.

'You have stared into the face of death, have you not? You are calm now, and you accept your fate.'

Merrivale smiled a little. 'Perhaps you are right,' he said. 'I am not unduly concerned about my own fate.' The smile faded. 'It is the fate of others that haunts me,' he said.

—

Back at the *alcázar* that evening, Ficaris and Warin played endless games of *kanjifah* by lamplight. Eleanor picked up the lute and began to play. Restless, Merrivale walked across the courtyard out into the garden, where he stood looking up at the net of stars. The heady scent of roses drifted around him. After a moment, he realised that inside the music had stopped and Eleanor was standing beside him.

'It is very peaceful here,' she said quietly.

'Perhaps.' Merrivale spoke without thinking. 'I don't like gardens. They bring back too many memories.'

'Memories of people?' she asked.

'Yes.'

'Back at al-Jazīra, I asked you a rather insensitive question about whether you had ever been in love. This is what you mean, isn't it?'

'She loved gardens,' Merrivale said after a while. 'She loved music, too. She would often sit in the garden and play the lute, and sing. Not *Aucassin and Nicolette*, or the chansons, she loved the music of the troubadours and trobairitzes. Azalais was one of her favourites. "My heart is in such disorder that I turn away from everyone. I know how much I have lost, in less time than it took to gain it." And there was a couplet from Beatriz de Dia that she used to like to quote to me, especially when she was teasing me: "Go and tell him, messenger, that many people suffer from too much pride."'

'And did you?' Eleanor asked.

'Of course I did. I was a gentleman's son who fell in love with a king's daughter, further above me even than those stars we see now. I was dust beneath her feet, and yet I dared to think I was worthy of her.'

'Of course you were,' Eleanor said. 'Which would you rather, Simon? To have loved her and lost her? Or to never have experienced, no matter how briefly, the happiness you made for one another?'

'I often ask myself the same question.'

There was silence for a long time, both of them thinking the same thing. 'Arundel is prepared to sacrifice his soul for you,' Merrivale said finally. '"What need have I of Paradise? I have no wish to enter there." Those were his words.'

In the starlight, her face was wry. 'Aucassin... But where does that leave me? What about *my* immortal soul?'

'I don't know,' said Merrivale. 'But I have learned not to worry unduly about such things. I will consider my own soul when it comes time to pay the ferryman. Until then, I have too many other things to occupy me.' He paused. 'Which is, I suppose, a form of answer to your question.'

Surprisingly, there was humour in her voice. 'It is. And you have resolved my dilemma as well. I will confront my feelings about Richard when we return to al-Jazīra. Not before.'

20

8th of October, 1343

Another message came the following morning, this time from Fra Moriale.

> *I have news. Meet me in the Plaza del Malcocinado at midday.*

It took them some time to find the plaza, at the heart of a maze of turning, twisting lanes even more complex than the ones in Xerez. It was market day in the plaza, with stalls selling vegetables and fruit and fish just caught in the river and men and veiled women haggling in Arabic. Fra Moriale, dressed for once in a plain tunic and hose, was sitting in the shade of a tree eating snails in pepper sauce out of a wooden cone. 'Try these,' he said. 'They are delicious.'

Merrivale and Ficaris sat down. 'What is your news?' Merrivale asked.

'I found out about one of the caravans from Garnāta. It didn't come to Córdoba. It stopped at Almodóvar.'

Ficaris shook his head. 'I thought that castellan was behaving oddly.'

'What do you think the caravan was carrying?' Merrivale asked.

'I don't know,' said Fra Moriale, 'but I think we should find out. Remember, Queen María is said to be wanting gold. What if she is hiding it at Almodóvar?'

'What do you propose to do? Take *Santa Creu* downriver and storm the place?'

'No, you and I will ride there tomorrow. Arrange some horses, and then think up a pretext for our visit.'

'Just like that?'

'Lies and deception are what you're good at,' Fra Moriale said. 'Have a snail.'

Back at the *alcázar*, Merrivale asked the chamberlain for two horses to be made ready for the morning. The chamberlain returned an hour later to say that none of the queen's horses were available, but he would arrange for mounts to be hired. Throughout the afternoon, Merrivale made further polite inquiries about progress, and was told the matter was in hand; there was no need to worry, horses would be found.

'They don't want you to go,' said Eleanor.

'That much is self-evident.'

Merrivale walked out of the *alcázar* and into the narrow lanes of the *judería*, doubling back several times to ensure he was not being followed before coming to the Plaza de Teberiades and knocking at Duran ben Shlomo's door. The big man looked up in surprise as he was shown in.

'I need to hire two horses,' Merrivale said. 'Secretly.'

Duran wiped the ink from his finger. 'There is a livery stable near the Plaza de la Trinidad, not far from the gates. The owner is a *mudéjar*, and a friend of mine. Mention my name and he will attend to you.'

9th of October, 1343

The following morning, Merrivale and Fra Moriale collected their horses from the stables. The sentinels at the city gates looked surprised but made no move to stop them and they rode on down the track beside the river towards Almodóvar. 'What will you do if we do find gold at the castle?' Merrivale asked.

'Find out where the gold comes from, and set up an ambush.'

'Will it be that easy?'

'My friend, I've been robbing caravans for twenty years. I learned at my father's knee. This is what *I'm* good at.'

The guards on the gates at Almodóvar did not look especially pleased to see them. 'I bear a message and a gift from my lady of Lancaster,' Merrivale said, holding up a purse and shaking it so they could hear the money jingle. 'She was unable to thank your master properly when we left, as she had lost her money when our boat sank. She sent me to repair this fault.'

The sentries looked at each other. Regrettably, they said, the castellan was absent on duties elsewhere. 'A Dominican brother was here,' Merrivale said. 'I assume he is your chaplain? May I speak to him?'

After a short pause the postern opened and the friar walked out to join Merrivale and Fra Moriale. Merrivale repeated his errand, and the friar looked at him with dark suspicious eyes. 'Why did the lady wait until now to send you?' he demanded. 'Your story sounds like a falsehood to me.'

Merrivale weighed the purse again. 'But this money is real,' he said. 'Did a caravan come here at any time in the last couple of months?'

The friar looked at the purse, trying to calculate how much money was in it and, Merrivale thought, how much he could remove for himself before passing it on to the castellan. 'Yes,' he said finally. 'About three weeks ago. A pack train of horses and mules.'

'What freight did they carry?'

'Bricks of salt. They are the queen's property, but we are storing them here until she sends for them.'

Merrivale and Fra Moriale looked at each other. 'Salt?' the latter demanded. 'Where did it come from?'

'I assume it came from one of the royal *salinas*.' The friar hesitated. 'I did not ask too many questions.'

He knows something is wrong, Merrivale thought. 'Who led this caravan? Who guarded it? Can you describe them?'

'The leader was a Knight of Calatrava, a bearded man with deep-set eyes. The men with him were Moorish mercenaries, I think. Their captain was a tall man with a patch over his left eye.'

The Knight was clearly Garcíez; the other man did not match any description Merrivale knew. 'Is the salt still here?' he asked.

'Yes, *señor*. It is guarded night and day.'

'A moment,' Fra Moriale interrupted. 'Why do you say the escort were Moors?'

'Because I heard them speaking Arabic,' the friar said. 'One of them said something about *al-abidu mina al-Ghaba*, the slaves from La Algaba, although that makes no sense. Everyone at La Algaba was killed in the raid.'

Merrivale handed over the purse. 'Remember that generosity is a virtue in the eyes of God,' he said, mounting his horse. They rode back towards Córdoba through the dusty heat, ideas flickering like lightning in the back of Merrivale's mind.

'Salt?' demanded Fra Moriale. 'Where is the queen getting salt?'

'Perhaps she is stealing it from the king.'

'And selling it in order to raise money.' Fra Moriale nodded. 'Very clever. But we still don't know where the gold is.'

'No,' said Merrivale.

They returned to Córdoba in the middle of the afternoon and handed over their horses at the stable. Fra Moriale returned to his ship. Merrivale waited until he had gone and hurried to the *judería*, where he found Duran and his uncle examining an Arabic translation of Aristotle's *Nicomachean Ethics*. 'Forgive the intrusion,' Merrivale said, 'but I have a question for each of you.'

'We will help if we can,' said Gershon.

'Master Duran, did your correspondents in Garnāta ever mention a raid on a manor called La Algaba, near the town of Palma del Río?'

Duran nodded. 'Yes, there was much talk about the second raid. Several hundred Christians were slaughtered by the Warriors of the Faithful. Men being what they are, some applauded this as an act of holy war, but most were shocked by the brutality.'

'Wait a moment. The second raid? There was another?'

'Yes, a couple of weeks before, I think. This was carried out by the sultan's own troops, led by a commander known as al-Awaru. A few unfortunate souls were taken back to Garnāta to be sold as slaves, but there was no killing.'

'Al-Awaru? Doesn't that mean the one-eyed man?'

'Yes.'

Merrivale's mind raced. He turned to Levi ben Gershon. 'Master, you are one of the wisest men I know. How would you conceal gold so that no one could find it?'

'An interesting question,' the older man said gravely. 'I would seek answers from an alchemist.'

'Alchemists transmute base metal into gold. At least, they claim to be able to do so.'

Gershon shook his head. 'That is what everyone thinks, but there are many other alchemical processes as well. In the case you have mentioned, instead of turning something else into gold, I would seek to turn gold into something else, in order to hide it. Something that no one would suspect could really be gold.'

'Thank you,' said Merrivale. 'That leaves quite a wide range of possibilities.'

Gershon smiled. 'God will show you the way when He is ready.'

Back at the *alcázar*, Merrivale called the others together. 'The hunt is back on,' he said quickly. 'Mauro is still alive, I am certain of it. This captain from Garnāta, al-Awaru, took him from La Algaba before the Warriors came. The same man also escorted the salt caravan to Almodóvar.'

Eleanor smiled. 'Simon! I have never seen you this excited.'

'I have, my lady,' said Warin, 'and it never ends well. Sir, back at al-Jazīra you said quite definitely that we were not going to Garnāta.'

'Perhaps we won't have to go,' Merrivale said. 'Not if we can get the truth out of Garcíez.'

'What are you going to do?' asked Ficaris.

'Denounce Garcíez to the queen, and see what happens.'

—

The palace lay on the far side of the gardens, its gates flanked by dark cypresses. The guards refused to admit him. 'We are sorry, *señor*, but we have orders. No one is admitted without the queen's permission. You must apply to her chamberlain.'

'If I cannot see the queen, perhaps I could speak to her physician. If Señor Reyes is within, would he see me?'

'We will send a message, *señor*.'

Dámaso Reyes, white-bearded and red-robed, came down to the gate a few minutes later. 'Señor Merrivale. How may I assist you?'

Merrivale glanced at the guards. 'I will be answerable to Her Grace,' Reyes said. 'Come with me, *señor*.'

Behind the gate was a colonnade surrounding another garden, shimmering in the late afternoon heat. Reyes turned to Merrivale. 'What is this about?'

'Garcíez is betraying the queen,' Merrivale said. 'I must see her, at once.'

'Betraying her? How?'

'I must see her,' Merrivale repeated.

Reyes hesitated. 'Wait here,' he said finally, and walked along the colonnade and through an arched doorway at the far end. Merrivale waited, listening to the trill of birdsong from the garden and the distant thump of mill wheels from the bridge.

The physician returned half an hour later. 'She will receive you now.'

Polished and venomous, Queen María sat in the same gilded chair with her hands resting on its arms. Her face was absolutely still. This time there were just a few attendants with her, all of them armed. One of them was Garcíez.

Merrivale bowed to the queen. 'What have you to say to me?' she demanded.

'Pero de Garcíez has stolen a consignment of salt from one of the royal *salinas*,' Merrivale said. 'He brought it to your friends in the garrison at Almodóvar.'

Her expression did not change. 'What of it? I am the queen. When I become regent for my son, the salt monopoly will fall into my hands. I am merely taking a downpayment.'

'But Garcíez wasn't supposed to bring you salt, was he?' Merrivale demanded. 'He was supposed to be bringing you gold, gold from Timbuktu, conveyed by his allies the Warriors of the Faithful. What do you think has happened to the gold, Your Grace? Has Garcíez kept it for himself, perhaps, or shared it with the Warriors?'

The queen's hands clenched suddenly. Garcíez stepped forward, eyes glaring. 'You have no idea what you are talking about,' he said.

'Don't I? Let us send for the Dominican friar who is chaplain at Almodóvar, and hear what he has to say.'

Dámaso Reyes intervened. 'Salt is a valuable commodity, Señor Merrivale. As Her Grace indicated, the salt will be sold and the profits remitted to her exchequer. There is nothing untoward about that.'

'Salt is valuable in Timbuktu,' said Merrivale. 'Not here in Castile, which produces more salt than any other realm in Christendom. The salt would need to be sold overseas, and that would take too long. Her Grace needs money now, to pay her own allies before Leonor de Guzmán can strike.' He turned to Garcíez. 'What did you do with the gold you promised the queen? Where is it?'

Garcíez turned to the queen and bowed. 'Your Grace, I refuse to listen to these wild accusations. With your permission, I will withdraw from court for a few days. I have pressing matters to attend to.'

'You may go,' the queen said. She raised a hand and pointed at Merrivale. 'You and the lady Eleanor will remain in Córdoba. You will not leave the city.'

Merrivale schooled his face, concealing his surprise. 'Are we prisoners, Your Grace?'

'You are my guests,' María said. 'You will remain so, until I give you leave to depart.'

Back at the guesthouse Merrivale slammed his hand down on the table in frustration. 'That did not go well,' he said.

Eleanor frowned. 'She wants to stop us from following Garcíez. Why?'

'Because whatever Garcíez is up to, she is in it up to her neck,' Merrivale said. He shook his head in anger. 'I should have seen this coming. God knows there were enough signs. Garcíez isn't betraying anyone here, not at all. He is planning to divide the Knights of Calatrava and bring his faction over to her side. It is even possible that the Warriors of the Faithful will join them.'

'And hell will break loose in Castile,' Ficaris said grimly. 'What shall we do, Simon?'

Across the city, church bells were ringing vespers. Merrivale looked at the garden falling into shadow. 'It is growing late,' he said. 'Let us see what tomorrow brings.'

10th of October, 1343

During the night a fog rose from the river, and dawn came grey and misty. The servants who brought food were new and, unlike the ones who had greeted them on arrival, were unsmiling and unresponsive. Two more men worked in the garden, snipping dead flowers from the roses.

He waited until the servants had withdrawn, and spoke in a low voice. 'Stay here, do nothing out of the ordinary. Play *kanjifah*, play the lute or do whatever you want, but don't let on that you think anything is wrong.'

'What are you doing?' asked Ficaris.

'I'm going to find a way out of the city,' Merrivale said.

Ficaris nodded. 'Fra Moriale's ship is moored not far away. Perhaps he can help us get away downriver.'

'Perhaps,' Merrivale said.

They were prohibited from leaving the city, but not the *alcázar* itself. The men working in the garden pretended not to notice him leave, and the guards at the gates made no move to stop him as he walked out into the city still veiled in mist. The narrow streets were busy with veiled women and men in long white robes on their way to shops and markets; once again, most of them were speaking Arabic. *Duran was right*, Merrivale thought. *Castilian rule is a thin veneer. Even the palace servants were speaking Arabic to each other. If civil war does erupt, whose side will the* mudéjars *be on? Or will they choose their own side?*

He did not go towards the river. Instead, he walked at random through the narrow streets until he was satisfied that no one was following him before turning into the quiet lanes of the *judería* and coming once again to the Plaza de Teberiades.

Duran ben Shlomo and his uncle were hard at work on the manuscript of Aristotle. Merrivale realised he had never seen a woman in the house, and he wondered if women were secluded or if Duran was simply unmarried. 'Can I trust you?' he asked.

Duran seemed amused by the question. 'What do you say, uncle?' he asked. 'Can Señor Merrivale trust me?'

'Insofar as any man can be trusted,' the old scholar said calmly. 'Why do you ask, Señor Merrivale?'

'My friends and I need to escape from Córdoba,' Merrivale said. 'Then, we must go to Garnāta.'

Duran looked pensive. 'The journey is easy enough. It is three days' journey on foot to al-Qal'at on the *frontera*. The

Castilians took it last year and renamed it Alcalá. There is a big garrison there now. From there, it is another day to Garnāta.'

'Can we get across the *frontera* without being noticed?'

'There are ways,' Duran said. 'Why do you wish to go to Garnāta?'

'Do you recall that I mentioned the name of Pero de Garcíez?' Merrivale said. 'He was here in Córdoba, but he has now departed and I need to track him down. I can tell you more, but it will take some time.'

Duran glanced at his uncle. Gershon nodded a little. Duran leaned forward, resting his arms on the table, biceps bulging under his tunic. 'Save it for the journey,' he said.

Merrivale stared at him. 'You are coming with us? Why?'

'Because my uncle has told me a great deal about you,' Duran said. 'He says you are a righteous man.'

'The men I have killed might not agree with you.'

'There is no righteous man on earth who has not sinned,' Gershon said gravely. 'Were I younger, I would go with you myself. But I commend my nephew to you. He knows the way to Garnāta and you do not. When do you wish to depart?'

'As soon as possible.'

Duran hesitated. 'It will take a little time to make the arrangements. And tomorrow is Shabbat.'

'I am a rabbi,' said Gershon. 'I shall give you dispensation, nephew. Go safely. I shall remain here, and pray that God watches over you.'

The sun was burning through the mist as Merrivale walked back to the *alcázar*. He found Eleanor sitting in the garden in her red gown, playing the lute and humming softly to herself. 'What did Fra Moriale say?' she asked. 'Did he agree to help us?'

Merrivale lowered his voice. 'I didn't go to see Fra Moriale.' Quietly, he outlined the plan that he and Duran had devised. 'I would have preferred to leave Córdoba under cover of darkness, but Duran says that is impossible. Since the raids on La Algaba and Palma del Río, there are so many guards on the gates at night that not even a mouse can get past them. We'll have to go in daylight. Duran will make the arrangements today and we will leave tomorrow morning.'

'What happens once we are out of the city?'

'Duran knows ways to get across the frontier and into Garnāta. Once there, he has contacts in the city. We take it from there.'

Eleanor smiled a little. 'This sounds like another plan that could get us killed.'

'I know what you said at Teba, but you don't have to come with us. A ship can take you down to Sevilla, and from there you can go wherever you like.'

'Of course I'm coming with you,' she said with quiet firmness. 'Warin will pine without me. And what about Call-me-Jac? What will he think of this plan?'

'I don't know,' Merrivale said. 'But don't tell him. Let it come as a surprise.'

The Red Fortress

21

11th of October, 1343

Morning brought fog again, and the damp air was chilly. The same unsmiling servants brought food and, at Merrivale's request, a charcoal brazier for warmth. One of the men placed the brazier on the table and the other leaned forward with a taper to light it. Merrivale's staff descended on his skull at the same moment as Warin's fist connected with the jaw of the other. Both slumped unconscious to the floor.

Ficaris stared. 'What in the name of God?'

Merrivale called to the two men working in the garden. 'Come quickly! The brazier has started a fire! Help us!'

Both men dropped their tools and ran upstairs to the refectory, where two more solid blows knocked them senseless. 'Take their clothes and change into them,' Merrivale said, pulling off his tabard and coat. 'Put your own clothes into your travelling bags, weapons too. My lady, if you go to your bedroom, we will bring clothes to you.'

'There isn't time!' she snapped. They undressed quickly, pulling on loose trousers and long white tunics. Eleanor tucked her hair under her turban, folded her red gown and laid it on the table beside the lute, and pulled off her rings and laid them down too.

'Very conscientious of you,' said Ficaris.

'They aren't mine,' Eleanor said simply.

Merrivale tucked his staff under his tunic and wrapped a turban around his head, covering his lower face. 'Let us go,' he said.

They walked out into the misty garden, bags over their shoulders. The guards at the gate were huddled around another brazier, rubbing their hands for warmth. Merrivale recognised two of them and bowed his head, covering his face still further, but neither made any connection between this ragged servant and the English herald, and they paid him no attention. One of the others, a little more alert, looked suspiciously at their bags. 'You! Stop! What have you there?'

Merrivale folded his hands. '*Salaam, saīdi*. These are the clothes of the English. We are taking them to the laundry.' He pulled his bag off his shoulder and opened it, showing the guard the sweat-stained coat and hose and tabard inside.

Another guard walked out of the gatehouse, carrying a steaming jug and a stack of wooden bowls. 'Hot wine, *chicos*! Come and warm your guts. Bernal! Leave those filthy Moors alone and have a drink.'

'You may go,' the guard said, and he turned away.

Merrivale folded his hands again and shuffled away down the street, the others following. 'Come,' Merrivale whispered. 'Walk slowly until we are out of sight. Do not attract attention.'

Slowly, shuffling a little, they passed the wall of the *alcázar* and entered the courtyard of the cathedral. Palm trees hung darkly over their heads, shrouded with fog. Ficaris stopped and pointed towards the river. 'Fra Moriale's ship is that way,' he said.

'I know,' Merrivale said. 'You may join him, if you wish.'

Anger clouded Ficaris's face. 'You're going after the gold,' he said. 'And you don't trust me.'

'I'm not interested in the gold,' Merrivale said. 'I want Garcíez, and I want Mauro. But I suspect that when we find them, we will find the gold as well, and I don't particularly want Fra Moriale and his merry band of pirates trampling after us. This calls for subtlety, and subtlety is not one of Fra Moriale's virtues.'

'And you don't trust me,' Ficaris repeated.

'No man can serve two masters, Jac.'

'Ah, yes. According to Saint Matthew, the choice is between God and money. Fra Moriale represents money. Are you setting yourself up as God, Simon?'

Merrivale said nothing. Slowly, Ficaris lowered his hands. 'That was uncalled for,' he said. 'I am sorry. Send me away, Simon, if you wish. But I too made a promise to Juan Moreno. I vowed that we would find Mauro. Juan's death has not released me from that vow, any more than it has released you.'

Silently, Merrivale rested his hand on Ficaris's shoulder for a moment. They walked on, crossing the courtyard and going out through the eastern gates into a small plaza. A half-built church stood on the far side, scaffolding rising like dark skeletons in the mist. A big man with a long cloak over one shoulder walked out from behind the scaffolding and stopped in front of them. 'I see you were successful,' said Duran ben Shlomo Catalan.

Merrivale introduced the others. Duran bowed to Eleanor. 'We must go quickly now,' he said. 'We need to be away from the city before the fog burns off.'

They walked through another maze of narrow lanes, past a row of tanners' workshops and the low domed roof of a bathhouse and came down to the foreshore of the river. Boats were drawn up here, men working around them. Nets hung on wooden racks, glistening with dew like coarse spiderwebs. Duran led the way to one of the larger boats, gesturing towards another man standing and watching the river. He was not as tall as Duran, but his shoulders were broad and square. 'This is my friend Haym,' Duran said. 'He owns this boat. We sometimes compete in wrestling contests. Well... I compete. He tries.'

Haym smiled. He and Duran clasped hands briefly with a grip that would have cracked lesser men's bones. 'Ready, brother?' he asked.

Duran nodded. 'Get into the boat and lie down,' he said to the others. They climbed into the boat, lying down behind the thwarts so they could not be seen. 'What about the other men working here?' Merrivale asked.

'I know them all,' Haym said. 'They will tell no one.'

Duran pushed the boat off from the shore and climbed in. He and Haym took up the oars and rowed slowly across the river, the fog hanging over them. After what seemed like quite a long time but was actually only a few minutes, the boat grounded again and Haym and Duran jumped out and pulled it up onto the shore, dragging the heavy boat like it was made of feathers. The others stepped out into the soft mud, and Haym reached into the stern of the boat and brought out bags of food and waterskins. The city was a dim shape on the far bank; downstream, a few arches of the bridge could be seen but the windmills were just dark bulks in the fog. Fra Moriale's galley was invisible.

Merrivale slung one of the water sacks over his shoulder. 'Thank you,' he said to Haym. 'You must allow us to pay you.'

Haym smiled and shook his head. 'God commands that we be generous to strangers. Look after my little friend Duran. He is a weak and feeble fellow, more fit for the scriptorium than the real world, but he means well.'

Duran laughed, and he and Haym clasped hands again. 'Make yourself ready,' Duran said. 'I will return in time for the next wrestling tournament.'

'Which you will lose, of course. Go with God, my brother.'

—

The road south from Córdoba was a caravan trail, a meandering path through stubbled fields and olive groves and pastures lined with low stone walls. By late morning the sun had burned away the fog and Córdoba was over the horizon, the hills beyond it blue in the distance.

The olive groves were full of men bringing in the harvest, and there was plenty of traffic on the trail, most of it mules laden with panniers full of shiny green olives heading for the markets of Córdoba. A few other travellers passed too: packmen with loads of merchandise slung over the backs of their horses, a white-haired priest, stinking of wine and vomit, who insisted on blessing them in slurred Castilian. A column of light-armoured horsemen trotted up from the south, lances pricked like porcupine quills against the sky. Merrivale looked at the devices on their surcoats, wondering if they were the queen's troops sent out to find them, but the horsemen wore a red lion on white, the badge of Ponce de Léon's men from the north. Their leader reined in and looked at Duran.

'Where are you going?' he demanded.

'Al-Qal'at,' Duran said. 'We heard there was work there.'

'Alcalá, you mean? Keep a close watch once you get south of Castro. Warriors of the Faithful have been spotted between there and Alcalá.'

'Thank you, *señor*,' Duran said. 'Have you seen a Knight of Calatrava on the road in the last few days? A man riding on his own?'

The leader frowned. 'Yes, one of the Knights passed through here yesterday morning. What's your business with him?'

'He owes me money,' Duran said.

'Good luck getting it out of him. Miserly bastards, those Knights.'

At midday they halted near a watchtower and opened their food bags, squatting by the roadside and eating cold mutton and snails in green sauce and passing around a waterskin. A small taverna crouched in the lee of the tower, and some of the garrison sat in the shade drinking wine, their helmets on the table beside them. Duran went across to talk to them, and after a moment they answered him.

'It was definitely your friend Garcíez,' he said when he returned. 'One of those men recognised him. He didn't think Garcíez was going to al-Qal'at, though. He thought he heard him say something about Jayyān.'

'You mentioned that his family come from Jayyān,' Merrivale said. 'Where is it?'

'Away to the east. Jaén, the Castilians call it. I don't think that soldier can be right, though, because this isn't the road to Jayyān.'

—

They camped in an olive grove that night and set off again at sunrise, walking south as the heat began to build around them. A fresh range of mountains rose over the southern horizon. Later in the day a dry wind came up, swirling dust devils around them. The land was less populous now, the olive groves untended, the villages empty. Watchtowers began to appear on the hills around them, a sign that they were nearing the *frontera*.

Castro, when they reached it, was a collection of houses huddled around a small castle on the top of a low hill. Roman columns protruded from the soil of the nearby fields. This village too was empty, the flat roofs of the houses mostly fallen in, but the castle had a garrison from the commune of Córdoba. 'Will you admit us for the night?' Duran asked the sentinels at the gate.

'Sorry, stranger, not while the Warriors of the Faithful are prowling around. Captain's orders. Jesus Christ and the Twelve Apostles could walk up to this gate, and we still wouldn't open it. If I were you, I'd turn around and go back to Córdoba.'

Duran shook his head. 'We need work, you see. Look at me, six children to feed and another on the way.'

The sentinel looked him up and down. 'Maybe they could eat part of you. There'd still be plenty left over.'

Duran chuckled. 'Have you seen a Knight of Calatrava pass this way? Yesterday afternoon, perhaps?'

'Yes, that's right. He didn't stop, just rode on south towards Bayana.'

They camped for the night in one of the ruined houses, eating the rest of the mutton and snails and finishing them off with a handful of roasted almonds. 'Do you really have six children?' Eleanor asked.

Duran shook his head. 'No, my lady. I'm not married. My life is devoted to scholarship.'

'And wrestling,' said Ficaris.

Duran looked wry. 'Actually, I do not greatly enjoy wrestling. I do it to keep myself fit to fight, waiting for the day when we must defend ourselves.'

'I hope that day never comes,' said Eleanor.

'We have a saying in the *judería*, my lady. Hope that the sun shines, but prepare for rain.'

'Very wise,' said Ficaris. 'What happens when we get to Garnāta?'

'I insisted on coming with you, Señor Ficaris—'

'Please,' said Eleanor. 'Call him Jàc.' Ficaris grinned and nodded.

'I insisted on coming with you, Jac,' Duran said, 'not only because I know the way, but also because I have friends in the city. One is a clerk at court named Ibn al-Khatīb, and the other is a physician and scholar called Ibn al-Rāzī. They find manuscripts for me to translate. Your concern, as I understand it, is to learn more about this trade in gold and salt and how it is being used to finance rebellion. One or the other of these men should be able to help you.'

'I have heard Ibn al-Rāzī's name,' Merrivale said. 'Tell me more about him.'

'He is a great scholar, much greater than myself. He is a physician and alchemist, but he also studies astronomy and physics, and much else besides. He is also physician to the sultan's grandmother.'

Kahina had spoken of the Grandmother, who had once been her friend. 'And the other man, Ibn al-Khatīb?'

'A scholar too, and a poet. He is secretary to the vizier of Garnāta, the second most important official after the *hajib*, Abū Nu'aym Ridwan.'

'You have friends in high places,' Warin said.

'Scholarship admits to no rank,' said Duran. 'When it comes to the love of learning, we are all equal.'

A thought struck Merrivale. 'Have you heard of a royal official called al-Rumani? The superintendent of the salt works?'

'Abdallah al-Mu'min al-Rumani? Yes, I have heard of him. He is an ally of the vizier, I believe. His appointment to this high post caused some jealousy, because al-Rumani is not an Arab or an Amazigh. He is a *renegado*, a Christian who arrived in Garnāta only recently, and has now embraced Islam. He is called al-Rumani because he came from Rome.'

'Ah,' said Merrivale.

There was a little silence. 'Is that significant?' asked Duran.

'More than you can begin to imagine,' Merrivale said.

—

They set off at dawn once more, when the eastern sky was melon green and cold stars sparkled in the west. The mountains ahead were dark ramparts streaked with silver mist hanging in the valleys. The wind had died away, and the air was clear and cool, enough to make their breath steam as they walked. All around them lay a vast silence.

The sky brightened and the last stars faded. The eastern skyline was flooded with fire, and the dark mountains blazed with sudden light. As the sun rose, Duran pointed to a hill at the foot of the mountains, crowned with another castle. 'That is Bayana. There is another garrison there, but after that we will be in the wild mountains. Stay alert.'

The clear air made the mountains seem much closer than they really were, and it was mid-morning before they reached Bayana's hilltop fortress with the inevitable ruined town on the slopes below. Bones lay scattered in a field nearby, some equine, some human. Beyond the field were olive trees, branches heavy with unharvested fruit. None of the trees had been cut down; the country was depopulated, but there had not been the wholesale destruction they had seen further west.

A bright banner with the red lion of Córdoba flew from the gatehouse of the castle, but the gate itself was firmly shut.

Leaving the others behind, Merrivale and Duran climbed up through the ruins to the gate. A suspicious sentry answered their hail. 'Who are you? What do you want?'

Duran repeated the story about travelling to Alcalá to find work. 'Have you seen a Knight of Calatrava ride through here?'

'Calatrava? You wouldn't catch any of those pricks this deep in the *frontera*. No, they stay well back, keeping away of danger and counting their money. Stay safe on the road, *amigo*. The Warriors of the Faithful are out in those mountains.'

They moved on. The track began to climb through more abandoned olive groves with dry weeds growing knee-high among the trees, following a watercourse towards a narrow pass through the mountains. A trickle of water ran down between the stones. On the heights above them, more stone watchtowers rose towards the sky.

Warin held up a hand. 'Sir. I think we are being followed.'

'The queen's men come to haul us back to Córdoba?' asked Ficaris. 'Or Warriors of the Faithful? I know which I would rather face.'

To the right was a steep hill forested with oak trees. Motioning to the others to wait, Merrivale climbed partway up the hill until he could see the castle of Bayana a few miles behind them. Shading his eyes against the sun, he scanned the valley and the olive groves. At first he saw nothing, but then came a movement, and another; men in black robes, using the olive trees as cover as they skirted the castle. He waited motionless, watching as more and more men emerged: a dozen, fifteen, twenty.

He scrambled back down the hill. 'Warriors,' he said. 'We need to get off the main track. Up into the hills.'

Another watercourse, this one completely dry, ran down from the hills to the right. They scrambled over bleached stones, climbing steadily into the mountains. The night may have been cold, but the afternoon sun was blazing hot and sweat ran down their faces and into their eyes. After an hour they halted to draw breath and drink water. Warin climbed up the slope beside the stream and looked back down the valley. 'They're still following,' he said.

'Do you think they've seen us?' Merrivale asked.

'I don't think so, sir. They're moving slowly and scanning the ground.'

'How can they be tracking us over these stones?' demanded Ficaris.

'I don't know, but they are,' Merrivale said. To the left lay a steep mountainside covered with more scrub oak trees growing out of crevices in the stone. 'Let's get up onto the heights. Jac, lead the way.'

The crest of the mountain was two thousand feet above them. They climbed, sometimes on their hands and knees when the slope grew too steep, not speaking, drenched with sweat, swatting at the flies that followed them. Once, Merrivale dropped back and paused, listening for any sound from the trees below, but he heard nothing. He moved on, bracing himself with his staff and climbing quickly after the others.

Just before they reached the crest of the mountain he called a halt and this time they all sat still, listening. No sound came. 'Have we lost them?' whispered Ficaris.

'For the moment.' Merrivale looked at the sun, which was sinking into the west. 'We need to find shelter for the night.'

Warin pointed. 'I think there might be a cave over there, sir.'

The entrance to the cave was partly hidden by trees, impossible to see from above or below. They scrambled across the slope and entered the cave one by one, and found themselves in a high chamber with a narrow vent through the top, letting in the final rays of sunlight. The air was damp and smelled of wet limestone and something else, sour and pungent. The floor was slippery with a thin layer of mud. From deeper inside the cave there came the steady tap of dripping water.

'Are we safe here?' asked Duran.

'For the moment,' Merrivale said. 'It will be dark in another hour, with no moon, and I don't expect the Warriors will climb these mountains by night. We will have to move on early in the morning.'

Eleanor sat down on the stone, leaning back against the wall. 'Move on to where?' she asked. 'The garrison at Bayana hadn't see Garcíez, and we can assume they are keeping good watch.'

The stone behind her head was dark red, and after a moment Merrivale realised the wall had been painted, a crude figure of an animal that might have been a goat. Further up was a single staring eye, looking down at them. He was not a superstitious man, but he shivered nevertheless.

'I wonder if those soldiers yesterday were right,' he said finally. 'Garcíez is going to Jaén.'

'What are you thinking?' Ficaris asked.

'Either Peruzzi is intriguing with both Leonor de Guzmán *and* Queen María, playing them off against each other and using Garcíez as his agent, or Garcíez is playing some game of his own, probably with the support of the Warriors of the Faithful. Perhaps this is part of his scheme to rebel against his own grand master and seize control of the order.'

'Are we really certain about that?' Eleanor asked. 'Garcíez and Núñez were together that day in the mountains.'

'Yes, but Garcíez was blowing smoke in Núñez's eyes. Núñez is said to be greedy, and my guess is that Garcíez is giving him part of the profits from the slave trade to keep him happy. Garcíez's family come from Jaén. Duran, you said his brother was executed for rebellion?'

'Yes. He was one of the nobles who joined Don Juan Manuel's revolt ten years ago.'

Merrivale came to a decision. 'In the morning we will start for Jaén. Duran, can you guide us there?'

Duran nodded. 'And if Garcíez isn't there?' asked Ficaris.

'Then we continue to Garnāta,' Merrivale said. 'It isn't far.'

Night fell. Inside, the cave was inky black, lit only by a glimmer of starlight coming through the entrance and the vent overhead. Something rustled in the air, invisible wings fluttering in the night. More followed, accompanied by a distant squeaking. The hair rose on Merrivale's neck. The rustle of wings rose to a murmur, then a deep whirring noise coming from the depths of the cave. He looked at the entrance to the cave and saw the silhouette of a bat flitting out into the night.

'Get down on the floor,' he hissed. They flattened themselves on the muddy stone, listening to hundreds of bats flying overhead and out into the night. It took an age for the last of them to pass and silence to fall again.

'This mud stinks,' said Ficaris.

'This isn't mud,' Warin said. 'This is bat shit.'

The reek was powerful; the bats had contributed more droppings during their flight out of the cave. 'I want to vomit,' Ficaris said, his voice choked.

'Go ahead,' said Eleanor. 'It can't smell any worse.'

—

Between the smell and the flutter and squeak of returning bats, they slept very little that night. As soon as there was light enough to see, they left the cave and made their way cautiously along the hillside until they were overlooking the track to Alcalá once more. Their clothes and bags were stained black and reeked even in the morning cold.

They waited for a long time, scanning the valley but seeing no sign of movement. The forested slopes of the mountains behind them were silent. 'The Warriors must have moved on,' Ficaris murmured. 'Perhaps they are searching for us further south.'

'All the more reason to go east,' Merrivale said.

They descended the steep slope into the valley still in shadow. The hills on the far side were less steep; they climbed the forested slopes, passed over the crest and went down again. The rest of the day followed the same pattern, one hill giving way to the next, higher mountains rising steep to the right, glimpses of the plains leading towards Córdoba opening out to the left. From the mountain crests, deserted watchtowers looked down at them with empty eyes.

Sweating, reeking, exhausted and with their water running low, they clambered down one final slope. Sheer cliffs rose in front of them. At the bottom was a dell with a series of pools full of vivid blue water, partly enclosed by a crumbling stone wall. A powerful smell of rotten eggs drifted up from the water.

Warin sniffed. 'That stinks even worse than I do,' he said.

'Brimstone,' said Merrivale. 'Never mind the stink. At least it is clean.'

Eleanor walked along the rim of one of the pools. 'This one is mine,' she said. 'There's another pool down the hill for the rest of you.'

Despite the smell, the water was surprisingly refreshing. Once they were clean, they emptied their leather travelling bags and washed them too. The clothes they had taken from the servants at Córdoba were ruined, but their own travelling clothes, though not exactly clean, were at least wearable. Warin climbed the slope in search of clean water to refill their skins. Eleanor rejoined them, dressed once more as Buscador the crossbowman. The walnut stain had largely gone from her skin, but her face and hands had been exposed to so much sun that it hardly mattered.

'How far are we from Jaén?' she asked. 'Or Jayyān, or whatever we are calling it?'

'As the crow flies, only about ten miles,' Duran said. 'But the ground is still difficult.'

Merrivale nodded. 'We need to stay out of sight as far as possible. Closer to Jaén those watchtowers on the hills will be manned. Garcíez mustn't learn that we are following him.'

Some of the food had been spoiled by the bats, but there were enough almonds and olives to make a meal of sorts. As they were out in the open, Merrivale insisted that they post a night guard, and he himself took the first watch with Warin to follow him in a couple of hours. The others stretched out exhausted on the grass beside the pool and fell asleep. Merrivale stood, leaning on his staff and listening to the night. Thanks to the pool the little dell was warm; insects chirred in the shadows, and once he saw the flicker of a glowworm. Far away in the high mountains, a wolf howled at the circling stars.

Warin relieved him as instructed and he lay down to sleep. He woke again to find dawn flushing the sky. 'Anything?' he asked Duran, who had taken the final watch.

The big man shook his head. 'All quiet. Even the wolves finally went to sleep.'

'I'll rouse the others.' Gently, he shook Warin, Ficaris and Eleanor awake, and they rose and stretched. 'This is the last of the food,' said Ficaris, handing around the olives.

'We can buy more in Jaén,' Merrivale said. He still had some of the money Queen María had given them in Córdoba; unlike Eleanor's jewellery, he had no qualms about keeping it. Eleanor herself came out from behind the wall where she had been performing her ablutions.

'Simon,' she said quietly, 'there is something you need to see.'

The weathered stone of the building had been cut more than a thousand years ago, but the mark she showed him was bright and new: a tiny ξ symbol, scratched into the stone.

'I saw one like it at the mouth of the cave yesterday morning,' she said. 'How far can we trust Duran, do you think?'

Merrivale looked at the symbol. 'We're about to find out,' he said.

—

Dressed all in black, wearing a fur-trimmed hat despite the heat, Donato di Pacino de' Peruzzi stalked into the audience chamber in Córdoba where Queen María sat in her gilded chair. He bowed, with the least possible reverence, and stood with his arms folded across his chest.

'You have allowed Merrivale to escape,' he said. 'Who is responsible for this blunder?'

'How did you get here?' the queen demanded.

'As soon as I heard Merrivale had arrived in Córdoba, I hired one of the Genoese captains from your husband's fleet. His ship brought me to Sevilla and thence upriver. I see Fra Moriale has also departed.'

'I have no idea who you are talking about.' The queen's dark eyes were wide with anger. 'You deceived me, Peruzzi. You promised gold. Where is it?'

'I have not yet sent the gold, Your Grace, because you have failed in your side of the bargain,' Peruzzi said. 'You in turn promised that you would raise a rebellion against your husband. Don Juan Manuel and all the nobles who follow him would join you, you said. But Don Juan Manuel sits quietly at Algeciras, reading books of philosophy and thinking noble thoughts. Where is the rebellion?'

She studied him, and there was something in that hard, proud face that made him uneasy. 'I need gold to finance the rebellion, Peruzzi. Surely that is self-evident.'

'And I will not give you gold unless you first raise an army. Well. We seem to have reached an impasse.'

The queen smiled, and Peruzzi's unease deepened. 'Oh, I will raise an army,' she said. 'With or without your aid. I know more than you think, Peruzzi, and I have more power than you can dream of. Think twice before you defy me.'

'Think twice? Your Grace does not appear to have thought even once. If you are referring to your misconceived attempt to win over Pero de Garcíez and back him to overthrow his own grand master, you are sadly wrong. Grand Master Núñez has a backer who is just as strong as you.'

'Núñez is humping my husband's whore. I know. As I said, I know more than you think.' Her eyes narrowed a little. 'You asked whether I let Merrivale escape. Perhaps I didn't. Perhaps I sent him after you. He is your nemesis, is he not? He is the one who brings all of your plans to ruin.'

'You are playing with fire, Your Grace.'

'And while we are using tired old metaphors, Peruzzi, you are walking on thin ice. Be careful not to put a foot wrong. The hell that waits below is dark and deep, and for you, death will be only the beginning.'

22

15th of October, 1343

The fortress of Jaén perched on a spur of rock jutting out from the larger mass of mountains, towering over the plain below. The town, protected by thick walls, clung to the hillside beneath the castle. A few villages and isolated farms lay around the foot of the hill, surrounded by olive trees. Herds of cattle grazed in the distance.

The five of them halted in the shade of an olive grove. 'It all looks very peaceful,' said Eleanor.

Duran pointed to the castle. 'There is a powerful garrison there, strong enough to keep even the Warriors of the Faithful at bay. Wait here, *mi çaida* and *señores*, and I will scout the town.'

Duran walked away towards the town. The other four withdrew into the olive grove and sat down on the grass in the withering heat. The grove had been harvested recently, and a few bruised olives still lay on the ground under the trees. Insects buzzed around them, and cicadas chirred a monotonous chorus. Ficaris leaned back against the withered grey bark of an olive tree and fell asleep.

After a while Eleanor rose and began walking around the trees, studying their rough bark. Merrivale got up and joined her. 'Have you found anything?' he asked.

'No, but I'm worried. I recognised that symbol we saw at the pools, I saw it in the tattoos of some of the women at Teba. It's a Tamazight letter.' She paused. 'Does Duran speak Tamazight?'

'I don't know,' Merrivale said. 'If Duran wanted to betray us, why would he come with us?'

She looked at him. 'Don't you think you've answered your own question?'

For so big a man, Duran could move in surprising silence; he came through the trees and joined them almost before Merrivale was aware of his presence. 'I have found Garcíez,' he said low-voiced.

Ficaris sat up at once, rubbing his eyes. 'He is in the town?'

'No, at one of the *fincas*, the farms at the bottom of the hill. I was on my way up to the gates when I looked down and saw a horse in the courtyard of the *finca*, with a saddlecloth in the livery of Calatrava. So, I went to the gates and asked who lived there. They said the *finca* was owned by a widow, Señora de Garcíez. She must be the widow of Garcíez's brother.'

Ficaris gave a low whistle. 'Praise be to God,' he said. 'It's about time our luck turned. What shall we do, Simon?'

'Is the *finca* guarded?' Merrivale asked.

'Not that I could see. It looked rather dilapidated, as if the owner was quite poor.'

Merrivale rose to his feet and smoothed out the creases in his tabard. 'Show me which *finca* it is,' he said. 'Then, come back here and wait with the others. If I am not back by sundown, make your way back to Córdoba.'

'Simon,' Eleanor said quietly. They looked at each other for a moment. 'Garcíez will be armed,' she said finally. 'Take a sword.'

Merrivale picked up his staff. 'I have all that I need,' he said.

The *finca* was a two-storey manor house with a flat roof, surrounded by barns and sheds. A wooden stair led up to the main door of the manor house, which was recessed into the wall with arrow slits on either side. One of the sheds held an olive press, a heavy structure of wood and iron and stone; judging by the dust and debris, it had not seen use for some time. Chickens clucked in the courtyard, but there was no sign of the horse Duran had seen.

Merrivale climbed the stair and rapped on the iron-banded door. After a moment a wary face appeared in one of the arrow slits. 'Who is it?' a boy's voice asked.

'My name is Simon Merrivale, from England. I wish to speak to la Señora de Garcíez, if she will receive me.'

'What is this about?'

'It concerns Pero de Garcíez, the Knight of Calatrava.' Merrivale looked at the young face in the arrow slit. 'Is he your uncle?'

'Yes,' the boy said after a moment. 'Do you mean to harm him?'

'I mean to harm no one, least of all you or your mother.'

'Uncle Pero said he was in danger,' the boy said.

'Not from me,' Merrivale said. 'I give you my oath that I will not harm him.' *You were right, Moriale*, he thought. *Lies and deceit are my stock in trade.*

'I will speak to my mother,' the boy said.

Merrivale waited. The chickens clucked, stalking around the courtyard pecking at insects. Flies hummed in the hot afternoon.

From inside he heard a bar being lifted and the door swung open. The boy stood in the doorway, barefoot in ragged hose and a coat with torn points and one sleeve hanging loose. 'You may enter.'

Merrivale bowed and followed him through the hall and into a smaller room, a solar with tall windows looking towards the town and the castle hundreds of feet above, a massive dark silhouette against the sun. A woman sat in a chair beside the window, gazing vacantly into space, holding a piece of embroidery in her lap. A little stack of gold maravedís stood on the table beside her. The room was plain and bare, the tile floor unswept; cobwebs hung from the ceiling timbers in long strands coated with dust.

'Here is Señor Merrivale, *madre*,' the boy said.

Merrivale bowed. 'Welcome,' the woman said. 'Have you come to help Pero?'

'Your son said his uncle is in danger,' Merrivale said. 'Did he say from whom?'

'No. He said only that a time of strife was coming, and that his enemies would try to kill him. But he would emerge victorious, he said, and when it was all over, he would be able to look after me and my children. Our family would be restored to our old position, he said.'

Merrivale looked at the dusty room. 'Things have been hard for you since your husband died,' he said gently.

'Most of his property was confiscated. I was left only with this *finca*, which does not earn enough even to feed me and my son.' Her hand groped across the table for a moment, finally coming to rest where her fingers touched the coins. 'Without the money Pero brings me, we would starve.'

'I am sorry,' Merrivale said.

She looked directly at him for the first time, and he saw the empty dark eyes and realised with a shock that she was blind. 'Have you come to help Pero?' she repeated.

'Yes,' he said, swallowing the sick taste in his mouth. 'I am his friend, and I am trying desperately to find him. The enemies you refer to are on Pero's trail, and I must warn him. I only pray that I can get to him in time.'

'If you can, *señor*, then may Jesus Christ and his mother the Virgin cast their blessings upon you. I am glad to know that Pero has friends like you.'

Merrivale swallowed again. 'I was told in Córdoba that Pero might come here. Have you seen him?'

Her fingers touched the gold again. 'He was here only this afternoon, but he has ridden away again. If you have a swift horse, you might catch him.'

'Did he say which way he was going?'

'South,' she said. 'He is going to Wadi 'Ash. He is meeting someone there, he said, a Moorish lord who can help him. It is strange to deal with the Moors, I know, but Pero says that in times of danger, we cannot always choose our friends.'

'Quite true,' Merrivale said. 'I believe I know the man you mean. When I find Pero, is there any message you wish me to give him?'

'Tell him to come home safely,' the woman said. 'That is all I ask.'

Back in the olive grove he told the others what had happened. 'We will camp here for the night,' he said. 'Jac, go into the town and buy food. Duran, go with him, please.'

The two men departed. Merrivale closed his eyes for a moment and stood leaning against an olive tree, breathing deeply. Warin and Eleanor watched him, their eyes full of concern. 'What is it?' Eleanor asked.

Merrivale opened his eyes again, staring at the rough grey bark of the tree. 'Of all the despicable things I have done, lying to a blind woman comes high on the list.'

'You are doing your duty.'

'That does not help. If we kill Garcíez, and we will probably have to, who will care for that woman and her son? They will be destitute, just as my father and I were. When I looked at her sitting there in that dirty little room, I saw also my father in his cell at Frithelstock. Not blind, but so wandered in his wits that he no longer knew what was in front of him. I didn't just betray Señora de Garcíez, my lady. I betrayed my father, and I betrayed myself.'

'What is the alternative?' asked Eleanor. 'That Garcíez goes scot-free? That civil war erupts in Castile, and possibly Garnāta as well? That thousands perish needlessly? That Mauro remains a slave and is never found?'

Merrivale raised his hand, but Warin caught his arm before he could slam his fist into the trunk of the tree. Merrivale was strong, but Warin was a tin miner and was stronger still. Gradually he forced Merrivale's arm down. 'Don't do it, sir,' he said. 'You're no use to any of us with a broken hand.'

'Leave me alone,' Merrivale said harshly. 'Both of you.'

He stood alone for a long time, hearing Duran and Ficaris return and watching the shadows lengthen under the olive trees. Eventually Duran came to find him. 'We have brought food,' the big man said simply. 'You should eat.'

Merrivale said nothing. Duran waited for a little while, and spoke again. 'I could remind you of what my uncle said. There is no righteous man on earth who has not sinned. Or I could quote from Aristotle's writings on ethics. "The beauty of the soul is seen when a man bears with composure one great misfortune after another, not because he does not feel the pain of fate, but because he is a man with a strong and noble soul." Of course you feel pain. You would be a much lesser man if you did not.'

'Have you any idea how patronising that sounds?' Merrivale asked.

'If that is how you hear my words, I apologise. I meant to say that pain is part of the sacrifice we make. Not just you, but everyone. All of us try to do the right thing, and all of us suffer the consequences.'

'Not all of us,' Merrivale said.

'True. For those who do *not* do the right thing, there is Simon Merrivale to hunt them down and chastise them. Come and eat, and I will tell you what I know about Wadi 'Ash. That is where Garcíez is going, Warin says.'

Duran and Ficaris had brought flatbread and mutton sausage and olives, and a small flask of wine. They ate hungrily, tearing the bread to pieces with their hands. 'Wadi 'Ash is on the caravan route from al-Mariyya to Garnāta,' Duran said. 'I have not been there, but I am told that the country is very dry and Wadi 'Ash is one of the few places with good water. Al-Mariyya is the second port of the kingdom, after Mālaka. In times of peace it does good trade with the Maghreb and even with the Christian kingdoms.'

'Why might Garcíez be going there?' asked Eleanor.

'The caravans sometimes carry salt to ship overseas,' Duran said. He paused. 'Is that significant?'

'Possibly,' Merrivale said after a moment. 'According to Fra Moriale, gold is still coming across from Africa to Suhayl, so salt must still be going out. Garcíez could be going to arrange the shipment... But why, when the Warriors of the Faithful or the superintendent of the salt works, al-Rumani, could do it? Surely Garcíez has more important work to do, like starting a civil war.' No one answered him.

'Do you know the way to Wadi 'Ash?' Merrivale asked Duran.

'I think so. I have never made this journey, but I have seen maps.'

'Very well. We start in the morning.'

16th of October, 1343

The road south from Jaén led straight past the town and was in full view of the castle, but Merrivale decreed that they would circle around behind Jaén and pick up the main road further south to avoid being spotted. 'More climbing,' said Eleanor.

She was right. They climbed through the cool air, the northern plain vast behind them and the mountains rising like walls to their front, the oak forests giving way to pine woods where cones crunched under their feet. Once the castle was behind them they descended into a deep valley, and from there back up and over another spur of the mountains. They were at higher altitude now, and even in full sunlight the air seemed cooler.

Another descent, into a narrow pass through the mountains. A green river bubbled in its bed below cliffs that rose to dizzy heights. Crows cawed, echoing off walls of stone.

More echoes, a drumming sound that reverberated like distant thunder. 'Horses,' Warin said.

'Get off the trail!' Merrivale snapped. 'Over there, to the left.'

Another stream tumbled downhill, carving a gap through the cliffs where it joined the larger river. They splashed through the shallows and climbed up beside the smaller stream, emerging at the top of the cliff and crouching as they looked down into the valley below. A column of riders came down from the north, men in black robes and chainmail and spired helmets riding small sturdy horses. Ficaris's breath hissed.

'Warriors of the Faithful,' he said.

The leader of the column held up his hand, and the riders halted. The leader looked around, shading his eyes and scanning the cliffs. Even at this distance it could be seen that he was missing several fingers from his left hand. 'Aksal ben Mellal,' Merrivale said grimly. 'Our old friend. This time, I don't think he means to take prisoners.'

'The Warriors are bold to go so openly this close to Jayyān,' Duran said.

'Bold, or desperate,' Merrivale said. 'That stream bed we climbed is too steep for horses, so we have bought a little time. Let us make the most of it.'

Crawling back from the cliff edge, they rose and hurried up the hill, pushing through thickets of scrub oak and clambering over rocky outcrops. More mountains rose in front of them, six thousand feet or more in height, crags and cliffs shining in the sun. Lower hills tumbled down to the south and east. Duran pointed.

'Those mountains are called al-Mājīna. If I remember the maps correctly, if we cross the hills keeping the high mountains to our left, we will come to a town called al-Habar. From there, a track runs down to the plains, and we can go south to Wadi 'Ash.'

'Perhaps the Warriors of the Faithful will carry on towards Garnāta,' Ficaris said hopefully.

No one responded to this. They climbed on through a harsh wilderness full of trees and stones. Reaching the top of another pass they stopped for a moment, sweating in the rising heat, looking around at the wild landscape and the buzzards circling overhead.

'How careless,' Eleanor said.

'What's that, my lady?' Warin asked.

She pointed. 'There's a hill over there with no watchtower on it. Someone must have forgotten.'

Once again, the towers on each peak were crumbling into ruin. 'This is an empty land,' Duran said. 'Between Castile and Garnāta is a country that everyone fights for, but no one can take or hold. Once there would have been herdsmen in these woods, and villages and farms down in the valleys. Now, the herds have all been slaughtered, and the people carried away and enslaved by one side or the other.'

'Or both,' Ficaris said. 'I cannot stop thinking about that bastard Garcíez selling his own people.'

'Forget about Garcíez for the moment,' Merrivale said. 'Watch the trail behind you.'

Another valley, another river flowing slowly over a pale stone bed. Stone crags, eroded by the wind, rose on either side of the river. A pair of towers surrounded by curtain walls perched on the crags, facing each other across the river. The lion and castle banner of Castile flapped from the roof turret of one tower; the other, a bowshot away across the river, flew the scarlet and gold of Garnāta. Another ruined town lay below them, windowless houses lining the riverbanks. The remains of a mill wheel protruding from the water.

'That is al-Habar,' said Duran. He paused. 'Or, what remains of it.'

Eleanor looked at the banner of Castile. 'We could ask the garrison for protection,' she said doubtfully.

Merrivale shook his head. 'We would get the same answer we did at Castro. And even if they did admit us, we would be trapped there. The Warriors would simply wait for us to come out. We need to keep moving.'

'If we hail the Castilians, that will alert the Garnātan garrison,' Ficaris said. 'And if we try to slip past without hailing the Castilians, they'll think we're the enemy.'

'Then we must hope that neither side spots us,' Merrivale said. 'Let us hope they are too busy watching each other to think about us.'

There was no way past the two castles except through the town. They forded the shallow river and skirted the cliffs below the Castilian tower and began to move cautiously past the buildings, keeping low and using the broken walls as cover. A narrow street led past a bathhouse and thence to a plaza lined with elm trees whose leaves were turning yellow. Merrivale looked around, but there was no other cover and no other way through the town.

'Run,' he said.

They ran across the plaza, boots thudding on the cobbles. High above, voices shouted in Arabic and Castilian. A crossbow bolt struck the stones with a shower of sparks and skidded away; another thumped into a stone wall and fell to the ground, and then they were safe, sheltering in another narrow street on the far side of the plaza. Ficaris slid down onto his knees, gasping. Breathing deeply, Merrivale looked up and saw smoke rising from the top of the Garnātan tower.

'Beacon,' he said. 'They are signalling to the Warriors.'

Ficaris staggered to his feet. 'Are you all right?' Warin asked.

'No, but I'm not staying here to meet Aksal again. Let's go.'

There was no question of following the track down to the plains. They climbed again, and again, up onto the high slopes of the Mājīna mountains across pine forests and talus slopes of broken stone, skirting the monstrous cliffs that towered above them. Once again, no horse could follow them and the Warriors of the Faithful would struggle to track them in this stony wasteland, but Merrivale was taking no chances. All through the rest of that hard, hot, bitter afternoon he pushed them on, right to the limits of their endurance, and his own.

And the others responded, as much to his implacable determination as to their own need for survival. Warin the miner's son was the strongest of them all; he had grown up on Dartmoor and was used to hardship, and now he dogged Eleanor's heels, ready to catch her if she should fall. He was not needed. Eleanor had been a pampered lady of the court, but her childhood of riding and climbing and shooting had given her whip-like strength and never once did she falter. Ficaris staggered, his breath rasping in his throat, but sheer determination and force of will drove him onwards. Surprisingly, it was Duran who struggled the most. The big man was formidably strong, but he lacked endurance; wrestling bouts seldom last for more than a few minutes, and hour after hour of grinding effort on top of the five previous exhausting days had taken its toll. Once, he stopped, sweating and shaking, blinking his eyes, and it was Ficaris who moved over to him and put an arm around him, propping him up.

Merrivale turned. 'Enough,' he said. 'We will rest for a while.'

Duran straightened, wiping his face with the back of his hand. 'No,' he said. 'We go on.'

Night brought them to a ruined castle in the shadow of the highest peaks. They pushed through the weed-infested courtyard and found shelter inside the gatehouse, where they ate cold food and drank stale water from their skins and slumped down to sleep. Merrivale again took the first watch and stood outside the empty gateway, staring out at the hills lit by a million stars. He saw again the face of the blind woman at Jaén, and his own father, eyes uncomprehending, in his little cell at Frithelstock in Devon. He heard Duran's words in his mind. *We go on*.

—

'*Salaam*, Saīda Buthayna,' said Hamou Ou Akka ibn Zayani, *amir* of the Warriors of the Faithful. 'Welcome to my humble home.'

They were standing in the courtyard of a house in al-Bayyāzīn, the oldest part of Garnāta city. Below the house the ground sloped sharply down to a river and then up again to the al-Qal'a al-Hamrā, the palace of Sultan Yūsuf on the opposite hill. A fountain bubbled gently in the jasmine-scented evening.

The lady Buthayna, one of the concubines of Sultan Yūsuf, was small and slender, robed in black with a veil drawn across her face so that only her eyes could be seen. Another man, pale-skinned and inclining to fat under his white robes, stood beside and a little behind her. 'What have you to report, Amir Zayani?' Buthayna asked, her voice sharp with tension.

'We received another shipment of gold just before the end of the month of Rabī ath-Thānī. We have resumed sending salt to Murrākush, but we are forced to use the salt pans at Mutrayil now, so the quality is not as good and we will receive less money. We have been forbidden to use the mines at al-Mallāha by the Grandmother.'

'The sultana!' The dark eyes were furious. 'How dare the old bitch interfere?'

'Be calm, *saīda*,' the man in white said. 'The important thing is that the trade goes on. We have rid ourselves of Kāsim al-'Aswad, at least, and we now have caravan masters we can trust.'

'And who do not know too much,' said Zayani. 'We made a mistake in trusting Kāsim, but we will not make that error again. The new caravan masters know the cargoes that they carry and their destination, but no more.' He nodded to the other man. 'Al-Rumani you have done your job well. We are indebted to Saīdi Peruzzi for introducing you.'

'What of the vizier, and the *hajib*?' Buthayna asked. 'Are they prepared to support us against Rīm and the sultana?'

'They are with us.'

'You mentioned Peruzzi,' said Buthayna. 'I do not trust him. Dispose of him, and we will keep the gold for ourselves.'

'That would not be wise, *saīda*,' said al-Rumani. 'We still need him, for the moment. Without his backing, the trade dries up.'

'More importantly, he is undermining Castile on our behalf,' Zayani said. 'When Castile collapses into civil war and the

Knights of Calatrava turn on each other, then our moment comes. We proved that the defences of Castile are weak when we slaughtered the people of Palma del Río. Soon it will be the turn of Qurtuba, Sharīsh, perhaps even Hims al-Andalus. You and your son will restore glory to your kingdom, *saīda*.'

'What about this man Merrivale, the one who eluded you at Runda?'

'Aksal and Mouha are hunting him now in the mountains south of Jayyān. If he escapes he will make for Wadi 'Ash, where a fresh trap is being set for him. I will escort the next caravan myself, and see that it is done.'

'Good. No mistakes this time.'

Zayani inclined his head. 'You should return before you are missed. My men will escort you home.'

Buthayna held up a hand. 'There is one other thing. I want you to kill my rival, Rīm.'

'Is that necessary?' asked al-Rumani. 'Can we not send her into exile in Murrākush?'

Buthayna pulled down her veil. Her face was round, her skin fair with rosy cheeks and lips like rosebuds. A livid red scar ran from one cheek down to the soft line of her jaw.

'Rīm did this to me,' Buthayna said. 'Between her and myself there can be no peace, no forgiveness. A sea of hate lies between us, and one of us will die. It will not be me.'

23

17th of October, 1343

The Warriors of the Faithful came at dawn. There were only two of them, making their way cautiously across the stony ground towards the castle. Warin, on watch, spotted them and roused the others and they crouched behind the gatehouse, waiting. They let the Warriors get to within twenty yards of the gate, and Eleanor stepped out from cover, raised her crossbow and shot one of them in the chest. The other halted in astonishment, and Warin's thrown knife took him straight through the throat. He fell, gouting blood.

'Christ,' said Ficaris, low-voiced. 'How did they find us?'

Merrivale turned to Eleanor. 'Are you all right?'

She stood staring at the body of the man she had shot, which was still twitching a little. 'I've never killed a man before,' she said.

'The first time is the hardest,' he said quietly.

She shook her head in surprise. 'Hard? Why would it be hard? It was them or us.'

After a moment Merrivale bowed his head. 'My lady,' he said quietly. 'Warin, fetch your knife. I reckon Aksal has lost the trail and is sending out scouts to comb the country. It will be some time before those two are missed. We have a chance to put some distance between ourselves and the Warriors. Let us go.'

There followed another long day struggling through the mountains. Finally, aching, tired and sunburned with blistered feet, they reached a pine forest on the southern slopes of the Mājīna range and slumped down in the evening light. There had been no sign of the Warriors all day.

'I think we have lost them,' Merrivale said. 'We need to get to Wadi 'Ash, but we also need rest. We will stay here tomorrow.'

'I am grateful,' Duran said. 'Tomorrow is Shabbat.' He smiled. 'We have no rabbi, but I will do what I can.'

There was no wine, but there was a goatskin full of water, and some stale flatbread and sausage and olives, and Duran laid these out quietly and stood over them and softly recited the kiddush. *And the heavens and the earth and all that filled them were complete. And on the seventh day God completed the labour that he had performed… Blessed are you, the Lord our God, King of the Universe, creator of the fruit of the vine.*

'Amen,' Merrivale said quietly, and the others followed him.

He'd taken the first watch as usual, listening to the wolves howl in the mountains as darkness fell. Warin took over from him a couple of hours later; Eleanor following at midnight.

Merrivale slept uneasily, and just after midnight was woken by the sound of another wolf, close by. He sat up just as Eleanor's crossbow went off with a sharp crack. Something whimpered in the night, and was still. Merrivale hurried to where Eleanor stood in the shadows, looking down at a dead wolf. 'I was hoping it would pass us by,' she murmured, 'but it picked up our scent and was coming straight towards us.'

'Is it dead?'

'I think so. I don't suppose it would be practical to take the skin, would it? I've always wanted a wolfskin.'

'We have wolves in Devon,' Merrivale said. 'When we get home, I will show you where to hunt them.'

They rested through the heat of the following day, and on the second morning they rose and ate the last of the bread and sausage, and Duran filled their waterskins from a nearby stream. Casting around through the forest, Merrivale came to a pine tree that had shed a piece of its bark. A small ꙅ symbol had been carved into the resinous wood.

They descended cautiously from the hills and started south across a dry open plain, baked earth with stunted shrubs and clumps of grass. The wind stirred up clouds of fine powdery dust which seeped into their eyes and noses and mouths, but it also hid them from eyes in the omnipresent watchtowers, and for this they were grateful. Towards evening the wind died away and the air cleared, revealing the shapes of mountains looming on the southern horizon. They camped in a narrow *arroyo* full of dry grass, looking at the mountains. 'That range is called al-Bussarat,' Duran said. 'The mightiest mountains in Andalus. You see there the highest peaks, al-Balata, al-Qasabah, al-Tell.'

The high peaks were sheathed in white, glowing briefly with streaks of flame as the sun began to set. Warin shaded his eyes. 'Is that snow up there? It seems a bit early, given how hot it is down here on the plains.'

'The mountains are high, of course, but the snow comes earlier every year. When my father was young, al-Bussarat rarely saw snow before December, and some winters not at all. But over the past thirty years, that has changed. The sun's heat is fading, it seems, and the world is growing colder.'

Ficaris stood with his hands on his hips, gazing at the mountains. 'I have heard of these peaks. Sierra Nevada, the Castilians call them. The Snowy Mountains.'

'Well,' said Eleanor. 'Let's hope we don't have to climb them.'

Duran pointed to a pass running through the mountains to the west. 'No need. That way leads to Garnāta. The city is only about forty miles away.'

'Too close for my liking,' muttered Warin.

—

Dawn came clear and sharp. They rose and ate a meagre meal and trudged on across the undulating plain. The mountains, blue with white caps of snow, filled the southern horizon now.

Just before midday they came to a green valley running south, with a river trickling along its bottom. Suddenly they were back in the land of the living; the valley was full of fruit trees and olive groves with little heavily fortified hamlets, each with a whitewashed watchtower. They stayed out of the valley, sticking to the arid, unpopulated high ground to the west. Herds of goats grazed here and there, tinkling with bells. Warin pointed to a stone structure ahead. 'There's another castle.'

They studied it for some moments before Ficaris shook his head. 'That's no castle,' he said. 'At least, it wasn't made by the hand of man.'

Wind had eroded the soft stone into columns and towers. As they moved slowly forward they encountered more and more of these rock outcrops and escarpments all sculpted into fantastic shapes, colonnades and cones and pyramids, their faces incised by the wind to form elaborate friezes. Merrivale was reminded suddenly of the ruins of Rome, temples and churches and palaces shattered by war and time, carved walls and rows of columns rising from the ground. This place looked much the same, but as Ficaris had said, no man dwelt here; the hand of God had carved these stones. Hushed and silent, they walked on, and the mountains rose ever higher before them.

The castle of Wadi 'Ash, when it did appear, looked almost puny by comparison. Square, with crenelated ramparts and corner towers and a central keep, it squatted on a hill overlooking a ford of the river. A small town surrounded it: a cluster of white houses, a mosque with a stubby minaret, the domes of a bathhouse, a few flat-roofed buildings down by the ford with horses and mules picketed in the meadows beyond. Crouching behind another outcrop of rock, Duran pointed. 'That is a *funduq*,' he said. 'Caravans halt there to let men and animals rest.'

The faint clopping of hooves came to their ears. A caravan was coming in from the west, a long column of horses and mules laden with panniers strapped to their backs, each led by a man on foot. Horsemen rode guard on either flank, men in black with lances and chainmail tunics and steel helmets that sparkled in the sun. Hidden behind the rock, Merrivale counted over fifty animals, and nearly as many men in the escort.

'They must be carrying something very valuable, to have so many guards,' Duran murmured.

'Yes,' said Merrivale. 'I'd like to know what it is.'

The leading horsemen reached the *funduq* and dismounted. The pack animals arrived and the panniers were lifted from their backs and stacked carefully on the ground. Another man dressed in plain brown walked out of the *funduq* and greeted the leader of the escort. The hair rose on the back of Merrivale's neck. It was too far away to see their faces clearly or make out their features, but he was quite certain from their movements and their stance that the leader of the escort was Zayani, and the other man was Pero de Garcíez.

More hoofbeats and a jingle of harness. Crouching lower still, they watched another column of black-clad horsemen ride down the valley from the north. They passed almost directly below the rocks where Merrivale and his party were hiding, and this time they saw plainly that the leaders of the column were Aksal and Mouha. They too rode to the *funduq* and dismounted, joining Zayani and Garcíez. Mouha turned and pointed back to the north, and the four of them walked inside the *funduq*.

Beyond Wadi 'Ash the ground rose again with more wind-carved ridges and columns of stone. 'We'll circle around to the west,' Merrivale said. 'We'll need to stay well clear of that castle, I don't want Zayani learning of our presence here. Once we're away from the town, we'll find a hiding place and wait until night.'

The sun was bright and hot, the sky its usual flawless blue, but the leaves on the oak and elm trees were turning orange. They used the trees as cover to avoid the gaze of the castle, and once they were well past it they crept out into the open again, moving cautiously through undulating hummocks of ground fenced in by more strange eroded banks of stone. There were fields here, and more herds of goats with jangling bells.

Ficaris sniffed the air. 'I smell charcoal smoke,' he said. 'But I can't see where it is coming from.'

The ground sloped down into a natural amphitheatre, a long open space with steep banks crowned by more eroded pillars of stone. They walked down into this, looking around curiously. Warin pointed to a thin spiral of smoke, issuing from a tiny hole in one of the banks. 'There's a fire underground,' he said. 'Is there a mine nearby?'

Merrivale stopped, holding up a hand. 'We are being watched,' he said.

An invisible door in one of the banks slid open and a man stepped out, raising a short spear and levelling it at Merrivale's chest. Around them more doors began to open and more people came out, men and women carrying spears or long knives. Some had short bows, others were armed with leather slings and bags of shot. Merrivale put his staff on the ground and spread his hands to show they were empty, and the others laid down their weapons.

'*Quis ais?*' the man with the spear demanded.

It took Merrivale a moment to realise that he was speaking Latin, a Latin so heavily accented as to almost be a different language. 'I am Simon Merrivale, herald to the Earl of Derby from England,' he said. 'These are my companions.'

'What is your business here?'

People crowded around him, weapons raised, waiting for an answer. Their clothes were plain leather and undyed wool; some wore rough leather sandals, but many were barefoot. Their faces were broad, almost square. Many had missing teeth or fingers, and one man had an empty eye socket. *These are not Imazighen*, Merrivale thought. *But who are they?*

He decided to take a chance. 'A caravan has just come in from Garnāta. I am interested to know what cargo it carries. I would prefer that the Warriors of the Faithful do not know that I am here.'

A murmur ran through the little crowd. Some of the faces around him showed anger. 'What do the Warriors want here?' another man demanded.

'Some of them are guarding the caravan. Others have been hunting my friends and I through the mountains for the past week.' Merrivale looked at the leader. 'May I ask who you are, *domine*?'

'My name is Euric, and these are my people, the Wesi.' The spearpoint lowered, just a little. 'Why are the Warriors hunting you?'

Merrivale looked up at the sun sinking towards the western hills. 'If we remain out here for too long, someone might see us,' he said. 'Is there somewhere we could talk?'

'Take them to the *ecclesia*,' said a woman carrying a bow with an arrow at the nock. 'We all want to hear them.'

Euric walked towards a steep rock face topped with another eerie wind-eroded colonnade. There was no sign of a door, only a rough stone wall with desiccated weeds hanging down over it. Euric pressed against the stone and part of the wall slid inwards, revealing an arched doorway. He motioned with his spear for Merrivale to enter. Merrivale walked through the arch and into a surprisingly large underground cavern with a barrel-vaulted roof and walls of rough stone. Paintings decorated the walls, processions of bearded saints with yellow halos, the Lamb of God gazing down from the roof, Christ Pantocrator robed in blue on the end wall above a stone altar bearing a gilded crucifix decorated with polished coral. Two plain tallow candles sat on either side of the crucifix.

Of all the things I expected when I stepped through the door, Merrivale thought, *this was not one of them.*

Eleanor, Ficaris, Warin and Duran followed him inside. The Wesi crowded in too, crossing themselves as they faced the altar but never letting go of their weapons. Euric knelt before the altar and bowed his head for a moment before rising and turning to face Merrivale.

'Tell us why you are here,' he said.

'Civil war is coming,' Merrivale said. 'In Castile, and maybe in Garnāta as well. The Warriors of the Faithful are intriguing with their own enemies. What their intentions are, we do not know, but this bodes no good for the sultan. Already they are stealing the sultan's gold. It may be that they have designs on his throne.'

The crowd murmured again, sound echoing in the stone vault like buzzing bees. 'The Warriors have attacked us before,' said Euric. 'They have taken some of our people as slaves.'

'The Warriors know about this place?'

'They know it exists, yes, but they have not yet attacked our village directly. The people they have captured were herdsmen and hunters caught out in the open.'

'Could you resist them if they did attack?'

'We are not strong enough,' said another man. 'We have tunnels that will allow us to escape.'

'Escape to where?' asked the woman with the bow. 'This is our only home.'

Euric shrugged his shoulders. 'The *muhafiz*, the governor in Wadi 'Ash, protects us so long as we pay our taxes, but if he were gone, I believe the Warriors would try to exterminate us.' Unlike the others, he was pensive rather than angry. 'Our people are vanishing, our numbers decreasing. We accept this. But we ask God to let us slip peacefully into the twilight, rather than being slaughtered or dying as slaves.'

'How long have you been here?' Ficaris asked.

'We have always been here. We remember the Poeni, the Romani, so many others. We remember the time when the Moors came... What was it? Five, or six...'

'Five or six years?'

'No, no. Five or six centuries. We co-existed at first, but then the Imazighen came out of Africa and imposed harsh rules upon us. Gradually we moved underground. Others joined us, Christians, Jews, even Moors fleeing persecution by their own people. We welcomed them all.'

'And now you have welcomed us,' Merrivale said gently. 'We thank you for this kindness.'

A little sigh ran around the group, and the last weapons were lowered. 'What do you intend?' Euric asked.

'With your consent, we will remain here until night falls. I will attempt to discover what cargo this caravan is bearing. I think I know already, but I need proof. If I am right, I will take what I know to King Alfonso and Sultan Yūsuf. The power of the Warriors will be broken, and there will be no civil war.'

He had not mentioned Garcíez or Peruzzi. *No point in complicating things needlessly*, he thought. Euric looked at his people and read their faces. 'You must be tired after your long journey,' he said. 'We would be honoured if you would accept our hospitality.'

Euric took them to his own house, ushering them inside. The woman with the bow and a couple of barefoot boys in their teens followed them in, closing the stone door and fitting it into place so that it was invisible from outside. The house itself had been carved out of the rock and was windowless; only a tiny chimney above a central hearth admitted light. A charcoal fire glowed on the hearth, showing stone walls blackened with centuries of smoke, a few iron tools and pots hanging from hooks, straw mattresses on the floor at one end of the room. The other end of the house was enclosed; behind the fence, several small goats stared bellicosely at the strangers. The combination of charcoal smoke and goat was a musky, acrid scent that grated in the back of the throat.

Olive oil lamps were lit, adding to the smoke. The woman, whom Euric introduced as his wife, brought them flatbread and olives and curdled goat's milk. They ate, gratefully, and Duran fell asleep. Ficaris pulled out his playing cards, now rather sweat-stained and the worse for wear, and showed them to the two boys, Euric's sons; they looked at the cards in fascination, examining the painted faces of the kings and viziers. Eleanor rolled her eyes and turned to Merrivale.

'You think the caravan is carrying gold,' she said quietly in English.

'It must be. Peruzzi has promised support for both Leonor and María, and indeed the king himself, but he has no intention of providing support to any of them. He sent a caravan of salt instead of gold to María, and kept the gold for himself. Now he is sending it to al-Mariyya, where doubtless a ship is waiting to carry the gold away to his new bank in Rhodes.'

She thought about this. 'Something doesn't make sense. Why bother sending the salt to María?'

'I don't know. There is a still a great deal that we don't know.'

The light coming through the chimney hole grew fainter and died away to nothing. Merrivale took off his bright surcoat, rolling it and putting it into his battered travelling bag. The others watched him in silence. He picked up his staff and turned to Euric.

'I must go,' he said. 'I will be back by compline. If I am not, help my friends to get away.'

'I will guide you,' Euric said.

'Thank you, but you need to remain here with your people. I will find my way.'

Duran stood up. 'Let me come with you, at least.'

Merrivale shook his head. 'A single man has less chance of being spotted.'

They opened the door and let him out into the night, and pulled the stone back into place. He stood for a moment, letting his eyes adjust to the night and getting his bearings. The last faint glow of sunset was dying in the west. Overhead the Milky Way was a river of stars flowing across the sky, pointing straight towards Wadi 'Ash. Good, he thought. That will be my guide.

He started to walk towards the town. Despite the starlight the shadows were deep; he probed them with his staff, looking for pitfalls. Once, just as he was about to step into a dark place, his staff met with empty air. He stepped back hurriedly, realising that he had nearly fallen over one of the escarpments. He went even more cautiously after that, and it took him over an hour to skirt the walled town and castle and approach the river below.

Here he halted for quite a long time, lying on his belly and watching the *funduq*. The main building was rectangular, about three storeys high. Torches wavered over its gate, and more light came from the interior courtyard. Another torch burned by the stables. He saw the horses and mules of the pack train, picketed on the grass, and the panniers stacked in the open. It was curious that Zayani's men had not taken them into the *funduq*'s storeroom; unless there were too many of them? Fifty animals with a pannier each side meant a hundred panniers, and perhaps it was too much work to shift them inside and then out again in the morning.

The panniers would be guarded, especially if, as he suspected, they contained gold. He watched the shadows around the *funduq*, looking for any sign of movement. He picked out two guards outside the gates, four more watching the pack animals, another three leaning on their spears next to the stacked panniers. Not enough, he thought; it if were me, I would have an entire company on patrol. Can Zayani really be that overconfident?

Still on his belly, he began to crawl down the slope towards the *funduq*. Moving to his left, he reached a point where the panniers were between himself and the torches; more importantly, they were also between himself and the nearest guards. Slowly and silently, holding his breath, he inched forward until he could touch one of the wicker panniers.

A voice broke the silence, startlingly close by. He froze, gripping his staff hard in his hand. It was Zayani, speaking in Castilian. 'The caravan is all yours now, Señor de Garcíez. You have your safe-conducts from the vizier, and Saīdi Peruzzi's ship will be waiting for you at al-Mariyya. You have arranged an escort, I hope, for such a valuable cargo?'

'Peruzzi has arranged it,' Garcíez said. 'The escort arrives tomorrow. You are returning to Garnāta?'

'I am. There are still a few arrangements to be made. What about you?'

'My orders from Peruzzi are to see the cargo on board the ship and then return. We too still have arrangements to make.'

Zayani chuckled. 'Are you tempted to take the ship and cargo for yourself? You could buy yourself a kingdom somewhere, if you wished.'

'My kingdom is here. I intend to overthrow my grand master and take his place. Queen María will reward me too. And you and I still have our own venture, of course.'

'Slaves are becoming harder to find,' said Zayani. 'The *frontera* has been nearly stripped of people, and the supply is drying up. You need to aim higher, Garcíez. As I do.'

'The next sultan of Garnāta?' Garcíez said mockingly. 'Does Buthayna know of your ambitions?'

'She will, when I am ready to tell her. But I am glad to hear that you wish to continue our alliance. When I go on to conquer Murrākush as well, it would be useful to have the Knights of Calatrava by my side. You could even dress it up as a crusade, to get the pope's support.'

'I think we are getting ahead of ourselves,' Garcíez said dryly. 'You haven't overthrown the sultan, and I have not yet deposed the grand master. And we still have Merrivale to deal with.'

Their voices were growing fainter; they were moving away. Merrivale waited until silence had fallen, and sat up and reached for the nearest pannier. It was heavy; good. It was not locked, which was surprising, but perhaps Zayani's men were unable to procure so many locks. He shifted the pannier a little, feeling the weight, and unfastened the straps securing the lid. Taking a deep breath, he opened it and reached inside.

He had expected to touch cold metal. Instead, his fingertips brushed across something granular and rough. A faint saline smell came to his nostrils. Disbelieving, he wetted his fingertips, rubbed the object for a moment, and brought his hand back up to his mouth. There was no mistaking the taste of salt.

But salt is not heavy. This pannier weighs four stone if it weighs an ounce.

Hoarse breathing behind him, light footsteps moving fast. He rolled sideways onto his back just as a knife slashed through the air where he had been kneeling. Starlight showed him a snarling face, a hand missing three fingers, the knife coming down again, and he raised his legs and kicked Aksal hard in the midriff. Aksal staggered, the wind knocked out of his lungs, and Merrivale lunged for his knife arm and twisted his wrist hard, forcing the knife from Aksal's hand. Two fingers jabbed towards Merrivale's eyes, but he ducked under the strike and hit Aksal a shattering blow on the jaw with his balled fist. Aksal catapulted backwards against the panniers and slumped to the ground.

Groping in the shadows, Merrivale found his staff. More footsteps; the guards had heard the scuffle and were coming to investigate. The time for stealth was over. Merrivale fled across the dark fields and uphill past the town. Men ran after him, shouting in Arabic and Tamazight; one of them was Garcíez, yelling for someone to bring torches.

He ran on, following the line of the Milky Way. The ground began to undulate, hillocks and crags of eroded rock looming out of the night. Once he tripped over a heap of stones and fell, rolled over and scrambled up again, hearing the drumming of hooves as horsemen swept up behind him, knowing he had very little time left. He fell again, down a steep bank and landed on his back with a jolt. As he looked around in the starlight, he realised he was back in the long amphitheatre.

He groped along the wall, hearing the hoofbeats coming nearer, and found the rock face outside the church. He pushed hard on the stone and the door grated open, so quickly that he lost his balance and tumbled through the arch onto the floor. Rolling over, he pushed the stone door and pressed it back into place. He lay on the floor in pitch darkness, breathing hard, waiting to see what would happen next.

The hoofbeats were directly overhead. They stopped, and he heard men sliding down the steep bank around him. 'Bring the torches!' he heard Garcíez call, and he held his breath, hearing men moving around outside the church door.

'It's no use,' he heard Mouha say finally. 'This place was created by devils, not men. Once these people melt into the rock, we will never find them. Especially not at night.'

'We will find them,' Garcíez said. He raised his voice. 'Señor Merrivale! Can you hear me?'

Merrivale said nothing, but he sat up and reached for his staff, lying on the floor beside him. 'I know you are there!' Garcíez shouted. 'You cannot escape now!'

A long silence followed. 'Very well,' Garcíez said. 'I grant you one last night. I will return in the morning. You will come out and face me then, or else your friends will suffer. We know how to smoke them out. You have until dawn, Merrivale.'

More sounds of movement, men climbing back up the banks, and the hoofbeats began again, fading away. Absolute silence fell. The enemy would not have gone far, Merrivale knew; they would have watchers all around the underground village, and if he stepped out into the open he would be spotted. He leaned back against the cold stone, imagining the painted saints and the bearded figure of Christ watching him in the darkness.

He knew that darkness had saved him, but he knew also that Garcíez would keep his word, and in the morning he would return. The Wesi had concealed their homes with great skill, but a determined enemy would still find them. *Smoke them out,*

Garcíez had said. Chimneys could be stopped up, battering rams could be used to break down stone doors, and then it would be Palma del Río all over again. He had a few hours of respite, no more.

He realised he had no idea what time it was. Hopefully it was after compline, and Eleanor and the others would be on their way into the hills... One of the Wesi had mentioned tunnels; if he could find one of these, he too could get away. Sitting in the dark, he pondered this notion for a while, and rejected it. If he escaped, Garcíez and Zayani would take revenge on the Wesi. He would be abandoning Euric and his people to their fate.

He was a lone man, unarmed and surrounded by enemies. There could only be one outcome. So, he thought, this is what the end looks like.

He thought of Yolande the last time he had seen her, trembling with fear and shock, her face streaked with tears as her father's men-at-arms dragged him away. He thought of his own father, eyes vacant and sad as he stared at the fire. He remembered Dartmoor, and the shrouded bodies of his mother and sisters lowered into their graves in the empty church. He heard in his mind the voice of Mercuriade of Salerno, the physician who had saved his life and rescued his soul, quoting from a Gnostic text. 'The one who remains ignorant will become a delusion of forgetfulness, and dissolve into oblivion. Those who have no root also have no fruit. They think of themselves as existing, but they will dissolve in a moment. They exist only like the shadows and phantoms of the night.'

On the heels of that thought came another voice: Asach, the old scholar in Xerez. 'The wise know that enlightenment comes in unexpected places,' Asach had said, and he had quoted too, from the *Ghāyat al-Hakīm*: 'When I wished to find knowledge of the secrets of Creation, I came upon a dark vault within the depths of the earth, filled with blowing winds. There appeared to me in my sleep a shape of most wondrous beauty. I said to him, "Who are you?" And he answered, "I am your perfected nature."'

Well, Merrivale thought wryly, I am within the depths of the earth. Perfected nature? Hardly that. I never really learned how to live, apart from those few short months with Yolande. But I know how to die.

Feeling strangely at peace, he lay down on the stone floor and fell asleep.

—

No light penetrated the underground church, but Merrivale knew it was morning; years of travelling in wild places as a King's Messenger, much of it on the run from enemies too numerous to mention, had taught him a keen sense of time. He woke and rose to his feet, stretching his arms and picking up his staff. The sense of peace he had felt last night remained with him. His mind was clear and calm.

From outside came Garcíez's voice. 'Señor Merrivale. It is time.'

Merrivale waited, listening. He could hear no other footsteps. 'I am alone,' Garcíez said. 'Come out and face me. If you do, you have my word of honour that the troglodytes will not be harmed. If you fail, we will drop Greek fire down their chimneys and burn them to death.'

Merrivale took a deep breath and let it out slowly. Opening the stone door of the church, he stepped out into the open.

The weather had changed during the night. Heavy grey clouds sealed off the sky, and a cold wind kicked up dust in the amphitheatre. Garcíez stood at the far end, in the same plain brown cote and hose he had worn yesterday, a sword and dagger belted at his waist. Merrivale planted his hands on his hips. 'I am here,' he said. 'Where is Zayani? Where are Aksal and Mouha?'

'Searching the hills for the lady Eleanor and the rest of your friends. We think they escaped during the night with the help of the troglodytes. It seems they abandoned you to your death. Such lack of loyalty, after all you have done for them.'

'Let them go free. They know nothing.'

Garcíez's voice was dry. 'That is unlikely.'

'I saw your brother's widow,' Merrivale said. 'She told me you were a good man.'

'Goodness is a matter of perception, *señor*. You of all people should know that.'

'Why did you take service with Peruzzi? What hold does he have over you?'

'He has no hold over me. When I am grand master of the Knights of Calatrava, it is Peruzzi who will bow to me.'

'And Queen María? Why choose to ally with her?'

'We share similar aims,' Garcíez said. 'And we both understand injustice. Enough now.' He drew his sword, blade flashing dimly in the light. 'I am offering you an honourable death.'

Garcíez began to walk down the length of the amphitheatre towards Merrivale. After a moment Merrivale responded, walking towards the other man with slow deliberate steps. The silence was so intense that Merrivale could hear his own heart beating. In his mind he heard the tolling of a bell.

They halted a few paces apart. The wind whistled suddenly around the fantastic eroded rocks, singing like an Aeolian harp, plucking fine streams of sand from the tops of the cones and columns. 'You have no sword,' Garcíez said.

'I do not carry one.'

Garcíez drew his dagger and tossed it on the ground by Merrivale's feet. 'I told you before, I am not a murderer. Give yourself a chance, at least.'

Merrivale nudged the dagger with his foot and pushed it away. Standing quite still, leaning on his staff, he stared straight into Garcíez's eyes. He saw a moment of wonder, even a little fear, hardening swiftly into determination. Garcíez raised his sword.

Behind Garcíez, the door of one of the cave houses opened. Eleanor of Lancaster stepped out into the open, raised her crossbow and shot Garcíez in the back.

24

22nd of October, 1343

Garcíez dropped his sword and fell onto his knees, clutching at his back. Blood began to dribble from the corners of his mouth, staining his beard. He fell onto his face, twitching faintly, and lay still.

Eleanor ran towards Merrivale, fitting another bolt to her crossbow and winding it. 'What in the name of God are you doing here?' Merrivale demanded.

'Rescuing you. Come, we must get to the tunnel.'

'Too late,' Merrivale said.

Hoofbeats echoed all around them. Black-robed Warriors of the Faithful galloped into the amphitheatre, swords and lances levelled, converging on Merrivale and Eleanor. Merrivale felt suddenly sick. 'My God,' he said. 'You didn't think Garcíez would be stupid enough to come here alone, did you?'

Someone shouted from the depths of the earth, an eerie long-lost battle cry that echoed off the carved rocks and floated in the wind: '*In hoc signo vincis!*'

Others took up the cry, punctuated by a clash of metal. The door of Euric's house opened and Euric himself ran out carrying his spear, followed by his wife with her bow and their sons whirling slings around their heads. Duran, Ficaris and Warin followed, swords in hand. Other doors opened and more of the Wesi came after them, a hundred or more waving a motley assortment of weapons and shouting over and over, *In hoc signo vincis!*, the ancient war cry of the Roman legions: by this sign, you shall conquer.

Eleanor shot one of the Warriors, who tumbled into the dust, and knelt to reload her crossbow. Another man rode at her with upraised sword; Merrivale swung his staff two-handed, breaking the man's sword arm. Howling with pain, the rider hauled his horse around with his good hand and galloped away. Merrivale turned to see Duran dragging another man from his saddle by brute force, raising him overhead and smashing him to the ground. Ficaris, Warin, Euric were all in the middle of the fray, while Euric's wife stood to one side, bow raised and shooting rapidly with calm precision.

Caught by surprise, the Warriors had not expected resistance. They turned and galloped back out of the amphitheatre, leaving half a dozen men on the ground. The fight was over before it had barely begun.

'You didn't think I'd be stupid enough to come here alone, did you?' Eleanor asked, gentling a loose horse with her hand.

Merrivale turned to face Euric who stood breathing hard, bloody spear in hand. 'Thank you,' he said.

'You are our guest,' Euric said simply. 'It is our duty to protect you.'

Merrivale nodded. 'We will depart now. For the moment, the Warriors will follow us rather than molesting you further. But I worry about the future. They may come seeking revenge.'

'We will send word to the *muhafiz* in Wadi 'Ash and tell him the Warriors have attacked us. We will ask him to take us under his protection.'

An image passed before Merrivale's eyes: Diago and his fellow slaves waiting for death in the water mine. He pushed the thought away. This was different; at least Euric and his people had some means of escape. A voice in his mind said, *They chose this path. Are you disappointed that your chance for martyrdom has gone?*

The Wesi were rounding up more of the riderless horses and leading them forward. Merrivale and his companions mounted, and Euric's sons brought their bags and waterskins out from the house and handed them up. Merrivale looked down at Euric. 'May God watch over you,' he said, 'and may He grant that your village endures.'

'Nothing endures,' said Euric. 'But we are in God's hands.'

They rode hard through the windy morning, knowing that the Warriors of the Faithful would quickly regroup and follow them. As they climbed into the oak forests where dead leaves spun gently to the ground, Merrivale looked around. 'I assumed you had departed through the tunnels, as we arranged,' Merrivale said. 'Why did you come back?'

'Euric sent his sons to follow you, sir,' Warin said. 'When they saw what happened at the *funduq* and that you were being pursued back towards the village they ran back and sounded the alarm and we all hid in the tunnels. Then we realised that you were trapped in the church. When he realised that we weren't leaving without you, Euric decided to stay and help us.'

Merrivale was silent for a moment. 'I am grateful,' he said finally.

'What now?' asked Ficaris.

'Garcíez is dead. Everything now rests on finding Mauro. We must go to Garnāta, and hope that Duran's friends there can help us.'

'I knew it,' Warin said, not quite under his breath.

'Can we outrun the Warriors?' Ficaris asked.

'We must,' said Merrivale.

The hills became steeper, and several times they had to dismount and lead their horses up slopes littered with broken stone. From the crest of the last hill they looked down to see another village surrounded by orchards and vineyards at the bottom of a long valley leading to the west. Eleanor pointed. 'Look,' she said.

Black-clad horsemen were riding hard from the east, the direction of Wadi 'Ash. Even as they watched, the horsemen reached the village and halted. After a moment scouts began moving out to the west and south. Merrivale looked at Duran. 'How well do you remember your maps?'

'I am trying to think.' The big man rubbed his forehead. 'This range of hills is a spur that runs down from the high peaks of al-Bussarat. That valley running west is the only direct route to Garnāta, and they have cut us off from that. We can try to go over the hills, but it is very rough country. And if we go too far south, we will be up in the high peaks.'

'And if we follow the valley we will ride straight into the arms of the Warriors,' Eleanor said. Her eyes were bright. 'Is this another trap, perchance?'

Warin pointed to the left. 'There's a side valley coming down from the south, sir. We could follow that for a while, and see if we can find a way over the hills.'

Ficaris, listening, held up a hand. 'More of the bastards,' he said urgently. 'Coming up behind us.'

They rode hard, using the folds of ground to stay out of sight of the village. The side valley Warin had spotted was dry and arid, with even tufts of grass struggling to survive in the stony soil. Jagged cliffs rose around them. Crows cawed raucously as they passed.

Afternoon found them in another strange and haunted landscape, a maze of canyons and crags and sawtooth ridges, winding and twisting at random. The clouds hung low over them, blotting out the sun. It was easy to become disoriented, and twice they discovered that they had been travelling in circles, finding their own hoofprints in the dust. 'Let's hope Zayani is having the same problem,' Ficaris muttered.

Cold dusk fell early under the clouds. They reached the edge of the maze and climbed into another forest, where deer started nervously in the shadows and oak leaves rustled in a hundred shades of bronze. Turning west as the light began to fade, they dismounted and led their horses over a high ridge and down into another deep valley. Dark shadows flitted through the twilight: Warriors of the Faithful, riding up from the north.

'What about the ones behind us?' Ficaris asked.

'They're still coming,' Merrivale said.

They turned south once more, dismounting and leading their horses through the forest as night fell, climbing all the time. The smell of sulphur came to their nostrils, and they heard bubbling water in the darkness and felt a wash of stinking, heated air. 'Stop,' Merrivale murmured. 'It's too dangerous to go on. We'll wait for daylight, and see where the hot pools are.'

'The Warriors may still be hunting,' Duran said.

'They aren't hunting,' Merrivale said. 'They're herding us. Eleanor is right. They think they have us trapped.'

An outcrop of rock gave them shelter from the relentless wind. Groping in the dark, they tethered their horses and sat down with their backs against the rock to eat the last of their food. Merrivale took the first watch while the others fell into an exhausted sleep. Up in the mountains, the wolves began to howl.

—

'We have them in the palm of our hand,' said Zayani. 'Tomorrow, we will crush them.'

Around them, campfires were flickering to life among the trees as the Warriors of the Faithful settled in for the night. 'I reckon they are about two miles ahead of us,' Mouha said. 'Why not ride on, and take them now?'

'The hills are steep and treacherous in the dark, and you can hear the wolves. There is no need to take risks. All we need to do is cut Merrivale off from Garnāta and keep forcing him south until he reaches the high mountains. From there, he will have no escape.'

Mouha scowled. 'He escaped from Runda, *saīdi*. And Garcíez thought he had Merrivale trapped at Wadi 'Ash, but he wriggled free.'

'This is different. Down here in the valleys, my friend, it is autumn, but up on those heights it is winter. And no one crosses al-Bussarat in winter.' Zayani clapped Mouha on the shoulder. 'I leave this to you and Aksal. I must return to Garnāta.'

'The death of Garcíez changes things,' Mouha said.

'Our task is more difficult, but not impossible. When you have killed Merrivale, go back to Wadi 'Ash and take charge of the caravan. See that it reaches al-Mariyya as planned.'

'We could keep the gold for ourselves.'

'Greed is the enemy of the soul, Mouha. It corrupts the faith. We take what is necessary for ourselves, and no more. It is thus that we will triumph.'

23rd of October, 1343

At first light Merrivale stirred and woke. Warin was standing watch nearby, a dark shadow against the pale light. 'Anything to report?' Merrivale asked.

'Nothing, sir. Quiet as the tomb.'

'Very apt.' They roused the others, Ficaris groggy, Eleanor alert in an instant, Duran stretching and flexing his biceps. Untethering his horse, Merrivale looked at the rock face. So tiny and faint as to be almost invisible, a Ƨ symbol had been scratched into the stone.

The light was strong enough now to see where the hot sulphur pools lay. They mounted and rode past the steaming water, and pressed on up the valley. The slopes grew narrower and steeper. Oak trees gave way to forests of stunted pine trees clinging to the stony ground. Dark clouds drifted overhead, and a fine misty rain began to fall.

At Merrivale's signal, Warin dropped back to see if the pursuit was following. He rejoined half an hour later, spurring his horse up a steep slope. 'They're about a mile back,' he said. 'And there's more of them following the high ground to the west. They're nearly opposite us, sir.'

That meant the way to the west was still barred. Merrivale looked at the steep mountain slopes ahead. 'We'll have to leave the horses,' he said. 'Hopefully they'll make their way back downhill before the wolves get them. Leave most of your gear, too. Carry only what is absolutely necessary.'

For himself, that was his staff and his herald's tabard, badges of office that he stubbornly clung to. Eleanor's crossbow and quiver were strapped to her back, and the others kept their swords. Abandoning the horses, they climbed on through ever-increasing rain.

Soaked and shivering, they reached a high crest and halted. Ahead lay another mountain, with narrow valleys running down past its right and left flanks. Right would take them west, closer to the enemy. 'We'll go left,' Merrivale said, 'and see if we can put this mountain between us and the Warriors. If we can throw them off the trail, we might be able to double back and get down to the lower levels. From there, we can find a way to the west.'

'And get out of the rain,' Ficaris said with chattering teeth.

They descended into the valley, a steep slope of five hundred feet that led to a roaring brown stream fed by the rain, only to find that they would have to climb again. They scrambled up over wet rocks, and gradually the pine trees dwindled and were gone, leaving only the stony spines of the mountains rising like broken towers through the rain.

Another high ridge. They paused at the summit, Merrivale trying to remember the mountains as he had seen them from below. The highest peaks must be off to their right. Al-Tell and al-Qasabah were, he knew, connected by a high saddle of rock; al-Balata was a little further to the west. They needed to avoid those if possible because that was where the snowfields lay. He gestured with his hand, and they began to make their way cautiously around the side of the mountain, stones crumbling and rolling under their feet. Again, Warin dropped back, and again he returned with bad news. 'They've left their horses, but they're coming fast. I think that bastard Aksal is leading them.'

The rain turned to sleet. Icy pellets stung their faces and hands. The mountain slope curved sharply away to the west, and they looked out through the falling sleet to see more black shapes creeping along the far side of the mountain. Merrivale's heart sank. 'They have us in a vice,' he said. 'We'll have to go higher to avoid them.'

The wind whipped sleet around them. Eleanor said something under her breath. A perilous descent over icy rocks led to another climb, this one so steep that once again they often had to scramble on their hands and knees, groping for handholds with numb fingers. There was one blessing; the sleet was so thick that they could not see the ground below them, or know how far they would tumble if they slipped and fell.

The sleet turned to snow, fine white powder at first, rapidly developing into thicker flakes. Soon snow lay thick on the ground and they had to plunge their hands into it to find holds for climbing. Merrivale's back ached, and sparks flashed in front of his eyes. His lungs fought for air. It was impossible to know how high they were. The crest of the ridge was a steep spine of rock sheeted with ice. Panting, lungs burning, they fought their way up it and reached the crest, where they sank down into the snow.

The wind moaned around them. Snowflakes flew into their eyes and matted on their clothing. Gasping for breath, Merrivale realised that they had climbed right into the heart of the mountains; this was the saddleback ridge that connected al-Tell to the left with al-Qasabah to the right. He sensed a great void beneath his feet, but could not see it through the blinding snow.

Out of the snowstorm came men in black, floundering through the snow and snarling with upraised swords. Instinct took over. Eleanor raised her crossbow and shot the first man, the bolt lodging in his neck. Blood flew through the snowflakes, staining the snow as he fell over the side of the ridge and disappeared from sight. She knelt, trying to reload with freezing hands. Another man ran at her with levelled sword, but the snow hampered him and gave Merrivale time to raise his staff and bring it down on the man's head. He fell unconscious. Two men were attacking Duran, who dropped his sword and seized both by the neck, smashing their heads together. Ficaris and Warin were fighting two more Warriors; Ficaris was already bleeding from a wound to his hand and visibly tiring. Merrivale moved towards them, swinging his staff to parry the blow from the Warrior's sword before reversing his grip and driving the butt into the man's midriff, knocking the wind out of him. Another blow to the man's face sent him staggering backwards with blood spurting from his nose. Merrivale turned towards the Warrior attacking Warin, and realised that the other man had three fingers missing from his left hand.

Aksal snarled. Warin was hurt too, a cut on his cheek, and despite his strength he was growing weary. Aksal had also struggled with the climb and the cold, but the sight of blood drove him on. He attacked Warin repeatedly, Warin parrying each blow with difficulty. The ridge here was thin as the edge of a knife, too narrow for Merrivale to come up alongside Warin and intervene. To the right lay the steep slope up which they had climbed; to the left was a ledge of rock and a sheer drop.

Aksal lunged again. Knowing he had to make an end, Warin seized his sword arm and twisted it. They wrestled for a moment, each trying to throw the other, Aksal's face rigid with strain and rage. At first they were locked together, frozen and immovable, neither able to gain an advantage, but after a moment, very slowly, Warin began to force Aksal back. Aksal fought him like a wildcat, shifting his feet in the snow, trying to keep his balance, and suddenly Warin released his grip and stepped back, kicking the other man hard on the knee. Aksal's leg collapsed and he fell shouting. The snow gave way beneath him, sending him sliding over the ledge. He managed just in time to cling on with his fingers, but his maimed hand could not get enough purchase to haul himself back up. Holding on with his right hand, he glared up at Warin with bloodshot eyes.

'*Rebbi d ameqqran!*' he shouted.

'Pull him up,' Merrivale said.

Warin shook his head. 'No, sir. I don't think I will.' Standing over Aksal, he raised his booted foot and stamped brutally on Aksal's right hand, breaking the other man's fingers. Aksal lost his grip and fell into the void, his body turning over once and disappearing into the falling snow.

They were almost too exhausted to move, but to remain on the ridge for much longer meant certain death from cold and exposure. Inching along the ridge, they found a shoulder of rock that allowed them to descend onto its western slopes into a little dell with a couple of frozen lakes. The wind was less fierce here, meaning they could recoup some strength, and they moved forward through the falling snow, only to find more dark rocks looming in front. A cliff of unguessable height towered over them, barring their way. They flattened themselves against the rocks for a few minutes, resting and catching their breath. Ficaris shivered and cradled his hand; blood had frozen on Warin's cheek. Duran staggered and looked on the edge of collapse. Once again, Eleanor seemed as strong as any of them, and not for the first time Merrivale marvelled at her indomitable will.

'Señor Merrivale,' said a voice from behind the curtain of snow. 'We have found you at last.'

A dark shape emerged from the veil of white; Mouha, with a drawn sword in his hand. Five more Warriors followed. Merrivale staggered upright, the others following him.

'No speeches,' Merrivale said. 'We're too tired to listen. Do what you came to do.'

'I am not an inhumane man,' Mouha said. 'You are people of the book, and I respect your faith. You may have a moment of prayer, to commend your souls to God.'

'Thank you,' Merrivale said, and he took a firm grip on his staff. With his other hand he made the sign of the cross in the air and looked at the others. '*In hoc signo vinces,*' he said.

Eleanor whipped her crossbow from behind her back and squeezed the trigger. The bolt missed Mouha, but hit the man behind him in the shoulder. He spun around and fell into the snow. Merrivale started towards Mouha, but Duran threw back his head and screamed into the sky. Roaring like a bull, he surged past Merrivale and hurled his own sword at Mouha's head. Mouha ducked, and for a split second, his guard came down. Duran tore the other man's sword from his hand and lifted Mouha like he was a child, holding the Warrior flailing over his head as he ploughed through the snow down towards the frozen lakes. The rest of the enemy hesitated, and another crossbow bolt pierced one through the hand, knocking his sword away. Screaming like fiends, Ficaris and Warin ran towards the others, and they fled through the falling snow and disappeared.

Duran reached the lake. Standing on the bank, he threw Mouha down onto the ice. With a crash, the ice broke, plunging Mouha into the water. He came to the surface quickly, struggling to climb out. Duran jumped into the icy water beside him, seizing Mouha's head and dragging him under, holding him fast. The water surged as Mouha struggled, but Duran's iron grip did not cease. A trail of bubbles broke the surface for about a minute, and stopped.

Merrivale and Warin pulled Duran out of the water and the big man sank to his knees. 'Get up,' Merrivale said harshly. 'If we don't move now, we will die here.'

Duran did not speak. Ficaris knelt beside him, wrapping his arms around him and holding him close, trying to impart some of his own body heat. 'Come on, my friend,' he said. 'What did Aristotle say? "The hardest victory is over the self." Back in Córdoba you have friends who love you, and a scriptorium full of books that still need reading and translating. Don't leave your work unfinished by dying on this damned mountain.' After a long moment Duran lurched to his feet.

'What do we do now?' Eleanor asked. 'We can't possibly climb that cliff.'

'The ground to the right slopes away downhill,' Merrivale said. 'We'll go that way.'

'What about the Warriors?' Warin asked. 'There must be more of them out there.'

'We'll have to take our chances. We have about two hours of daylight left, maybe less. If we don't get down to lower levels and find shelter before nightfall, we will all be dead.'

They floundered through the snow, keeping the cliffs to their left. The ground sloped away steeply. Rugged boulders loomed up in front of them; they struggled past these, slipping and sliding on sheet ice. More cliffs rose on either side, and Merrivale realised they were in a watercourse running down off the mountain. Time passed with infinite slowness, every second a torture of fatigue and cold. A haze descended on Merrivale's mind; he moved like an automaton, planting his feet slowly and deliberately, using his staff as a crutch to drag himself down the mountain. Every now and then he turned to see if the others were all still there, and it took a powerful effort of will to count them, *one, two, three, four.*

Ficaris's voice croaked. 'The snow has stopped.'

Merrivale had not noticed. The snow had stopped, and a fine rain was falling through a cold fog. A river bubbled among rocks, tumbling down towards the distant plains. The ground became softer, and the pine forests reappeared, interspersed with high alpine meadows.

Something square loomed up out of the fog. Focusing his eyes, Merrivale saw a stone hut with no windows and a single wooden door, and a lean-to shed at one end; a herdsman's hut, at a guess, used when the herders drove their animals up to the high pastures in summer. They stumbled towards this. Merrivale knocked once on the door and, receiving no answer, opened it. Inside the room was cold but dry. They entered and sank down on the floor, unable to move or even speak for a moment.

Once again, Merrivale roused them. 'We must have a fire,' he said. 'I saw wood in that shed outside. Warin, fetch some in. The rest of you, look around for a tinderbox.'

There was no tinderbox to be found. Warin came in and dumped an armload of wood on the floor beside the hearth. 'The wood is still good and dry. Let's get that fire going.'

Ficaris sat hunched over on the floor. 'It's no good, Warin. We can't light a fire without flint and steel.'

'We can,' Eleanor said. 'Lend me your knife, Jac.'

They watched as she shaved paper thin peelings from a block of wood and piled them on the hearth. Larger pieces of kindling followed, with the rest of the block of wood on top. Still shivering, she trimmed the bottom of another piece of kindling until it was roughly round, and picked up a second block of wood and carved a small circular hole in the top of it.

'Where did you learn this?' asked Ficaris through chattering teeth.

'My father's huntsman.'

Holding the stick of kindling between her hands, she inserted it into the hole and rubbed it vigorously back and forth. Within a minute smoke was curling up from the tip of the stick; another minute and the tip was glowing bright. She plunged this into the wood shavings which ignited immediately. Soon the kindling was crackling, the wood burning merrily. They huddled around the fire, soaking in the warmth and not minding the smoke in their faces.

'I may live now,' Ficaris said.

Duran smiled a little. 'Until tomorrow,' he said.

'I'll take that. An hour ago, I didn't think we would see tonight.'

The firelight showed them a string of sausages hung from a hook in one corner, desiccated and rock hard. It was impossible to know what meat they were made from, and no one cared. 'Shall we set a watch tonight, sir?' Warin asked.

'We all need rest,' Merrivale said. 'If the enemy come, they come. We won't be able to resist them.'

They ate some of the sausage and slumped on the floor beside the fire, sinking into an exhausted sleep.

They rose the next morning, aching and weary, and carried on down the valley. More streams tumbled out of the hills, fed by the rain and snow, and the river grew in size, running through a steep canyon with a narrow trail along its bank. Duran scratched his head. 'I think this river may be the Nahr Sinnil,' he said. 'If so, we are fortunate. It runs through Garnāta.'

'What do you propose to do when we get there?' Merrivale asked.

'I will guide you to the old city, the al-Bayyāzīn. Friends will give us shelter.'

Eleanor pointed at the hills above them. 'Watchtowers,' she said.

'Christ,' said Merrivale, 'get under cover.' They dodged behind a cleft of rock in the canyon wall, but they were too late. Smoke was already rising from the beacons on the towers. They heard horsemen coming up the valley towards them, and more riding down from behind. The slopes of the canyon were too steep to climb.

'After all that pain and agony yesterday,' Ficaris said softly. 'After everything we have been through. It isn't right.'

The horsemen closed in. They wore white tunics instead of black, and spired helmets with chainmail lappets and steel grilles, and their light lances were tipped with deep red pennons. A banner floated over the leader's head, crimson with writing picked out in gold: *Only God is victorious*.

Thank God for that, Merrivale thought wearily. *At least they are not Warriors of the Faithful*. He laid his staff on the ground and spread his hands. The others dropped their weapons. '*Salaam*,' Merrivale said. 'We come in peace.'

'Seize them,' the leader said. 'Take their weapons. We shall take you to Garnāta, *kāfir*, and there you will suffer the fate that awaits all Christian spies.'

25

24th of October, 1343

The wind blew steadily at al-Jazīra, rattling the canvas pavilions and scattering dust through the camp. The rain and snow in the mountains had not yet reached the coast.

Henry, Earl of Derby, stood in his pavilion, arms folded, staring at the canvas wall. Richard, the Earl of Arundel, sat on a bench nearby, his head in his hands. Neither spoke. They had gone beyond the point where words were of any use. The end of October, when they would be obliged to depart for England, was just over a week away.

One of Derby's esquires entered and bowed. 'My lord, Signor de Peruzzi requests to see you.'

Arundel raised his head. 'Peruzzi? What does that vulture want? Send him away, I am in no mood to see him.'

Derby shook his head. 'It might be important, Richard. Show him in.'

Robed in sombre grey with a sable-trimmed hat, Peruzzi entered the pavilion and inclined his head in the briefest of bows. 'My lords, I will not trouble you for long. I fear I bear bad news.'

Derby tensed. 'What is it?'

'Your sister the lady Eleanor, my lord. She is dead.'

Arundel closed his eyes, leaning forward like he was about to be sick. 'What happened?' Derby asked.

'It appears that your herald Merrivale found the lady, but instead of returning her to you, her brother, he insisted on dragging her with him while he pursued his private vendetta with me. For some unknown reason they entered the emirate of Garnāta and got lost in the mountains, where they died in the snow.'

'Have their bodies been recovered?' Derby asked, keeping his voice steady.

'No. It is unlikely that they will be found until spring.'

'How did you learn of this?'

'Abū Nu'aym Ridwan, the chancellor of Garnāta, wrote to tell me. He expresses his profound sorrow and regret at your sister's unnecessary death. Merrivale, of course, is entirely to blame. What a pity that he too is dead, and cannot be held to account.'

'You are enjoying this,' Derby said. 'Aren't you?'

'I too deeply regret the loss of the lady Eleanor,' Peruzzi said. 'Merrivale is another matter. Had I known that you intended to welcome this reckless and unbalanced man into your household, my lord, I would have advised you against it.'

'Get out,' Derby said.

Peruzzi bowed and withdrew. Arundel raised his head, his eyes wet with tears. 'I cannot believe this is true.'

'Perhaps it isn't,' Derby said. He put his hands together, thinking. 'Why did Ridwan write to Peruzzi? Why not send word directly to me, her brother? Speaking personally, my friend, I'll believe Simon Merrivale is dead when I see his body, and not before.'

Arundel sat up a little. 'Why would Peruzzi lie?'

'Perhaps in hopes of persuading us to give up and go home now, rather than waiting. He wants us out of the way before whatever he is planning comes to fruition.'

Arundel drew a deep breath, sobbing in his throat. 'I pray to God you are right.'

'That's all we can do,' Derby said, a little grimly. 'Wait, and pray.'

In the courtyard of Leonor de Guzmán's house, the flowers were starting to fade. Peruzzi waited while her servants announced him, and entered the hall to find her seated beside a charcoal brazier. Rings glistened on her hands and gems flashed on her jewelled cap. 'I have some interesting news for you,' Peruzzi said. 'Pero de Garcíez is dead.'

There was a little pause. 'Why would that interest me?' asked Leonor.

'As you know very well, Garcíez was intending to challenge your lover Juan Núñez for control of the Order of Calatrava. Had he succeeded in becoming grand master, he would have thrown the Order's support behind Queen María, and you would be as good as dead. Now you have a fighting chance once more.'

Leonor rose to her feet. 'What are you talking about?' she demanded. 'You assured me that María is weak. The *fidalgos* who promised to support her would never dare to rise against the king.'

'I did say that,' Peruzzi agreed. 'I also told María much the same thing about you.'

'You spoke to *María*? My God, Peruzzi, have you betrayed me? You are supporting her?'

Peruzzi's eyebrows rose. 'I have no interest in factions. I am an interested onlooker, no more. You see, *mi çaida*, I do not greatly care which of you wins. The mere fact that you are fighting is enough.' He paused. 'Although, I must say, if I were a gambler I should back María. She is ice to your fire.'

'Fire melts ice,' said Leonor.

An expression of contempt crossed Peruzzi's face. 'And water douses flames. Do not waste my time with childish games of words. Fortune's wheel has been set in motion, my lady. Prepare your forces, and fight to the best of your ability. It is all you can do now.'

'You *have* betrayed me. Where is the gold you promised me?'

'If you triumph over María, I shall see to it that you have all the gold you could wish for. You see, no matter which of you loses, I shall win.'

Peruzzi bowed and left the hall. Leonor de Guzmán sat down again, resting her hands in her lap and staring at the glowing charcoal in the brazier. 'Fight to the best of my ability,' she repeated softly. 'Oh, I shall fight, Peruzzi. And when I win, I will show you just how much I need you, you faithless pig.'

Garnāta, the city of pomegranates, lay at the confluence of two rivers, surrounded by orchards and olive groves. The minarets of its mosques rose slender and tall over the packed white houses. The old town, al-Bayyāzīn, perched on a hill above the newer city. Opposite, on a wedge of rock between the rivers, stood the high crenelated walls and towers of al-Qal'a al-Hamrā, the Red Fortress, the seat of the sultans of Garnāta.

Their escort had bound their hands and forced them to walk to Garnāta. The journey was only about five miles, but they were exhausted and hungry and it had begun to rain again. The guards at the gates looked at them with contempt. Inside the encircling walls of the fortress was a small city; workshops, stables, aqueducts, barracks, even a marketplace. They passed through an arched gateway and into a courtyard with a long ornamental pool of water pocked with raindrops. Here, their escort dismounted and an officer, ornately armourted in a spired helmet and breastplate both inlaid with gold calligraphy, approached and stared at them with dark, hostile eyes.

'Take them to the vizier,' he said.

They were marched across the courtyard, through a door and down a long corridor, past more guards and into a big, high-ceilinged room that glowed like a box of jewels. Every wall and every beam in the ceiling was carved and painted with intricate geometric and floral patterns. Cartouches with exquisite calligraphy and shields all bore the same motto: *Only God is victorious.* Their escort marched them forward and halted them. They stood for a moment, dripping water onto the glazed tile floor. Even Eleanor's head was down.

Two men faced them. One, seated in a high-backed chair, was fair-skinned with a lined face and snow-white hair and beard. The other, dressed all in black with cold dark eyes, was Zayani.

Merrivale studied Zayani. *He is surprised to see us,* he thought. *He thought Mouha and Aksal had killed us.*

The captain of their escort folded his hands, bowing his head. 'We found these men in the hills, *saīdi*. We believe these are the spies who were reported at Wadi 'Ash.'

'You are correct,' said Zayani. 'Their leader is that man, Simon Merrivale.' He pointed at Eleanor. 'That one is a woman. An Englishwoman, Saīda Eleanor of Lancaster.'

The white-bearded man pursed his lips in disapproval. 'I am Abū al-Hasan ibn al-Jayyāb, vizier of his highness Sultan Yūsuf, may God send him reward. You will answer my questions truthfully.'

'Yes, *saīdi*,' Merrivale said.

'How did you come here? Our men are patrolling the road to Wadi 'Ash. How did you escape their notice?'

'We did not follow the road, *saīdi*,' Merrivale said. 'We came over the mountains.'

There was a short pause. 'This is untrue. No one has ever crossed al-Bussarat in winter.'

Merrivale raised his head. 'If you doubt my word, send men up to the slopes between Al-Qasabah and al-Balata. You will find there the bodies of two officers of the Warriors of the Faithful, Aksal ben Mellal and Mouha ben Tirga. They followed us into the mountains, as their surviving men will attest.'

Zayani took a step forward, one hand dropping to the hilt of his sword. 'You killed my captains? That is impossible!'

Merrivale shrugged. 'One fell off a cliff, the other drowned. The mountains can be dangerous, especially at this time of year.'

Zayani turned to the bearded man. 'They should be executed immediately, *saīdi*.'

'I am inclined to agree,' said Ibn al-Jayyāb. 'If they can cross al-Bussarat in the snow, they are not just spies but devils as well. Simon Merrivale, have you anything to say before I pass sentence?'

'Yes,' said Merrivale. He pointed at Zayani. 'I accuse Hamou Ou Akka ibn Zayani, *amir* of the Warriors of the Faithful, of treason and inciting rebellion against the sultan, and of conspiring with the Order of Calatrava. If you will permit me, *saīdi*, I will lay out my case against him.'

The vizier's lips pursed again. 'The *amir* is a loyal servant of the sultan, may God look kindly upon him. You accuse him, I think, to deflect us away from your own guilt. God dispenses justice to the righteous, but to evil-doers He shows no mercy. You and your companions will be taken to the place of execution, where you will be flayed alive. Your skins will be stretched on the walls above the gate to serve as a warning to others. Take them away.'

'No!' Ficaris said. 'Wait!'

The captain of the escort spun around and hit Ficaris a violent blow to the point of the chin. Ficaris sagged, his eyes rolling back in his head, and he fell unconscious onto the tiles.

'Stop,' said a firm voice behind them. '*Saīdi*, my orders are that you deliver the prisoners to me.'

There was a long silence. Zayani stood with clenched fists. 'Who gives these orders?' the vizier asked.

The man who had spoken walked forward. He was tall, Merrivale saw, slender but strong, dressed in long white robes with a hauberk and helmet with mail lappets. He wore a black patch over his left eye. A dozen other white-robed men stood behind him.

'The Grandmother gives the orders,' he said. 'Do you contest her authority, Ibn al-Jayyāb?'

The vizier looked down at his hands for a moment. 'I do not,' he said. 'But I hold you responsible for the prisoners, Faraj ibn Muhammad. If they do harm to any of our people, you will suffer the consequences.'

'Of course,' said Faraj. He bowed briefly, and pointed to the still unconscious Ficaris. 'Carry him. Saīdi Merrivale, Saīda Eleanor, you and your companions will come with me.'

They walked out of the audience chamber, two of Faraj's men carrying Ficaris between them. Merrivale could feel Zayani's eyes boring into his back. In the courtyard, Faraj turned to Duran.

'There is no reason to detain you further, Duran ben Shlomo. You may go where you please.'

'I would like to stay with my friends,' Duran said.

'That would not be wise. Go. No man will hinder you.'

Weary, head bowed, Duran walked away. Faraj turned to Eleanor, ragged and dripping. '*Saīda*, it is not fitting that you should stay with the men. The Grandmother orders that you be taken to the *harīm*. The servants will show you the way.'

Eleanor opened her mouth to protest. Merrivale shook his head and she closed it again. *Something is happening,* Merrivale thought, *something that I do not understand. Let it play out.*

Faraj snapped orders to his men. Two of them escorted Eleanor away. Faraj himself guided Merrivale and Warin, followed by the men carrying Ficaris. They passed through another courtyard, this one still half-built with masons working in the colonnade, and into a garden planted with pomegranate trees surrounded by ornate stone buildings. A stair led up to a big room on the first floor of one of these, its walls hung with carpets woven in intricate patterns of black and white, red and blue. One window looked out over the garden; another faced the valley and the white houses of al-Bayyāzīn on the opposite hill.

Bronze lamps stood on carved wooden side tables. A brazier rested on a tripod in the middle of the room, glowing with heat. Low beds stood against the walls. Merrivale stared at these, trying to remember when he had last seen a bed.

Ficaris was coming around. The escort set him down and helped him to his feet; he stood, rubbing his jaw and swaying a little. 'Rest now,' said Faraj. 'Food will be brought to you.'

'What will happen to us?' asked Merrivale.

Faraj looked at him, and Merrivale read the expression in his eyes. *He is not doing this because he is our friend. He is doing this because he has orders.*

'That will depend on the Grandmother,' Faraj said.

—

The *harīm* was in a separate wing of the palace, its doors guarded by big dark men with heavy swords. They opened the doors for Eleanor, admitting her into a tiled antechamber, and closed and locked the doors behind her. She stood for a moment in her wet, ragged clothing, trying to restore the circulation in her numbed hands and breathing in the scents of jasmine and attar of roses.

Another door opened and a woman with veiled hair entered the room and knelt at her feet. 'Welcome, Saīda Eleanor. If it pleases you, I shall show you to your quarters.'

They walked into a hall, once again lavishly decorated with ornate carpets on the walls and a painted and gilded ceiling. Two little girls, barely more than infants, sat playing in a corner, stacking wooden blocks one on top of each other; they did not look up as Eleanor passed. A tiled stair led to a suite of rooms on the first floor with windows looking out over a deep ravine. Towers and colonnades could be seen on the far side of the ravine, with cypress trees rising beyond them.

The woman knelt again, bowing her head. 'What is your wish, my lady?'

'I want to sleep,' Eleanor said.

One of the rooms was a bedroom with a soft bed with a wolfskin cover next to a brazier radiating warmth. Eleanor looked at the wolfskin for a moment, fighting down the urge to laugh insanely. She took off her clothes, lay down on the bed, pulled the cover over herself and lapsed into unconsciousness.

When she woke it was night. Her clothes were gone, replaced by a light silk under-robe and a long woollen tunic woven in intricate patterns of red and blue and white. The serving woman came into the room and knelt again. 'Food has been prepared for you, *saīda.*'

Eleanor reached for her clothes, but the woman took them and indicated that she should stand. She rose, and the woman settled the robes over her head and pulled them gently down into place, and knelt to put a pair of soft slippers on her feet. *My God*, Eleanor thought, *we were pampered at court, but at least we dressed ourselves...* The woman conducted her into another room and seated her on a pile of cushions in front of a low table and served food, little skewers of mutton flavoured with pepper and cinnamon, chicken with lemon and rosewater, meatballs of partridge breast with pepper, olives and spices, fried cakes dipped in honey and a silver ewer of pomegranate juice. For a brief moment, she wondered if she had actually died in the mountains, and this was the beginning of paradise.

On the other hand, she recalled that Aucassin had been rather dismissive of paradise: 'None go there but the halt and the lame, those that wear rags and tattered old cloaks, shivering and dying of hunger and cold and misery.' *Now* that, she thought, *sounded like the mountains.*

The woman remained kneeling while she ate. 'What is your name?' Eleanor asked.

'I am called Auria, *saīda.*'

Auria. In Latin it meant the golden one. Quietly, Eleanor realised that this woman was a slave.

Lights twinkled in the buildings on the far side of the ravine. 'What is that place?' she asked.

'That is the Jannat al-Arīf,' the woman said. 'The summer palace.'

'Summer palace? There appear to be people there now, and it is hardly summer.'

'No, *saīda*,' Auria said, and she bowed her head, but not before Eleanor saw the fear in her face.

Having eaten all that she reasonably could, Eleanor sat back. 'Do you wish to go to the bathhouse, *saīda*?' Auria asked.

'That really would be paradise,' said Eleanor.

More stairs led down to the bathhouse, brilliant with azure and green tiles on the floor and walls. Eleanor stood in the antechamber while Auria undressed her and then, disconcertingly, slipped out of her own clothes as well. Painted columns with horseshoe arches led into the warm room where she sat down on a tiled bench and was given a bowl of honey water flavoured with a mix of spices; she recognised cloves and ginger and galangal, and others she was not familiar with. Auria fetched a pot of red henna and a brush and painted Eleanor's fingernails, while Eleanor herself once again fought down the urge to giggle.

The hot room was glazed with more brilliant tiles. A lattice screen, fine as lace, separated the room from a huge bronze cauldron of boiling water that generated clouds of steam. Humbly, Auria asked Eleanor to stand again, and used a bar of sticky black soap to coat her entire body before sluicing her with hot water. Feeling both clean and scalded, she sat and leaned back against the tile wall, surrounded by steam and listening to the gentle bubble of the cauldron. For the first time in many days, she knew a moment of peace. She closed her eyes.

Movement, the steam swirling against her skin. She opened her eyes as another woman sat down opposite her. The woman was younger than herself, with fair skin that glistened like alabaster with little beads of moisture, and a mass of tumbling black hair. Vivid dark blue eyes stared out of a beautifully sculpted face. Her full figure reminded Eleanor of ripe fruit. She too had an attendant, a dark-skinned girl with curling black hair.

'Greetings, Lady Eleanor,' the other woman said in fluent Castilian. 'My name is Rīm.'

Eleanor sat up slowly. She remembered the name; during their stay at Teba, which now seemed a lifetime ago, Kahina had spoken about the bitter rivalry between the sultan's two concubines, Buthayna and Rīm.

She groped for the right words. 'It is an honour to meet you,' she said.

'The honour is mine, *señora*. I hope you have been made comfortable?'

'I have lacked for nothing,' Eleanor said truthfully.

'Only for some company, perhaps. The *harīm* is quiet these days. The sultan's grandfather, may God light up his tomb, had more than fifty concubines. In these straitened times, Sultan Yūsuf makes do with just two.'

'Yourself and the lady Buthayna,' Eleanor said, watching her face.

The flash of fear in Rīm's eyes was covered quickly. 'I am told the Grandmother herself asked for you to be brought here. I am curious to know why.'

'I have no idea,' said Eleanor. She had not really had time to think about it; part of her was still coming to terms with the fact that she was not going to be skinned alive. 'I only know that a man Faraj ibn Muhammad rescued us, and brought me here. Who is Faraj? Is he sometimes called al-Awaru?'

'Yes, though he does not like the name. He is the half-brother of the sultan. The Grandmother is his grandmother also, and he commands her bodyguard and carries out her every wish.'

'I see,' said Eleanor. Her mind was beginning to stir again. 'I have heard that the Grandmother is the enemy of Hakou ben Zayani, the *amir* of the Warriors of the Faithful. Is this so?'

The fear was back, and curiosity too. 'You ask many questions, *señora*.'

Steam condensed on Eleanor's skin and ran down her body in little rivulets. 'I will be truthful,' she said. 'My best chance of getting out of here alive is to understand why I am here in the first place. Zayani's men imprisoned me and my companions, and they have tried several times to kill us. I need to know where I stand.'

Rīm paused, and Eleanor could see the calculation in her face. 'Zayani has formed an alliance with Buthayna. He intends to help her overthrow the sultan and place her own son on the throne, with herself as regent. That would mean the end of the Grandmother's power.' She paused again. 'I think you already know something about this. That is why you are here.'

'I know very little,' Eleanor said.

'But you know something. I need your help, *señora*. I need to win the favour of the Grandmother.'

'For what purpose?'

'I need her favour,' Rīm repeated. 'Help me, *señora*, and I will help you. You say that you wish to leave this place alive. I can help you, but not many others will come to your aid.'

26

25th of October, 1343

Merrivale, Ficaris and Warin had been well cared for; food was brought to them, along with a salve for Warin's cut cheek and a bandage for Ficaris's hand. Ficaris slept through most of the day and the ensuing night; Warin fretted about what might be happening to his princess before he too fell asleep. Merrivale had sat for a long time, staring out at the soft rain falling in the garden.

Morning found the al-Hamrā shrouded in cold fog. The servants brought more braziers, and torches flickered in the courtyard, misty haloes surrounding the flames. A little apprehensively, Ficaris opened the leather bag containing his *kanjifah* cards and took them out, exhaling with relief as he saw they were damp but had suffered no further damage. Given what they had endured on al-Bussarat, Merrivale thought, the survival of the cards was little short of miraculous.

'What do you suppose they will do with us?' Ficaris asked, spreading out the cards to let them dry.

'You heard Faraj,' Merrivale said. 'It depends on the Grandmother. Sooner or later, she will make her will known.'

An hour passed. The fog lifted a little. Footsteps sounded on the stairs outside and they all turned as the door of the room opened. 'Saīdi Merrivale,' said Faraj ibn Muhammad. 'You have been summoned.'

Two of Faraj's men escorted Merrivale to another audience chamber, high up in the newest wing of the palace. The tap of masons' hammers came faintly from the courtyard below. A carved stone latticework screen closed off one end of the room from floor to ceiling. Lamps burned behind the screen, showing the shadowy outline of a person seated cross-legged on cushions. Braziers flickered, and the air smelled of charcoal smoke and sandalwood.

Merrivale folded his hands and bowed, rehearsing Arabic words in his head. 'Whom have I the honour of addressing?' he asked.

A woman's voice, slow and creaking with age, responded in Castilian. 'I am the Sultana Fātima bint Muhammad bint al-Ahmar,' she said. 'What is your business here, Simon Merrivale?'

'I think you already know, Your Highness,' Merrivale said. 'I am searching for a Christian slave, a man who goes by the name of Mauro.'

'What is your interest in this man?'

'He is the nephew of a friend, who is now dead. I wish to find Mauro and purchase his freedom.'

'That does not answer my question,' the sultana said.

Staring at the screen, Merrivale spread his hands. 'What do you wish me to say?'

'I am told that you accused the *amir*, Hamou ibn Zayani, of treason. Have you evidence of this?'

'Not yet,' Merrivale said. 'I came here hoping to find it.'

The old voice became dry. 'Perhaps we shall flay you after all.'

'Zayani is conspiring with the Knights of Calatrava,' Merrivale said. 'They are selling salt from your royal mines in exchange for gold. Several days ago, I saw a caravan passing through Wadi 'Ash. Ostensibly it carried a cargo of salt, but I believe it was also transporting gold.'

'That is not unlawful.'

'No, but stealing salt from the royal *salinas* is. Your superintendent of the salt works, al-Rumani, is cheating you.'

There was a long pause. 'Where is this caravan now?'

'On its way to al-Mariyya,' Merrivale said. 'A ship chartered by the king of Castile's banker, Donato de' Peruzzi, is waiting for it. Your officials are stealing your salt, exchanging it for gold, and sending that gold to your enemies. Does that not qualify as treason?'

The silence that followed dragged on for a long time.

'You know of Peruzzi,' Merrivale said finally.

'I have heard his name.'

'Where is the lady Eleanor of Lancaster? What have you done with her?'

'She is safe and well.'

'I wish to see her.'

Another silence. 'I will permit it,' the old voice said finally. 'You may go.'

After Merrivale was escorted away, another door to the audience chamber opened and Faraj ibn Muhammad entered and bowed towards the screen. 'Arrange for Merrivale to meet the lady Eleanor,' the sultana said. 'Ensure that it is done discreetly. No one must see them.'

'Yes, *saīda*.'

'When that is done, take a strong force of men and ride to Wadi 'Ash. A caravan passed through there, bound for al-Mariyya. Find this caravan, quickly, and take possession of its cargo. Let no one stand in your way.'

Faraj bowed again. 'I live to serve you, Grandmother,' he said.

—

It had begun to rain again. Raindrops whispered through the leaves of the pomegranate trees, and dripped steadily from the carved and painted colonnade. Merrivale pointed to a cloaked figure at the far end of the row of columns. 'Who is that?'

'Auria,' said Eleanor. 'My servant. For the moment, at least, they are looking after me very well.'

Merrivale glanced at her painted nails. 'So I see.'

Eleanor held up her hands. 'I had already refused the offers to have my eyebrows plucked and my nether parts shaved. I felt that this was the least I could get away with.'

'Why did you refuse?'

'Because I tried to imagine Richard's reaction when I showed him, and failed.'

He told her about his meeting with the Grandmother, and she told him about Rīm. 'We have walked into a hornets' nest,' she said finally.

Merrivale's voice was wry. 'It reminds me of England in my youth.'

'Indeed. I was four years old when they dragged my uncle Thomas out to face the headsman at Pontefract, and nine when the king's father was murdered by his wife's agents at Berkeley. Twelve when the king overthrew his own mother and sent Roger Mortimer to be hanged. I thought life would always be like that, full of chaos and violence. We have been fortunate these past few years.'

'Fortunate to have a king who has a knack for making himself popular with most of his people, most of the time,' Merrivale said. 'For the present, we may have done ourselves some good. I am willing to bet that the sultana will send men after that caravan, and if they find it and it really is laden with gold, she may look more kindly on us. Meanwhile, if Rīm comes to you again and asks for help, play along. We may be able to use her against Buthayna and Zayani, and in the process we just might save our own skins.'

'Literally,' she said dryly.

Merrivale looked at her for a moment. She had ridden or walked for hundreds of miles, fought for her life, climbed the ravine at Runda and scaled the heights of al-Bussarat, and now the spectre of a hideous death hung over her head, but outwardly at least she was perfectly calm and collected. She met his eyes. 'What are you thinking?' she asked.

'I was thinking of Nicolette, the wise, the brave. When this is over, will you make the journey to Beaucaire and rescue Aucassin?'

'Nicolette played the viol, not the lute,' she said cryptically. 'As I said before, I will make up my mind when this is over.'

—

Water trickled through the gutters of the streets of al-Bayyāzīn, running down to the river at the foot of the hill. Duran ben Shlomo Catalan stood in front of a window, arms folded across his massive chest, watching the rain.

'It is good to see you up and about, my friend,' said a voice behind him. 'Are you recovered?'

Duran turned. The room in which he was standing was part workshop, part library and scriptorium. Shelves were stacked with codexes and rolls of parchment written in Arabic and Hebrew, Greek and Latin, Persian and Chaldean. The walls were covered with star charts and rows of kabbalistic symbols. Tables were covered with rows of pottery jugs and glass retorts. A small iron furnace stood at one end of the room; opposite it was a still, a complex array of interconnected copper pots and glass tubes. Half a dozen bricks of salt rested in a wicker basket beside it.

'My strength has returned,' Duran said. 'You have looked after me very well, 'Ali my friend. I am in your debt.'

Ali ibn al-Rāzī smiled. He was a small man with a bulbous nose, and his hair and long beard were both dyed bright red with henna; he wore a black robe with signs of the zodiac picked out in silver, and rings with carnelian intaglios on his fingers. He pointed at the still. 'My saffron cordial is an infallible tonic. Ask the sultana. She turns eighty-three this year, but thanks to my potions she is in better health than ever.'

Duran picked up one of the salt bricks. It was heavy, far heavier than any block of salt should be. 'Where did you get these?' he asked.

Ibn al-Rāzī's eyes were bright for a moment. 'From the sultana. A gift to her physician.'

Duran replaced the brick. 'I am worried for my friends,' he said. 'I saw Ibn al-Khatīb before I left the palace and he promised to help, but I do not know how much he can do. Especially now that the vizier, his master, has declared for Buthayna and Zayani.'

'That presents a problem,' the physician agreed. 'Perhaps you should stay out of this, Duran. Go back to Córdoba and resume your work. You would be safer.'

Duran shook his head. 'How long before Zayani and Buthayna make their move?'

Ibn al-Rāzī shrugged. 'Who can say? Days, perhaps hours.'

'You have heard nothing?'

Ibn al-Rāzī bared his teeth in an unreliable smile. 'I am only a poor physician, my friend. No one tells me anything of importance.'

'My friends are looking for a Christian slave named Mauro. Have you heard of him?'

The physician shrugged again. 'There are many slaves.'

'This one was taken when al-Awaru's men raided al-Ghaba earlier this year. Come, 'Ali, you have access to the *harīm*. You must hear things.'

'Quite honestly, my friend, I have never heard of Mauro. And if Faraj raided al-Ghaba, he must have done so in great secrecy. Not a word has come to my ears. Did you ask Ibn al-Khatīb?'

'He too had heard nothing,' Duran said. 'I am not sure if I believe this. In Garnāta, even the walls have ears.'

'Even more importantly, my friend, the ears have walls. If men have not heard something, it is often because it is better and safer not to hear. Be careful, Duran. You are a scholar, not a soldier or a spy.'

'I seem to have become all three,' Duran said.

—

Mist hung over the trees on the slopes above the Jannat al-Arīf, the summer palace on the far side of the ravine from the al-Hamrā, and the long gardens were deserted in the rain. Four people met in the House of the Sultana, two robed in black and two in white: Zayani and Buthayna, the latter veiled once again so that only her eyes showed, facing the portly al-Rumani and the white-bearded vizier, Ibn al-Jayyāb.

'Faraj ibn Muhammad has left the palace,' said the vizier. 'He has taken most of his men, and is riding to Wadi 'Ash.'

'He will find nothing there,' Zayani said confidently. 'By now the caravan will be at al-Mariyya.'

Buthayna looked at him. 'You are still determined to keep your word to Peruzzi? You are a fool. As I told you, we should take the gold for ourselves.'

'And lose Peruzzi's support, and his money? You are the fool, *saīda*.'

'You are both fools,' al-Rumani said sharply. 'Your caravan never left Wadi 'Ash, Zayani.'

'How do you know?'

'A courier from al-Mariyya came through this morning. He reported the caravan is still at the *funduq*, guarded by a few of your Warriors. It will fall into Faraj's hands.'

Zayani drove his fist into his palm in sudden rage. 'You are right. I *am* a fool. After Garcíez was killed, I instructed Mouha and Aksal to take command of the caravan after they had killed Merrivale. But, of course, they never returned.'

'And Peruzzi will not get his gold,' the vizier said. 'Now what?'

'We organise another caravan. There is more gold at al-Mallāha.'

'The sultana's men have taken control of al-Mallāha,' said Rumani. 'I have been barred from entering the works there.'

'I will send to Suhayl and instruct my men to send another caravan,' Zayani said. He had recovered from his fit of anger. 'A fresh shipload arrived from Murrākush a few weeks ago.'

'Then you had better do it soon,' Rumani said. His voice betrayed his tension. 'Peruzzi will demand his share. I know this man better than any of you. People who cross him or betray him do not live for long.'

'And what do we do about Merrivale?' asked the vizier.

'Kill him,' said Buthayna.

Furious again, Zayani rounded on her. '*I have tried!* He escaped from Runda, which is impossible! He has killed two of my best captains! If you think you can succeed where I have failed, *saīda*, you are welcome to try.'

'Perhaps I will,' said Buthayna.

—

The door to Merrivale's room opened abruptly and two men in the black robes of the Warriors of the Faithful entered. '*Tamettut Buthayna tessawel-ak-d*,' one of them snapped, pointing at Merrivale.

Ficaris and Warin, who had been playing cards, rose to their feet. 'The lady Buthayna summons you,' Ficaris translated. 'This is almost certainly a trap.'

Merrivale looked at the Warriors. 'I am under the sultana's protection,' he said.

Ficaris translated this, and the reply. 'You will be safe. The lady gives her word.'

Merrivale nodded. 'I'm coming with you, sir,' Warin said.

'No. Stay here. If it is a trap, there's no point in anyone else getting killed.'

The Warriors escorted him across gardens full of soft rain. A stone stair with water flowing in channels beside it brought them to a smaller palace, less finely ornamented, with a prayer room overlooking the ravine and the white buildings of the Jannat al-Arīf on the far side. A small woman veiled in black stood with her back to the *mihrab*, facing him. The two Warriors took up positions behind her.

'Welcome,' Buthayna said, speaking in Castilian. 'This is the al-Bartal palace. It is rather fine, do you not think? Small, but then so am I. When I am sultana and regent for my son, I shall live here.'

Merrivale bowed. 'I am sure it will suit you very well, *saīda*. And your rival Rīm? You will hand over the rest of the Hamrā to her?'

'I shall feed Rīm to the wolves,' Buthayna said. 'There are many of them in the mountains.'

'So I have noticed.'

She approached him a little, holding the edge of her veil in her hand. 'What do you fear, Saīdi Merrivale?'

'The same things most men fear. Failure. The loss of love. The loss of honour.'

Her eyes opened wide. 'Honour? It seems strange to hear a *kāfir* talk of honour. Why are you so interested in this man called Mauro? He is only a slave.'

'Even slaves deserve kindness.'

'Do they? I was a slave once. My family farmed in the *vega* of Jaén. At the age of nine I was captured by the Knights of Calatrava and sold to the Moors. Of course, I was terrified at first, but I soon learned to accept my situation. Now, I too am a Moor.'

Merrivale paused. 'The Knights sold you to the Moors?'

'Please do not think that I bear them any ill will. Had I stayed in the *vega*, I would have spent the rest of my life picking and pressing olives. Now, I shall soon be a queen.' She paused. 'I hear that Garcíez is dead. Did you kill him?'

'No,' said Merrivale.

'I wouldn't have minded if you had. He was beginning to outlive his usefulness. Too many people want to be part of my future. There isn't room for all of them.'

'Will there be room for Donato de' Peruzzi?'

Her answer was calm. 'Forget about Mauro, *señor*. Forget about all of us. Go home, go back to your people. What happens here is none of your concern.'

'Is that what you summoned me to say?' Merrivale asked.

'Go home,' she repeated, and she turned her back, facing the *mihrab*.

Merrivale bowed and turned away too, walking back across the gardens. Someone stepped out from behind a line of orange trees, motioning away the two Warriors. They hesitated for a moment, and bowed and withdrew.

The newcomer was wearing a hooded cloak to ward off the drizzle. His face was young, but there were shadows under his dark eyes. 'Greetings, Señor Merrivale,' he said. 'I have been looking for you. My name is Lisān ad-Dīn ibn al-Khatīb.'

Merrivale was alert. 'You are the vizier's secretary.'

'That is my official post, yes.' The other man was also wary. 'Duran asked me to help you. What is it that you need?'

'I am searching for a Christian slave called Mauro. I believe he was taken at La Algaba – al-Ghaba as you would call it – by Faraj ibn Muhammad's men.'

Ibn al-Khatīb shook his head. 'I know nothing of al-Ghaba, or this slave. I am sorry.'

'Have you heard of Kāsim al-'Aswad?'

The wariness increased. 'Yes. He is dead.'

'You are certain of this?'

'Abdallah al-Rumani, the superintendent of the salt works, told me this. Where his information comes from, I do not know.'

Merrivale watched the other man's eyes. 'Mauro was a slave in Kāsim's household. He served on the caravans across the desert to Timbuktu. I believe he knows what Kāsim knew. Unlike Kāsim, someone is keeping him alive. Who?'

'I cannot help you,' said Ibn al-Khatīb. He rubbed his eyes. 'You spoke with Buthayna just now. Be wary of her.'

'Why her in particular?'

Ibn al-Khatīb was silent for a moment. Behind him, the orange trees dripped in the rain. 'A storm is coming to al-Hamrā,' he said finally. 'The rivalry between Buthayna and her fellow concubine Rīm is about to explode. The fire that follows may consume them both, and many of us as well.'

'Why?' Merrivale asked. 'What will happen to Buthayna?'

'She is a gazelle. Zayani is a wolf. You understand my meaning, I think.'

'Have you heard of a man named Donato de' Peruzzi?' Merrivale asked.

Ibn al-Khatīb did not reply, but his face gave the answer. 'Come,' he said. 'I will guide you back to your quarters. If I learn anything about Mauro, I will send word to you.'

Back in the room overlooking the courtyard, Ficaris and Warin greeted him with relief. Briefly, Merrivale told them what had happened. 'Buthayna is walking into a trap she cannot see. I feel sorry for her, but as she said, what happens here is none of our concern.' Ficaris and Warin glanced at each other. 'Ibn al-Khatīb knows much more than he was prepared to tell me,' Merrivale continued. 'He is also frightened of someone, or something.'

'His master the vizier is supporting Zayani and the Warriors,' Warin suggested. 'Perhaps the secretary is backing the other side, and doesn't want his master to find out.'

'Yes,' Merrivale said slowly. 'I wonder if that is it.'

—

At the end of the day the clouds parted and a pale sunset lit up the palaces and mosques of Garnāta. The evening call to prayer echoed off the surrounding hills. *I don't remember hearing it since we arrived*, Eleanor thought. *Too exhausted to pay attention, probably.*

Auria entered the room and knelt in front of her. 'The sultana sends for you, *saīda*.'

Silently they walked through the painted halls of the *harīm* to a chamber high up in the northwest corner of the palace. Attendants opened the carved wooden doors and ushered her inside. She found herself in a quiet room lit by silver lamps, where carpets glowed with brilliant colours and the gilded roof beams were painted with ornate Arabic calligraphy. Braziers burned softly, perfuming the air with sandalwood and rosemary. The two little girls she had seen the previous day were playing with the same blocks of wood in a corner, their small faces still with concentration.

A woman sat cross-legged on a cushion facing a low table of carved wood. She was very small, shrunken with age; her hair was snow white, and her face was lined and seamed by time, but her black eyes were bright. She wore a simple black robe with rings on her fingers. One word came to Eleanor's mind: *formidable*.

Unsure of the etiquette, she knelt and bowed her head. 'You know who I am,' said Sultana Fātima. 'And I know who you are, so we need not spend time on introductions. At my age, time is not to be wasted.'

'At any age, *saīda*,' said Eleanor. 'None of us knows how much time we have been granted.'

'Azrael the angel of death approaches on silent wings, so we do not hear him coming. Tell me about your companion, Simon Merrivale.'

'There is not much to say. He is a loyal servant of his king, and faithful to whatever cause he is pursuing at the time. He believes in justice and honour, and he will never desert a friend.'

The sultana watched her. 'In some men, these things are strengths. In others, they can easily turn into weaknesses.'

'In Simon, they are a little of both,' Eleanor said.

'Are you in love with him?'

Eleanor was genuinely startled. 'Absolutely not. I admire his qualities, but no more.'

'Who is it that you love?'

There was a pause. 'Is it so obvious?' Eleanor asked.

The sultana said nothing. Her face was expressionless, but Eleanor could feel the dark eyes boring into her soul. 'I love Richard Fitzalan, Earl of Arundel,' she said. 'Unfortunately, he is married to another woman.'

'And you are not content to be his concubine, so instead you are here, following Simon Merrivale. You can see why I asked the question.'

'I too believe in justice and honour,' Eleanor said. 'And I like to think that I also would never desert a friend.'

'But you did desert your lover,' the sultana pointed out. 'None of us are who we think we are, lady of Lancaster. All of us are capable of delusion.'

Eleanor saw the opening for a riposte. 'And what is your delusion, *saīda*?' she asked.

'I once trusted a man,' the sultana said. 'He warned me of a plot against myself and the throne of Garnāta, led by the Warriors of the Faithful. With my support, this man killed the *amir* of the Warriors and took his place. Only much later did I learn that he had lied, and there had been no plot. Now, this man is betraying me.'

'You mean Hamou ibn Zayani,' Eleanor said. 'The *amir* he killed, was that Musa ben Uthman?'

'How do you know this?' the sultana demanded.

'Musa's widow told me,' Eleanor said. 'Kahina.'

'Ah, you have met Kahina… Yes. Vengeance burns like a flame in Kahina. She dreams of killing Zayani.'

'I would gladly help her,' Eleanor said. 'How do you know that Zayani is betraying you?'

'Today, my grandson Faraj ibn Muhammad seized a caravan belonging to Zayani at Wadi 'Ash. He also found the corpse of Pero de Garcíez, a Knight of Calatrava who had been colluding with Zayani. Unfortunately, I have no evidence to bring a case against Zayani himself. What a pity Garcíez is dead. Had he lived, perhaps he could have been persuaded to confess.'

'Yes,' said Eleanor. 'Well. Some things can't be helped. You could arrest Zayani and put him to the question.'

'Any attempt to arrest Zayani now would lead to a revolt of the Warriors of the Faithful, along with the followers of the concubine Buthayna. The concubine Rīm and *her* supporters would then rise up and attack Buthayna and the Warriors. Do you see those two children playing in the corner?'

'Yes,' said Eleanor. 'I wondered who they are.'

'They are my great-granddaughters. One is the child of Buthayna, the other is the daughter of Rīm. They are dear friends and playmates, and they know nothing of war and treachery. But when the fighting between Rīm and Buthayna is over, at least one of them will die.'

Eleanor said nothing. 'I am attempting to control events,' the sultana said. 'Arresting Zayani would provoke chaos. Do you understand me?'

'I do,' Eleanor said. 'I have met Rīm. She asked me to persuade you to support her.'

The sultana's voice was contemptuous. 'Rīm is playing a game whose rules she does not understand. Buthayna will destroy her.'

'That was my impression too,' said Eleanor. 'Unfortunately, as you say, much else will be destroyed along the way.' She glanced again at the two children. 'Do you know who is behind Zayani and Buthayna's revolt?'

'Yes,' said the sultana. 'So do you, and so does Simon Merrivale. And I think you know now why I have detained you here.'

Eleanor returned to her own rooms, her mind whirling. Darkness had fallen; the same pale lights glimmered in the Jannat al-Arīf. Taking a deep breath, she looked at Auria. 'Do you know where my friends are?'

'Yes, *saīda*.'

'Go to Simon Merrivale and tell him to meet me in the same place as before. Then return, and escort me there.'

The colonnade was dark and cold, the trees silhouetted against the faint reflection of light from elsewhere in the palace. 'They found the caravan,' Eleanor said. 'She knew who Garcíez was, which leads me to suspect she also knows about the schemes in Castile. I'm also fairly certain she has heard from Kahina, which is why she knows so much about us. And she knows Peruzzi is behind all of the plots.'

'What does she want from us?'

'She can't proceed openly against Zayani, not yet. She needs us to weaken him, I think.'

Merrivale rubbed his chin. 'The only way is to find Mauro. And I believe she already knows where Mauro is.'

'She does not trust us completely,' Eleanor said. 'She does not trust anyone completely, so she keeps her secrets close. But I will do what I can to persuade her.'

'You should go back before we are seen. My lady?'

'Yes.'

It was too dark to see Merrivale's face, but she could hear the humour in his voice. 'If you decide not to go back to Arundel, you would make a very good King's Messenger.'

27

26th of October, 1343

The *qasaba* of the al-Hamrā was the original fortress of Garnāta, out on the very tip of the spur of rock on which the palace had been built. The palace guards and servants lived here, and like the al-Hamrā itself it was a bustling little town in its own right, with a bathhouse and marketplace full of people haggling heaped baskets of walnuts and almonds and shiny green olives brought up from the plain below. Duran ben Shlomo asked for directions to the barracks of Faraj's men, and a man in a long white kaftan helpfully pointed out the building. 'You'll find no one there, though. Faraj and his men rode out to Wadi 'Ash yesterday. They'll be back tomorrow, I hear. Not before time.'

'What do you mean?' Duran asked.

The man glanced around. 'The Warriors of the Faithful are gathering. Coming in through the gates in twos and threes in the hopes that no one would notice them. It's been happening for a couple of days now. Word is that there's a hundred or so at the Jannat al-Arīf.' He paused. 'The summer palace should have been shut up for the season, but we keep seeing lights there at night.'

'Thank you,' Duran said briefly. Hurrying back through the *qasaba*, he saluted the guards at the palace entrance. 'I have business with Ibn al-Khatīb. I have been here before, I know the way.'

The guards recognised him and motioned him inside. Ibn al-Khatīb's scriptorium was a pleasant, untidy room with a single window looking out towards the mountains. The clouds had lifted and the mountains could be seen clearly now, white with new snow. Ibn al-Khatīb himself sat cross-legged behind his low desk. A pair of Venetian spectacles was perched on his nose, making him look like a surprised owl. 'Do you know what is happening, Lisān ad-Dīn?' Duran asked directly.

The secretary removed his glasses, laying them carefully on the desk. 'That depends,' he said.

'Don't play word-games with me. Faraj and his men are out of the city. The sultana and the *harīm* are all but defenceless, and Zayani's men are gathering. He may be intending to strike while Faraj is away.' Silently, Ibn al-Khatīb looked down at his hands. 'You knew this already,' Duran said.

'It was not hard to guess.'

'Lisān ad-Dīn, I have no interest in the fate of most of the people in this palace, yourself excepted, but if Zayani seizes the throne, my companions will die. The vizier has already sentenced them to be skinned alive. If Zayani is victorious, that sentence will be carried out.'

'It won't,' said Ibn al-Khatīb. 'It will not come to that.'

'How can you be so certain?' Duran demanded.

Silence again. Duran looked down at his friend. 'Which side are you on?' he asked. 'Are you for Buthayna, Lisān ad-Dīn?'

'No,' said the secretary. 'You know me, Duran. I was never very good at picking winners.'

'I need a favour. Authorise me to take a horse from the royal stables.'

Ibn al-Khatīb looked up at the big man and smiled a pale smile. 'It will need to be a very strong horse.'

'The strongest and fastest there is. Quickly, my friend. Time is passing, faster than we can imagine.'

Fifteen minutes later Duran was on his way, riding down past the foot of the al-Bayyāzīn hill and turning onto the road to the east. He turned from time to time, as if expecting to be followed, but no one had spotted his departure. By nightfall he had reached the *funduq* at Wadi 'Ash.

Eleanor stood at her window, watching the pale walls of the Jannat al-Arīf. There had been lights there again last night, and something about those lights had roused her suspicion. Today she could see people moving around, walking through the gardens and into the palace. The distance was too great to allow her to see who they were.

They might be workers, repairing walls and roofs while the summer palace was not in use. Equally, they might not.

A whisper of movement behind: Auria, entering on silent feet and kneeling. 'The lady Rīm wishes to see you, my lady.'

Rīm fully clothed was even more lusciously beautiful than she had been in the bathhouse, Eleanor thought. Why *do* some women have all the luck? She dismissed the thought at once; the fear in Rīm's eyes was vivid and real.

'I asked if you would persuade the sultana to grant me her favour,' Rīm said. 'Has she done so?'

Eleanor shook her head. 'I think she is trying to avoid taking sides.' *Part of the truth*, she thought.

'Will you speak to her again? I beg you.'

'Why not speak to her yourself?'

'Because if I go to her as a supplicant, I will look weak. She will think Buthayna is stronger and should win out over me. As I said, she brought you to the palace for a reason. She will listen to you. *Saīda*, I am desperate. I do not fear death for myself, but I will do anything to protect my children.'

Something was wrong, Eleanor thought. She turned to Auria. 'Send word to the sultana, and ask if she will see me.'

Sultana Fātima sat on the same cushion as before, facing another woman in black with a veiled face. Silver glasses of pomegranate juice and a tray of candied fruits dusted with sugar lay between them. A man with shockingly bright red hair and beard, in a black robe covered with astrological symbols, knelt to one side mixing something pungent with a mortar and pestle.

'*Salaam*,' said the sultana. 'Join us.' She gestured to a servant to pour Eleanor a glass of pomegranate juice. 'What gives us the pleasure of your company?'

Eleanor glanced at the other woman and the red-haired man. 'You may speak freely,' the sultana said. 'This is my physician, Ibn al-Rāzī. And this is my honoured guest.'

The other woman lifted her veil, and Eleanor looked into a steely face with hard, imperious eyes. It was María of Portugal, queen of Castile, whom she had last seen in Córdoba.

She bowed her head to hide her shock. 'Greetings, Your Grace,' she said. 'I did not expect to find you here.'

'Nor I you,' the queen said coolly. 'I assumed by now that you were dead. Quite frankly, it is something of a disappointment that you and Merrivale are still alive.'

'She is my guest,' the sultana reproved. 'Saīda Eleanor, you have not yet answered my question.'

'Rīm is in danger,' Eleanor said. 'I am asking you for protection for herself and her children.'

'Whom does she fear? Buthayna? She is strong enough to protect herself from Buthayna. When they fought a few months ago, Rīm won.'

'She cannot protect herself from the Warriors of the Faithful,' Eleanor said. 'I presume it is they who are gathering in the summer palace.'

There was silence. The physician stopped mixing his potion and sat quietly, watching.

'You are perceptive,' the sultana said finally.

'Thank you,' Eleanor said. 'I assume also that they intend to attack the al-Hamrā while your grandson and your bodyguard are absent. But you have loyal servants, and you can bar the doors. Invite Rīm here and give her sanctuary. The Warriors will not dare to attack the sultan's grandmother.'

'If you believe that, you do not know the Warriors of the Faithful,' said the sultana. 'We must keep the peace for three more days. In the meantime, we shall do whatever is needful to prevent them from attacking.'

'Including offering up Rīm and her children to be butchered, in exchange for a three-day truce?'

'What would you do in my place?' the sultana asked calmly. 'Rīm is weak. You said so yourself.'

'*You* said that you were trying to prevent chaos.'

'More correctly, I said I am trying to control events. Be assured that I will not order Rīm's death unless it is essential. We have other counters with which to bargain.'

Eleanor ignored this. 'Three more days, you said. What happens then?'

'My army arrives from the north,' said Queen María. 'My loyal troops along with the Knights of Calatrava will enter Garnāta and drive the Warriors out. If God smiles on us, we shall exterminate them completely and deliver Garnāta from its greatest threat.'

'Your army? Paid for with Peruzzi's gold?'

'Peruzzi promised much but sent me nothing,' the queen said coldly. 'Not so much as a single maravedí. It is the sultana to whom I owe my largesse.'

A light dawned in Eleanor's mind. 'I see,' she said slowly. 'The sultana's grandson delivered a cargo of what everyone thought was salt to Almodóvar, but in reality part of the cargo was gold. In exchange, you promised to come to the sultana's aid if she requested it. You came ahead of your army to reassure her that you were keeping your side of the bargain.'

'As Sultana Fātima says, you are perceptive,' said the queen. 'Once the Warriors of the Faithful are defeated, my army will crush Leonor de Guzmán. My husband will meet with an unfortunate and extremely painful accident and my son will succeed him. Peace will return to both Castile and Garnāta.'

'Mm,' said Eleanor. 'I'm afraid it won't be quite that simple. You assumed that Pero de Garcíez will oust Juan Núñez and replace him as grand master, thus bringing the Knights of Calatrava over to your side, but that is no longer possible.'

'What do you mean?'

Eleanor glanced at the sultana. 'Has no one told you? Garcíez is dead.'

'*What?*' For once, Queen María had lost her composure. 'How did he die?'

'I shot him,' Eleanor said.

'*Why?*'

'He was becoming tiresome. He kept trying to kill *us*, or get Zayani to kill us, and enough was enough. Also, Your Grace, you may have been unaware of this but Garcíez had a connection with Zayani that goes back many years. I'm not convinced that he would have remained loyal to you. He might have decided to join his old ally Zayani and turn against you. Garcíez was playing his own game, not yours.'

Queen María looked at the sultana. 'You knew Garcíez was dead.'

'Yes,' the sultana said. 'I was waiting for you to tell me what alternative plan you have devised. I am sure you have one.'

The queen bit her lip. 'Oh, dear,' Eleanor said. 'Apparently not.'

'Even without the Knights, my men can still defeat the Warriors of the Faithful,' María said.

'That is a hope, not a plan,' said Eleanor. She rose to her feet, looking down at the small, withered figure of the sultana. 'If Zayani asks for Merrivale and myself, will you hand us over as well?'

'Peace be with you,' the sultana said. 'You may withdraw, *saīda*.'

After Eleanor had departed, Ibn al-Rāzī cleared his throat discreetly. 'You did not answer her question, sultana.'

'I did not need to. She is right, of course. Zayani desires revenge for the death of his two captains. More than ever, he wants to kill Merrivale and his men.'

'Hand them over now,' said María. 'It might buy us time.'

'I have other plans for them,' the sultana said. She looked at Ibn al-Rāzī. 'Zayani has sent to Jubayl for a new caravan of gold, to replace the one lost at Wadi 'Ash. Go to al-Mallāha and wait for it. Deal with it as before.'

'Zayani's men will be guarding the caravan,' Ibn al-Rāzī said. 'They will be alert this time.'

'Kahina will take care of them,' the sultana said. 'You need not worry.'

Ibn al-Rāzī bowed his head. 'And the gold that is already at al-Mallāha? What is your wish concerning it?'

'You are an alchemist,' the sultana said. 'Make it disappear. Before you depart, send the vizier Ibn al-Jayyāb to my audience chamber. I wish to speak with him.'

—

The garden of the summer palace was full of cold sunlight. Birds sang in the nearby forest and water bubbled gently in the fountains.

Ibn al-Jayyāb the vizier, white beard resplendent in the sun, faced Buthayna, Zayani and al-Rumani. 'I come directly from the Grandmother,' he announced. 'She bids me tell you that she is aware of your plan to depose Sultan Yūsuf. You will fail, she says, because the sultan is with the army and will be protected by the *hajib*, Abū Nu'aym Ridwan.'

Zayani smiled. 'You did not tell her that Abū Nu'aym already supports us.'

'I thought it best to conceal that fact for the moment. The sultana also says that she wishes all parties to be reconciled. As a gesture of peace, she is re-opening the salt works at al-Mallāha and restoring it to the control of the superintendent of salt.' The vizier turned to al-Rumani. 'You should go there yourself. Make preparations to receive the new caravan coming from Suhayl. Ibn al-Rāzī will be there to help you.'

Al-Rumani nodded. 'We carry on as before.'

Buthayna shook her head. 'Be wary. The old witch is up to something, I know it. She has not survived this long without being crafty as the devil.'

'Yes,' said the vizier. 'There is one more thing. A Castilian force has marched south from Qurtuba, and is approaching the frontier. We estimate their numbers at about three thousand men.'

'Queen María's men,' Zayani said. He stroked his chin. 'I have only a few hundred men here. If I call in the garrisons from Runda and Zaharra, we will have more than enough strength to face them, but that means leaving the frontier wide open.'

Al-Rumani spread his hands. 'What are we waiting for? Faraj and the warriors of her bodyguard have gone. The sultana and Rīm have no one but a few slaves to protect them. We could walk into the palace now.'

'Not yet,' said Zayani. 'Saīda Buthayna is right, this could be a trap. Faraj and his men will be gone for several days while they escort the caravan back to Garnāta. We have time.' He looked at Buthayna. 'You said you were going to kill Merrivale.'

'Yes,' Buthayna said. 'I shall return to the palace tonight to make the final arrangements.'

—

Seething with suspicion and anxiety, Eleanor waited until night fell before sending Auria to contact Merrivale. The final call to prayer of the day floated over the rooftops as they met in the colonnade.

Merrivale listened to her story with concern. 'What you did was very dangerous,' he said at the end.

'Everything we have done since leaving Xerez has been dangerous,' she said impatiently. 'Mother of God... The queen and the sultana are aligned, and presumably Don Juan Manuel and his friends are aligned with them. The Warriors of the Faithful have made common cause with our Christian soldier-monks. Can *anyone* be trusted?'

'No,' said Merrivale. 'These twisted webs of loyalty go far beyond fealty or faith. The powerful and the mighty are driven by greed, self-interest and hatred. Knowing this, we can turn these into weapons to use against them.'

'You are being even more cryptic than usual,' Eleanor said. 'What are you thinking?'

'At the moment, I am thinking that our fate, and the fate of at least two nations, rests in the hands of a rather timid secretary. If Ibn al-Khatīb decides to tell me what he knows, we might yet avert catastrophe.'

Back in his own room, Merrivale looked at Warin and Ficaris, playing endless games of *kanjifah* to calm their nerves and pass the time. 'Is the princess well, sir?' Warin asked.

'As well as any of us can be. A storm is about to break.' He told them what Eleanor had said about Queen María and the Warriors of the Faithful gathering in the summer palace. 'I told them about the caravan at Wadi 'Ash in good faith, but that may have played into the enemy's hands. We need Faraj back here.'

The night deepened. Stars glimmered in the sky above the courtyard. Ficaris and Warin put the cards away and fell asleep. Merrivale paced the room quietly, thinking hard.

A soft tap at the door. He opened it to find a servant kneeling in front of him. '*Salaam, saīdi,*' the man said. 'The esteemed Lisān ad-Dīn ibn al-Khatīb, secretary to the vizier, sends for you.'

Well, Merrivale thought. *This is where it gets interesting...* He followed the servant through the dark gardens and bright painted chambers to Ibn al-Khatīb's scriptorium, bathed in lamplight. The secretary sat on a cushion before a low desk, spectacles balanced on his nose, writing lines on paper with a wooden pen. He looked up when Merrivale entered.

'Good evening, Señor Merrivale. You are welcome, of course, but I did not send for you.'

The servant had vanished. Merrivale's scalp began to tingle. 'My apologies,' he said. 'I have been misinformed. I shall withdraw.'

'Please, stay if you wish.' Ibn al-Khatīb pointed to a silver jug and cup on one end of the table. 'Have wine with me. I would welcome some company.'

Merrivale poured a cup of wine and sat down on a cushion. His nerves were still jangling. 'Does your faith allow you to drink wine?'

'No, but I am a poet. That gives me special dispensation, in my own eyes at least. Although I doubt that the *imams* would agree.' Ibn al-Khatīb removed his spectacles, rubbing his eyes. 'Also, I suffer from insomnia. The wine helps me to sleep.'

Merrivale looked at the paper. 'What sort of poetry do you write?'

'Poems about misery and unhappiness, mostly. Shall I read you one?

She made me a promise and broke it
For she knows not the meaning of loyalty.
She made me a promise and broke it
She does not care that she is unfair.
Why does she show me no kindness
When my heart has never stopped loving her?
Why does she show me no kindness
When I worship the light in her eyes?

Have you ever been unhappy in love, *señor*?'

'My experience of love was both happy and unhappy,' Merrivale said.

'Happy and unhappy, simultaneously. Yes, I can understand that... One day, perhaps, I will write about happier things. At the moment, all of the good commissions go to the vizier, Ibn al-Jayyāb, but he is an old man and will not last forever.'

'He is also a poet?'

'No,' said Ibn al-Khatīb, 'but he has managed to convince people that he is. Even the sultan.'

Merrivale smiled a little. 'I take it you do not enjoy working for him.'

'He is a pompous, corrupt fool. But working for him gives me access to power, and without love, what else is there except power?'

'What sort of power?'

Ibn al-Khatīb tapped his head. Merrivale wondered how much wine he had already drunk. 'Knowledge,' he said. 'The truly powerful are those who know more than the others. The sword and the arrow are useless without knowledge.'

'And what do you know?' Merrivale asked quietly.

Ibn al-Khatīb drained his cup and refilled it slowly. 'More than I should,' he said finally. 'After we spoke... I made some inquiries. Very discreetly, of course.'

'I am glad to hear it,' said Merrivale.

'When Kāsim al-'Aswad fled Murrākush, he turned to his associates, Zayani and al-Rumani, for help. He demanded they provide him with assistance and money, or he would make public some secret about the salt trade. I assume that this secret is that both of them are skimming off money from the salt exports for themselves.'

'And in retaliation, they betrayed him to the Knights of Calatrava, and began employing other caravan masters.'

Ibn al-Khatīb nodded. 'Kāsim and his household were sold into slavery at al-Ghaba, as you said. And Faraj ibn Muhammad did indeed raid al-Ghaba, on the orders of the sultana. Those orders specified that he should find and bring back a slave named Mauro.'

Merrivale sat forward. 'And did he?'

'Yes,' said Ibn al-Khatīb.

In the silence that followed, Merrivale could hear his own heart beating. 'Why did the sultana want him brought back?' he asked finally.

'He knows what Kāsim knew, that is all I can tell you. The inference is that Kāsim is dead, but Mauro knows that Zayani and al-Rumani are stealing salt.'

Merrivale shook his head. 'The sultana would not go to such lengths over a minor matter of corruption. What *are* Zayani and al-Rumani protecting?'

'I do not know.' Ibn al-Khatīb smiled a little hazily. 'There are limits to my power, you see.'

'Where is Mauro now?'

'That, I have been unable to discover. I will keep trying. In the morning.'

'Tell me about al-Rumani. Duran said he is a *renegado*, who comes from Rome.'

'That is correct. He had been working in secret for the vizier for many years, but eventually his spying was uncovered and he was forced to flee from Rome. He sought refuge here and converted to the true faith. He was given the post of *musharaf* of the salt works as a reward for his services.'

'What post did he hold in Rome?'

'He was a priest, though he cannot have been a very faithful one… He was in the household of a great man of your church, Cardinal Orsini.'

Merrivale looked down at his hands for a moment. Napoleone Orsini had been killed in the riots in Rome back in the summer of this year. It was rumoured that he had been importing gold from Spain, though very little was found in his palace when it was ransacked by the mob. But Orsini's banker was Donato de' Peruzzi.

The chain of evidence was nearly complete. Only one element was still missing.

'You know what is about to happen in the palace,' Merrivale said. 'Are you in danger?'

Ibn al-Khatīb was nodding. 'It is happening already,' he slurred. 'We are all in danger now.'

Something crawled down the back of Merrivale's spine again. 'It has been a most interesting evening,' he said, rising to his feet. 'I will leave you now. Thank you for the wine.'

He stepped out into the corridor, closing the door behind him. The palace was silent and dark around him. He found his way down to the ground floor and started to walk through the dark courtyards, navigating by the stars. Two dark shapes loomed up in front of him, and he saw the blue glow of starlight on the blades of drawn swords.

'Mmut, ay ilef,' a voice growled.

Before Merrivale could move, hard hands from behind seized his arms and pulled them behind his back. One of the sword blades rose high, ready for the killing stroke.

A thump, the rasp of steel on bone, the terrible liquid sound of steel withdrawn from flesh. The man with the raised sword collapsed, his weapon falling into the shadows. The other swordsman stood stunned; a faint ripple of light, and his head parted from his neck and tumbled into the darkness. A blood fountain rose black in the light, pouring over his shoulders as he fell. In the same moment, the man holding Merrivale's arms grunted and was ripped away from him. Merrivale turned in time to see Duran ben Shlomo lifting him and hurling him to the ground.

The night air reeked of jasmine and blood. Another swordsman stepped out of the shadows, holding up his dripping blade. 'We arrived just in time,' said Faraj ibn Muhammad. 'Those were Buthayna's men.'

'Thank you,' Merrivale said, rubbing his bruised arms. 'How did you know?'

'Your friend Duran learned that Zayani's men are gathering at the Jannat al-Arīf, and rode to find me. I left a few of my men to protect the caravan and returned with the rest. Your companions told me you had gone to see Ibn al-Khatīb, and we came to find you and escort you back to your room.'

'Is Buthayna in the palace?'

'If so, we have not yet found her. I have given orders for her arrest.' Faraj paused. 'The palace has been sealed off and strong guards posted on every gate. If Zayani wants to enter the al-Hamrā, he will have to fight.'

'Zayani does not strike me as a man to shy away from conflict,' Merrivale said, but he felt relief all the same. 'You found the caravan? And the gold?'

'There was no gold,' said Faraj. 'The mules were carrying blocks of salt, yes. Sealed inside each block was a lump of lead.'

Merrivale stared at him. '*Lead!* How did it get into the salt bricks?'

'I hoped you might know,' said Faraj. His voice was full of suspicion.

That explained why the panniers were so heavy, Merrivale thought, but it did not explain anything else. 'But where is the gold?'

There was anger in Faraj's voice now. 'Again, *kāfir*, I hoped that you would know.'

'It appears that I know absolutely nothing,' Merrivale said after a moment. 'What will you do now, captain?'

The man Duran had thrown was moaning, trying to sit up. Faraj stepped forward, lifted his sword and stabbed once. The moaning ceased. 'I shall do my duty,' Faraj said abruptly. 'You will be safe, *kāfir*. No harm will come to you. The Grandmother has ordered it so.'

Faraj strode away into the darkness. 'There is more,' Duran said.

Merrivale waited. 'As we rode back from Wadi 'Ash, I asked some of the men about al-Ghaba. You were right. They had specific orders to abduct Mauro, and those orders came from the sultana herself.'

Merrivale's fists clenched. 'Ibn al-Khatīb has just told me the same thing, but he didn't know where they had taken Mauro. Do you?'

'He was taken to a place called al-Mallāha, ten miles from the city. I know where it is.' Duran looked up at the stars. 'There is no moon. If we leave before dawn, Zayani's men will not see us go.'

'Eleanor is in the *harīm*,' Merrivale said. 'Can we get a message to her?'

The big man nodded. 'I know some of the palace servants.'
'Good. Here is what she needs to do.'

―

Sultana Fātima sat alone in her painted and carpeted chamber, reading a paper scroll with elegant flowing calligraphy, mounted on brass scroll bars. The soft notes of an *oud* flowed through the perfumed air. She did not move as Eleanor knelt before her.

'The hour is late, sultana,' Eleanor said. 'Can you not sleep?'

'The black gazelle has bewitched me,' the sultana said. 'She has stolen my sleep, and denies me all repose.'

'I do not understand.'

'It is a line from the poem I am reading,' the sultana said. 'Apt, as poetry tends to be.' She laid the scroll aside. 'What do you desire, my lady?'

'I wish to go to al-Mallāha,' Eleanor said. 'And to take my friends with me. Only for a day. Then we will return.'

The older woman said nothing. 'We must know what Mauro knows,' Eleanor said. 'Help us find the truth. But we must go soon, while it is still night.'

The sultana looked again at the scroll. '"The moon rises through black clouds,"' she said slowly. '"The dawn has lost a brother, and full of sorrow has garbed itself in mourning…" I have tried to play my part. I have tried to tame the whirlwind, as I have done so many times before. I have lost sons, grandsons, a husband, but always I have endured. But now, my powers are fading.'

'Let us help you,' Eleanor said softly. 'That is why you kept me here, is it not?'

'You may go.' The sultana slid a ring from her finger, polished gold with a bright cabochon ruby, and handed it to Eleanor. 'Show my servants this. They will procure horses for you, and the guards will let you pass.'

28

27th of October, 1343

Dawn found them riding through a verdant countryside lined with rows of olive trees and speckled with white-washed villages; a place of peace, unlike the *frontera* thirty miles to the north where Queen María's army was approaching. War had not come to this plain for many years. In the next few days, that might change.

'What if it turns out that he really does know nothing?' Ficaris asked.

'We will take him to a place of safety,' Merrivale said, 'and we will buy his freedom. It is the least we can do.'

The olive groves parted and Duran pointed to a cluster of buildings, stark white against the blue mountains that encircled Garnāta's plain. 'There it is. That is al-Mallāha.'

The village lay on a low rise in the ground on the far side of an acrid salt marsh. A handful of flamingos stalked through the marsh, hooked bills hovering above the water. Part of the marsh had been cleared and enclosed. Square pools were laid out in a grid, separated from each other by low stone banks. Some of the pools were dry, glistening white with salt. Men worked here, raking the salt into piles and shovelling it into baskets. They glanced up at the riders approaching, and moved closer together for safety.

A big stone shed stood at one end of the pools, flat-roofed with a brick chimney. A horse stood tethered outside the shed. Duran frowned. 'I recognise that horse,' he said.

A man in a plain brown robe walked out of the shed to greet them as they dismounted. His hair was covered by a loose turban, but his long scarlet beard was like a banner against the brilliant white of the salt pans. 'Duran! What are you doing here, and who are your friends?'

Duran made the introductions, and explained. Ibn al-Rāzī looked at the ring on Eleanor's finger, and stroked his beard. 'Were you followed here?'

'Not that we know of,' Merrivale said, but even as he spoke he heard the murmur of hoofbeats. He turned east, shading his eyes against the glare of sunlight off the snowfields on the high sierra, and saw a thin stream of dust, coming closer.

'Were you expecting visitors?' he asked.

'Them, yes, but not you,' said Ibn al-Rāzī. 'Your coming here complicates things. Go inside, and stay out of sight. Yufayyur! Come quickly!'

A big, broad-shouldered young woman robed in black with a bow and quiver slung across her back came around the corner of the shed. Her face was veiled, but there was no mistaking the tattooed symbols on her wrists. Other veiled women followed her, armed with swords and bows. 'Yufayyur, there has been a change of plan,' Ibn al-Rāzī said quickly. 'Abdallah al-Rumani, the superintendent of salt, is about to pay us a visit. Arrest him and bring him to me, and dispose of his escort.'

'*Ih, a sidi.*' As Merrivale and the others watched from inside the shed, Yufayyur sent her warriors running out to right and left through the olive groves, quickly disappearing from sight. Yufayyur herself followed them. The murmur of hoofbeats grew louder. The dust cloud resolved into a cavalcade of horsemen riding down the Garnāta road, Warriors of the Faithful in black led by a rotund man in white. The horsemen slowed a little, and Merrivale saw the man in white point towards their own horses, still tethered in plain sight.

Faster than thought, the ambush came. Yufayyur stepped out into the road, holding her bow with an arrow at the nock, and in the same instant her warriors closed in from right and left, raising their bows, ready to shoot in an instant. '*Hbes!*' Yufayyur screamed. '*Ssers imrigen-ik!*'

'What is this?' the man in white demanded in Arabic. 'I am a royal official! Let me pass!'

'You are under arrest!' Yufayyur snapped. 'And the rest of you, unless you drop your weapons *now*, you are dead!'

One by one, the Warriors drew their swords and dropped them onto the ground. Yufayyur ordered them to dismount, and her own warriors came forward and tied their hands, herding them away. Yufayyur prodded the man in white with the tip of her arrow and ushered him towards the shed. Ibn al-Rāzī walked out to meet them, followed by Merrivale and the others. The physician opened his arms wide in welcome, smiling.

'Abdallah al-Rumani! Welcome, my friend! I was expecting you.'

Al-Rumani stared at him. 'Who are these women? What is the meaning of this?'

'They are Kahina's people. The sultana sent them to help me.'

'To help you do what? I am the superintendent of the salt works, not you!'

'That is about to change,' Ibn al-Rāzī said. 'It would be helpful if you told us everything you know about Kāsim al-'Aswad and the king of Castile's new banker, Donato de' Peruzzi. It might save you from a rather unpleasant death.'

Al-Rumani's jaw dropped. 'Have you gone mad?'

'People often ask,' al-Rāzī said. 'The answer is, not so far as I know, but then, I would be the last to know, would I not? We shall do this another way. Yufayyur, bring the prisoner inside.'

Merrivale looked at Yufayyur. 'Where is Kahina?'

Her eyes smiled at him over the rim of her veil. 'Waiting at Arsiduna, thirty miles to the west of here. Do you recall she said she would find out more about the gold at Suhayl? She has done so. A caravan is coming north as we speak, and Kahina is preparing to seize it.'

'The sultana knows about this?'

The eyes smiled again. 'You will have to ask Kahina.' Yufayyur looked at Eleanor. 'Greetings, Lady Tizemt. I recognise the ring you wear. Kahina has one like it. The Grandmother gave it to her husband, many years ago.'

Ibn al-Rāzī smiled too. 'Come,' he said. 'You shall see the secret of al-Mallāha.'

Much of the floor of the shed was covered in trays loaded with wood boxes, each the size of a brick of salt. Each had been filled about a third full with wet salt, which was slowly drying. Further along were more stacks of boxes full of hardened salt bricks, snow white and crystalline in the sunlight reflected off the waters outside. Scattered across the room were high wooden tables with racks of iron tools, hammers and chisels, tongs and heavy files.

'Everything in the world, with all of their qualities and features, are aspects of the moon and the sun,' Ibn al-Rāzī intoned. 'From the sun and the moon and the fixed stars come mutations. Things suffer change, receiving benefit from the good qualities and harm from the bad ones. The sun and the moon receive no harm to their nature, only their nature in turn affects the four elements and everything that is made of them. These are the words of the *Ghāyat al-Hākim*, the Goal of the Sage.'

'"After the intellect comes the spirit,"' said Merrivale. '"And after the spirit comes matter, the base material."'

Ibn al-Rāzī smiled and picked up the salt brick. 'White for the moon,' he said. 'White for purity.' He set the brick down on a wooden table, and picked up a hammer and chisel and split the brick open. Inside, gleaming like the sun, was a solid bar of gold.

'Very clever,' said Merrivale.

The physician smiled again. 'Thank you. My friend Dámaso Reyes in Qurtuba was the first to suggest the principle of transmutation, but I am pleased to say that the final plan was mine. We let a layer of liquid salt harden in each box, place a gold bar inside, and then fill the rest of the box with more liquid salt and wait for it to harden as well. At the end there is a single block of salt, its contents invisible and distinguishable only by its weight.'

'Gold is heavy,' Merrivale agreed. 'So is lead.'

Ficaris stared at him. Ibn al-Rāzī's smile grew broader. 'Indeed,' he said.

'The gold from Suhayl. What form does it come in?'

'It arrives on our shores in the form of fine dust with occasional nuggets. We melt it and cast it into bars. There is a furnace elsewhere in this shed.'

Merrivale nodded. 'Let me see if I have this right. Al-Rumani and his allies called for your help because they wanted to make the gold from Suhayl disappear. You cast the gold bars and concealed them in salt bricks. Zayani's men then took a caravan loaded with these bricks towards Wadi 'Ash, unaware that you had created a second cargo of bricks where you substituted the gold for lead, and passed this off to Zayani's men. Part of the real cargo of gold was sent to the sultana's ally, Queen María, who used it to buy an army that would march to Garnāta and help the sultana defeat the Warriors of the Faithful. The rest remained here for the Grandmother to use as she chose. Stop me if I am wrong.'

Ibn al-Rāzī continued to smile. Ficaris shook his head. 'Zayani's men didn't check the cargo?'

'They had no reason to distrust me,' said Ibn al-Rāzī. 'Also, the caravan was led by Mouha and Aksal, neither of whom had what one might call a spirit of scientific inquiry. They believed what they wanted to believe, as men so often do.'

'You are a traitor!' al-Rumani snapped.

'Treason is a point of view, my friend. Yes, I betrayed you and Zayani, but I was loyal to my sultana. Are you willing to confess now?'

'I will see you perish in fire,' al-Rumani hissed.

'Perhaps we will go there together,' said Ibn al-Rāzī. 'What is written will be done.' He raised his voice. 'Dāwūd! Bring the man called Mauro to me.'

The silence that followed hummed with tension. Ficaris stood beside Merrivale, fists clenched, his body rigid. Al-Rumani had gone pale, and looked like he wanted to vomit.

Two of the salt workers led Mauro in. He was tall, with brown skin and curling black hair, and had once been strongly built but was now emaciated with fatigue and hunger. His forehead was lined, and there were wrinkles at the corners of his eyes. The resemblance to Juan Moreno was there, Merrivale thought, in the firm mouth and the dark sorrowful eyes.

He remembered Moreno's pulse, flickering under his fingers and dying. He remembered Philippe of Navarre, dead in his bath. Peiro d'Iguna falling shot from his horse. Diago's voice in the water mine saying 'you are out of time, *señor*'. Sifredo falling and falling and falling, tumbling down the slope into the torchlit gorge, while the Warriors of the Faithful screamed in triumph.

The skeletons among the trees at Palma del Río, a skull with a rotting orange in its eye socket.

Garcíez, lying face down with a crossbow bolt in his back. A blind woman cowering in a house at Jaén. The white hell of the mountains, bubbles rising to the surface in a frozen lake, and stopping.

Has it been worth it? I do not know.

The man in front of him shuffled to a halt and stood, head bowed. Merrivale realised that his mouth was dry. 'Are you Enrique Cavador?' he asked.

Slowly the head came up. The dark eyes searched Merrivale's face. 'I do not know that name.'

'Are you Mauro?'

'…That is what the masters call me. Are you my new master?'

'No,' Merrivale said. 'As of this moment, you are free.' He looked at Ibn al-Rāzī. 'I will pay whatever is required.'

'That will be for the sultana to determine,' said the physician.

'Let him sit down,' Merrivale said. 'Bring him water.'

A cup of water and a wooden bench were brought and Mauro sat down, drinking the water in slow gulps. Merrivale reached into his coat and drew out the little rock salt crucifix, and pressed it gently into Mauro's hand. 'Do you recognise this?' he asked.

A long silence, the heartbeats ticking by. Very slowly, Mauro raised the crucifix into the light. Fire flashed in its crystalline depths. Watching his face, Merrivale saw memories tumbling like a cataract over rocks, memories of love and fear, of hope and horror. 'Where did you find this?' he whispered.

'Your uncle was given it in Murrākush after your mother died. After he too died, I took it so I could give it to you. It belongs to you now.'

'My uncle?'

'You will not remember him, I think. Later, we will tell you about him and his quest to find you.'

'He was a good man,' Ficaris said quietly.

'I think I remember my mother,' Mauro said. His voice was slow, like a man newly wakened from sleep. 'I remember her holding this in her hands, and praying.' He raised the crucifix to his lips and kissed it. '*Christos eleison*,' he murmured. 'She used to say that, over and over. Christ have mercy upon us.'

Tears glistened on Eleanor's cheeks. 'Tell me what you remember,' Merrivale said gently.

'I remember the screaming. The houses burning. The smell of blood. Men in black robes, killing… I remember the slave pens, the auction blocks, men shouting, so many times, so many times... We crossed the sea, I remember that, because soon after I was separated from my mother. She wept so much when they took me away. I was young, and assumed I would come back one day. But I never saw her again.'

'Where did you go?'

'They took me to Murrākush. I was sold again there. To *him*.'

'Kāsim al-'Aswad?'

A shudder passed through Mauro's body. He clutched the crucifix tight to his chest. 'I was taken over the mountains with a hundred others to Sijilmasa, where the caravans depart. There we became beasts of burden. They loaded us with packs, so heavy they nearly crushed us, and drove us south over the desert. I remember the heat, the dust, the sand and stones spreading out forever, featureless, empty... But we never got lost, for the trail was always clear. The way was marked by the bones of camels and of men who had died along the way.'

'Did Kāsim accompany the caravans?'

'He and his men rode beside us on camels, beating us if we faltered, killing those who tried to run away. After a while we lacked the strength to run. Heat and thirst killed far more. A hundred of us made that first crossing. Only sixty returned to Sijilmasa.'

'How many times did you make the journey?'

'Twelve times,' Mauro said.

Two words, Merrivale thought, two simple words that spoke to an eternity of suffering and horror. *I hope Garcíez is burning in hell.*

'Were you ever more than just a beast of burden?' he asked.

'Later, yes. Kāsim... He was a rich man, but he came from the mountains where they have no ink or parchment, and he could not read or write. One of his slaves was a scribe who wrote letters and accounts, but he died in a sandstorm near Taghaza. Kāsim knew that my mother had taught me to write in Castilian, and I had learned Arabic in captivity. He ordered me to take the scribe's place.'

Eleanor wiped her eyes. 'Did this mean you got better treatment?'

'No. I still carried burdens every day. We all did. If you could not work, you were killed.'

'But you learned a great deal about Kāsim's business,' Merrivale said.

Al-Rumani started forward, but Yufayyur whipped out her knife and held it to his throat. He stepped back again. 'You learned that Kāsim was in partnership with Hamou ibn Zayani, *amir* of the Warriors of the Faithful, and a *renegado* known as al-Rumani, the Roman,' Merrivale said. 'They were exporting salt to Timbuktu and taking payment in gold. Was this trade legitimate? Was it carried out on behalf of Sultan Yūsuf?'

Mauro looked at the crucifix and said nothing. 'Give him more water,' Merrivale said.

Ibn al-Rāzī picked up a waterskin and refilled the cup. 'No one will harm you,' Merrivale said. 'I have said you are a free man, and you are under my protection. I want to see justice done. Will you help me?'

Mauro looked at the crucifix again, and then up into Merrivale's eyes. He nodded.

'I asked if the trade was legitimate. I assume it was not.'

'No.' The words were coming more fluently now. 'Zayani and his friends were stealing salt from the royal salt works. The gold was divided between Zayani, Kāsim and al-Rumani.'

Merrivale sighed, releasing some of the pent-up tension. 'I think we know the rest,' he said. 'Kāsim joined the rebellion against the sultan of Murrākush, and was forced into exile. He demanded that Zayani and al-Rumani help him, and threatened to reveal the thefts of salt if they did not. They responded by betraying Kāsim and all of you to the Knights of Calatrava. I think they intended that the Knights should kill you all, but the man who captured you got greedy and sold you instead.'

'Why didn't you tell the Knights you were a Christian?' Ficaris asked.

'One of the other slaves tried to do so,' Mauro said. 'The Knights held him down and cut his tongue out. After that, we kept our silence.' He paused. 'They did not care about our faith, you see. They saw us only as merchandise.'

The *alcalde* at al-Jazīra had used the same term. 'What happened to Kāsim?' Merrivale asked.

Mauro paused again. 'He was a cruel and brutal master. I saw him kill many of his own slaves. It did not matter, he was rich and could always afford more... After we were taken to La Algaba, they put him into the slave pen along with the rest of us. In the morning he was dead.'

There was a moment of silence. 'But someone knew you were his scribe, and therefore you knew the contents of his letters,' Merrivale said. He turned and looked directly at Ibn al-Rāzī. 'Who exactly are you working for, physician?'

Ibn al-Rāzī smiled. 'I told you,' he said. 'I am a faithful servant of the sultana.'

Merrivale disregarded this. He looked at Mauro again. 'There is one more name I want to hear from you,' he said. 'Kāsim, Zayani and al-Rumani were part of a plot, but another man planned the entire thing, the theft of the salt, the smuggling of the gold to Suhayl and then here to Mallāha, where it would disappear. This man also is a Christian. Do you know his name?'

'I heard it only once or twice,' Mauro said. 'They referred to him as al-Pirs, the pears.'

Merrivale turned to al-Rumani. 'Confirm the evidence just given. Admit that your master is Donato di Pacino de' Peruzzi, and I will ask the sultana to spare your life.'

'You are right,' al-Rumani said with a sigh. 'It was Peruzzi's plan from the beginning. He knew that salt was in high demand in Timbuktu, and saw the potential for riches. He persuaded me to defect to Garnāta, and used his influence to make me superintendent of salt. Once in post, I was able to remove salt from the royal mines and set up a clandestine trade.'

'Why start a revolt?' Merrivale asked. 'The trade would have made all of you rich for life. Why risk it?'

'The revolt was inevitable,' al-Rumani said. 'Zayani's desire for power and Buthayna's hatred of her rival Rīm are stronger even than the lust for gold.'

'No,' Merrivale said. 'We are returning to Garnāta to stop them.'

Ficaris's eyes widened. 'We are?'

'Yes, we are,' said Eleanor. 'I made a promise to the Grandmother.'

Merrivale watched al-Rumani's eyes, and saw his spirit break. His shoulders slumped suddenly. 'Do not go back,' he said. 'Do not take me back, I beg you. If we return, our fate is death.'

'Why?' Merrivale demanded. 'What will happen?'

'It is happening already,' al-Rumani said. 'This morning, the Saīda Buthayna disappeared from the palace. The vizier's men searched for her, but she has vanished. No one knows where she is.'

It is happening already, Ibn al-Khatīb had said, in the exact same words. *We are all in danger.*

29

27th of October, 1343

Yufayyur and her warriors remained behind to guard the prisoners and the gold. Merrivale, Eleanor, Ficaris, Warin, accompanied by Ibn al-Rāzī and al-Rumani with his hands bound in front of him, rode back to Garnāta. Mauro came with them; Merrivale had offered him the chance to remain behind, but he had insisted that he wanted to bear witness.

'When I first saw him, I thought his spirit was broken entirely,' Warin said quietly. 'But with every passing minute, he heals a little more.'

'Look after him,' Merrivale said.

'Of course, sir.'

They returned to Garnāta at midday, just as the call to prayer began to echo from the minarets of the city's mosques. The guards at the gates of the al-Hamrā were tense and nervous, looking over their shoulders, but they admitted Merrivale and the others. 'Has the Saīda Buthayna been found?' Merrivale asked.

'Not yet, *saīdi*.'

They dismounted outside the palace, and Duran pulled al-Rumani down from his horse. 'What shall we do with him?' the big man asked.

'Take him to our chamber,' Merrivale said. 'We can keep him secure there. Then I will find Ibn al-Khatīb. If anyone knows what is going on, it will be him.'

There was no need to search for Ibn al-Khatīb; he was waiting for them in the chamber overlooking the courtyard with the pomegranate trees. He gaped at the sight of al-Rumani, hands bound, sweating through his white robes. 'In the name of God, what are you doing?' he asked Merrivale.

'I am executing justice,' Merrivale said. 'What is happening? Has Zayani's coup begun?'

'Not yet. It is Rīm. She has decided to strike first.'

Eleanor stepped forward. '*Rīm!* What has she done?'

Ibn al-Khatīb began to stutter. 'Her servants t-t-took Buthayna last night. The vizier's m-men searched the palace but they c-could not find Buthayna and finally the vizier called off the search and withdrew his men. Now, Rīm will kill her rival. Her servants have taken Buthayna to the bathhouse in the *harīm*.'

Merrivale was already moving towards the door. 'What are they going to do to her?'

'They are g-going to put her in the cauldron,' Ibn al-Khatīb said. 'They are going to boil her alive.'

'Show me the way,' Merrivale snapped. 'Warin, Jac, guard al-Rumani.'

They ran through the maze of courtyards and painted passageways, Ibn al-Khatīb leading with Merrivale, Eleanor and Duran behind him. Unexpectedly, Ibn al-Rāzī and Mauro followed them too. They reached the entrance to the *harīm* and found the doors standing open. There was no sign of the guards.

'God grant that we are not too late,' Ibn al-Khatīb gasped.

They hurried through the soft painted and carpeted chambers of the *harīm*. The two little girls sat in a corner of one room, playing patiently with their wooden blocks, absorbed in their own world. Eleanor pointed. 'The bathhouse is this way.'

The bathhouse door was open too; the attendants had vanished. Paid off, or frightened off, Merrivale thought... Noise could be heard coming from beyond the hot room, voices speaking urgently, a noise like someone groaning in pain, the bubble of boiling water. A narrow service passage ran beside the warm room and the hot room. They followed it, and came to a room full of steam where charcoal glowed like an inferno beneath the great bronze cauldron that stood nearly as high as a man, resting on an iron tripod. A set of steps led up to a stone platform beside it.

Two women stood on the platform, partly veiled in steam from the cauldron. One of them, her hands tied behind her back and her veil ripped away to reveal the livid scar on her cheek, was Buthayna. She had been gagged to stop her screams, and now her muffled cries of terror as she looked down into the boiling water at her feet were like the moans of a wounded animal. The other woman, standing behind her with a gleaming knife in hand, was Rīm. A group of palace servants, most of them looking nearly as frightened as Buthayna, stood below the platform watching the scene unfold.

'*Stop!*' Merrivale shouted.

Rīm wheeled around to face him. Duran was already bounding up the steps, and before Rīm could move again he seized Buthayna around the waist and jumped down to the floor. Screeching with rage, Rīm ran down the stairs after him, knife upraised, but Mauro stepped forward and caught her arm, twisting the knife out of her hand. Eleanor grabbed her other arm and pinned it behind her back. Ibn al-Khatīb stood petrified by the door. The physician, Ibn al-Rāzī, turned to the cowering servants. 'Leave us,' he said.

Pounding footsteps in the corridor, and before anyone could move, armed men ran into the chamber, levelling their spears and pointing them at Merrivale and the others. Behind them came the white-bearded vizier, Ibn al-Jayyāb, who rapped his gilded staff on the floor.

'God is merciful,' he said, 'Saīda Buthayna, we have found you in time. Saīda Rīm, you and your confederates are under arrest.' He pointed his staff at Merrivale 'This time, you will not escape.'

'You are mistaken,' Merrivale said. 'We rescued Saīda Buthayna.' He turned to the woman, who knelt gasping on the floor. 'Tell him, *saīda*.'

Buthayna said nothing. Ibn al-Jayyāb was contemptuous. 'I will not listen to your lies. You and your companions are hereby sentenced to death for treason and attempting to murder the sultan's concubine. The sentence will be carried out immediately. Seize them, and take them to the place of execution.'

Rough hands seized them all, Rīm included. Ibn al-Jayyāb helped Buthayna to her feet. 'Come, *saīda*,' he said. 'You will wish to witness their deaths, I think.'

'Nothing will please me more,' Buthayna said viciously. 'I shall wield the flaying knife myself.'

The guards dragged them down the corridor and back through the *harīm*. The screams of frightened children followed them. Reaching the entrance to the palace, they were pulled out into the courtyard where fountains bubbled in a long pool. A row of men, all robed in red, stood facing them with drawn swords. In front of them was another man in silver-shot black, his dark beard streaked with grey and his arms folded across his chest: Abū Nu'aym Ridwan, the chancellor of Garnāta.

'In the name of Sultan Yūsuf, our master, I command you to stop,' said Ridwan.

Ibn al-Jayyāb's jaw dropped. 'Abū Nu'aym! Why are you here? I thought you were still at al-Jazīra!'

'Ibn al-Rāzī has informed me of events,' Ridwan said. 'I rode straight here with three companies of warriors. Amir Zayani's men have been ordered to disperse, and Zayani himself has been taken into custody. All of you are now under arrest, including the women.' He nodded to the men in red. 'Bring them to the audience chamber.'

Even though the sun was shining brightly outside, the audience chamber glowed with lamps. The walls and ceiling beams were brilliant with colour, red and blue, black and white and green, with gilded scroll-like calligraphy repeating the message, *Only God is victorious.*

Others were already in the room. Ridwan's red-robed guards stood around the sides of the chamber, with a cluster of them near the door. The sultana, veiled in black, sat on a cushion at one end of the room, her attendants behind her. Queen María, also veiled, stood to one side; the slave woman who had attended on Eleanor knelt behind her. Zayani stood on the opposite side of the room, arms folded, rigid with anger. The door opened and al-Rumani entered, followed by Warin and Duran. Sighing with relief, the superintendent of salt walked over to stand beside Zayani. Warin moved up behind Merrivale. 'Sorry, sir,' he murmured. 'We couldn't resist them.'

'I know. Never mind.'

'What happens now, sir?'

'Ridwan will decide our fate.'

All eyes followed Ridwan as he walked forward, bowing to the sultana and turning to stand at her right hand. 'Ibn al-Jayyāb,' he said without preamble. 'You will explain.'

The vizier bowed. 'I received word that the concubine Rīm was plotting to overthrow the sultan and proclaim her son as ruler of Garnāta. To achieve her aim, she called for help from the *kāfirs*. Simon Merrivale and Saīda Eleanor of Lancaster are among her allies, and they in turn have corrupted my own secretary and compelled him to assist them. Rīm also paid Queen María to invade Garnāta. All of this was achieved by the theft of salt from the royal mines. Rīm and her companions sold the salt for gold, which they used to bribe the sultan's loyal servants and pay their allies. Last night, she began her campaign of treachery by abducting the loyal concubine Saīda Buthayna, and only moments ago she attempted to murder Buthayna with the help of Merrivale and Saīda Eleanor. All of them have worked against Garnāta and our gracious sultan, may God always watch over him. Abū Nu'aym, they must die.'

'I did not intend to overthrow the sultan,' said Rīm, shivering. 'I only wished to defend my children.'

Ridwan ignored her. 'All present have heard the case against Rīm and her allies. Does anyone wish to present a rebuttal?'

'Yes,' said Merrivale. 'I do. Before I present it, I would remind you and all those others present that I am a herald and ambassador, and therefore my companions and I have immunity. I ask you to release us at once.'

'Your request is denied,' Ridwan said calmly.

Merrivale bowed. 'The vizier's case is entertaining, excellency, but is sadly lacking in factual basis. There *is* a plot to overthrow the sultan, but it is led by Hamou ibn Zayani, the *amir* of the Warriors of the Faithful. He has promised the concubine Buthayna that her son will rule, but there is little doubt that once Sultan Yūsuf is dead, Zayani will kill them both and take the throne for himself.'

Zayani started forward. 'Lies! Silence him!'

'It is you who will be silent, Hamou Ou Akka!' Ridwan snapped. 'You may proceed, Merrivale.'

'The theft of the salt is also real,' Merrivale said. 'The theft was undertaken at Zayani's behest by the *musharaf* of the salt works, Abdallah al-Rumani. It is one of many schemes that Zayani has used to raise money to pay for his revolt. For example, he has for many years collaborated with the Knights of Calatrava in the slave trade. Al-Rumani is a *renegado*, as you know. What you may not know, excellency, is that he is still in close contact with his old master Donato de' Peruzzi, who is now banker to King Alonso of Castile. Zayani, however, is well aware of this. I have the word of two witnesses that the theft of salt from the royal mines was directed by Peruzzi. One witness is the former slave Mauro, who knows all of the details from his time in the household of Kāmal al-'Aswad. The other is al-Rumani himself.'

Al-Rumani was sweating heavily again. 'Your pardon, Abū Nu'aym, but these are lies—'

'Hold your tongue,' Ridwan said curtly.

Silence fell in the room. Ridwan steepled his fingers. 'Well,' he said finally. 'We have two different stories. Either could be true, either could be false. Or, both could be true. I could convene a court and ask the learned judges to hear evidence, but that would take time, and time I do not have. I need to settle this matter quickly and return to al-Jazīra.'

He paused again. 'There can be no question of blame or fault attributed to Sultana Fātima. As the sultan's grandmother she is above the law. Likewise, I find no reason to blame her faithful servant Ibn al-Rāzī, whose message brought me here today.'

No reason? Merrivale thought. *That is interesting...*

'The rest of you fall into two camps. Amir Zayani, you have conspired with the *musharaf* of the salt works, the concubine Buthayna and my own vizier. Silence!' he snapped as Ibn al-Jayyāb opened his mouth. 'In the other camp, the conspirators are the concubine Rīm, the secretary Ibn al-Khatīb who has supported her in secret and spied for her, the Englishman Simon Merrivale, Saīda Eleanor of Lancaster and their servants and followers. And you also, Queen María. You have chosen to meddle in the affairs of another state, and you must suffer the consequences.'

María looked at the sultana. The latter did not speak or move. The queen turned and looked at Merrivale, and he saw her eyes burning above the rim of her veil.

'We shall let God show us the way,' Ridwan said. 'There is a practice in Christian lands known as trial by combat, which I have long admired. Each party will be represented by a champion, the Amir Zayani on the one side, the Englishman Merrivale on the other. God will give strength to the righteous champion, who will prevail.'

'This is not permitted in our law,' the vizier said.

'I am here today, Ibn al-Jayyāb, as the representative of the sultan. Therefore, *I* am the law. Zayani and Merrivale will fight until one of them prevails. The defeated champion will then be executed, along with everyone else in their camp. Is that understood?'

'I agree on one condition,' Merrivale said. 'There has been enough killing already. If I prevail, no one will be executed. Everyone in this room will walk free.'

'My terms are not open to negotiation,' said Ridwan.

'Neither are mine,' said Merrivale.

Their eyes met for a long moment. Finally, Ridwan nodded. 'You have no weapon,' he said, motioning to one of his men. 'Give him a sword.'

The man started forward, but Merrivale held up a hand. He walked over to Ibn al-Jayyāb and took the gilded staff out of the vizier's hands. 'This will do,' he said.

Zayani stared at him. 'You will fight me with a stick?'

'Yes,' said Merrivale.

'I will slice you to pieces,' Zayani said, drawing his sword.

'You will try,' Merrivale said calmly.

'Step back,' Ridwan ordered. 'Give them room.'

The others moved back towards the walls. Merrivale glanced around briefly and saw them: Ficaris tense and rigid, Duran leaning forward a little, Warin standing with his fists clenched, Eleanor's lips moving in what he thought might be a prayer, Mauro motionless and still. *We rescued him from slavery*, Merrivale thought. *Let us hope his freedom is not too brief...* Ibn al-Jayyāb was hesitant; al-Rumani looked again like he wanted to be sick. Buthayna glared at her rival; Rīm turned her back, unable to watch. The sultana's eyes were expressionless above her veil.

'Begin,' said Ridwan.

Catlike, stalking on the balls of his feet, Zayani approached Merrivale. The herald waited for him, taking a quarterstaff grip on the staff. Zayani made a couple of quick feints to test Merrivale's reaction, and then came the stab, hard and low, the sword point aiming for Merrivale's belly. Merrivale slid sideways; the gilded staff flashed in the light and struck the side of Zayani's head with a crack. The blow was not particularly hard but Zayani was furious; he stepped quickly back, and Merrivale watched him control his temper. *He did not expect me to touch him at all...*

Composed once more, Zayani returned to the attack, but always the tip of the staff circled just inside his line of vision, distracting him. Each time he prepared to lunge, the staff came down and forced him to step back. Watching his eyes, Merrivale saw the anger starting to rise again. He slashed at the staff, trying to cut it with his razor-sharp blade, but each blow met with empty air as Merrivale pulled the staff back and retreated. Seeing his enemy withdraw, Zayani pressed forward, his eyes on the gilded staff, determined to either break it or smash it from Merrivale's hands. His eyes narrowed and he clasped both hands on the hilt of his sword, swinging with all of his strength.

Even before he began his move, Merrivale pulled the staff back, transferring his weight to his left foot and ramming the butt of the staff into Zayani's jaw. Zayani stumbled and stepped back, moving just in time as Merrivale reversed his grip and swung the staff two-handed like a broadsword at Zayani's skull. This blow missed, but the first hit had opened up a cut on Zayani's jaw. Blood dripped down onto his black tunic and splattered on the tile floor. Snarling a little, Zayani returned to the attack.

He had been tricked into fighting the staff, not the man, and he did not make this mistake again. Three times he lunged towards Merrivale, cutting at the other man's body, and each time Merrivale slid to the left, driving the staff back towards Zayani's head before he could parry, forcing the other man to duck and disengage. On the fourth lunge Merrivale moved early and Zayani followed him, the point aiming for Merrivale's heart. Merrivale, who had been watching Zayani's face, read the move and stepped back to the right, reversing his grip on the staff. This time he did not miss; Zayani, extended at the end of his lunge, could do nothing to stop the staff cracking into his ribs. Grunting with pain, Zayani staggered and Merrivale changed grip again and rammed the butt of the staff into the side of Zayani's head. More blood flowed from a ruptured ear.

Furious, Zayani fought back. A series of lunges and slashes forced Merrivale to retreat, and once or twice he knocked splinters out of the staff without ever making full contact. Both men were tiring, and Merrivale had already ridden twenty miles since the small hours of the morning. Twice in succession Zayani's sword pierced his defences and cut him on the arm, and his sleeve was quickly soaked with blood. A third lunge aimed at his head, and he saved himself only by dropping to the floor. Luck favoured him; Zayani overbalanced and stumbled, giving Merrivale time to rise to his feet. *Time to make an end*, he thought. *Now or never.*

He watched Zayani's face again. The successful attacks of the last few minutes had restored the *amir*'s confidence, and he pushed Merrivale back still further. Merrivale let his guard drop and immediately Zayani lunged, taking instinctive advantage of the opening. Merrivale dodged and riposted with a long sweeping blow towards the other man's head; Zayani ducked under it, but his own guard came down, and Merrivale hit him a savage blow across the wrist of his sword arm. The sword dropped from numbed fingers, clattering on the tiles. Merrivale kicked it away before Zayani could reach for it and hit him again, three shattering double-handed blows to the body and head that knocked Zayani onto his back. Merrivale stood over him, pressing the end of the staff hard into Zayani's larynx.

'If I press any harder,' Merrivale said, 'I will collapse your windpipe and stop your breathing. Do you yield?'

Zayani's eyes gazing up at him were black with hate. 'I yield,' the *amir* said finally.

Merrivale stepped back, wiping the sweat from his forehead. Bleeding and dazed, Zayani sat up but he did not immediately rise. Merrivale turned to face Abū Nu'aym Ridwan. 'I will hold you to your pledge,' he said. 'No one dies today.'

Silence. Merrivale stood, staring at Ridwan and listening to the sound of his own heartbeat.

'I will honour my word,' the chancellor said finally. 'Many of you in this room can count yourselves fortunate that I am doing so. All of you will depart with your lives, but there are conditions. Hamou ibn Zayani, I hereby deprive you of your title of *amir* of the Warriors of the Faithful. You will leave this place and not return to court again, on pain of death.'

Zayani struggled to his feet. Without looking at Merrivale, he picked up his sword and walked out of the room.

'Abdallah al-Mu'min al-Rumani,' Ridwan continued. 'I hereby deprive you of your post as *musharaf* of the salt works. You too will not return to court on pain of death. Abū al-Hasan ibn al-Jayyāb, I do not believe you played a leading role in his conspiracy. You may keep your post, for the present, but if ever I have cause to doubt your loyalty in future, I will hand you over to the executioners. You will be reconciled with your secretary, Ibn al-Khatīb.'

Both vizier and secretary bowed, not looking at each other. 'Saīda Buthayna and Saīda Rīm, you too will be reconciled,' Ridwan said. 'If you should again fail in your loyalty to your master the sultan, rest assured that you will be punished. You will now return to the *harīm*. Queen María, I advise you to return to your own country as soon as may be. Simon Merrivale, Saīda Eleanor, that applies to you also. Your weapons will be returned to you and horses provided. Depart within the hour.'

'We shall,' said Merrivale. 'I have one further request. Enrique Cavador, who is called Mauro, was a slave at the salt mines of al-Mallāha. I request permission to arrange his ransom so that he may be manumitted.'

'I also wish to ransom Auria, the slave of the *harīm*,' said Eleanor, white-faced but calm.

'You are both impertinent,' said Ridwan. 'However, I admire courage. God has made his will plain today. You may take both slaves freely, without payment. I discharge them into your care. God grant you safe passage back to your own people, and if God wills it, you will never return to Garnāta again.'

Merrivale bowed and turned to Ibn al-Jayyāb, standing mute and silent as a statue. He held out the battered staff. 'Thank you,' he said.

Only Ibn al-Khatīb came to say farewell. He held out a small bound codex and pressed it into Merrivale's hands. 'These are my own poems,' he said. 'One day, perhaps, you will translate them from Arabic into your own language. As thanks go, this is quite inadequate, but it is all I have.'

Ibn al-Rāzī had dressed the wounds on Merrivale's arm and he now wore a white swathe of bandage from shoulder to elbow. The cuts stung but were not debilitating. Merrivale smiled. 'I think you have learned a lesson.'

'I have. From now on I will stick to poetry and scholarship, and leave the fighting to big men like Duran.'

'I too intend to stick to scholarship,' Duran said. 'Wrestling for pleasure is one thing. Fighting and killing rot the soul. I too will take my leave, my friends. I shall go home now, and purify myself with Aristotle.'

'I have a book for you also, before you go,' Ibn al-Khatīb said. 'Ibn Rushd's commentary on the *Posterior Analytics*. It was written in Qurtuba, centuries ago, and it should return there.' Ibn al-Khatīb turned back to Merrivale. 'Believe it or not, I am sorry to see you go,' he said. 'In another life, we might have become friends.'

'We might,' Merrivale agreed. 'Write to me from time to time, when you can.'

'I will send you pomegranates, so that you remember Garnāta more kindly.' The young man smiled and turned away, walking back inside the palace. Duran turned to the others. 'I don't know what to say,' he said.

'There is nothing to be said,' said Ficaris, opening his arms. Duran embraced him, and the rest of them too, whispering farewells in words choked with emotion, and followed Ibn al-Khatīb in to the palace. The others waited for a long time, collecting their thoughts.

The autumn sun shone brightly around them, reflecting off the fountains in the gardens and the snow-covered mountains to the east. 'It feels strangely peaceful now,' Eleanor said.

Ficaris laughed a little. 'Don't worry,' he said. 'It won't last.'

30

28th of October, 1343

They made camp that night in the lea of an outcrop of rock a few miles west of al-Mallāha. Yufayyur and the other warrior women from Teba accompanied them. They were no longer needed; Ridwan had sent a detachment to the salt works to take charge of the gold.

'You are still in danger,' Yufayyur said. 'Zayani will not forget that you have humiliated him yet again. You should have killed him when you had the chance.'

'And deprive Kahina of the pleasure?' Merrivale asked.

Once again Yufayyur smiled with her eyes. 'Rest now. I will post guards.'

Beside Merrivale, Eleanor stirred a little. She was back in her old clothes again, crossbow on her back; Ridwan had kept his promise to return their weapons, including Merrivale's staff of office. 'Who was Ibn al-Rāzī really working for?' she asked.

'Everyone, it would seem,' said Ficaris.

Merrivale smiled a little. 'He is a clever man who took dangerous risks. As the most famous alchemist of his day, it was perhaps inevitable that Zayani and al-Rumani would approach him. He offered his services, I presume in exchange for payment, but he also informed the Grandmother, who saw an opportunity to forestall the rebels by stealing the gold out from under their noses.'

'She was spying for the sultana all along,' Warin said.

'Yes, but there is more. What the Grandmother didn't know was that Ibn al-Rāzī, her own physician, was also spying on *her*, for Abū Nu'aym Ridwan. I suspect that he kept Ridwan informed from the beginning, and that Ridwan's timely arrival at the al-Hamrā was no coincidence. He and his men were probably just over the horizon the entire time, waiting for Ibn al-Rāzī's signal.'

'A twisted web of loyalties, you called it,' Eleanor said. 'Do you think Ridwan knew about the smuggling?'

'Of course he did,' Merrivale said, 'and he was profiting from it. That's why he too tried at first to stop us from finding Mauro, and pretended not to know who al-Rumani was. Once things started to unravel he distanced himself from the plotters, which I don't think they were expecting. But I know Ridwan was involved, and he knows I know it. We can turn that to our advantage.'

He looked across at Mauro, squatting on his haunches by their little campfire. He had barely spoken on the ride from Garnāta. Beyond him, Auria, the slave woman Eleanor had redeemed, stood on the edge of the circle of firelight, gazing up at the stars. Merrivale rose stiffly to his feet and walked over to join her.

'When we have finished our business here, we will return you to your home,' he said. 'If you wish to go, that is.'

'Home was a village in the *frontera*,' Auria said after a moment. 'I do not think it exists now. I am content to go where the lady Eleanor goes.'

'She has spoken to you?'

'When she returns to her own people, she says, there will be a place for me in her household. I could not ask for more.'

'She is generous,' Merrivale said quietly. 'And she has given me an idea.'

He turned and walked back to where Mauro crouched by the fire and sat down beside him. Mauro had the little crucifix in his hands, he saw, but was not looking at it; his eyes were focused on the flames, gazing into the heart of the fire. 'What is on your mind?' Merrivale asked quietly.

'I am thinking of the thousands of campfires I stared into while we crossed the desert. Part of me is still there, struggling with the heat and the wind and the sand... Part of my soul is out there in that desert, and always will be.'

'I went to your village,' Merrivale said. 'Prado del Rey. It is deserted now, I am afraid.'

'I know. Warin told me.'

Ficaris, who had been so vehement about finding Mauro, now seemed to be avoiding him, but Warin had been far more solicitous. Out of the corner of his eye Merrivale saw Warin now, watching them. 'He is taking care of you?'

'A brother could not be kinder than Warin.' Mauro swallowed suddenly. 'I never had a brother. There was only my father, my mother and me. Now they are gone.'

'My mother died in the famine when I was young,' Merrivale said quietly. 'My sisters died also. My father is lost in a world of his own and no longer knows my name. I understand this kind of pain, Mauro. I also know that, just as we lose people, we also find them. Perhaps you have truly found a brother.'

'Perhaps for a little while, *señor*. But one day you and Warin will return to England and I... I have nowhere to go.'

'Come with us,' Merrivale said.

There was a long silence. 'What are you saying, *señor*?' Mauro asked finally.

'I am a herald,' said Merrivale. 'There is a place in my household if you wish it.' He smiled a little. 'And if you stay with me... perhaps that brother will be there for you, too.'

Mauro's eyes were wet. 'Thank you, *señor*,' he said simply.

Merrivale looked towards Warin. The groom nodded a little, and smiled.

Was it worth it? Yes.

29th of October, 1343

'I sent scouts ahead earlier,' Yufayyur said. 'The Warriors of the Faithful are waiting at al-Hajar on the road to Arsiduna. The scouts counted about a hundred of them. Zayani is with them and so is the fat *renegado*.'

Dawn was a greenish glow in the east, silhouetting the distant mountains. Overhead the Milky Way blazed like a banner from horizon to horizon. 'That was to be expected,' Merrivale said. 'Is there another way to Arsiduna?'

'Preferably one that does not involve climbing over a mountain range,' said Eleanor.

'Only a small one,' Yufayyur said cheerfully. 'Do not fear, Lady Tizemt. After that there is a good road that I know well.'

'Lead the way,' said Merrivale.

Sunrise came, accompanied by a hurrying wind from the west. High scattered clouds drifted across the sky. The mountains Yufayyur had referred to were no more than high hills; they dismounted and led their horses up steep dry slopes dotted with pine trees, descending on the far side into a narrow valley full of scrub and grass. A stream trickled slowly along the bottom; the recent rains had begun to fill up the watercourses. A narrow defile led them into a broader valley flanked by higher mountains with steep cliffs hanging over them. Buzzards circled in the air above.

Late afternoon brought them to the valley's mouth. The higher mountains were well to the south now, but a high, steep-sided hill reared out of the plain a few miles to the north. Another jagged hill with steep cliffs, like a giant anvil that had been thrown down onto the plain, lay a few miles to the west. Yufayyur pointed to the first hill, crowned with a white-walled castle. 'Arsiduna. Kahina awaits us there.'

A rough track wound back and forth up the slope to the top of the hill. The women guarding the castle gates recognised Yufayyur, and spotted Eleanor at once. Cries of 'Tizemt! Tizemt!' echoed around the courtyard and Eleanor was surrounded by smiling faces as soon as she dismounted. Kahina stalked forward to face Merrivale, the tattoos on her forehead black in the evening light. Jidji was with her, beaming with delight.

'Well met,' said Merrivale.

'It is a good hour,' Kahina said. 'Jidji and her warriors have been tracking the caravan since it left Suhayl. Tonight the caravan makes camp outside Madīna Antaqira, ten miles from here.' She pointed to the anvil-like mountain to the west. 'Tomorrow we shall take them there at the Rawīka al-Ushāaqa.'

Eleanor had joined them, followed by a phalanx of her friends. 'The Rock of the Lovers?' she asked. 'An odd name.'

'The towns of Arsiduna and Madīna Antaqira have always been at feud,' said Jidji. 'Centuries ago, it is said, a girl from Arsiduna and a man from Madīna Antaqira married against their parents' wishes. They tried to get away, but the girl's father hunted them and drove them up the mountain. Rather than be parted, they jumped from the cliffs and perished.'

Merrivale looked at Eleanor. 'Nicolette would never have given in so tamely.'

'She would have found a way,' Eleanor agreed. 'What is your plan, Kahina?'

30th of October, 1343

Next morning they waited in the shadow of the gigantic rock, watching dust devils whip across the plain. Far in the distance, a bright banner on the walls of the castle at Arsiduna was raised and quickly lowered. 'They are coming,' Kahina said. 'Jidji, you know what to do.'

The tactics Kahina had devised were ones that the Warriors of the Faithful had used many times themselves. There was a risk that the Warriors would recognise this but, Kahnia reasoned, once they realised they were fighting mere women, they would throw caution to the wind. Jidji and a handful of horsewomen raced yelling towards the caravan, shot a few arrows at random, and then turned and fled. The greater part of the caravan's escort galloped after them, following Jidji around the corner of the rock and straight into the main body of Kahina's warriors.

Volleys of arrows emptied half the saddles of the escort and brought horses tumbling to the ground; the rest turned and bolted across the plain. Kahina, Jidji, Merrivale, Eleanor and the others rode around the rock to find that Yufayyur, who had circled around behind with thirty more warriors, had persuaded the few remaining guards to surrender and effortlessly taken possession of the caravan, a column of about seventy laden mules who stood swishing their tails in the sun.

Merrivale dismounted and opened one of the saddle bags, and pulled out a soft leather bag sealed with lead. He broke the seal and poured a little of the contents of the bag into the palm of his hand. Gold dust glittered like sparks of fire in the sunlight.

The warriors yelled with delight, dancing and waving their weapons in the air. Merrivale turned to Kahina, gesturing to the caravan. 'Half of this is yours,' he said. 'Dispose of it how you will. As soon as it is safe to do so, send the other half to al-Mallāha and hand it over to the authorities.'

'What about yourself?' asked Kahina.

Merrivale smiled. 'I can't imagine transporting that much gold back to England. There are too many pirates around.'

Kahina turned, giving orders to her people. Ficaris stared hard at Merrivale. 'Have you forgotten your arrangement with Fra Moriale?'

'I am sending my share to the government of Garnāta, its rightful owner. I am donating Fra Moriale's share to Kahina and her people.'

'He won't be pleased with you. Or me, for not stopping you.'

'He'll be pleased enough when he hears the rest of my plan.'

'Which is?'

'All in good time,' said Merrivale.

Far away on the walls of Arsiduna the banner was fluttering again, a bright speck of red against the sky. '*Kahina!*' Jidji shouted. '*Iɛdawen ttasen-d!*'

Ficaris tensed. 'Enemies are coming,' he said. 'Zayani has discovered that we slipped past him.'

Kahina was barking orders, sending Yufayyur and some of her archers up onto the lower slopes of the rock where they concealed themselves behind fallen stones, directing a solid core of mounted warriors down into a nearby stream bed where they waited out of sight. She herself, with Jidji and a company of dismounted women with swords and lances, stood in a long line in front of the caravan. Merrivale, Eleanor, Ficaris and Warin stood with them; Eleanor pushed Auria behind them, and loaded her crossbow. They waited.

'Will you fight?' Merrivale asked quietly.

'It is written in the stars that one day I shall kill Zayani,' Kahina said. 'I pray to God that this may be the day.'

Dust boiled on the horizon, swept away quickly by the wind. Out of the dust came a phalanx of horsemen riding under a black banner emblazoned with white flowing letters proclaiming the greatness of God. Zayani rode at their head, sword in hand. The bruise on his jaw and his bandaged ear were plain to see as he rode closer. Beside him, sweating and dusty, was the erstwhile superintendent of salt, Abdallah al-Rumani.

Fifty paces from the line of women, Zayani reined in his horse. The others halted behind them. 'You have taken what is mine,' Zayani said harshly. 'Release the caravan to me, Kahina, and I may let you live.'

Kahina raised one hand. '*Tura!*' she screamed.

Up on the slopes of the rock, Yufayyur's archers rose from cover, arrows at the nock and covering the men below. From behind Zayani came the hammer of hoofbeats as the company of horsemen rode up from the stream where they had waited, cutting off his retreat.

'Honour compels me to make this offer,' Kahina said. 'If you drop your weapons, Zayani, I will let *you* live. But I pray that your arrogance and pride will overcome your intelligence, and that you will not see reason.' She dropped a hand to the hilt of her own sword. 'I have practised at arms every day since you killed my husband, Zayani. I am waiting for you.'

Zayani spurred his horse. A shower of arrows came down from the rocks, spilling more men from their saddles; one of them was al-Rumani, shot in the back as he tried desperately to turn his horse and get away. He leaned forward over the neck of his mount, scrabbling for the reins, but the strength went out of his body and he fell heavily to the ground. Yelling and ululating, Kahina's mounted warriors charged into the rear of Zayani's men, who could not turn in time to face them. The phalanx burst apart, the Warriors of the Faithful trying desperately to escape the arrows and lances that pursued them like furies.

Zayani charged towards the line of women facing him. At twenty paces, Eleanor squeezed the trigger of her crossbow. The bolt missed him but it hit his horse in the flank and the animal reared up in pain. Zayani did not wait to be pitched from the saddle; he jumped, hitting the ground and rolling over, coming to his feet with sword in hand. Jidji attacked, light on her feet with little dancing steps, looking for an opening. Zayani's sword swung; Jidji tried to duck under the blow, but the blade slid past her guard and bit into her arm. Crying out with pain, she stumbled back and Zayani turned to face Kahina.

'Surrender, Zayani,' Merrivale said quietly. 'Your men have broken. All that is left of them are fleeing for their lives.'

Zayani gave no sign that he had heard. He lunged at Kahina, who parried the blade, her face expressionless. Zayani raised his sword again; and staggered as Jidji, her right arm still streaming blood, raised her left hand and plunged her dagger into his back. He swayed, gasping for breath and struggling to say upright, and raised his sword once more, and Kahina took a long pace forward and stabbed him through the chest. For a moment they stood, locked together by the steel blades, before blood started to pour from Zayani's mouth and he fell without a sound into the dust.

Kahina stood for a long time, looking down at him, oblivious to the screams of victory all around her. Merrivale came up quietly beside her. 'We gain much pleasure from anticipating revenge,' he said. 'But the moment, when it comes, is never as satisfying as we hope.'

'Revenge?' said Kahina. 'Perhaps. I consider this to be justice.'

'And that, as a wise man once said to me, is altogether more complicated,' Merrivale said. A few yards away, Eleanor was kneeling and tying a bandage around Jidji's arm. 'What will you do with your share of the gold?'

'Keep a little, to feed my people. Send the rest to Mallāha. It belongs to the sultan, and I value the favour of the sultana. I may need her goodwill in future.'

Merrivale nodded. 'Go with God,' he said.

31

4th of November, 1343

'Here come the ships,' Warin murmured.

A mile out to sea, three ships were making their way through the windless night in the light of the westering moon: a pair of roundships under oars and a big galley with its sail lowered, its own banks of oars rising and falling steadily. 'We were only expecting two,' murmured Eleanor. 'Who is in the other one?'

Ficaris's voice was tense. 'What if they're waiting for us? What if this is an ambush?'

'How could it be an ambush?' Merrivale asked. 'Who could have warned the Warriors that we were coming?'

'Ridwan, for a start. You're mad to trust him, Simon.'

'Ridwan has everything to gain and nothing to lose,' Merrivale said. 'Watch, and wait.'

The six of them lay on their bellies on a low hill overlooking the sea, fringed with a long sandy beach. A rectangular castle with crenelated walls and squat, square towers stood on a rise in the ground above the beach, a quarter of a mile away: Suhayl, stronghold of the Warriors of the Faithful. A small river ran down from the hills and emptied into the sea below the castle. Beyond the river were the ruins of what had been a small town.

The past few days had been, by the standards of recent weeks, relatively uneventful. From Madīna Antaqira they had ridden through narrow mountain passes down to the port of Mālaka, where they had prevailed upon a ship's captain to carry a message to Abū Nu'aym Ridwan in the camp near the Jebel

Tāriq. Ficaris had been puzzled. 'Why not send a message straight to the Earl of Derby?'

'Because no Garnātan captain will want to go near our camp,' Merrivale said. 'He will remember what happened to the crew of the ship Garcíez captured. Also, we can test Don Juan Manuel's reaction. Don't forget, the plot in Garnāta has been broken up, but Leonor and María remain very much at war. Peruzzi still has the power to cause chaos.'

The herds of sheep and goats had come down from the high pastures now, and it was an easy matter to find an empty herdsman's hut in the hills where they could wait. At sunset that evening, they had crept down through the hills to the high ground overlooking Suhayl. Merrivale's greatest fear had been that the message would fail to reach Ridwan at all. The appearance of the ships had been a source of vast relief; and unlike Eleanor, he was fairly certain he knew who was in the third ship.

Down in the castle a drum began to beat. A fortified stone stair connected the castle to a landing place at the head of the beach, and men began running down this, forming up on the beach and preparing to repel any landing. Another drum sound from out to sea, and the big galley began to pick up speed. In his mind Merrivale could hear Fra Moriale calling to his officers, *padrun! Colp de guerra! Batè a quart!*

At a range of two hundred yards the archers on the beach began to shoot, the whack of bowstrings clearly audible in the still night. The galley came steadily on. The drum stopped and the oars lifted out of the water, and the galley ran up onto the stand. The archers advanced, still shooting. Merrivale held his breath.

A long tongue of fire lanced out from the forecastle of the galley. Hurtling through the air, it landed on the beach and splattered still burning across the sand. Two of the archers were caught in the flames and burned like human torches. The others ran back, stumbling in the soft sand, and another snake of flame landed among them. Even from a quarter of a mile away, Merrivale could hear men screaming.

A third wash of flame splattered across the stone stairway, greasy flames continuing to burn. 'In the name of God,' Eleanor said. Mauro watched in fascination; Auria had put her hands over her eyes.

'Greek fire,' Ficaris said softly. 'Fra Moriale is very fond of it.'

As hell unfolded, the two roundships grounded quietly on the beach. Men jumped over the sides of one of them, splashing through the water. The surviving archers continued to shoot, but Englishmen in russet and green ran up onto the beach, nocking and drawing their longbows and shooting back. Men-at-arms followed, and Merrivale saw the lions of Derby and Arundel and the red and ermine bars of Sir John Sully leading them. From the other ship more men-at-arms swarmed, led by the unmistakeable golden winged hand holding a sword, the device of Don Juan Manuel. The galley's crew were coming ashore, Fra Moriale's white cross on red well to the fore as he ran up the beach. Within a few minutes the men-at-arms were fighting their way up the stairs, covered by the deadly fire of the English archers behind them.

'Fra Moriale is determined to get to the gold first,' Ficaris said.

Merrivale rose to his feet. 'I think we can go down now,' he said. He smiled at Eleanor. 'Are you ready?'

'No,' she said, her voice shaking a little. 'But I must go.'

By the time they reached the beach the fighting was over, the last defenders slain or fled. Fires burned here and there in the courtyard of the castle. The surprise attack, the horror of Greek fire and the speed and accuracy of the archers had been too much even for the Warriors of the Faithful. The men-at-arms and archers fanned out, throwing out a cordon in case the enemy should recover and try a counter-attack. Fra Moriale was at the foot of the stairs, supervising parties of his men dragging heavy, locked wooden chests down to the beach. Derby,

Arundel, Sully and Don Juan Manuel stood nearby, leaning on their swords. They looked up as Merrivale approached, his tabard bright in the dying light of the Greek fire burning on the sand.

'In the name of all the saints that ever lived,' Sully said, grinning. 'Simon Merrivale is back.'

'I brought someone with me,' Merrivale said.

Eleanor of Lancaster stepped forward, dropping her crossbow onto the sand. She was dressed in the same ragged coat and hose she had worn on the march to Jerez; her hair was mostly still black, though growing out blonde at the roots. Her brother closed his eyes for a moment. Richard Fitzalan, Earl of Arundel, gazed at the woman he loved, his mouth opening and closing as he tried to find words.

'Are you glad to see me?' Eleanor asked, her voice still shaking.

'Am I... Oh, my beloved, where have you been?'

'Many places,' Eleanor said. 'Xerez, Córdoba, over the mountains. There was a lot of climbing. I shot a wolf. Oh, and some men.'

Arundel dropped to his knees. Reaching out, he took her hands in his. The moon shone silver on the tears on both of their faces. 'Never leave me again,' Arundel said softly. 'I will do anything you ask, anything you bid. My honour, my soul matter nothing. Your happiness is the only thing in the world to me.'

'You won't make me happy if you give up your honour and your soul,' Eleanor said. She too was weeping. 'This is Auria, by the way. She is coming with me—'

Arundel rose to his feet and swept her into his arms and they stood locked tight together, swaying a little. Warin leaned over to Auria. 'You do realise that if you stay with her, there will be a lot more of this,' he murmured.

'I don't mind,' said Auria, and for the first time since Merrivale had seen her, she smiled.

Derby embraced Merrivale, and there were tears in his eyes too. 'Thank you,' he said. 'I will never forget this.'

'Neither will I, my lord,' said Merrivale, with a certain amount of feeling.

Derby walked away to join Fra Moriale. Sully clapped Merrivale on the shoulder and grinned at him. 'Well done, boy,' he said.

Merrivale turned to face Don Juan Manuel. 'You received my message, *señor*.'

'I received both of them,' Juan Manuel said. 'The one you wrote to Ridwan, and the other unwritten one that was between the lines. If we continue down the same path, we shall be playing into Peruzzi's hands. I have written to Queen María, advising her that I and my followers will no longer support her and suggesting that she returns to Portugal. I have also advised Leonor de Guzmán that she should distance herself from both Grand Master Núñez and Peruzzi.'

'What do you suggest we do with them?' asked Merrivale.

'I will speak privately to Núñez. The death of Zayani has robbed him of his ally in the slave trade; he will not go back to it. What happens to Peruzzi is up to you. You have earned the right to decide his fate.'

'Thank you,' Merrivale said.

Fra Moriale strode up, surcoat flapping around his legs. 'Simon! Congratulations, my friend. Your plan was perfect. As you suspected, Zayani had withdrawn so many men from Suhayl to protect his caravans that there was only a small guard here at Suhayl. We overcame them without difficulty.' He looked around. 'Where is Jac?'

Ficaris was nowhere to be seen. 'I don't know,' Merrivale said. 'Don't be too hard on him. He tried to communicate with you, but we were in some very wild places.'

'On the contrary, I am quite pleased with him. There is plenty of gold here, not as much as I had hoped, but enough to take me on the first step to my kingdom. I calculate that your share is about twenty thousand maravedís. What will you do with it?'

'Half will go to my lord of Derby, who will take it back to the king in England. At least the embassy won't have returned empty-handed. The other half will go to a blind widow, Señora de Garcíez, who lives just outside Jaén. Don Juan Manuel, will you see that it is delivered to her?'

'On my honour, I shall,' said the old man. 'This will be my sacred trust.'

The flames were dying down. The men on the perimeter were being called in; they would sail soon. Merrivale walked along the beach until he reached the river and turned, following its bank under the walls of the castle. The hillside sloped down steeply to the water here, with lumps of stone jutting up from the ground. His ears were alert, listening for the sound of footsteps behind him, but even so he was taken by surprise when a voice spoke from above him.

'This is where it ends,' Ficaris said.

Merrivale searched the shadows and found the other man, standing high on an outcrop of rock a few yards away. 'What do you mean?' he asked.

'You said in Córdoba that when it was all over, you would consider taking me into your service. What do you say?'

Merrivale considered the matter for a moment. 'On the whole, I think you would be better off with Fra Moriale,' he said. 'Unfortunately, though, I don't think he will want you back.'

'I see.' Ficaris's voice was calm. 'I've risked a great deal for you, you know. For both of you. I deserve some loyalty.'

'Ordinarily, I would say yes. But when Fra Moriale finds out that you were spying on both of us for Donato de' Peruzzi, he won't be very pleased. Similarly, I would sooner walk through hell than take you back into my service.'

Ficaris moved, bringing Eleanor's crossbow out from behind his back and pointing it at Merrivale's chest. 'Where did you encounter Peruzzi?' Merrivale asked. 'Oh, on Rhodes, I suppose. When you returned from your Egyptian captivity, you had no money and no future prospects. He offered you riches and high position if you would work for him, and you were greedy. Peruzzi used you to gather information, which I am certain you did very well.'

'How did you know?' Ficaris asked.

'Well, someone was carving Tamazight letters into the stones or the woodwork everywhere we went, and the only one who knows the language is you. But I first worked it out in Runda, when Aksal threatened to throw you into the gorge. If they had really wanted to shake me and get me to talk, they would have followed through on the threat, and killed you.'

'I fought the Warriors, if you recall. I even killed some of them.'

'Of course you did, because by then it was kill or be killed. If Zayani's men had succeeded in killing me, you would not have lasted for much longer. Peruzzi doesn't like leaving witnesses. You are right, though, you did good service at times. I would almost be tempted to forgive you, but you murdered three people, Jac. And two of them were friends of mine.'

'Rubbish. Garcíez killed them.'

'Garcíez did many wicked things, but he was never a poisoner. You had spent time in the east, so you were familiar with the properties of laurel water. In small quantities it can be used as a medicine, but in larger doses it is immediately fatal. You stole some of Alameda's stock and used it to poison a cask of Moreno's favourite wine, having first forged a letter from Eleanor of Lancaster and paid a boy to deliver it. Later, at Xerez, you left Warin to search for Garcíez and came back to the palace, where you poisoned the king's wine too. This time Alameda discovered the theft. Fearing he would be blamed, he tried to flee. In turn, you feared that he might be captured and tell the truth, so you killed him. Poor Alameda. We all blamed him for Philippe's death, but he was entirely innocent.'

Ficaris laughed. 'Do you really believe that anyone is entirely innocent?'

'Well... In one respect, you are. You were a fool to believe Peruzzi. You really ought to know that he never keeps his promises.'

'He'll keep them to me,' Ficaris said. He paused. 'If you were so certain I was Peruzzi's spy, why did you keep me on? Why not turn me away, or kill me?'

'It was inevitable that Peruzzi would send someone to spy on me,' Merrivale said. 'Once I knew it was you, it made things much easier. I could keep an eye on you, and more importantly I could conceal knowledge that I didn't want you to have. If I had got rid of you, Peruzzi would have sent someone else and I would have had to start all over again working out who it was. In a way, you did me a favour.' It was Merrivale's turn to pause. 'I'll make you a bargain, Jac. Lay down the crossbow and walk away. I won't tell anyone I have seen you.'

Ficaris shook his head. 'Where would I go? Back to poverty and obscurity? Back to the slave pens? Peruzzi will reward me for killing you, and that is better than nothing. I'm sorry it has to end this way, Simon, but there is no choice.'

He raised the crossbow. Suddenly he stiffened, throwing his head back. For a moment he stood, rigid, the crossbow slowly falling from his fingers and clattering down across the rocks. Mauro appeared behind him, pulling his knife from Ficaris's back and shoving the body forward. Ficaris pivoted and fell headfirst towards the water. As he fell, his coat opened and the bag containing the *kanjifah* cards upended in midair, spilling its contents. His body hit the river with a splash, bobbing gently, and the painted cards fluttered down after him, spreading out like flower petals on the water.

6th of November, 1343

Rain swept across the bay, hiding the rock of Jebel Tāriq from view. Reaching the gates of Peruzzi's house, Merrivale refused a servant's offer to take his dripping hat and cloak. 'Show me in to your master. This will not take long.'

Peruzzi stood in the blue painted hall, more vulpine than ever, hands clasped behind his back. 'Spare me the long and tedious explanation of how clever you have been,' he said. 'What do you propose?'

'No explanations, but a couple of questions,' Merrivale said. 'You promised gold to King Alfonso, to Leonor de Guzmán, to the Knights of Calatrava, to Queen María, to Abū Nu'aym Ridwan, to Zayani and Buthayna... to Rīm as well? No? That may have been a miscalculation, and you should certainly have bribed the sultana. The question is, did you have any intention of ever paying any of them?'

'Some of them,' Peruzzi said. 'I had already paid some money to Zayani and al-Rumani, and Ridwan. The rest, I simply wanted to keep interested.'

'So that they would fight each other, and while they were fighting, you could take your pick of the spoils. And with minors on the thrones of both Castile and Garnāta, you could have become the power behind two thrones. When did you first have the idea?'

'In Rome, several years ago, when I discovered that al-Rumani, or Father Giovanni as he was then, was spying for Ridwan in Rome. I knew about the salt trade already, and persuaded al-Rumani to defect and take over the trade, with a bribe to Ridwan to make sure he was given the post of superintendent. Zayani had connections in Murrākush, and promised to guard the gold once it reached Garnāta.'

'And you hired Ibn al-Rāzī to disguise the gold as salt,' Merrivale said. 'Once this was done, you intended to send it by caravan to al-Mariyya, where a ship would take it to Rhodes and the new bank you were establishing there with the help of the Knights of Saint John. You would have the best of both sides, power and riches in Garnāta and Castile, and enough gold in Rhodes to start meddling in the affairs of other countries as well. I must say, Peruzzi, you have never lacked for ambition.'

'Have you informed King Alfonso?' Peruzzi asked, and for once his voice had lost some of its arrogance.

'I will do so, tomorrow. I am giving you a day to get clear.'

'Why? What have I done to earn your clemency?'

'Do you call this clemency? King Alfonso would merely hang you, possibly after chopping some pieces off of you first, but you would be dead and out of your misery. I am inflicting a far worse punishment on you, Peruzzi. I am going to let you live. You have no money now, no gold, no power and no friends. You will die in poverty, alone, haunted by all of the times you failed; by all of the times I caused you to fail. I am your nemesis, Peruzzi, and you will live with that knowledge for the rest of your sorrowful, pitiful life.' Merrivale touched the brim of his hat. 'Farewell, Peruzzi. I do not think we will meet again.'

Warin and Mauro were waiting outside the gates. 'It is done,' Merrivale said.

Warin nodded. 'My lord of Derby asks you to hasten back, sir. We depart for Xerez within the hour.'

It was not quite done, not yet. There was still the need to find the house of the Erlantz Gebara, merchant of the San Nikolas quarter in the city of Iruña, and return a little wooden cross to his daughter Arrosa, who would now never marry the man she had loved. After Philippe died, he had thought he would never go to Navarre, but this was a duty that could not be avoided. And then, home, to whatever awaited him there.

'I have never thanked you both for saving my life,' he said as they walked down the hill.

'You saved *my* life, *señor*,' Mauro said. 'I am glad I was able to return the favour.'

Warin snorted. 'Don't worry, Mauro. Master Merrivale tends to keep interesting company. You'll get plenty more chances to save his life, in the years to come.'

Merrivale smiled a little. 'I certainly hope so,' he said.

Historical note

The siege of al-Jazīra al-Khadrā (the Green Island), known today as Algeciras, lasted from August 1342 to March 1344 when the city finally surrendered to the Castilian army led by King Alfonso XI. The siege was part of a much longer series of campaigns that the historian Joseph O'Callaghan has dubbed 'the Gibraltar crusade', which was essentially a contest between Castile and the principal Muslim leaders, the sultans of Garnāta (Granada) and Murrākush (Marrakesh, the modern Morocco) for control of the Strait of Gibraltar. In practice, this was a contest for control of three key ports: Tarifa, al-Jazīra and the Jebel Tāriq (Gibraltar). Tarifa had been seized by Castile some years earlier; the Jebel Tāriq had been held briefly before the forces of Murrākush drove them out.

Three years before the events of this book a powerful army from Murrākush, accompanied by forces from Garnāta, advanced and laid siege to Tarifa. They were attacked by a numerically smaller Castilian army, reinforced by troops from Aragón and Portugal, and suffered a catastrophic defeat at the Río Salado. Momentum passed to the Castilians, and although King Alfonso managed to alienate the kings of Aragón and Portugal so that they withdrew their troops, he decided to press on with the siege of al-Jazīra regardless. By the summer of 1343 the siege had been going on for nearly a year, and the Castilians had suffered heavy losses.

Desperate for money and reinforcement, Alfonso appealed to the rest of Europe for help. The response was lukewarm. The papacy declined Alfonso's pleas to declare an official crusade, which would have meant significant financial assistance. A party of French crusaders arrived, got caught up in heavy fighting and took so many casualties that they withdrew. Genoa contributed a squadron of galleys on the condition that Alfonso pay the wages of their crews, which he was often unable to do. The English embassy and a small company led by the king of Navarre (see below) arrived in 1343; otherwise, foreign assistance was limited.

Alfonso's own nobles, the proud and independent *fidalgos*, were restive. The chief among them, Don Juan Manuel, had just been reconciled to the king after a long rebellion, but his loyalties were uncertain. The powerful military-religious Order of Calatrava had just ended its own civil war and was still riven with divisions. (There were two other military orders, Santiago and Alcantara, who both played significant roles in the siege.) Alfonso's mistress, Leonor de Guzmán, openly cherished hopes of supplanting the king's estranged wife, María of Portugal, and putting her own son on the throne, and the nobles divided into two camps, each supporting one woman or the other.

Alfonso did eventually take al-Jazīra, but he died of the Black Death in 1349. Queen María and her allies placed her son Pedro on the throne, and Leonor de Guzmán was murdered on María's orders. Unfortunately, Pedro turned out to be a vicious tyrant, and María herself joined the revolt against him before finally retiring to Portugal. The ensuing civil war between supporters of Pedro and of Leonor's son, Enrique de Trastamara, dragged on for years and resulted in foreign intervention from both France and England. Castile was gravely weakened, a major factor in bringing the wars in Andalusia to a halt and allowing the sultans of Garnāta some breathing space. Garnāta finally fell into Spanish hands in 1492.

Garnāta itself occupied an uncomfortable space, caught between the Christian Spain to the north and powerful Murrākush on the far side of the Strait of Gibraltar. Alliances did not always fall along religious lines. Only thirty years before the events in this story, Castile and Murrākush had joined forces in a war against Garnāta; even more recently, Garnāta had given sanctuary to rebels fighting against King Alfonso of Castile. In the past, even the great Spanish hero El Çid had taken service with Muslim kings after rebelling against his own Christian overlords. Intermarriage between Christian and Muslim families was not uncommon. Sultan Yūsuf's concubines, Rīm and Buthayna, were both born into Christian families, as was his powerful chancellor, Abū Nu'aym Ridwan.

Garnāta also gave sanctuary to rebels against the sultan of Murrākush, who arrived in such numbers that they sometimes became an embarrassment. Imazighen warriors who arrived in Garnāta from the late thirteenth century onwards formed a volunteer corps known as al-Ghuzāt al-Mujāhidīn, meaning the Volunteers of the Faith or – our preferred translation – Warriors of the Faithful. Under their influential leader Uthman ben Abi al-Ula, they became a reliable force for the defence of Garnāta, and Uthman was close to both Ridwan and Sultana Fātima, the powerful kingmaker in Garnāta known as the Grandmother. After Uthman's death, however, the Warriors became increasingly independent of central authority and a thorn in the side of the sultans. Sometime around 1370, the post of *amir* of the Warriors was abolished and they were absorbed into the army of Garnāta.

In the early years of the Hundred Years War, Edward III of England expended a great deal of effort and money trying to acquire allies against France. Despite the fact that Castile and France had long been aligned with each other, in the summer of 1343 Edward dispatched an embassy led by three of his prominent nobles, the earls of Salisbury, Derby and Arundel, to King Alfonso's siege camp outside al-Jazīra, hoping to persuade Alfonso to form an alliance with England. Salisbury fell ill and retired to England, leaving Derby and Arundel to carry on. Like most of the western contingents who came to the camp, the English occasionally joined in the fighting and engaged in a few skirmishes. During one of these, King Philippe of Navarre was wounded and withdrew to recuperate, but died at Xerez before he could return home. Predictably, Derby and Arundel made no headway whatever, and were recalled in October.

Arundel's lover, and Derby's younger sister, Eleanor of Lancaster accompanied the embassy. A few years later, Arundel succeeded in gaining an annulment of his marriage to Isabel Despenser, to which neither bride nor groom had consented in the first place. He and Eleanor lived the rest of their lives together and were buried together in Arundel cathedral.

Acknowledgements

Thanks go first of all to Kit Nevile, who has been our editor at Canelo throughout this series, for his unwavering support and clear-sighted critique. Kit has now moved on to another post, and he is very much missed. Thank you, Kit, for everything over the years.

Thanks also to Craig Lye for stepping in to guide the project calmly through its final phases. Craig, your support too has been very much welcomed. Jon Wood our agent has always been there to help when needed.

Thanks to the rest of the team at Canelo, especially to Hannah Boursnell for a detailed and patient line edit, to James Macey of Blacksheep Design for a splendid cover, and to Chere Tricot for copy-editing the manuscript.

Thanks must go to Jane and Ian Colbourne who joined me on our road trip through Andalusia to look at the ground, and to all of the people of Andalusia we met along the way who fed us, watered us and gave us information. Andalusia is a beautiful land. We hope we have done it justice.